Prologue

Akira Mano pressed his arms a little closer to his body, slowly moving from one foot to the other. His boots flattened the same patch of snow that he had been standing on for almost an hour. He turned, spitting a thick globule of chewing tobacco on to the ground in front of him, and grunted.

'Where hell are you?' he hissed in broken English. He cursed again, but this time in his native Japanese. After so long working on the same Antarctic research project, he was even starting to think like the rest of them.

Five miles distant stood a line of mountains, their jagged peaks curving in an arc like a row of teeth. The Englishman, Sommers, had been gone too long. Something was wrong.

A huge, red tractor faded orange by the sun stood directly behind Akira. Its caterpillar tracks were enormous, towering above his head. The engine gave only an occasional splutter, belching out a smudge of exhaust into the otherwise cobalt blue sky. Taking a step backwards, Akira huddled closer to the exhaust, letting the dirty flow of air wash over his back.

The fumes were noxious, drying out the back of his throat, but at least they were warm.

There was a glimmer of light – metal winking in the sun. He could see the faint outline of a Ski-Doo making its way towards him, then a few seconds later hear the high-pitched whine of its two-stroke engine. Finally, the hunched figure of Harry Sommers pulled it to a standstill.

'I was right!' he exclaimed, the words escaping his mouth before he had even shut off the engine. Pulling a balaclava from his face, he revealed ruddy cheeks, flushed from cold, and a short, greying beard. Striding towards Akira, he clenched his fist in triumph.

'I bloody knew it!' he shouted. 'What do you say to that, Akira-san?'

His thick Lancashire accent made the pronunciation of the Japanese man's name almost unrecognisable, but Sommers was too excited to notice.

'I knew there was something past that ridge,' he continued. 'I could make out a kind of structure. Whatever it is, it's definitely man-made, and I'll tell you something for nothing – it wasn't our lot that built it.'

Akira blinked, trying to piece together the Englishman's grammar. A moment passed before he looked up.

'So?'

'What do you mean "so"? It means that someone else is here on *our* lake. At *our* drill site!'

Akira shrugged, unable to conceal his lack of interest. He was cold, and that was all there was to it. It had been three days since he had last had a shower or even changed his socks. Without replying, he motioned towards the tractor, his shoulders hunching with indifference.

'Bloody hell,' Sommers hissed, trying to fight back his annoyance. 'Look, I don't know how you do things in Japan, but that structure isn't on any of my charts. It shouldn't be there! We should go and investigate.'

Akira scratched the side of his neck, pulling at the Gore-Tex hood of his jacket and revealing the very tip of a tattoo that surged up from his shoulder to his jawline. The indelible ink was intricate and subtle, merging with his naturally dark skin.

'We here too long,' he said, refusing to make eye contact. 'If other structure, then it's not our problem.'

'Look, we've got to put something in the report. Wouldn't it be better to know what we're talking about, rather than running home like a couple of schoolgirls? Another few kilometres around that ridge and we'll be able to see it.'

Akira turned towards the new route, scanning his eyes across the perfect white landscape. The surrounding mountains funnelled the snow, blanketing the whole lake area in a flat, unbroken expanse. For once, the interminable wind had ceased and Antarctica looked like a different place entirely. It was peaceful, pleasant even.

'Road OK for Ski-Doo but not for tractor. It too heavy,' said Akira, before turning back towards the larger vehicle and clambering up on to its steps. Sommers watched as he slowly heaved open the door, before settling himself in the passenger seat without another word.

'Soft, sushi-eating bastard,' muttered Sommers, his top lip

curling in disdain. He waited for a moment more then, with a shake of his head, stalked back to the Ski-Doo and drove it round to the rear of the tractor. Stamping down on the locking mechanism of the tractor's tow bar, he secured it tight before following Akira and clambering up into the main cabin.

'Guess you should learn how to drive the tractor, Akira my old son, if you want to make the decisions around here.'

With that, Sommers wiggled the gear lever out of neutral, finding first with a grinding of cogs. Before powering off, he reached up to the breast pocket of his jacket and pulled out a squashed pack of cigarettes, jamming one into the corner of his mouth. Almost immediately, the dry filter absorbed what little moisture was left in his chapped lips, breaking the skin. Sommers winced, feeling a bead of blood well out and dribble down across his chin. He ignored it, lighting the cigarette anyway and drawing the smoke deep into his lungs.

Releasing the clutch, he then sent the tractor lurching forward with its steel tracks tearing at the fresh snow. Akira had already turned away from him in protest, but Sommer knew it wouldn't last long. Jiggling the packet in his direction, he waited several seconds before Akira slowly turned back, taking the last cigarette.

The tractor rumbled on.

The two men were scientists and had been working in Antarctica for the last ten months. It had taken them a long time to become accustomed to the scale of their

BENEATH THE ICE

PATRICK WOODHEAD

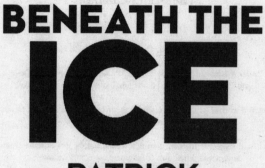

arrow books

Published by Arrow Books 2015

2 4 6 8 10 9 7 5 3 1

First published in Great Britain in 2015 by Arrow

Random House, 20 Vauxhall Bridge Road,
London SW1V 2SA

www.randomhouse.co.uk

Addresses for companies within The Random House Group Limited
can be found at: www.randomhouse.co.uk/offices.htm

The Random House Group Limited Reg. No. 954009

A CIP catalogue record for this book is available from the British Library

ISBN 978 1 84809 079 8

Penguin Random House is committed to a sustainable
future for our business, our readers and our planet.
This book is made from Forest Stewardship
Council® certified paper.

Typeset in Electra LT Std Regular by Palimpsest Book Production Ltd,
Falkirk, Stirlingshire
Printed and bound by CPI Group (UK) Ltd, Croydon, CR0 4YY

environment and the time it took to travel anywhere. But now, it was all part of the journey. Conversations would start then naturally fade, before continuing some minutes later. Time was in abundance. The landscape infinite. With the last of the cigarettes gone, Sommers drummed his fingers on the steering wheel as he whistled the chorus line of some half-forgotten tune. He knew that both actions would annoy his travelling companion, but they had been working together for too long not to indulge in petty torments.

Craning his neck towards the windscreen, Sommers raised one gloved hand to wipe the condensation off the glass, only succeeding in smearing it a little more. Suddenly, the indistinct outline of a structure appeared on the horizon.

'There it is!' he shouted, jolting Akira from his daydream. Stamping down on the brakes, Sommers pulled the mighty tractor to a standstill and threw open the side door.

'What do ya suppose it's for?' he asked, raising an arm to shield his eyes from the blinding glare. 'Is that some kind of tower to the left?'

Akira craned his neck out of the open window, but didn't bother to get out. Finally, he gave a soft grunt, but offered nothing more. A few minutes passed with Sommers trying to discern the exact nature of the distant shapes, before his head snapped back round and he glared at Akira like a father might a petulant child.

'Come on, Akira-san, stop sulking and help me out here. We've got to see what this is.'

'I not sulk,' Akira protested, suddenly raising himself in the seat. 'No road! No road! This tractor weighs five tons! It

5

too dangerous to continue.' He jabbed his forefinger against the windscreen. 'We need GPS route or no carry on!'

'Jesus,' Sommers muttered, rolling his eyes skywards. He had rarely seen Akira so agitated, nor, for that matter, animated.

'Why don't we just . . .' he began, but his voice trailed off. Despite Akira's quiet demeanour, Sommers knew that he was as stubborn as an ox and, once a decision had been made, there was little point in trying to talk him round. Eventually, Sommers raised his hands in defeat.

'OK, have it your way,' he said and, heaving the tractor round in a slow, right-hand turn, he pointed them back in the direction they had come. 'We always have it your bloody way.'

They continued in silence for nearly two hours, following their own tracks back towards the base. As they reached the end of the lake, a hill led up to a low mountain pass. The diesel engine of the tractor revved higher, sending vibrations across the whole cabin as the machine powered its way through the deep snow. Just as they passed the apex, Sommers finally cracked.

'Are you thinking what I'm thinking?' he asked, waving his hand behind him vaguely. 'It's another drill site, right? We should ask the Russians if they know anything about it.' He reached towards the radio handset, then paused. 'Better wait a bit, eh? Reception's bloody rubbish over here. When we get back, I'll see if . . .'

There was a jolt. Then the nose of the tractor pitched down so violently that both men were flung against the dashboard. The horizon went from sky blue to grey as the entire front end of the machine broke through the snow and down into a crevasse hidden just beneath the surface. Immense walls of ice stretched below them, channelling their eyes down towards the belly of the glacier itself. It was black, like the throat of an enormous beast.

Sommers groaned. He had split the skin above his eye and now blood streamed down the side of his face. His head was crooked against the cold glass of the windscreen and he blinked several times, trying to focus on Akira.

'You all right?' he shouted, reaching out an arm, but Akira's body lay slumped forward. The force of the blow had caved in his right cheek, leaving splinters of bone protruding through the skin. Sommers called again, but there was no response.

'Oh, shit,' he said, reaching out and grabbing Akira by the scruff of his jacket. Jabbing two fingers down on to his neck, Sommers tried to steady his own heartbeat and listen. Come on! There had to be a pulse!

There was a secondary jolt as the enormous shock wave from the fall cracked the snow under the tractor's rear axle. The machine listed to one side then suddenly it was free, and tumbling downwards.

Forty feet lower down, a column of ice jutted out from the main wall of the crevasse like a tree branch. As the full weight of the tractor crashed down upon it, the column splintered, collapsing in on itself, but it was enough to arrest their fall. Everything went still, with only the soft tinkling sound of loose shards of ice spinning off into the depths below. The tractor was stuck, wedged to a standstill between the sidewalls of the crevasse.

Sommers opened his eyes. It was as if everything were moving in half time, every sense straining from adrenalin. He could feel the pulse beating at his throat, while his vision seemed sharper somehow, heightened by fear. His own body was jammed into the driver's footwell, while next to him the passenger door swung loosely on its hinges – Akira was gone.

Grabbing the VHF radio off the dashboard, Sommers pressed down on the comms switch and spoke quickly. There was only static. He tried again. Nothing. Checking the frequency on the miniature console, he read the numbers out loud – 145.15. It was correct, but nobody was replying.

Craning his head out of the open window of the tractor, Sommers looked up. A halo of dazzling white light poured in through the tear in the surface snow, illuminating the upper reaches of the crevasse. There, the ice was a deep, iridescent blue – the same mesmeric colour as the shallow waters of the Indian Ocean.

The hole in the surface looked impossibly small to have allowed their tractor to pass through, but then he realised just how far they had fallen. They were too deep to transmit a radio signal. Here, the ice had faded in colour. It was black, and deathly cold. 'Sommers!'

He turned to see Akira wedged into the sidewall of the collapsed column. He was about twenty feet lower down, with only his head and shoulders visible. The force of the fall had jammed his legs under his torso, twisting his body unnaturally to one side. 'Sommers!'

The sound of Akira's voice was high-pitched and panicked, making it difficult for Sommers to think. He had enough experience of the mountains to know that he should take things slowly and not rush into any rescue plan. He had to think how to get them out of there and, as his eyes passed across the massive bonnet of the tractor, he suddenly remembered the winch. The steel cable was easily capable of getting Akira out.

Yanking open the glove box, he found the winch remote hidden under a clutter of charts and old clothing, and jammed it into the breast pocket of his jacket. Raising his head once more, he paused, the rush of blood making him reach out to steady himself. Blood streamed down his face and into his neckline, soaking his thermals. He was going to have to take this slowly. Focus on each step.

Carefully opening the door, he couldn't resist glancing downwards. The walls of ice were so linear and unbroken that the perspective was dizzying. Everything looked so still, the air absolutely static, as if unchanged for hundreds of years.

Clambering up on to the tractor's bonnet, Sommers inched his way along it, his entire body pressed flat against the freezing metal. Reaching forwards to the winch cable, he heaved hand-over-hand until the heavy metal hook appeared. Then, twisting his body round, he managed to jam the toe of his climbing boot inside and, gripping tight, moved out towards the edge.

Every instinct screamed against the thought of swinging out over the side of the tractor. All he could see was the yawning darkness below. He hesitated, willing his body to comply. He could see his hands shaking, while his breath came in quick, shallow bursts, condensing in the air above.

'Sommers!' The sound of Akira's voice drifted up towards him once again.

'For Christ's sake!' he snapped. 'Give me a bloody minute.'

He inched closer to the edge, letting his body slip the final few inches. The drop was sudden, jolting him to a halt just beneath the line of the tractor's giant caterpillar tracks. He let himself swing for several seconds, too scared to do anything but grip onto the steel cable, before finally his right hand crept higher, searching for the remote in his pocket.

The winch lowered, the steady release of the cable his one reassurance. In only a few moments he was at the site of the splintered column and the broken body of his colleague.

Akira was staring up at him, eyes wide with shock. His fleece hat had been ripped off by the fall and now his long, jet-black hair fanned out around him, with clumps already frozen to the sidewall of ice. An open flap of skin hung from his chin, whilst his shattered cheekbone distorted his face. As Sommers' climbing boot came to rest on the slab of ice next to him, Akira desperately grabbed on to it.

'You're OK. You hear me? You're OK,' Sommers soothed, but even he could hear the flatness in his own voice. The fall had forced Akira's entire body into an impossibly tight crack, pinning him from his waist to his feet. He was trembling, the onset of hypothermia only minutes away, while his body heat had already begun to melt the ice around him, soaking his clothes until they were wringing wet. Sommers stared down at him, amazed by how pale Akira looked. His lips had drained of colour, becoming a cold and bloodless blue.

'This winch can move a five-ton truck, mate,' Sommers said, forcing a smile. 'It's going to hurt like hell, but it'll pull you free.'

Akira only nodded as Sommers knelt down on the ice and fed the cable underneath the injured man's thighs in a loop. It took several attempts to reconnect it, but finally he was done.

'I'm sorry,' Sommers whispered before pushing down on the button. The cable tightened, the immense power of the machine ratcheting tighter and tighter. At first, Akira gulped, the pain making him gag, and then suddenly he flung back his head and let out a sound that Sommers had never heard a human being make before. His mouth stretched wide as if about to vomit, then a gurgled hiss of agony escaped Akira's lips. 'Shit,' Sommers breathed. 'Come on!'

He could see his colleague's whole body being torn between the vice grip of the crevasse and the power of the winch. His eyes were wide with unspeakable agony as his spine seemed to buckle under the incredible pressure. Slowly, his thighs were being wrenched from their sockets, each muscle and sinew tearing beyond its limit. On it went, milli-metres at a time, the two opposing forces splitting his flesh and bone as if trying to divide it between them.

Sommers shook his head, unable to cope with the terrible pain he was inflicting. He pressed the remote once more and immediately the winch cable reversed, releasing Akira. His whole body slumped back, with the cable slackening off and lying innocently beneath him.

There was a long pause before Akira finally tilted his head up and stared directly into Sommers' eyes.

'Again,' he breathed.

'Just wait a minute,' Sommers pleaded, staring down at the top of Akira's head. 'Please.'

'Again,' he repeated, trying to raise his voice, but the sound was lost to the cavernous walls of ice.

Sommers pushed his thumb down on the remote once more. There was the same sound, the same immeasurable pressure on a human form. He counted the seconds as the cable pulled inexorably tighter with each one. It sawed through the soft flesh at the back of Akira's thighs all the way down to the bone, before there was a dull crack as his hip joint finally collapsed. But still, Akira did not pull free.

Sommers killed the winch, tears welling up in his eyes.

'Please,' he begged. 'I can't do this any more.'

Akira's eyes were half closed, while his breath came out in a horrid rasping sound from somewhere deep within his chest.

'I'm sorry,' Sommers whispered, kneeling down at his side.

'It OK,' Akira breathed, reaching up to grab his hand. Somehow both of them had lost their gloves and their bare fingers curled tightly together. Then Sommers' body began to shake. As he silently wept, tears rolled down his face mingling with a line of snot from his nose.

'It OK,' Akira repeated, the words coming out breathlessly.

His free hand moved up, tugging at the collar of his jacket. '*Bushido*,' he whispered, revealing a little more of the tattoo on his neck. Sommers could see the tip of a samurai's *katana* sword, wreathed in blossom. 'Death not the end.'

Sommers looked away, this mention of death too soon for him to consider. He swivelled round so that his back was against the ice and let his eyes run up the side of the crevasse. His vision settled on the aura of light pouring in from the outside world and he exhaled, watching the vapour hang listlessly in the air. The light seemed so very far away.

For the first time, he felt cold. Sweat and blood had dampened his thermal layers, leaving only his thin windproof jacket to retain body heat. It wouldn't be enough to see him through the next hour.

'Don't know how I expected to climb out of here anyways,' he said, more to himself than Akira. 'Nowt but tools and some rope in the tractor. Be bugger all help climbing to the surface.'

He was about to turn back to his companion when a shadow played across the interior of the crevasse, partially blotting out the light. Sommers tried to focus, pulling his vision back from a blur. There, at the top of the crevasse, was a figure. He could see it now, the silhouette haloed by blinding white light.

'Down here!' he bellowed, bringing his hands up to wave. The figure moved slowly, eyes scanning from one thing to the next as it took stock of the situation, but it did not respond.

'Hey! Down here!' Sommers shouted again, this time clambering to his feet. It was impossible that the other person couldn't see them. 'We're about sixty feet down and Akira's hurt . . . bad!'

The figure paused for a moment more, then vanished. As light flooded back into the crevasse, Sommers stared up towards the opening in confusion.

'What the hell's he playing at?' he asked, then switched his attention back to Akira. 'Don't worry, mate. The cavalry's here. We'll get one of them oxy-acetylene torches from the base, and a hammer drill. It'll crack this shit right open.'

As he looked closer, he saw that Akira's head had slumped forward. His eyelids drooped, the exhaustion and pain finally too much to bear. The last vestiges of colour had drained from his face, leaving only an ashen mask. He was barely recognisable. Sommers moved closer, gently slapping his hand across Akira's face.

'Come on!' he said, trying to shout, but his voice seemed somehow disconnected from himself. 'You've got to stay awake. *Bushido.* You told me all about that once. *The way of the warrior,* right?'

Akira didn't respond. His eyelids were closed.

'Come on, mate. One last fight.'

Taking off his own fleece hat, Sommers jammed it down on top of Akira's head, poking some strands of loose hair back under the warm brim.

'Akira-san,' he whispered. 'You're one of my only real mates. You've got to pull through this. Please, for me.'

Sommers exhaled a great cloud of air against his fingertips, but they were already numb from cold. He knew that his core was starting to protect itself, re-routing the warm blood from his heart so that it cut off his extremities. It was the first stage of hypothermia, and soon the rest of his body would systematically start to shut down.

He stared towards the light once more. Why was the figure up there taking so long to help them? And how had he found them so quickly? They were over two days' tractor drive from their base.

'Help!' Sommers screamed. He waited, then screamed again, this time louder. After a moment more, he sat down next to Akira and curled his legs up against his chest.

'Please,' he whispered. 'Somebody . . . help us.'

Chapter 1

Rain mixed with sleet hit the side of the helicopter window.

The North Sea was its habitual grey-blue, near perfectly matching the autumnal sky. The only discernible differences between the two elements were the breakers playing across the surface of the water like the strokes of a paintbrush, but even they faded from view as the helicopter passed into yet another bank of heavy cumulus cloud.

Kieran Bates sat bolt upright in his seat, trying to focus on anything other than the flight. The austere cabin lights accentuated his already pale features, while his auburn hair was slicked back from his face, partly from sweat. Every few seconds the helicopter lurched in a new bout of turbulence and Bates' eyes would drop to his watch, willing the time to pass. He could feel the sweat slowly running down his back and collecting in between his buttocks, dampening the seat of his suit trousers.

Far below, there was a small collection of lights – the only feature for hundreds of miles in the desolate sea. They were nearing the oil rig.

The helicopter whined, the pilot feathering the collective, as first one skid, then the next, clumsily banged down on the concrete helipad. As he opened the door of the helicopter, Bates drew the thick sea air deep into his lungs, trying to steady his nerves. This had better work.

A surly rig worker, as indifferent to Bates' presence as he was to the weather, led him across the metal grating of the main platform and out towards one of the lower decks. Bates could hear the roar of the seawater swelling up from beneath them and smashing into the rig's mighty supports. His eyes followed the line of the scaffolding towers as they reached up into the turbulent sky, hundreds of feet above where he stood. The sheer scale of the structure was monstrous.

As they entered through a storm-sealed door, his guide suddenly turned to face him.

'Matthews, right?' he asked, the pitch of his voice unexpectedly high.

'Right.'

They followed the tunnel through one prefabricated module and into another, twisting down two flights of stairs to a lower level.

'Like being in a bloody rabbit warren this,' Bates offered, but his guide pressed on without comment. Arriving at what was obviously the canteen, the man simply gestured forwards and then left, leaving Bates with the smell of old cigarettes and recently fried food.

The canteen was nothing more than five rows of tables with coffee cups grouped in their centre. The movement of countless workers could be mapped by the grimy footprints zig-zagging across the linoleum floor, while heavy gas piping ran around the canteen's circumference. The room's sole redeeming feature came from the row of heavy-rimmed windows that faced out to sea, each accompanied by an old armchair, battered by age and neglect.

Bates stepped further into the room, passing a serving hatch surrounded by notices and official reminders. At the centre, as if enshrined by them all, was the front page of an old *FHM* magazine featuring a provocative, bikini-clad girl airbrushed to perfection. Bates' eyes lingered on her for a second, before the image was lost to a waft of steam curling up from a dented urn standing directly beneath. The smell of old, boiled tea rose up to meet him.

Bates smiled. It was exactly as he had imagined, only grubbier. The entire oil rig was like a repository for lost souls, isolated by hundreds of miles of seawater. Here, the workers existed in a kind of stasis – no past, no future, just each day blurring into the next while the machines sucked the oil from the ground with unending thirst. People came here to escape the outside world. They were cut off and far removed from any semblance of a normal, functioning society. His old school friend, Luca Matthews, must have sunk low indeed to have ended up in such a place.

In the farthest armchair, half turned from him, he could see the crooked knees of someone staring out to sea. He moved closer, surer with each step that the legs belonged to the man he had travelled so far to see.

'I thought you always hated the water,' Bates began, hovering just beside the chair.

Luca Matthews looked up, eyes hazy from staring out of the window for so long. He looked distant and unfriendly; with unwashed hair that had matted into strands and now clung to the sides of his face. His cheeks had hollowed since they had last met, the skin tighter and creased at the outer corners of his eyes. He clung to a tin mug brimming with tea, his long, supple fingers bandaged in a vain effort to heal the deep cracks running over his knuckles.

A few seconds passed before Luca's expression softened. Then, slowly, the beginnings of a smile appeared.

'I hate the water because you nearly drowned us once in your father's boat.'

'You know, he never forgave me for losing that boat.'

After carefully putting down the mug, Luca got to his feet. Bates could see his long, muscular limbs through the threadbare T-shirt he was wearing. His abdomen was utterly devoid of fat, uncurling like the body of a snake. As he reached forward to hug Bates, the smell of dirt and turpentine wafted from him. 'What the hell are you doing here, Norm?'

Bates smiled at the mention of his old nickname. On their very first day at school together, one of the older kids had taunted him that he must be related to the lead character in *Psycho* and the name had stuck. He hadn't heard it in almost three years – the last time he and Luca had met.

'That's a question I could very easily ask you. Real shithole you've found yourself here.'

Luca made no effort to refute this. Instead, he stared at his visitor for several seconds before suddenly seeming to check himself and raising his mug up to offer some tea. Bates winced, genuinely appalled by the idea.

'Guess there's no need to ask how the flight was,' Luca said.

'Weird, isn't it?' his friend replied, with a thin smile. 'I get motion sickness from just about every form of transport and there I go, choosing a job in the bloody Foreign Office. You'd have thought I might have opted for something with a bit less travel as part of the job description.'

Luca didn't respond, his mind still preoccupied by Bates' unannounced visit. In all the time they had known each other, Bates had only ever come to see him for a reason, and already Luca was trying to guess what it might be. But as he stared into his old school friend's face, he was struck by how much Bates had changed. He looked softer, paunchier.

When they had first met, Kieran Bates had been obsessive about martial arts and his body had borne the hallmarks of strict training. He had been supple and lean, with explosively fast reactions. Now, he looked every ounce the drab office worker, beaten down by life and the daily commute. But as Luca studied him more closely, he wondered if there wasn't perhaps something more deliberate about this change in his friend. Anonymity was an attribute highly prized in Bates' line of work.

'You're looking well,' Luca lied.

'I look fat. But at least I've seen the inside of a shower room in the last month. You, my old friend, smell like the arse end of a donkey,' Bates replied while idly scratching his thinning hair. 'Still, I guess there aren't too many ladies to impress around here – aside from Miss November over there.'

Luca's eyes flicked to the *FHM* poster on the wall. He had passed it hundreds of times, but would never have been able to say what edition it was. Bates had always been like that. He had a photographic memory and could remember even the most spurious details of their childhood years.

'So how have you been keeping?' Bates offered, his smile widening.

Luca shrugged. 'Come on, Norm, we've known each other for far too long. You didn't come all this way to check up on me.'

'Fair enough. Same old Luca – straight to the point.'

Dragging the neighbouring armchair a little closer, Bates hitched up his suit trousers and perched on the edge.

'The truth is,' he said, 'there's been an incident. A couple of scientists out in Antarctica got themselves trapped in a crevasse last week. Messy business. They had to cut them out with a damn blowtorch. The closest one to a guide in the whole group was a man named Sommers. They found him with all the skin stripped off his fingers from where he'd tried to claw his way out.'

He looked to Luca for a reaction, but his expression remained blank.

'You see, the scientists were drilling into this lake – a very special lake. Nearly two miles under the surface of the ice, they've found *unfrozen* seawater. It's been there for nearly twenty million years, with all sorts of lost enzymes and bacteria locked within.' Bates crunched his fists together as if trying to trap the water in his own hands. 'Imagine it, Luca! Bacteria that was around when the world just began.'

'Bacteria?' Luca repeated. 'Since when did you give a shit about bacteria?'

'Don't knock the little stuff. Life's in the detail. Aside from finding unknown microbes, drilling down that low tells you exactly what the atmosphere was like all those years ago. Kind of important if you want to prove whether climate change is man-made or not.'

Luca's eyes passed over the ceiling of the canteen as if encompassing the entire oil rig.

'You need to drill into an Antarctic lake to tell you that?'

Bates ignored him, leaning forward in his seat.

'Four different nations have pooled their resources and come together on this project. We've been at it for three years now. And this January, the Russian team finally succeeded in drilling into the lake.' Bates shook his head in disbelief. 'Drunken sods actually made it on schedule. Then it was supposed to be the British team's turn and our boys were tasked with extracting the first samples. Only now, we can't get back to the damn drill site.'

'Why's that?'

'The route goes over this narrow pass and that's exactly where the tractor was swallowed. Those idiots had been driving over a crevasse field for years and not even realised.'

Luca blew the steam off his tea, already guessing what was coming.

'We need someone to get our boys back to the drill site before Antarctica closes down for winter in just over a week's time. The seasons are about to change. Soon, it'll be twenty-four-hour darkness down there and as soon as that happens, *nothing* moves in or out for the next ten months. So, if we don't get back to the drill site before then . . .'

'. . . the hole will re-seal,' Luca interjected.

'Yeah, the hole will re-seal. And three years of Russian drilling will be up in smoke.'

'So just plot another route.'

'Believe me, we've tried. The only way back to the lake is over a mountain. The lake sits right in the middle of a semi-circular range of them. They bar the drill site to one side, while the other is locked in by the sea.'

'Why not just use a boat then?'

'You ever heard of the barrier?' Bates asked, but his short pause suggested that the question was purely rhetorical. 'It's a two-hundred-foot-high ice sheet that surrounds most of Antarctica. There are only a few places where you can actually dock a ship down there, and this lake isn't one of them.' He gave a smile that faded as quickly as it had appeared. 'There's a good reason why ye olde sailors used to stamp *Here be Dragons* and have done with it. Bottom line, Luca – we need a climber.'

He had barely finished the sentence before Luca started shaking his head. 'Come on, Norm, choose someone current. I can name five guys who could do the job for you.'

'It's a walk, Luca. Barely any climbing involved,' Bates countered, ignoring his protests. 'All you have to do is babysit a few scientists across to a lake. That's it.'

Before Luca could interject, Bates continued, 'Job starts

in Cape Town. From there, it's a five-hour flight due south to the ice runway in Droning Maud Land.'

'Cape Town?' Luca asked, having been to the city many times before. All that time spent on the southern tip of Africa and he had never known that it was a gateway to Antarctica.

'That's right. And we'll pay you twelve grand a week. Starting tomorrow, with a minimum of four weeks guaranteed.'

'Twelve grand? That's a bit more than the going rate, isn't it?' Luca stared hard at his friend. 'You little shit. There's a catch, isn't there?'

Bates didn't answer. Instead, he stood up and, taking Luca's mug, walked back to the tea urn by the counter. He refilled it, careful not to get any of the noxious fluid on his suit trousers, before handing it back and sitting down next to his friend.

'I mentioned the Russians. Well, the head of this international base is a man called Vladimir Dedov. Everyone calls him "The Poet" because he's published one or two works. I read some of his stuff and it's actually not bad. Lacks the self-pity that most Russians love prattling on about. Anyway, he's been on our radar for a while now as he's been using the science bases to smuggle contraband.'

Luca sipped his tea, wincing slightly as the scalding liquid touched his lips. He pictured the scene in Antarctica; a web of isolated science bases, all operated by different nations and shipping hundreds of tons of cargo each year in machinery and supplies. If you wanted to move contraband from Russia to almost any other continent, it would be easy enough just to deliver it to their science base. There were no border controls or customs; there were barely any people. The package would then be forward shipped using the base's own logistics to get it where it needed to be. Who would even suspect that anything illegal would be coming out of a place like Antarctica anyway?

'So what's he smuggling?'

The tip of Bates' tongue wetted his lips.

'We've got a lot of history, Luca, so I'll tell you. But just so we are clear, this wasn't part of the brief.'

Luca's expression hardened. 'You came to see me. Don't forget that.'

Bates nodded. He sniffed the air before lowering his voice. 'He's smuggling weapons-grade uranium from the old Soviet bloc.'

'Fucking hell,' Luca hissed, instinctively looking towards the door.

'His brother-in-law is the military contact,' Bates continued, now speaking faster. 'They ship it via Antarctica as it's the only place on earth no one has eyes on. No spy satellites look that far south, which makes it impossible to track remotely. We just need you . . .'

Luca raised his hands, finally silencing him. 'Enough! Let me spell it out for you, Norm. I'm not going within a hundred miles of some Russian lunatic who smuggles nuclear fucking bombs!'

Bates glowered at him, willing him to lower his voice. He had already grabbed Luca's wrist, the strength of his grip whitening the skin around his fingertips.

'Stop being so damn melodramatic. This is a sixty-year-old

scientist who writes bloody poetry. He makes a bit on the side smuggling a few grams of very nasty stuff. All I am asking you to do is insert some spyware into the International Base's main computer.'

'Spyware? What the hell do I know about spyware?'

'You don't need to know anything. All you have to do is insert a memory stick and run the programme. It's that easy.' There was a pause before Bates continued, his voice steadying. 'Listen, Luca, this is the perfect chance for us to intercept Dedov's transmissions. Trust me, opportunities like this don't come around too often. Down in the science base, every email, phone call and text message has to flow through the same satellite connection. It's like it's all going through one pipe. Dedov is sending encrypted messages to his military contact and we've only been able to intercept a few of them. The reality is that if we're going to understand what's going on, we need to get the intel from source.'

Luca stared at him, his jaw clenching with hostility. 'Seriously?' he asked. 'You are seriously coming to me and laying this on my doorstep?'

Bates didn't respond, just waiting for him to calm down. A moment passed before he eased himself up from the chair, sighing heavily.

'I guess you're right. I shouldn't have come,' he said, seemingly more to himself than Luca. 'I just thought it wouldn't be a big deal for you to plug something into a computer. That you would have done it for an old friend.'

Taking a handkerchief from his trouser pocket, he dabbed at the top of his perspiring hairline.

'But I suppose this is a lot to ask. And this has all kind of happened out of the blue.'

After a moment he turned back to look at Luca, his expression softer. 'It's been a long time, huh? Since we climbed together.'

'A lifetime.'

'You know, I was always jealous of the way you climbed. I never said anything at the time, of course, but I just couldn't understand how you always made it look so easy. You could find handholds in a pane of bloody glass.'

Luca nodded at the compliment, but didn't like the sudden change of tack.

'But I was always there to belay you,' Bates continued. 'I was the one you trusted to secure your rope.'

'What's your point, Norm?'

'You needed me then, and now I need you. And I'd have thought you were the kind of guy I could depend on.'

'I don't owe you shit. And stop talking about our childhood as if it were a couple of days ago. What is it with you, Norm? You turn up out of nowhere and then suddenly expect me to up sticks and pack off to Antarctica. Things are different now. I have a life.'

'You've spent the last six weeks on this rig, even opting *not* to go back to the mainland on leave for the last two rotations. What is it, Luca? Can't get enough of the fried food?' Bates moved closer, his voice suddenly taking on an edge that Luca hadn't heard in years. 'If you stopped fucking moping around for one minute, you might realise that I'm offering you a proper job. And one that pays damn well.'

Bates exhaled, already regretting showing his annoyance. He knew that it was pointless to lock horns with Luca like this. The very attributes that had made him one of the finest climbers on the planet, also meant he was one of the most stubborn bastards Bates had ever known. He knew he had to come at it from an oblique angle, and he knew that there were still two things about Luca that might tilt the field in his favour.

Earlier he had seen a request from Luca for a transfer to another oil rig, citing 'personal concerns' as the reason for the move. It had been filed three weeks ago, and was a direct result of Luca clashing with the rig's foreman on just about every aspect of his job. Bates knew that Luca was treading water here, desperate for the paperwork to clear so that he could move on.

The second consideration was money. Over the last couple of years it was clear that Luca had amassed a nasty amount of debt. Now he was trying to save every penny, but it was barely enough for him to make headway on the repayments. Bates knew that the money he was offering would be enough to wipe the slate clean. It was a lump sum that Luca couldn't afford to ignore.

'Think about it, Luca. Fifty grand. That kind of money can change things around.'

His friend gave a humourless smile. 'Guess you know all about that, don't you? Been sniffing through my rubbish?'

'Yeah, a little. That's one of the things about my line of work. Got to get your hands dirty once in a while.'

'That sounds about right.'

Bates paused, in anticipation of playing his ace.

'Even if you discount what I'd be paying, you and I both know the real reason why you're here and it ain't for the climbing. I mean, it's not exactly a dream come true, is it – shinning up metal ladders in the freezing rain?'

'I like it,' Luca retorted. 'It's steady.'

'Bollocks. You hate it and you know it. You're here because you're doing the same thing you always do – hiding.'

Luca didn't respond, knowing full well that it was true. His frown deepened as he contemplated his own life for the first time in months. He had spent so long escaping from it all that Bates' questions made him feel completely disorientated.

'Just leave me the hell alone,' he whispered, but Bates only inched closer.

'You can't keep doing this,' he said. 'Sometime or other, you're going to have to face up to the fact that Beatrice has gone.'

Luca's eyes darkened at the mere mention of his ex-girlfriend's name, but he remained silent, sagging back into the broken armchair.

'She's a beautiful woman and you must miss her like hell,' Bates continued, sensing Luca's vulnerability. He had met Beatrice Makuru, or Bear as everyone called her, a few years ago on a stopover in Paris. He remembered the occasion well, as he had taken to her almost immediately. It was extremely rare for Bates to react to anyone in such a way and he had felt a burning envy for what Luca had had back then. They had been one of those perfect couples;

good-looking, adventurous, and, more than anything else, genuinely in love. Now that it was all over, it wasn't hard to imagine the pain Luca was going through.

'It'll hurt for a while,' Bates heard himself saying, an image of Bear still in his mind, 'but it will get better, I promise.'

'Just get out,' Luca replied, but his thoughts had already locked on the one person he had travelled such vast distances to forget – Beatrice.

'All I'm saying is, why not do something positive while you ride it out, rather than festering in this shithole? You'll be doing good, making money, and at the very least, a job in Antarctica will be the mother of all distractions.'

As Luca looked up, Bates could see his resolve finally start to waver. He watched as Luca blinked several times, slowly coming to the realisation that what Bates was offering was a chance to begin again. It was a new start – a way of finally dispelling the past.

'OK,' Luca said, nodding slowly as if to convince himself. 'I'll go. But when do I need to leave here? I've got a few things that I need to take care of.'

'Antarctica is shutting down in just over a week. This is it, Luca. The helicopter's here to take us both back.'

'You're serious? You want me to leave now?'

Bates went to respond, then paused. He could hear a sound coming from somewhere beyond the canteen door. A second later and the heavy clump of workmen's boots filled the air, followed by a deep, growling voice.

'Matthews!'

More footsteps.

'Where's that scrawny . . .'

The words trailed off as a giant of a man stalked into the room. He was wearing thick orange overalls, with a clipboard clamped in his right fist. As he came closer they could see that he was entirely bald, with a mixture of sweat and rain glistening off his domed head, which glinted under the canteen's fluorescent lights. His eyes blazed with undisguised annoyance, while his mouth looked to be somehow twisted. It was only as he halted in front of them that it became obvious he had a cleft upper lip, with the pull of his lips revealing a row of yellow-stained teeth.

'I got the safety report,' he bellowed. 'What the hell are you playing at? You have to wear two safety ropes on the scalf towers at all times. Not one, but two. And you unclipped from both!'

Luca raised himself off the armchair, eyeing him closely. As they stood in front of each other Luca looked even more wiry and lean, the antithesis to the foreman's barrel chest and brawny forearms.

'Look, we've been through this,' Luca said, keeping his tone measured. 'The drag on the ropes is too much. It would have been a two-hour climb pulling all that shit. Instead, I got the job done in twenty minutes.'

A vein started to pulse at the side of the foreman's neck. He raised his clipboard, pointing it like a weapon at the centre of Luca's chest.

'You free climbed over two hundred and fifty feet into the air! Who do you think you are? Fucking Spiderman?'

A globule of spit flew from the back of his throat, catching

Luca on the shoulder. He raised his hands defensively. 'Look, I told you . . .'

'No! I'm telling *you*,' the foreman shouted back, jabbing the corner of the clipboard into Luca's sternum. 'How do I explain this to the mainland?'

He jabbed again, causing Luca to step back a pace. As he did so his expression darkened, the thought of Bates' new job at last providing him with an alternative. He didn't need to put up with the foreman's bullshit any longer and the realisation triggered a long-simmering resentment to finally boil over.

'Have you any idea how many forms I've got to fill in?' the foreman continued, oblivious to the sudden change in Luca. He then pushed forward with the clipboard once more, but this time Luca slapped it out of his hand, sending it spinning across the floor.

'So go and write your fucking reports,' he said, nodding to where the clipboard lay. 'Go on. Pick it up.'

The foreman's eyes bulged incredulously and his sneer widened, exposing a couple more teeth.

'That's it!' he shouted, raising one arm to strike but finding it suddenly stopped by a stranger grabbing on to his wrist. The foreman turned, taking in Bates for the first time.

'Enough,' Bates said.

For a brief moment the foreman's expression clouded in confusion as he tried to figure out where on earth he had come from. But then his anger returned, redoubled by the thought of a total stranger issuing orders.

'Don't you . . .' he began.

'I said, enough,' Bates repeated, without releasing his grip.

The foreman's shoulders suddenly flexed as he swung his free arm round, his fist aiming straight at the side of Bates' head. Before it had time to connect, Bates grabbed on to the foreman's shoulder and, dropping his opposite knee, sent him sprawling in a classic jiu-jitsu roll. The foreman's huge body toppled forward, his own weight sending him crashing across the dining tables. He skidded to a halt against the service hatch as the last of the coffee mugs smashed to the floor.

'What the . . .' he began, more shocked than hurt. His eyes flickered between Luca and the nondescript office worker who had so easily bested him.

'You're suspended, Matthews!' the foreman bellowed, quickly finding his voice but still eyeing Bates warily. 'Suspended without pay! I'm going to make sure they throw the fucking book at you!'

Bates was the first to react, reaching forward and taking Luca by the shoulder. He bundled him out of the room and along the corridor, while from behind the sound of the foreman's voice echoed up the flight of stairs. As they passed through the neighbouring Portacabin and walked towards the storm-locked doors, Bates drew to a halt.

'Forget about that guy and focus on what's in front of you.'

Luca nodded distractedly, suddenly trying to imagine himself on a flight to Antarctica.

'And a word of warning,' Bates continued. 'Watch out for the Russian poet, Dedov. He's one of those larger than life, charismatic types – all smiles and hugs, until you peel back the façade of course. Watch him like a hawk.'

'I just have to put in this spyware thing, right?' Luca asked. 'That's it.'

'That's it.'

Luca turned so that he was staring at his friend straight on. 'And I've got your word I'll be working for you? No one else.'

Bates nodded. 'Just me. This doesn't go any higher up the chain.'

As he said the words, he dug his shoulder into the door, swinging it back on its heavy iron hinges. Once they were outside rain beat down on them, soaking their clothes in a few seconds. Bates smiled.

'And, trust me, I'll be a better boss. I don't even own a clipboard.'

Chapter 2

Snow fell. It was light, flurrying in the updrafts off the Seine River. It caught momentarily in the orange glow of the street lamps lining the Quai Voltaire before finally sinking down into the dark folds of freezing water. A single car turned left off Pont Royal and out towards the vaulted glass archways of the Musée d'Orsay. It moved slowly, tyres leaving fresh tracks in the otherwise empty road.

It was five-thirty in the morning, and Beatrice Makuru was out jogging. Despite the treacherous ground she ran fast, with her breath condensing and lingering in the night air. She cast her eyes up to the snow-covered rooftops of Paris before switching them back again to the road ahead.

'Come on, Bear,' she muttered, forcing herself on, but she could already feel her thighs starting to cramp.

It had been nearly six weeks since she had last slept properly. Every evening as she got ready for bed, she would feel the panic rising in her chest. It was the anticipation that was the worst part, the dreadful certainty of what was to come. She would lie in bed just waiting for the hours to pass, trapped in the grey half-light between consciousness and sleep.

She had never suffered from insomnia before, but now, after so many weeks, it was starting to take its toll.

Pulling the scarf a little higher across her cheeks, Bear crossed the Pont de la Concorde and jumped over the low iron railings of the Louvre Gardens. She passed a carousel to her right, the silhouettes of the fairytale horses stretching out across the grey lawn. Just ahead, a row of trees blocked out what little light remained, making the pathway appear entirely black.

Bear skidded to a halt. There was the sound of her running shoes tearing at the gravel beneath her, then silence. She waited, her eyes scanning the darkness ahead. So many years spent growing up in the Congo had instinctively made her fearful of the dark. It was always at night that the predators came out, always at night when bad things happened.

Suddenly Bear let out a low groan and doubled over. Her whole body convulsed as a wave of nausea hit her, welling up from the pit of her stomach. Raising her hand to her mouth, she gulped then suddenly vomited.

'*Putain!*' she hissed, wiping the side of her mouth with the sleeve of her running jacket. *Shit.*

Pulling her hair back from her face, she stared down at the stain in the snow, her surprise outweighing her revulsion. What the hell was wrong with her? She usually had a cast-iron stomach. Then it dawned on her – the new secretary.

That was it. She'd taken the last week off work because of a stomach bug, and now she had given it to her.

Staring up at the night sky, she watched the snowflakes slowly swirl down towards her. They caught on her eyelashes, blurring her vision as she counted the seconds, waiting for the nausea to pass.

Just great, she thought with a shake of her head. On top of everything else, she was now going to be ill as well. Spitting the last of the acid taste from her mouth, she turned towards the park's exit and forced herself back into a run.

Past the revolving door of the Legionnaires Club in Saint Germain des Prés, the staircase swept down in a long, uninterrupted arc. Heavy stone pillars stood either side of it like sentinels, shielding the interior from the clamour of the streets. Within the club there was a pervading sense of calm. It was a hushed, moneyed calm, with a small army of waiters and cleaning staff to ensure that it remained that way.

Bear sat in the changing room downstairs, her hands pressed against her forehead. A towel was draped over her naked back; each rib was visible along the line of her spine. Her lithe shoulders were pulled forward, revealing an old burn mark that ran in a neat rectangular scar across the width of her back. She was motionless except for the slow clenching and unclenching of her toes as she splayed each one on the cold marble floor.

Three work folders lay on the bench next to her, each filled with the preliminary notes for a new mining investigation. She was supposed to have reviewed them all and chosen her next assignment, but in the last three weeks she hadn't got past breaking the security seals. She just couldn't concentrate; the words seemed to blur on the page.

Time was running out. There was only so long her manager could cover for her. Her job was to uncover the truth behind major mining incidents happening around the globe, and Head Office only cared about one thing – productivity. If she didn't pull herself together soon and get to work on one of the assignments, it didn't matter how good her track record was, she would be out on the streets.

Bear looked up. In the far corner of the room was an older woman, possibly sixty but with the slight tug of plastic surgery at the corners of her eyes. She had her face pressed against a mirror and was trying to make the best of the light, while her right hand expertly pencilled in the sharp acute of her eyebrows. She glanced up, catching Bear's reflection in the mirror. What would have been a smile of greeting quickly hardened into one of loosely disguised contempt. Her nose wrinkled as if catching an unpleasant smell before she abruptly turned back to her own reflection.

Bear stared at her in disbelief. After all the years of coming to the Legionnaires Club, she still caught the same glances, the same mutterings of disapproval. It was always the same – a black woman in the club! How perfectly scandalous! She would see the searching look in their eyes and sense the air of anticipation, as if they half expected her to burst into some kind of tribal dance.

Shutting her eyes, Bear cursed herself for letting it get to her. Who gave a shit what these people thought? She came to the club because of Edith, and Edith came because her father was one of the richest men in France. She had insisted Bear should join. It was that simple. She couldn't expect these people to relate to her. They had barely been outside the city walls, let alone grown up in a place like the Congo.

The Congo. Bear's lips moved silently, mouthing the words as if saying them for the first time. How would anyone here be able to understand what it had been like to grow up in such a place? The Congo questioned every moral certitude. It contradicted every absolute held so dearly by the West. Out there, life functioned on a totally different level, one where only the strong survived.

But it was an upbringing that had served Bear well later in life. Her mining assignments invariably led her to some of the most war-torn hellholes on the planet; from Sierra Leone to Nigeria, East Timor to the Sudan. In those kind of countries the situation was always fluid, always treacherous, and growing up in the Congo had habituated her to levels of danger that most people would have found terrifying. As a child, she had witnessed unimaginable horrors – no more so than when the Rwandese refugees had flooded across the border during the great genocide – so why did she always let something as petty as the racism of the club get to her? These people here would never change. They would never understand. 'Bear?'

She looked up to see Edith's smiling face, taking in the neat row of white teeth and heavy coating of lip-gloss.

'*Eddy? Comment ça va?*'

Edith's eyebrow rose as if she had been dying for someone

to ask her that question all morning. Disposing of her Chanel handbag with a quick flick of the wrist, she edged herself on to the bench next to Bear, squashing the work folders beneath her short skirt. Normally Bear would have objected, but she knew enough of Edith's unstoppable enthusiasm to comment.

'I have *got* to tell you what happened last night,' her friend began, eyes widening at the prospect. 'Henri and I were having a dinner party. You know, the usual banker mates of his and my cheeks were aching from smiling so goddamn much.'

Tucking a loose strand of hair behind her ear, she leant forward. 'Well, I went upstairs to check on little Frédéric as he was sleeping in our bed. A few minutes later, Henri comes up and we ended up talking in Frédéric's bathroom down the corridor. We were mouthing off about how boring everyone was, how fat his boss's wife is . . . you know, basically giving the whole room a good slagging off.'

Edith moved a fraction closer, her voice dropping conspiratorially. 'Then Henri starts getting horny, right? So we shut the door and do it right there on the bathroom floor.'

Bear looked skywards, perpetually amazed by how willing Edith was to share the intimate details of her marriage. 'And why are you telling me this?'

Edith grabbed on to Bear's shoulder in readiness to deliver the punchline.

'Because the fucking baby monitor was on!' Raising her hand to her mouth in delighted horror, Edith began to shake her head. 'Everybody heard everything. I mean, *everything*.

We dusted ourselves off and trotted downstairs like nothing had happened, only to find the dining room empty. *Putain de merde!* There was only the little flashing light of the baby monitor!'

Edith's finger bounced up and down as she mimicked the flashing light, before she looked up and cackled with laughter. Bear returned her gaze, trying to suppress her own smile. No matter how down she was, somehow Edith always seemed to make her see the lighter side of life.

'They were dull anyway,' Edith continued, smoothing down her skirt as she got to her feet. 'Does kind of scupper Henri's chances of promotion for a while though.'

They both fell silent as the older woman in the far corner of the room made an affected display of clearing her throat. She had already packed away her eyeliner. Marching past them towards the exit, she breathed the words, *'Petite salope,'* before sweeping out of the room. *Little slut.*

Edith's mouth fell open in shock. A moment passed in stunned silence before she gathered herself and leant forward so that she could call through the closing door: 'Shut it, you old hag!'

As the door finally eased shut, Edith flashed another smile at her friend. 'Don't worry, I know her. She plays tennis with my dad. *Complete* bitch.'

Edith then moved to the locker opposite and let her eyes settle on Bear. After a brief silence the frivolity seemed to ebb away, to be replaced by genuine concern.

'Nice to see you laugh, Madame Beatrice. Haven't seen it in a while.'

Bear shrugged.

'You know, you haven't phoned me in nearly three weeks,' Edith continued. 'Normally, I strike a friend out of my address book for that kind of behaviour.'

Bear raised her hands in self-defence. 'Sorry, Eddy, let's just say it hasn't been the best month.'

'Still thinking about Luca?'

At the mere mention of his name, the last of Bear's energy seemed to drain away. She turned her gaze to her feet, letting her vision blur.

'What the hell happened between you two?' Edith asked.

'Can we not talk about this?' Bear asked, not bothering to look up. It was as if each hour of insomnia was compressed into this one moment, making her feel utterly exhausted. Six weeks had passed. Six weeks, and still she felt raw. Bear slowly shook her head. Everything felt wrong. It was like she was on a path in life that she had never meant to take.

'Come on, Bear, you've got to talk to someone.'

'Yeah? Why?'

There was a long pause while Bear slowly closed her eyes. She could picture Luca at their flat in Paris, with his tousled blond hair and pale blue eyes. It was his eyes that she had fallen in love with, right from the start. They had always been so full of untapped energy. The way he used to look at her had been so uncompromising; as if life existed purely for them both.

But that was just it, it didn't. Bear had a son called Nathan, who was six years old and living in Cape Town with her ex-husband, Jamie. No matter how much she tried to rationalise her decision to live in Paris with Luca, it didn't ease the terrible sense of loss she felt. She could hear herself justifying it all, telling anyone who would listen that seeing Nathan once a month was an acceptable compromise for a short period while she focused on her relationship with Luca and her career. But even as the words left her mouth, she could feel the burning in her heart. Had she not been a mother, she could never have believed that the longing for your own child could cause physical pain.

And the worst part was, it wasn't even Luca's fault. He had only asked her to wait six months, just to get used to the idea of them as a couple before introducing her son into the same house. But with every reasonable call to wait, all Bear heard was 'no', and with it the desperate sense of separation from her child grew. On the last two occasions, her ex-husband had taken Nathan to his grandparents on exactly the dates she had flown to Cape Town to see him, just to spite her, and now there was only the gaping hole in her heart; from losing Nathan, from losing Luca, from life's relentless onslaught.

Resting her head against an oak-panelled locker, Bear stared across at her friend. A single tear welled up in the corner of one eye before running down the line of her nose. She sniffed, hating the feeling of being so exposed.

'I miss my boy, Eddy,' she whispered.

'Oh, *chérie*,' her friend replied, reaching forward to hug her, but even as Bear let herself be embraced, she could feel her breathing grow steady again. Why was she being so emotional? Why did everything that happened make her feel

like the world had just collapsed? It was the sleep deprivation. It was killing her, making her feel so damn vulnerable
all the time.

Detaching herself from Edith's arms, Bear stood up and
flipped the towel over her shoulder.

'Christ, I'm a mess,' she muttered.

Edith stood up too. 'Take it from someone who did a lot
of breaking up in their time, you've got to get back in the
game. It's the only way to forget Luca.'

'That's the last thing . . .' Bear protested, but Edith pulled
her over to the large wall mirror and stood behind her, eyes
scanning Bear's face like an over-zealous beauty therapist.
Bear stood naked but for the towel and a pair of frayed
knickers, greyed from age. Her eyes were cast down, refusing
even to acknowledge her own reflection.

After a moment's scrutiny, Edith frowned. 'I don't know
what the hell you are doing, girl, but this is the best I've
ever seen you look.'

'Oh, please.'

'I'm serious.'

'I'm sick and haven't slept in a week,' Bear countered, but
as she started to turn away her eyes caught her reflection in
the mirror and she stopped. It was the first time she had
really bothered to look at herself in almost a fortnight.

'You think it might be something else?' Edith added,
already suspecting the reason for the change, but Bear wasn't
listening. Instead, she let her eyes wander across her face
and neck, taking in every detail. Edith was right. Her skin
positively glowed. It was a deep, blue-black, glistening across

her neck and chest from the run, but shining with vitality. Bear moved closer, flicking her tongue out to the end of her lips and running it across the sharp points of her teeth. They looked whiter, the enamel stronger somehow.

Her forehead wrinkled in confusion, the unexpected discovery counter to everything she felt inside. Stepping back a pace, she glanced down at her breasts. They seemed fuller, weightier, as if they had filled out overnight.

'What do you mean . . . something else?' she asked, not taking her eyes off the mirror.

'I mean, you look pregnant,' Edith responded, as if the observation were entirely self-evident.

Bear's mouth opened in horror as her eyes followed the line of her body and rested on her belly. In that single moment, it suddenly became so obvious.

'Oh, shit,' she whispered. 'This can't be happening.'

Chapter 3

Vidar Stang brushed his fingers over his cheek. The entire lower half of his face was burnt black by the sun, blistered from his chin right up to his temples. As his fingers found a small strip of peeling skin, he gently tugged it, ripping upwards. It pulled more with it, exposing a bloody, thumb-sized patch of flesh.

Stang shut his eyes, screwing them up in annoyance. His thickset fingers were also black, this time from grime and engine oil. They poked at the open wound, dabbing it gently.

'No,' he said, the single word reverberating off the metal walls of the deserted Antarctic base. He paused, the bass note of his own voice surprising him. He hadn't spoken in weeks and it was deeper than he remembered.

Piles of equipment lay all around him. Closest were hundreds of packets of dehydrated food. Then came ropes and technical climbing gear, followed by his extra down clothing. They stretched off in all directions, everything neatly stacked by name and type with shoulder-width pathways snaking in between. Order was the one constant in Stang's life – a lesson he had learnt on the very first day he had landed in Antarctica.

He turned right down the nearest pathway, then left. His movements were fast and fluid, his body perfectly attuned to the space after so many months of living here. Within just a few seconds, he had pulled out a small aluminium panel with one side polished to serve as a mirror. Raising it to the light, he slowly tilted it from side to side to catch his reflection.

He grunted. His face looked even more haggard than he remembered. It wasn't just the burnt skin; a short beard now curled out from his jawline, the white-blond hair patchy and unkempt, making him appear more like a vagrant than a former naval serviceman. His eyes then moved up to his cheek to assess the damage and the nub of flesh hanging from the open wound. Nothing ever healed in Antarctica. The air was so damn dry it sucked the moisture from his skin.

Stang tilted the mirror lower. Despite the temperature in the room being a few degrees below zero, he was bare-chested. He ran the mirror slowly down the side of his torso. It was sheet-white from lack of sun, in direct contrast to his face, but Stang wasn't interested in that. Instead, he stared at the line of abdominal muscles running down the sides of his body, before his eyes settled on the great slabs of his pectorals. They curved across his chest like the flanks of a mighty racehorse and, as they filled the mirror, Stang instinctively tensed each one.

He had always been naturally strong, just like his father, Fedor Stang, before him. In fact, the months he had spent in Antarctica had given him the chance to train obsessively and he was quite sure that he was now even bigger than his father had been. He spent three hours every day, conditioning his body with narcissistic fervour, until his neck bulged and his thermal tops stretched to bursting at the seams. Grunting with satisfaction, Stang went to put the mirror down when he caught sight of his own eyes in the glass. He stopped abruptly, blinking as he took in their grey, almost translucent, colour. The eyes seemed to lack any recognisable form, only the pupils distinguishable as a dull speck dead centre. He peered closer, desperately trying to remember what colour they had once been.

He thought back to those first few days in Antarctica. He had been so unprepared, so pathetic. Without sunglasses or goggles, the sun's glare had been relentless, burning deep into his retina and causing him to go snow blind. For three whole days he had seen nothing but darkness then his eyes had become maddeningly itchy. On the second day, a viscous, pus-like fluid wept from their corners and he had thought he would never regain his sight.

Blind and alone in the middle of Antarctica – only then had he truly understood the meaning of fear.

He remembered the panic, the desperate sense of abandonment as he tried to search for the MSR stove through the tons of equipment he had brought with him. He needed it to melt the snow into drinking water, and with each hour that passed his thirst worsened. Eating fistfuls of snow only seemed to postpone the agony for a few minutes. Even before the numbness faded from his lips his thirst would return like some insatiable demon, causing his throat to swell up so badly that he could barely breathe.

Only on the third day did light begin to separate from darkness. Blurry patches came first, then solid shapes, and as each one grew more distinct, he redoubled his efforts to find the stove amongst the piles of unsorted supplies. But already he had become so weak. In only three days he had gone from being religiously fit and athletic, to a half-maddened wretch surviving on only a few sips of water.

Two things changed that day: Stang vowed never to be unprepared again and his eyes never recovered. Although his vision returned, his pupils were irreparably damaged, the colour permanently etched from them.

Stang lowered the aluminium panel and slowly tilted his head up towards the ceiling in thought. What colour had his eyes been? It was such a simple question. So obvious.

In a flurry of activity, he reached into the side pocket of his fleece trousers and pulled out a meticulously folded cellophane bag containing his Norwegian passport. Carefully holding it up to the light, he first read his own name printed neatly on the laminated page, then his date of birth. He scanned both slowly as if trying to commit the details to memory. Then he let his eyes turn to the image neatly stuck on the opposite side of the page.

There was a man in his late-thirties, with a rounded but strong face and cropped hair. The man looked determined and quietly resolved, as if the photographer had interrupted some deeply important task. Stang stared at the image, wondering what it was that he had been planning to do that day. It had been a Tuesday when the picture was taken, that much he remembered, and it had been raining.

Rain. Yes, he could still remember rain.

Stang peered closer, trying to discern the colour of the eyes beyond the shadow of the forehead. It was impossible to tell. The image was too small, the subtle tilt of the head too low. Why had he tilted his head down like that? Why would he have done such a stupid thing?

He could see his hand begin to shake with the effort of trying to remember. Exhaling a ragged breath, he tried to breathe in through his nose and out through his mouth, forcing the air through tight lips. That's what he had been trained to do at the Academy. All the pilots used it to combat the effects of negative G, when arcing through the sky in fighter jets. He could remember the briefing notes, even picture the diagrams that had been drawn on the white board in anatomy class. And now, he seemed to feel that exact same pressure, the weight pushing down on his chest. He had to take things slowly, step by step, not rush into something as important as remembering what colour his eyes had been.

It had been a Tuesday when the photograph had been taken. Tuesday. The word seemed to trigger something deep within his mind. Swinging round, he paced back to the main living area of the room and crouched down next to a low plastic table. Perched on one side was a large digital clock he had built, but instead of the numbers increasing they counted down in sequence. Five hundred and seventy-six hours to go. He did the calculations swiftly in his head, computing the numbers by rote.

Five hundred and seventy-six. That meant today was Tuesday 16 February.

The corners of Stang's lips pulled upwards hesitantly as though he were practising a new type of smile. His tongue then ran across his lips in anticipation.

A padlocked metal chest lay on the far side of the table and Stang reached across for it. He then stopped himself. Today was the day, but was there enough left? The last time he had been so foolhardy, so utterly carefree, he had almost used it all up.

Taking the key from a leather string around his neck, Stang clicked open the lock. His fingers groped within the deep chest, brushing past his hunting rifle and the boxes of ammunition, until finally they felt the glossy cover of a magazine. Pulling it triumphantly on to his lap, he stroked his hand across it before finally flipping it open. As soon as the sheaves of paper parted, the faintest hint of perfume wafted towards him from the open sachet within. Immediately, his nostrils flared as he drank in every part of the wondrous scent.

There was sandalwood and ochre, both infused by some kind of exotic Arabic spice whose top notes played across the whole magnificent symphony. Raising the magazine higher, he gently squeezed the sachet stuck to the page, oozing out a single drop of the precious liquid. It bled on to the glossy paper, slowly fanning out and releasing a deep, resounding aroma. Stang let his eyes close, giving everything to his olfactory senses and letting the perfume fill every part of his brain.

He dropped back on to his haunches, almost unable to process the sheer opulence of it all. His nostrils flared one last time, drawing in every hint of the scent into his lungs, before he forced himself to slam shut the magazine. In that one moment he tried to hold on to the absolute bliss, to keep the intensity of the fragrance alive, but already he could feel it wilting, slipping from his grasp like the end of a perfect sunset. Then it was gone; swallowed by the dead air all around him.

Stang sniffed deeply, then deeper again. There was nothing.

In all the years of research and planning that had gone into this mission, nobody had ever told him that Antarctica had no smell. It was an extraordinary truth, and one that, in its own way, was almost as debilitating as his loss of sight. Not as immediate or panicked, but far more insidious.

Ten months had passed, with the long dark of winter compounding Stang's misery. Now he hankered for smell almost as much as he had done for water. The food was no help. Every dehydrated pack was the same; a simple bureaucratic oversight, but one that had left him with hundreds upon hundreds of mashed potato sachets flavoured by some kind of ubiquitous, all-pleasing spice. He had eaten so many that he could no longer taste or smell them, his mind having long since blanked out the flavours.

In the mornings he would sometimes bury his nose in his

armpit, sniffing for the slightest trace of stale sweat or body odour. Just something to prove that he was still there. But after so many months, even his own odour had gone, as if Antarctica's dead air had finally succeeded in scrubbing him away.

After placing the copy of *Vogue* back in the metal chest and carefully padlocking it, Stang pulled himself to his feet. He stared at the digital clock, a snarl instinctively forming on his lips. Time was ticking away and Pearl would be here soon.

Richard Pearl. He forced himself not to think about the man any further. He had already lost days, maybe even weeks, to that. Finally, after so very long, time was running out.

And he still had so much to do.

Chapter 4

Luca stood by the snub nose of the Russian-made Ilyushin-76 aircraft. The bloated wings arced down from the top of the fuselage, giving the plane a squat, bulldog attitude. Across the trailing edge of the wings, Jet-A1 fuel leaked out through the rivets, instantly vaporising in the African sun.

Squinting against the glare, Luca walked around the front of the plane. He shook his head, never before having seen a relic of the Cold War so close up. He could see his reflection in the tinted glass of the navigator's hatch. The glass made it appear as if the fuselage had great, gaping jaws perpetually trying to swallow the air in front of it. The plane looked incongruous against the business jets lining the apron at Cape Town International, but then again, so was its destination.

'Go! Go!' shouted one of the Russian loaders. It was the single English word in his vocabulary, but all that he had ever needed when dealing with the melee of scientists and construction workers who usually boarded these flights. He eyed Luca cautiously, wondering why someone would be going *into* Antarctica so late in the season. The weather was already changing, the wind and dark of winter only a week or so away. Everyone was focused on getting home before the continent shut down, with even the pilots performing their safety checks with uncharacteristic haste.

The loader paused, wincing as the sound of the massive jet engines rose in pitch. He signalled impatiently for Luca to clamber up the metal steps, bundling his kit bag after him with a well-practised disregard for its contents. At the top of the steps Luca paused, staring back at the bustling airport. It was so alive – there was colour and sound everywhere he looked. Even the air was heavy. The sea was only a few miles away and he could almost taste the salt in the air. Luca took it all in, knowing only too well that this world was the diametric opposite of the one he was about to enter.

Inside, the plane was a mess of loose wires and tubing. Cyrillic lettering was stencilled over every clean surface, while cargo netting held down hundreds of barrels of fuel that stretched deep into the belly of the plane. As Luca pulled down one of the seat flaps, the loader grabbed on to his shoulder. The noise of the engines made it impossible for him to speak so instead he mimed smoking a cigarette and then shaking his head, pointed to the barrels of fuel.

'Yeah, I got it,' Luca mouthed, nodding his head.

The engines' roar intensified, each increment of power sending vibrations through the back of Luca's seat. The pilots were holding the plane with the brakes, wringing out every possible advantage for take-off. With a lurch, they surged forward along the runway, rolling and rolling, but barely seeming to go any faster. Just as it seemed they would plough off the end of Cape Town's three-kilometre runway, the nose pitched up and the last of the engines' power dragged the plane into the sky.

Once airborne, Luca pulled out the files Bates had given him on each of the British scientists he was to guide across to the drill site. There were three of them, ranging from mid-thirties to early-fifties, and none of them had a shred of climbing experience. The tractors would only be able to get them so far, then they would have to navigate the mountain range to get to the lake itself. Luca shut his eyes, already feeling a twinge in his lower back. That was always the thing about bloody scientists – they never travelled light.

Reaching for his kit bag, he pulled on his fleece layers and smeared a thick wadge of suntan cream over the bridge of his nose and cheeks. Sewn into the inside lining of his fleece jacket, he could just make out the memory stick with its spyware software that Bates had given him. Letting his thumb rub over its edges, he thought back to the helicopter ride from the oil rig.

Bates had briefed him on the route he should take to get the scientists to the drill site and had been insistent they travel west over the mountain ridge, even plotting a GPS route for him to take. But the wide-frame satellite imagery had been too hazy to see the relief in detail and, now that he had hours to kill on the plane, he wondered how Bates had been so sure of the route. And why was he insistent that they should travel *west*? Surely it would be better for Luca to check the lie of the land for himself once he had actually landed in Antarctica.

But that's the way it was with Bates. Luca could never tell whether he was holding something back or whether it was just his nature. Half-truths were his stock in trade after all. Perhaps even Bates could barely tell the difference any more.

Then again, what did it matter? Luca would load up the software on the main computer and get the scientists to the drill site. That was it. Anything more than that was none of his business.

He shut his eyes, letting the background hum of the plane wash over him. The noise and vibration were strangely soporific, while the heady fumes from the fuel barrels only intensified as the hours passed. He tried to keep himself awake, forcing his eyes open again and again, but already he knew it was hopeless. In that single moment, just as the blackness fanned out across his vision like a sunspot, he knew that he would think of Bear.

The image of her was never clear. It was more of an impression – the sensation of her next to him. He could feel her breath on his skin as she nuzzled into the crook of his neck, smell the faint scent of her long black hair. These moments were always so visceral, with Bear feeling so much a part of him that, for the first few seconds after waking up, he couldn't tell whether he had been imagining it or not.

All he had done was leave her a message. A single voice-mail informing her that he was off to Antarctica and that Kieran Bates was her point of contact if she needed to get in touch. Upon reflection, Luca didn't really know why he had left the message in the first place, but it had seemed to him that *someone* needed to know where he was going. He had no brothers or sisters, and had barely spoken to his parents since his teenage years. On the rare occasions when life did bring them together, all that remained was an unspoken animosity coupled with a genuine confusion as to how such different people could share the same genes.

So Luca had rung Bear, and even now could hear the recrimination in his own voice. It was that same perfunctory tone he used to shut everyone out. It was always like that. No matter how hard he tried to say what he felt, there was always this unspoken anger, this wall between them.

At the beginning of their relationship, Luca had been amazed by how quickly he and Bear had seemed to accept each other. There wasn't any of the usual fear he had experienced in the past. Instead, it felt entirely natural to have her with him, as if it had always been so.

But just in that one moment, that tipping point where their relationship would have taken shape and solidified into something more meaningful, it suddenly became much more complicated. The issue of her son grew and grew, gnawing away at every other part of their lives. It was terrifying how fast it all seemed to happen; the doubts and ill feeling spreading like a cancer. The very togetherness they had felt at the beginning of their relationship soon twisted into a resentment that was equally palpable. On it went, day after day, without Luca facing up to the real issues. Finally, all he could think to do was run.

He sighed, slumping back into the uncomfortable seat of

the plane. Why did he always cut away like that? Why did he always choose solitude over confrontation? Shaking his head, he wondered whether Bear had even listened to the message in the first place. With all that had happened, he wouldn't have blamed her if she had deleted it straight away.

'Go! Go!' came the loader's voice, rousing him from his thoughts. This time he was gesturing to Luca to don the last of his outer clothing. They were nearly there.

As Luca looked about him, he realised the light outside the plane had changed. Through the single porthole in the cargo bay, he could see the first ice as they passed through the Antarctic Circle and into perpetual daylight. Beneath him were immense tabular icebergs, forerunners of the mighty continent ahead, while a shimmering, yellow light haloed the horizon. It was the sun's rays being reflected back into the sky by the sheer mass of ice that was Antarctica.

Luca had seen mountains and glaciers before, but never anything on this scale. Antarctica was simply titanic. Stretching out before him was an entire new world, one that had been waiting there all along around the underside of the globe. Antarctica – the only land on the planet not owned by a single nation. The last great wilderness on earth.

There was a clunk as the landing gear unfurled. Then, as the plane descended on its final approach, a horizon of ice seemed to rise up above the porthole. Suddenly everything went white.

The plane thumped down on the runway, sending a metallic ripple through the fuel drums. As the engines roared in reverse thrust, clouds of loose snow blew up past the wingtips, reducing visibility to zero. On they went, the speed gradually bleeding off with each metre as they approached the end section of the runway, until the enormous machine finally ground to a halt. Before the noise of the engines had even wound down, the main door was heaved open and a bitter cold came rushing inside. It sucked out the warm, stale air from the flight, replacing it with a bone-dry cold that pierced Luca's lungs.

Getting to his feet, he grabbed his rucksack and moved over to the door. Beyond was a landscape of unending ice, stretching out as far as he could see. 'English!'

He looked down to see a man standing on the edge of the runway with his arms held wide. He was wearing a one-piece padded suit that seemed to accentuate his already bulbous waistline. Evidently the suit had once been bright red, but now the fabric more resembled the colour of the engine grease splattered across its knees and chest.

The man's bushy beard looked like a continuation of the fur lining of his jacket, while his cheeks were tanned the colour of mahogany. As Luca descended the steps of the plane, the man's dark brown eyes stared at him unflinchingly from behind a pair of thick-rimmed glasses. After a moment's reflection he grunted, as if he had been anticipating something more. Then he pulled himself to his full height and shook Luca's hand.

'I am Vladimir Dedov, base commander of GARI,' he said, crunching Luca's knuckles in a bear-like paw. He then wagged one finger of his gloved hand beneath Luca's nose as if about to impart a rare nugget of wisdom. 'And if *I* like you, you can call me "Poet".'

'Matthews,' Luca said, already wondering why someone as important as the base commander was here to collect him. It just wasn't the Russian way. He'd seen the strict sense of hierarchy before, like some hangover from the Soviet past. The base commander being here meant one of only two things: either somebody deemed Luca very important, or Dedov had lost control of the base.

The Russian sniffed loudly, wiping his nose with the back of his glove.

'It's cold out. Let's go.'

Motioning for Luca to get on board the tractor parked behind them, Dedov barked a few orders in Russian towards the plane loaders before clambering up into the driver's seat. They jumped at the sound of his voice, scurrying off without a second's hesitation.

'Now,' he said, half turning to Luca, 'if you are going to work at my base, I want to have a picture of your family and to know where they live.' He paused, locking his gaze on the newcomer. 'Just in case,' he added by way of explanation.

Luca stared at him, mind racing. The seconds passed in silence before Dedov suddenly grabbed Luca's shoulder, jostling it roughly.

'I make joke!' He beamed, his massive frame shaking with hilarity and causing his glasses to slip to the end of his nose. 'All Westerners think Russians are like gangster.'

'I didn't . . .'

'But I make joke on this,' Dedov continued, obviously

pleased with himself. As the shaking of his shoulders finally abated, he sniffed the air, nostrils flaring widely.

'Only *some* are gangster,' he added as an afterthought. 'Since collapse of Soviet times, only men with connections rise to top. They are like fat cream on milk. *They* are the ones that are gangster.' He spat the words out as if they were leaving an unpleasant taste in his mouth. 'A long time ago, I chose to come to Antarctica because, in this place, we have no such people. Here, we are free.'

He lit a cigarette, letting the smoke hang in the air for a moment before inching open the tractor's window.

'But even here, it is not like Lenin's dream. Everyone is not equal.' A smile passed across his face. 'How do your pigs say? Some are more equal than others!'

Dedov looked across to Luca for confirmation, but quickly realised that there would be little in the way of small talk.

'So, report says you are big climbing man. Real alpinist,' he queried, clearly doubting such an accolade. 'You climbed in Russia?'

'No.'

'Nowhere in whole of Russia?'

'It doesn't have any high mountains,' Luca replied. 'I climbed in the old Soviet bloc.'

'Hah! Russia. Soviet. You had your empire. We had ours. But tell me, what mountain?'

Luca remained silent for a moment, not feeling the need to justify himself by listing his climbing CV. In his prime, he had climbed all over the Pamir and Tien Shan Mountains, successfully summiting almost all of the most technically challenging routes. However, most people only knew the names of the highest peaks, so he kept it simple.

'I put a new route up Pobeda in the Tien Shan.'

'Pobeda? I heard of this mountain. It is famous in Russia as mighty seven-thousand-metre peak! If you climb it you have title of snow leopard, *da*?'

Luca nodded vaguely. 'Something like that.'

'Well, Snow Leopard,' Dedov intoned, as the glow of his cigarette faded, 'you have only a few days to get *your* scientists to drill site. We have done the hard work and broken into lake. But I will not allow that hole to re-seal without samples.'

With an air of finality, Dedov stubbed out what remained of the cigarette into an old pocket watchcase and snapped it shut, disposing of the crooked filter. His eyes tilted back to the horizon as he slowly shook his head.

'At least some good must come of all this,' he muttered to himself.

The Global Antarctic Research Institute, or GARI as it was commonly known, was a monstrous blue structure raised like a spider on squat, metallic legs. It looked futuristic, as if designed for another world entirely, with separate living modules connected via gangplanks and spaced out in a horizontal line. The closest module rose thirty feet above the top of the tractor, dwarfing the vehicle as they passed directly between the building's legs and into a garaging unit on the far side.

'New international base,' Dedov said, with obvious pride. 'GARI can accommodate ninety-two people in summertime, with two separate generator houses. Different modules mean if there is fire, you can close off and move to next one.'

'Incredible,' Luca muttered, peering out through the window at the underside of the beast. 'It's like something out of *Star Wars*.'

'Wars?' Dedov repeated. 'No wars in Antarctica! Only place on planet where we have no war. No military allowed here. Only scientist.'

As the garage roller door ground down towards the floor, Dedov pulled the tractor to a halt. Before Luca had a chance to open the passenger door the Russian turned towards him, grave-faced.

'Whole base was built by four governments. But only one task: to drill into special lake.' He reached out for Luca's shoulder. 'Now you see why it is important for you to succeed. If lake is lost, if hole re-seals and we fail to get samples, science will fail too.'

'I'll get the guys to the drill site,' Luca replied. Then, looking out to the far side of the vast hangar, he spotted the silhouette of a small helicopter, the front end covered in thick tarpaulin. 'Why don't you just use that thing to get there?'

Dedov followed the direction of his gaze. 'It is not ours, and it is broken. Apparently, it needs special part.'

'So fly the part in on the Ilyushin.'

'And who will fix it? You? Anyway, it is not one part. Apparently it is many.'

'What about other planes then? Aren't there smaller ones fitted with skis?'

'*Da*,' Dedov agreed, with a nod of his bulbous head. 'We have such planes in summer. We have Twin Otter plane, Antonov-2. Even, sometimes, there is DC-3 Basler.'

'So where are they now?'

'The birds have flown. Soon there will be last light here and small planes have to fly back to mainland before the start of winter. They hop along coast, from one science base to next, and go out of Antarctica via the peninsula.'

He slapped Luca on the shoulder, abandoning the topic. 'So you have to use the old-fashioned way, like a proper polar explorer! But you must move fast.'

Luca met his gaze. 'I can move as soon as the scientists are ready. I've already got a routing on my map that we can follow.'

'Map? Let me see.'

Luca pulled out the laminated paper, folded into a neat square. Dedov took it from his grasp. Tilting his head forward to peer over the top of his glasses, he followed the plotted course. After a moment's pause, he handed it back.

'This route is no good,' he said matter-of-factly. 'You have no time and quickest way is *east* around mountain rim. Not west.'

'I was given instructions. My contact was specific on this point.'

'Then your contact was wrong.'

Dedov was about to say something more when his head tilted forward. His eyes seemed to zero in on the single beam of light that shone through a skylight on the right-hand side of the hangar. His eyes watered slightly, while Luca could see a thick vein on the side of his neck start to pulse.

'Please go into the base and meet rest of team,' the Russian said, nodding slightly towards the door at the far end of the hangar. 'It is that way.'

'You not coming in?'

'Regretfully, I have a radio call to make.'

Luca hesitated, wondering why he would choose to sit inside the garage to make a call, but Dedov remained motionless, obviously waiting for him to leave. Luca swung open the tractor's door and, without another word, walked away into the main part of the base.

Only once he was out of sight did Dedov try to lift his hand off the steering wheel. His fist was locked tight, the muscles in his forearm straining.

'The light. Don't look at the light.' Dedov whispered the words out loud, but already he could feel his gaze being inexorably drawn towards the single beam flooding into the cavernous space. It was mesmeric, commanding his attention until his whole face twisted up towards it as if enraptured by the sight.

His jaw tightened, back molars grinding together. He groaned, knowing this was the precursor to yet another seizure. They were coming more regularly now, virtually every two days.

Suddenly his body snapped backwards, his back arching while his arms curled up close to his chest. His fingers wrung the air as if clawing at some imaginary foe. He gurgled, neck straining as spittle began to foam out of the corners of his mouth. The colour drained from his face while his upper lip pulled back from his teeth making it look as if a terrible, demonic force had suddenly taken hold of him.

He tried to hold on, to control the seizure in some way, but it ripped through him like an electric current. On it went, foam spilling out across his beard and pooling on the faded leather seat of the tractor. He could feel his peripheral vision darkening with just the single shard of light now visible before him. He clung to it, every part of his being reaching towards the light.

Twenty minutes later, Dedov woke. His eyelids flickered. Slowly he pulled himself up using the steering wheel for balance. He could feel the whole right side of his face was damp and his arms shook with the effort of simply raising himself vertical. He felt exhausted, so absolutely drained of energy that he barely had the strength to move.

Finally, his vision cleared and he stared towards the door of the hangar. It was still closed. Laying back his head on the seat rest, he let out a ragged breath. No one had seen what had happened. His secret was still safe.

But already he knew, it could only last so long.

Chapter 5

Despite being officially classified as 'operational', the interior of GARI was only just that. As Luca walked in, he could see wooden crates lying in the far corner of the room stacked in some long-forgotten order, while instructions for gas piping were scrawled in permanent marker across the sidewalls. He took a few paces further inside to where a makeshift couch had been positioned in front of the main heating vent. Everything about the scene looked unfinished, as if the builders had somehow got distracted halfway through the construction process.

A figure lay on an inflatable mattress next to the couch, with a sleeping bag pulled high across its chest. The hood concealed most of its face, while a single hand protruded from the covers, clutching a novel whose spine had been broken back so the pages could be turned using only one hand. The book was held only inches away from the figure's nose, leaving the eyes protruding above. The eyes blinked several times before switching focus and settling on Luca.

'So who are you?' asked the reader, his voice laced with boredom.

'Luca Matthews. I'm the new guide.'

It seemed to take several seconds for the information to be processed. Then, with a sudden burst of energy, the man tossed the book aside as if it had suddenly become contagious and tried to wriggle his body up through the innards of the sleeping bag. His elbows and knees strained against the heavy down fabric before he managed to jerk the zip lower and free himself. 'Shit,' he breathed. 'You're finally here!'

Now that he was vertical, Luca could see that the man was exceptionally tall, with long, bony limbs that seemed to unfold rather than bend. He had straggly hair, darkened by grease, which was pulled back from his face by an old Manchester United sweatband. It bunched up at his temples, making him look like a throwback to a 1970s tennis player, while the face itself was hawkish. He stared at Luca with bright eyes, set over a long, aquiline nose.

'I'm Joel. Joel Cable-Forbes,' he said, flashing a smile. For that brief moment his whole face seemed to light up, and he shook Luca's hand as if they were old friends. Luca guessed him to be in his late-twenties. He had the ingenuous manner of someone who had spent his entire adult life encased in academia.

Squinting a little, Joel reached for a pair of round glasses tucked into his top pocket. One end was secured to the frame by electrical tape.

'Better put these on or I could walk past you tomorrow and not even recognise you.'

He then raised his hands to indicate the building they were standing in.

'Guess I should say welcome to GARI. Well, the bits of it that are finished at any rate.'

'It's quite a place.'

Joel nodded. 'It's a beast. Truth is, we could have done the same job in half the space, but I guess that's not how things work as soon as people like Pearl are involved.'

'Pearl?'

'Yeah, Richard Pearl. He's the guy who funded most of this place. I actually met him once. Real smiley guy . . . seemed to know everything about me.' Joel paused, recalling the encounter. 'Yeah, he's one of those people who's everyone's best friend. Joking and smiling all the time. Well, that's Americans for you,' he concluded, as if it were all the explanation required.

Luca glanced down to the book Joel had been reading. The cover was so faded it was difficult to read the title, but looking closer he managed to piece together *Journey to the Centre of the Earth*.

'Inspiration for this place?' he asked.

Joel shrugged. 'Guess so. In the book, they find a prehistoric lake deep underground, so it kind of felt similar. Fewer dinosaurs here though. Unless, of course, you take the Russian base commander into account.'

Joel smiled at his own joke then the humour quickly drained from his eyes.

'If I were you, I'd watch what you say around Dedov. He's all smiles and jokes, but there's another side to him. And he has one *vicious* temper.'

As an old memory resurfaced, Joel exhaled deeply. A moment passed before he seemed to collect himself once again.

'I won't lie to you, Luca, I am glad you're here. Things have gone from bad to worse in the last two weeks. Since Akira and Sommers fell into . . . well, I'm sure you know all about that. Cabin fever's been getting to us all.'

'Is everyone holding it together?'

Joel arched his long back, stretching the stiffness out.

'Let me put it this way. When Admiral Byrd came to Antarctica a century ago, he brought twelve strait-jackets and only one coffin. And things haven't changed much since. The fact is – some people just can't handle this place. Mentally, I mean.'

'What about you?' Luca asked, his eyes passing over Joel's wiry frame and wondering how competent he'd be in the field. 'You ready to go for the drill site?'

'Well, I have the distinct advantage of being a bit of a dreamer. Means the days pass quicker for me. But it isn't the same for the rest of them. It's been so frustrating, having everything set up to extract the first samples, only to have to sit around waiting like this. Especially for the others.'

'You mean Andy and Jonathan?' Luca asked, remembering the files he'd been handed on the helicopter concerning the two other members of the British team.

'Everyone calls Jonathan by his surname – Katz. Don't

ask me why, but that's the way he likes it. And just so you know, they haven't spoken to each other in nearly a week. Fell out over the washing-up rota.' Joel raised an eyebrow. 'It's the little things, huh?'

'So I hear.'

'Actually they'll be OK, but that's no thanks to the Russians. They're real dicks when they're drunk, and since breaking through to the lake they've been doing a lot of celebrating. They don't really speak to outsiders much anyway.' Joel paused, gently setting the book down on a nearby crate. 'But we only need them to drive us to the mountain range. After that, it'll be over to you.'

Luca nodded thoughtfully, then pulled a notebook from his top pocket along with the folded map. 'You said everything was already set up to extract the samples, right?'

'Yeah. We had everything in place then the mother of all storms hit. You should have seen it. It was this massive front that came in from the coast.'

As he spoke, Joel's eyes blurred slightly, remembering the sheer ferocity of the wind.

'Joel,' Luca prompted, bringing him back to the present, 'I need to figure out some timings here.' He offered the other man the map showing the new route that Dedov had plotted. 'The base commander said it's about four hours by tractor to the edge of the mountains, then we have to find a way over. After that, I calculate it's a six-kilometre trek across the lake floor just to get to the drill site.'

'I'm not all that good with maps, but that sounds about right.'

'So how long are you going to need to extract the samples?'

Joel rubbed the end of his nose, turning his eyes skywards in thought. 'We need to re-open the borehole then feed down the piping. If everything goes well, then I'd say no more than three hours. Like I said, all the hard work's been done already.'

Luca scratched down some timings on his notepad, when Joel's hand shot out, stopping him mid-calculation.

'I forgot to mention that we left two Ski-Doos at the drill site. They'd be perfect to drive us back across the lake, which should cut a few hours off the return journey.'

'They in good condition?'

Joel shrugged, suggesting that there was no guaranteeing anything left outside in Antarctica.

'So what do you think?' he asked, trying to decipher Luca's notes.

'Crossing the mountain range is the big unknown, but assuming we find a route, then we're looking at nearly a whole day's worth of travel.' Luca looked up into Joel's eyes, which were magnified by the lens of his glasses. 'You think the others are capable of that kind of journey? It'll be tough.'

'Andy and Katz may bicker like children, but deep down they're both committed to this project. They've been working on it since its inception. That's three years' worth of work, so as much as they'll moan about their sore legs, they know how important this is.'

'And you?'

Joel cast his eyes down to the book lying beside them.

'Put it this way – if I have to read that bloody book one more time, I'll be joining Hiroko up in Module Four.'

Luca simply waited for an explanation, having realised that Joel hadn't met anyone new for a long time and seemed to refer to every facet of the base as if it were common knowledge.

'Oh, yeah, you don't know about her, do you? She's the other scientist from the Japanese programme, but since the accident she's really flipped. Now she's refusing even to step outside the base. I mean, we're talking full-blown agora-phobia and it's got so bad that she can't look outside the main windows without her legs starting to shake.' Joel paused, raising an eyebrow. 'Frankly, I don't know how things could have got so messed up so quickly.'

Breaking away from Luca's gaze, his eyes passed across the interior of the room as if the answer were to be found somewhere amongst the discarded crates.

'She's made this weird little nest for herself up near the top hatch on Module Four and only comes out to eat when the rest of us are asleep. She should have been rotated out on the last flight, but apparently orders from Japan were that she had to stay until we all leave next week. Idiots have no idea how bad it is. Mind you, I'd probably have gone the same way if it had been my partner who died down there.'

'She and Akira were a couple?'

'Yeah, a husband and wife team from Tokyo. And now his body is frozen stiff in the maintenance garage twenty feet below us.'

'The garage? Why not just store the corpse outside? You've got enough snow.'

'That's just it. We're getting a lot of storms at the moment, and that means massive snow accumulation. We'd either lose the bodies under a drift or spend days shovelling them out. Things are different now. The snow's not cold and dry like it used to be. It's too warm at the moment.'

'And humidity makes snow heavy, right?' Luca added, thinking ahead to their own journey. 'With enough wind, that kind of snow will destroy our mountain tents. If a front hits us out there, we'll be totally exposed.'

'You don't know the half of it. Winter's here. And I mean *now*. I mentioned that storm before – well, by the time we had made it back to base, the wind was gusting past hurricane strength. It peaked at over a hundred and ninety-five kilometres an hour, taking down the radio mast and rolling two shipping containers. They weighed over four tons each and were anchored with steel cabling.'

'Jesus Christ.'

Joel's eyes fixed on Luca. 'That guy? You're forgetting, we're men of science. He doesn't tend to like us much.'

Joel led Luca across a metal gangplank to the next module. As the door swung back, Luca could immediately hear the sound of drunk people talking loudly. They entered a room filled with stagnant cigarette smoke and the smell of human sweat. A group of Russians were conversing around a make-shift table, but as Joel clanked shut the door, they all fell silent.

Luca's eyes ranged around the room. There were seven men in total, all similarly dressed with the tops of their padded overalls pulled down at the waist to reveal faded white T-shirts stained yellow under the armpits and stretched tight across their paunchy waists. Although they varied in height and size, each man had pale, muscular arms and callused hands engrained with dirt. Their cheeks were a deep, windblown brown set below eyes rimmed red by drink and the hanging smoke.

Empty bottles of vodka had been placed beneath their chairs, while on the table several plastic tubs of gherkins and other snacks were being passed from one man to the next. They had stopped, some mid-chew, to stare at the newcomers in expectant silence.

Joel took a step closer.

'This is Luca Matthews,' he offered, forcing a smile. 'The new guide.'

The news was greeted with indifference. Then the silence was broken by a booming voice from the doorway. 'He is more than a guide. He is a great snow leopard!'

Luca and Joel turned to see Dedov on the gangplank directly behind them, beaming widely. As soon as his voice echoed out there was a bustle of movement from the Russians as they scrambled over themselves to make room for their base commander. The detritus on the table was quickly cleared and a chair vacated, causing the other men to bunch up so close that their shoulders touched.

'A *great* snow leopard!' Dedov repeated, with such theatrical aplomb that Luca thought the base commander might be mocking him. But then he remembered the Russian penchant for histrionics and allowed himself to be shep-herded to a seat next to Dedov. Shots of vodka and slices of cheese were summarily set before them both, while amongst the rest of the men smiles and conversation broke out once more. Dedov's patronage of Luca seemed to be universally accepted and the matter was immediately dismissed from the other men's minds.

As an obvious afterthought, Joel was offered a seat at the other end of the table, with the vodka and cheese taking longer to reach him. He sat with shoulders hunched, towering above the stocky Russians either side of him and smiling awkwardly as they talked across him. It was the first time he had been invited to sit with them and the solemnity of his expression made it clear that he was trying hard to make a good impression.

Luca watched the constant flow of food and alcohol as the Russians went back to their conversations in their native tongue. Secure in their own company, the cold exterior melted away. Instead they behaved more like excited Italians, slapping each other's knees at the punchline of a joke, or clutching each other's shoulders in commiseration as they reminisced about home.

'You must be ready to leave tonight,' Dedov said, pointing a finger at Luca. 'There is a weather front coming, but you have not enough time to wait for it to pass. The first darkness will be here soon and you must act.'

'I'd like to see the weather for myself. You got the latest satellite imagery?' he asked.

'Yes, yes,' Dedov replied impatiently. He then uttered a quick sentence in Russian and, without appearing even to have heard what was said, one of the younger men jumped up from the table and scurried out of the room.

'Sergei get you latest picture,' Dedov continued, leaning closer to Luca. 'Reach the site and get the samples. That is the number one priority. Science must come first. If you see anything else, you file a report to your government. Understood?'

'Else? What else could there be out there?'

'I said, you must file a report,' Dedov spat back, as if the remark were entirely self-explanatory. 'There is paperwork and there are rules. You cannot act like cowboy in these mountains. You have to work step by step.'

Shifting his weight round, he draped one bear-like arm across Luca's back.

'But first we toast success of mission,' he said, and, grabbing the vodka bottle, added a tiny dribble to Luca's already brimming shot glass. Luca stared at it, not wanting to do anything that would compromise his judgment out in the field, but at the same time knowing that to refuse would be tantamount to insulting Dedov. He had drunk with Russians in the past and knew that an event of any significance had to be sealed with a drink. The best defence was to show willing in the beginning, with the hope of an early exit once everyone else got stuck in.

'Your health,' Luca said, raising the glass. A wistful smile appeared at the corners of Dedov's mouth before he slugged back his vodka at a single gulp.

'And to your successful mission,' he countered, already re-filling the glasses. Luca hammered back the second shot with alacrity, trying not to wince as the liquid clawed its way down his throat. Beside him, Dedov watched closely. For the briefest of moments, the bonhomie drained from his face. Behind the hanging smoke, his eyes hardened with unreadable intent. The look only lasted a moment before he seemed to check himself and fished a gherkin from one of the Tupperware boxes on the table. He bit down on the anaemic-looking specimen, before offering the rest to Luca. The Englishman shook his head, feeling secure enough to refuse this part of the Russian's hospitality.

'You must eat otherwise you get drunk,' Dedov explained, swallowing the rest of the gherkin in a single mouthful. 'And here, we do not like drunks.'

There was a murmur of agreement from the nearest of his underlings as the remnants of the vodka bottle were metred out into the now-empty glasses. Another bottle miraculously appeared and the seal was broken before it had even reached the table. Tilting his head back, Dedov lit a cigarette, blowing the smoke upwards into the drifting haze above the table.

'You are climbing man,' he said. 'You understand mountains and nature. Already you have better understanding of Antarctica than this kind of scientist.' Dedov nodded to where Joel was seated at the opposite side of the table, still trying to follow the conversation out of some misplaced sense of civility. 'He is scientist, yes, but he does not *feel* Antarctica. He only look at this continent through thick glasses and the screen of his computer.' Dedov burped, banging the top of his chest to expel the last of the trapped air. 'But this is a place that you must fall in love with. It is like a mistress that is beautiful, even cruel. But most of all, she is fragile.'

He smiled indulgently. 'Yes,' he repeated, 'she is fragile.'

Taking another shot, he turned to Luca. Smoke had already tinged his eyes red and his pupils looked watery. The mask of bonhomie was gone.

'Antarctica must be protected, and we must do it together, like brothers-in-arms.'

Luca stared at him, almost unable to believe how swiftly a Russian's sensibilities could change. After only a few shots of vodka, Dedov was already speaking as if they were about to embark on a lifelong crusade together.

'Protect her from what exactly?' Luca asked.

'From us. From man – we protect Antarctica with our left hand, while trying to destroy it with our right.' Dedov held up his hands, idly inspecting his palms. 'But perhaps here the left has a chance to succeed. Perhaps *here* we tell different story.' With an air of finality, he squeezed his fingers closed. 'But one thing I do know for sure. Out here you have the chance to make your own destiny. Out here, you get to choose.'

He banged the tabletop, immediately killing the conversation.

'To the drilling expedition!' he shouted, raising his glass in a toast. To a man, the table got to their feet and held their glasses aloft. 'Now our British brothers will complete the work we have begun!'

There was a general nodding of heads, with even an encouraging glance offered towards Joel, before the shot glasses were drained. Through the smoke Luca could make out Joel's face, flushed from vodka and beaming with gratitude at this sudden, unexplained acceptance by their Russian hosts.

As they sat back down Luca slowly scanned one face then the next around the table, finally reaching Dedov's. Russians followed their leader. It was a singular truth that he had learnt from a two-month rigging job in the Caspian Sea. So why had Luca's arrival suddenly altered Dedov's attitude towards the British? Why should *he* make all the difference?

As their eyes met, Dedov smiled. There was something paternal about that smile, something ingratiating and easy. It was unlike any of the tight-lipped imitations Luca had encountered so frequently back home. Maybe it was because Dedov had spent so many years in the science bases of Antarctica, isolated from the real world, that he could behave with such openness

It was strange, nevertheless. If Luca had considered Dedov in his component parts, he would have said that the Russian was ugly and bloated, with a massive bushy beard that ran down into the hair poking out at his neckline. All that was true, and yet the sum of his whole seemed to be so much more. Bates had been right: Dedov did have a peculiar charisma to him. It was something innate, almost subconscious, to which other people found themselves drawn. Watching him was almost mesmeric, as though Luca were staring into the embers of a campfire.

Pulling at the collar of his jacket, he felt the fug of sweat and alcohol close in around him. The vodka was making him feel heady and relaxed, as though nothing else existed beyond the walls of the base. He could so easily let the shot glasses be re-filled and re-filled, settle back into the glow of the afternoon and let the rest of the world go on without him. But as he reached towards his glass on the table, his wrist brushed against the edge of Bates' memory stick sewn into the lining of his jacket.

Could Dedov really be the dangerous uranium smuggler Luca had been warned against? He seemed to be nothing more than a nostalgic old scientist in love with Antarctica. Even if he were making lots of money from this secret enterprise, Luca could barely imagine what Dedov would choose to spend it on. He gave the distinct impression that everything he needed in life was right in front of him.

The real enigma here was Bates. Now that he thought back to their first conversation, Luca felt sure that it wasn't so much concern that Bates had been hiding in his eyes as fear. He had been genuinely scared of something.

'Poet, I have latest weather report.'

They turned to see Sergei clutching a computer printout. As he handed it across to Luca, he shook his head.

'Same big system off coast,' Sergei added. 'I think it come here day after tomorrow.'

'Day after tomorrow?' Luca asked. 'I've done some calculations and it's a minimum of twenty hours' travel each way. And that's *if* we find an easy route across the mountains. Plus these guys aren't mountaineers. They'll need time to rest in between.'

He stared at Dedov, blinking several times as he tried to throw off the alcohol-induced apathy.

'I have seen such storms many times,' Dedov stated, his voice measured as if recounting empirical fact. 'They build for many days off coast before coming inland.'

Luca raised an eyebrow as he took the satellite image from Sergei's grasp. The entire mid-quadrant of the page was filled with a spiralling arm of cloud, with the isobars knotting together as a low-pressure gradient plummeted towards the centre. It was a monstrous storm that had been hovering off the coast for the last twenty-four hours, building in intensity and size. If they weren't back at GARI by the time it hit, they wouldn't stand a chance out in the open.

Dedov leant closer, casting his eyes over the same image.

'You must go now or there will be no time to make it back before the last flight.'

'And if we get caught out there?' Luca asked. 'We're not going to walk away from a storm like that.'

'You must understand,' Dedov countered, levelling a finger at Luca's chest, 'I would not send men into field if I thought danger too big. In my opinion, you have time if you go directly.'

'What about at the drill site? Could we shelter there if it gets bad?'

'Drill site only manned in summer months and so we took back living modules by tractor two weeks ago. There is only tower and technical piping equipment remaining.'

Dedov paused, casting his eyes down to the satellite image

once more. He sucked in air between his teeth as his eyes followed every line and contour of the page. Eventually, he nodded to himself. His voice dropped to a whisper as he added, 'If you are stuck in storm, there is abandoned Soviet base on east side of lake. It was only used in summer months, many years ago. But it is there.'

He signalled for Luca to pull out his map and, after a moment's deliberation, zeroed in on the exact point, scrawling the GPS latitude and longitude from memory with a pen extracted from somewhere within his grubby overalls.

'Don't go to base unless you absolutely have to,' he added. 'Old construction and building not safe.'

'Why didn't you mention this place before?' Luca asked.

'I mention it now,' Dedov replied flatly. 'But base very unstable and dangerous. You must stay clear unless no other option.'

With that, he scraped back his chair and stood up. Silence descended on the room once again.

'Our British brothers need us to drive tractors to mountain edge. We drop them there and return to base. Every man ready in fifteen minutes.'

There was a confused lull as the men around the table slowly took on board the fact that they were required actually to do something other than drink. Then, without a word of complaint, they staggered to their feet and started donning their outer clothing. The stocky Russian next to Joel repeatedly jabbed his gloves on to the wrong hands and, when Joel tried to correct him, swatted away any attempt at help, drunkenly protesting that they fitted better that way. One by one they filed out of the room and down towards the heavy machinery in the garage.

'Sure your men are up to it?' Luca asked as the last one stumbled over the metal doorplate.

'They eat lots of gherkin,' Dedov retorted, with no hint of irony. He then turned to Joel. 'Go tell other Englishmen and get them on board the tractors. We leave in fifteen minutes.'

'Can I at least meet them before we head off?' Luca asked. 'I'd like the chance to talk them through the expedition.'

Dedov swatted away the suggestion with a single wave of his hand.

'Talk! Talk! You have all time in the world to talk on mountain. We leave now.'

Luca inhaled deeply, knowing that there was little point in arguing. As Joel got himself together and left the module, Luca turned towards Sergei.

'I want to check one more thing on the weather,' he said. 'Where did the sat image come from?'

'We download satellite image in main communication room.'

'Good,' he said, reaching for the memory stick in his jacket. 'Take me there.'

Chapter 6

Bear Makuru closed the sliding door of the toilet and stalked into the small kitchenette set into the sidewall of her office. She pressed the button on the espresso machine while surreptitiously sliding a used pregnancy test wrapped in toilet paper into the pedal bin. Two lines. Two bloody lines! Edith had been right.

'Beatrice. A word, please.'

Turning at the sound of her manager's voice, Bear watched as Etienne du Val glided into the room. He was a trim man in his late-forties, who prided himself on always being immaculately dressed even outside the office. His eyes were the same colour as his jet black hair and, when he spoke, he did so through tight lips, enunciating each word with an affected sense of calm. But the calm was only skin-deep. On at least three occasions in the past, Bear had seen him scream with uncontrollable rage at office juniors over the most trivial of mistakes.

As he approached the far side of her desk, Bear could

smell the fresh wash of his aftershave. It was a smell she had grown to despise over the years.

'I didn't say anything in the meeting room,' du Val began, 'but we both know that you should already be on assignment. So, would you like to tell me what's going on?'

Bear raised herself to her full height. Even wearing flats, she was nearly an inch taller than her boss. Placing her hands on her hips, she let the full wattage of her gaze rest on him.

'Look, Etienne, I don't have time for this. I have a meeting starting in a couple of minutes.'

'It's been three weeks,' du Val interjected. 'Three weeks and I still have nothing to report to our friends upstairs.'

'You'll get . . .' Bear began, but du Val cut her off.

'You earn a good salary, Beatrice. In fact it's excellent, and that's because you get the job done. You jump in with both feet – always have.' He paused, breathing in deeply as if to sample the smell of coffee in the air. 'And yet here we are, still with no report.'

Du Val paused again, but this time in hesitation. He wondered if he should voice his next sentence. Normally he would never have challenged Bear so openly, but over the last few weeks he had noticed a change in her that emboldened him. She had been looking tired of late, unsure of herself even. Moving around the edge of the desk, he stepped a little closer. 'What happened to the woman we hired in Chile?'

'*Mon Dieu!*' Bear exclaimed, turning away from him to conceal the sheer depths of her loathing. Reaching forward to the coffee machine, she picked up the espresso and downed it at a single gulp. 'You know as well as I do, Etienne, I manage my own time. So don't worry – you'll have your damn report.'

'Well, naturally I'm concerned . . .' du Val added, as the slightest imprint of frown lines appeared on his forehead. 'And I am not the only one. You need to decide, Beatrice, and I mean now.'

Bear levelled her gaze. 'I'll come and see you when I have something to report. Now, if you'll excuse me, I have that meeting.'

Du Val nodded slowly, as if deliberating whether or not to give his consent. Then, after dusting off an imaginary speck from his cuff, his pursed lips tightened into what might have been a smile.

'I look forward to receiving it then.'

With that, he turned away from her, leaving Bear staring at the impeccably combed hair on the back of his head.

'Shit,' she whispered. As she spoke her hand traced across the upper part of her shoulder to the long, trailing burn mark hidden beneath her shirt. How dare du Val mention Chile after all this time?

Five years ago she had been inspecting a coal-seam gas mine outside the Torres del Paine when there had been an explosion. The onsite security detail earned little more than minimum wage and were not about to risk their lives for the seven men who had been trapped underground. On impulse Bear had suited up and gone down alone, eventually rescuing four of the seven miners before a secondary explosion closed down the entire site. She had been lucky to make it out alive and only later, once the adrenalin had died down, did she realise she had left open a thin, rectangular gap in her heat suit. It was not a mistake she would ever make again.

After Chile, her reputation as a fearless, if slightly reckless, mining investigator was all but secured. Soon afterwards du Val had appeared on the scene, offering her an enviable salary and her pick of assignments. During the course of the following year Bear had worked for him on four separate projects, proving beyond doubt that her tenacity and ability to react to danger were not one-off traits.

But as she watched du Val retreat through the ranks of partitioned desks towards his own office, she realised that he was right. She had been appallingly indecisive over the last couple of weeks and the sudden discovery of her pregnancy had only served to exacerbate the feeling. It was as if a cloud had descended over her, making it impossible for her to think about anything else.

Bear's eyes narrowed. She tried to recall whether she had felt the same with her first child, Nathan. But then she remembered. She had worked up until only a few days before the birth, and then only five months later, the whole Chilean escapade had occurred. Far from making her more risk-averse, having a child had barely impacted on her working life. Somehow she had been able to compartmentalise the two. Despite the love she felt for her newborn son, she was still able to take risks that other mothers would have considered unconscionable.

It was something her friends in the West never really understood. Growing up in Africa had imbued in her a different attitude towards life and children. There was an unyielding fatalism in her home country; the very antithesis to the mollycoddled children she saw in Parisian playgrounds, with their cashmere jumpers and over-protective parents.

So much had changed since Chile, and du Val was right. What had happened to her? Why did she feel so crippled by uncertainty? It left her spinning from one thing to the next, never committing to anything properly, never seeing it through.

Bear could feel sweat begin to prickle on her lower back and suddenly her office felt stifling. Christ, she hated these office blocks with their constantly recycled air. Shaking her head, she grabbed a Biro from her desk and used it to twist and pin up her hair. She glanced down at her stomach under the charcoal grey skirt she was wearing. It was fitted across her hips and, as she tilted her head to one side, she was suddenly aware that there was the slightest bump visible through the fabric.

Pregnant. How could she have been so stupid as to let herself get pregnant? She wasn't some naïve twenty-year-old, for Christ's sake.

All last night she had thought about getting a termination and even looked online for a nearby clinic. But as she had waited for dawn, watching the sun rise across the Parisian rooftops, she had been wracked by the need to tell Luca. Whatever had happened between them, this wasn't her decision alone. She had to speak to him about it and organise a time to meet up. This was something that had to be discussed face to face.

Digging into the side pocket of her handbag, Bear retrieved her mobile phone. She began dialling Luca's number while silently mouthing the beginning of a speech she had prepared late last night, though already the words felt flat and misplaced. But then she noticed a voicemail message. Thankful for the distraction, she connected through. Luca's voice. The message was short and perfunctory, informing her that he was off to Antarctica and an old friend called Bates was her point of contact in case of emergency.

Antarctica? What the hell was Luca up to now? As if the oil rig weren't escape enough, he had suddenly set off for the last damn continent on earth! Bear shook her head as her gaze blurred on some distant spot outside the window. This was just what she needed right now – Luca upping sticks and heading off to Antarctica!

Then there was the mention of Bates. Bear's eyes narrowed as she tried to picture his face, but it was surprisingly difficult. She could remember that he had stayed with them for a couple of days at their flat in Paris a few years back, but any more than that was a blur. Bates was kind of nondescript; average height, average build, with slightly receding reddish hair. The more she tried to picture him, the harder it became. All she could remember was his unfailing politeness. He was like some kind of ideal English gentleman. He had spoken quite a lot during his stay, but his conversation had been remarkable only by dint of the number of platitudes it contained. How he was suddenly involved in Luca's snap decision to go to Antarctica was beyond her.

Bear's gaze moved back to the phone, as if expecting an

answer to have suddenly appeared on the small screen. Antarctica! What the hell was Luca up to?

Scribbling Bates' number on the notepad in front of her, she dialled again. There was an international tone, then a pause as the call was re-routed through a separate switchboard.

'Bates,' said a familiar voice.

'Kieran, it's Beatrice Makuru. I was . . .'

'Of course! Bear. How on earth are you?'

She sat forward in her seat, pencil at the ready. 'Good, thank you.' She paused, trying to recall whether he had any family she should be asking about. Nothing came to mind. 'Listen, I just got this message from Luca saying he's gone to Antarctica. Can you tell me what on earth is going on?'

'Well, you know as well as I do, Bear, Luca's his own man. But he'll be back in a few weeks' time and you needn't worry. It's all routine stuff.'

'Routine? *Comment est-ce routine?* The last I heard he was in the middle of the North Sea!' Bear forced herself to be calm, jabbing the point of the pencil down so hard on to the page that the lead snapped. 'Look, is there a satellite number I can reach him on? I need to get hold of him quite urgently.'

'Nothing serious, I hope?'

'It's just a personal thing,' Bear replied, trying to keep the edge from her tone that suggested he should mind his own business.

'Thing is, Luca is in the field leading a group of scientists. They don't have their sat phones turned on during the day as they have to save the batteries. Bit cold down there, you see. We have to wait for them to switch them on each night. They usually do a scheduled call at eighteen hundred hours GMT. Just to check in and all that. Otherwise, if it's something urgent, we have to wait to hear from them.'

'OK, so I'll try him tonight. Can I get the number?'

Bates read out the Iridium prefix of +8816, repeating the rest of the number twice. After a moment's pause, he added, 'If you'd prefer, I can pass on a message. Just in case you don't get through.'

Bear thought about the message she could send. It wasn't easy saying that she needed to speak to Luca urgently without giving a reason why.

'Thanks, but I'd rather just do it myself,' she heard herself saying.

'Of course.'

After a slight pause, she switched focus.

'Tell me, Kieran, don't you need permits to get into Antarctica? I thought they took weeks, even months, to secure.'

'Well, normally, yes, but this is all going through the British Foreign Office and they're the ones who do the issuing. So the whole process was somewhat expedited.'

'And his reason for going?'

'There is this lake that some scientists need to get to that is surrounded by mountains. The winter is about to shut everything down and we needed someone to get in there and guide them.'

'Luca's guiding? Is it dangerous?'

'No, not at all. For a climber like him, this is all pedestrian stuff. He's probably whining right now about how boring it all is. You know how those science types drone on.'

The attempt at light-heartedness fell flat as Bear immediately switched tack. 'I remember you saying you worked for the Foreign Office, but when you say "we" – who do you mean exactly?'

'Sorry. Should have explained. I work for the British Polar Unit,' he replied. 'Well . . . truth be told, I'm actually in a part of the Foreign Office that bridges *into* the Polar Unit. I kind of sit between two stools.'

'Sounds uncomfortable,' Bear replied distractedly.

'Well, quite.'

'Antarctica sounds fascinating though,' she offered, prompting him to start talking. Something about the way he had given his job description jarred with her and Bear found herself instinctively pulling up the British Polar Unit's website on her laptop. Quickly scanning through it, she then clicked open the one for the British Foreign Office and did the same, keyword searching for Bates' name. Nothing came up.

On the other end of the line, he was still talking. '. . . but really, this is all because Luca kindly agreed to help us out. Routine stuff, of course, and he'll be home on the last flight out of Antarctica. I'll get him to call you as soon as he is back on dry land.'

'Routine' – there it was again. At first Bear had thought he was just trying to reassure her, but using that word for a second time? In all her investigations, when a person said 'routine' it usually meant anything but. Bear paused, trying to ignore the fact that something about Bates' manner was grating within her. But then again, perhaps it was just down to his English eccentricity.

'So whereabouts is Luca exactly? Did he go into Antarctica via South America?'

'No, no. They're at a new research station called GARI in Droning Maud Land, so they came in via Cape Town. Your old stomping ground, I believe?'

'Used to be,' Bear whispered, then shut her eyes. This was unbelievable. The two people on the planet whom she most wanted to see would soon be in the same city. Her son would be returning from a stay with his grandparents at the end of the week. Now Luca was passing through there too. After a short silence Bates chipped back in.

'I understand it must be disorientating, having him leave like that, but you know how much Luca loves the mountains. He practically twisted my arm off to get out there, so I'm sure he's having a good time.'

Bear went stock-still. 'Love them? That's what he said?'

'Oh, yes. Jumped at the chance. I am sure I don't need to tell you about his passion for getting up into the thin air.'

After a second more she heard herself say, 'Thank you, Kieran. Nice to hear Luca has an old friend looking out for him.'

'Not at all. Hope to see you again soon.'

Cutting the line, Bear gently put the phone down on the desk. The words 'loves the mountains' were still ringing in her head. She knew that Luca hadn't climbed in high mountains for nearly two years. Although the rig work involved climbing, it was always low-level stuff, more rock climbing than doing anything at altitude. The high peaks had been something he'd left behind the moment he came back from Tibet.

Mountaineering had become something unmentionable to Luca, with him refusing to talk to anyone about it, least of all Bear. He'd put all his climbing gear in storage; the boots, ice axes and carabiners, everything had been packed away in cardboard boxes and it had been all Bear could do to persuade him not to throw the stuff away.

On several occasions she had tried to coax him into talking about it, but had received little more than monosyllables in response. Only once, after they had got drunk together in a bar in Madrid, had he started to open up. That night she had seen a different side of him, one that had shocked her. It seemed that for him the mountains were filled with the memories of dead friends. Each cliff face had become a tombstone, each peak a memorial he would just as soon forget.

But despite it all, Bear had become convinced that he still wanted to climb again, if only to dispel the demons. She had booked flights, a hotel, and even rented climbing gear in an effort to surprise him, but when they had reached the airport and she had excitedly revealed their destination, Luca had flown into a rage. It was the only time she had ever been genuinely scared of him.

That day Bear had vowed never to try and manipulate him again. Hard as it was for her to understand, the simple truth remained: just because Luca had a spectacular talent for doing something, it didn't necessarily mean he wanted to do it.

So why had Bates said otherwise? Three years ago was the last time he and Luca had met, so perhaps he was still unaware of the change? Certainly, it was not a subject that Luca would have offered up in any conversation. One thing was for sure – if Luca had decided to go back to the high mountains, it would have been out of fundamental necessity. Love would have had nothing to do with it. Kieran Bates had been mistaken. But the real question was, how could he have got it so wrong?

Kicking off her shoes beneath the desk, Bear turned towards the window. From the fifteenth floor of the office block she could see the twin towers of Notre Dame rising above the morning mist. For nine years she had led investigations that uncovered the truth behind mining incidents all over the world. If there was one thing she was good at, it was telling when someone was holding back.

She checked her watch. Another eight hours before the scheduled call time and a chance to speak to Luca directly. In the meantime, she wanted some more answers.

Opening the door, she called to her assistant.

'Please ask Louis to come in. I've got some digging for him to do.'

Chapter 7

Kieran Bates leant back in his chair and let his mind linger on an image of Bear. He had anticipated that she might call, and hoped that the affable, 'English gent' routine he had affected had been enough to assuage any doubts she might have had. The last thing they needed was a professional investigator getting curious.

His eyes then passed across the features of his Whitehall office. The décor was tired and monotone, in direct contrast to the elegantly dressed woman sitting opposite him. She had her head tilted down, reading an open file on her lap, causing long strands of silver hair to fall across her face. After a moment more, Eleanor Page looked up and let her quick green eyes settle on him.

At fifty-nine years old, Eleanor still retained something of the attractiveness of her youth, and what age had diminished she had mostly compensated for with classic styling and impeccable tailoring. Her hair, although no longer dark brown, was thick and luxuriant, while the lines on her face had been carefully softened by a plethora of expensive moisturisers and even a few laser treatments. Perched on top of her head like a tiara was a pair of tortoiseshell-framed glasses.

For the last sixteen years, Eleanor Page had been chief adviser to the Director General of the FBI. In all that time she had witnessed a succession of new administrations come and go, and with each, had viewed their passing with unshakeable equanimity. Long ago she had realised that such events were mere blips in the course of history and that, for as long as the underlying factors remained constant, life would continue largely as is. It was this perspective alone that had kept her diastolic 80 under 120.

But in the last six months all that had changed. There had been a fundamental shift that would affect all US interests, both foreign and domestic. So far only four people in the US administration had seen the same report, with the Director General specifically labelling it a 'game changer'. The document had concluded with the warning that they would be able to keep the status quo for precisely eighteen months, after which time the full horror of their country's predicament would be laid bare on the world stage.

Eleanor had been personally tasked with finding a solution, and after a chance report had hit the desk of one of her contacts at the FBI, she felt she had one. It was a complicated plan, involving a number of third parties and big geo-political plays – all of which made her feel very uncomfortable. She would have preferred to keep this firmly within her own sphere of influence, but unfortunately that just wasn't an option. Instead she needed the British, and they in turn had assigned her Kieran Bates.

Staring across the desk at him, Eleanor brightened her expression into a smile, carefully masking the doubts she had about this man. Was Bates really up to the task? Then again, Parker himself had put him forward for the job.

When she had initially made contact with the head of MI6, Fabian Parker had told her that he had just the man for her. He had first pointed to Bates' aptitude tests, before going through his list of previous assignments. They had been impressive, with only one notable exception in the Yemen where one of his field operatives had been killed. But no career was perfect. If one seemed to be, there was usually something missing from the file.

But more than Bates' list of achievements was the fact that he had been physically absent from MI6 for the last three years. Continuous tours of Afghanistan and, prior to that, the Yemen had made him all but a stranger to his own department. It was exactly what Eleanor Page was looking for. She needed someone detached from the normal remit of MI6, but who could ensure that the British kept their end of the bargain.

With so much at stake, it was vital that as few people as possible knew of the plan's existence. Parker had even decided that the British Prime Minster need not be fully informed. Instead, a desultory report had been sent upriver that was as vague as he could make it without piquing the interest of the oversight committee.

Adjusting the glasses on top of her head, Eleanor's smile

widened a fraction. It was a knowing look, as though she and Bates had been friends for years.

'So, who exactly is this Beatrice Makuru?' she asked, her voice tinged with the slightest trace of a New York accent.

'My man's ex-girlfriend. She's a mining investigator for Anglo-Africa, so I thought a little reassurance wouldn't go amiss.'

'Well, I'm sure a man like you can handle her easily enough. No doubt you'll do whatever it takes to keep her from asking any more questions.'

Bates nodded, trying to ignore the flattery.

'And this contact of yours, Luca Matthews. You seem confident he'll get the job done.'

'He'll be fine,' Bates replied, nodding again, but almost as soon as he said the words, an image came to him of Luca crumpled into that decrepit armchair on the oil rig. Only now that everything had been set in motion did it really sink in that Bates was entrusting everything to a man who was all but broken. Was Luca really up to the challenge? Bates' single consolation was that the task itself was incredibly simple: insert the memory stick into GARI's satellite terminal. That was all Luca had to do. Whether the British scientists made it to the drill site or not was an irrelevance.

'An ideal opportunity presented itself, and it seemed a great deal neater than trying to hack in remotely to the Antarctic station as originally planned. We couldn't have sent in one of our own chaps. The Russians would never have bought it. Had to be a real climber, you see.'

Eleanor seemed to accept Bates' appraisal of the situation. She then shifted in her seat, her mind switching to the next item in a long list.

'We got word yesterday from the Chileans. They will follow the initial land claim of the British and ratify it. The only caveat is that they want the Argentinian claim rejected out of hand.'

Bates smiled knowingly. 'Nothing like hatred of one's neighbour, eh?'

Ignoring the quip, Eleanor widened her eyes slightly to ensure that she had his full attention.

'Everything has to follow one after the other, in the right order. Each land claim must fall in succession, like dominoes. The Russians will be too busy defending themselves to realise what's really at stake.'

'And the others?'

Eleanor shrugged. 'The only other major contenders are the Chinese and Indians, but relatively speaking they're still bit players in Antarctica. They are building a lot of new bases at the moment, with the Indians just having completed Larsemann Hills, but we're still ahead of the curve. My analysts suggest there shouldn't be too much fallout from them.'

Closing the folder that had been resting on her lap, Eleanor placed it on the desk in front of her.

'It's all in here. The Antarctic Treaty will be dismantled under Part Twelve, Protocol Seven.' She said the last words slowly, keeping her eyes locked on his. 'The Americans will be granted an official mandate to go in and clean up the mess. And that's when we will stake our claim.'

PATRICK WOODHEAD

'So everything is set?'

'Not quite. There's still one piece left.'

Bates waited for her to elaborate, but her expression remained fixed. Eleanor had previously decided she would disclose this part of the operation, but now old doubts resurfaced and she found herself instinctively holding back.

'The other piece?' he prompted.

Eleanor's lips pursed while she deliberated. Eventually she decided to stay on track. 'The final piece in all of this is to trigger the event itself. And that's all in the hands of a man named Richard Pearl.'

Bates' forehead creased as he tried to place the name.

'You mean, the US senator?'

Eleanor nodded.

'Isn't he the one who survived the submarine incident all those years back?' Bates added, trying to recall the details of an event that had been global news nearly a decade ago. 'He made it out with that other guy . . .'

'Fedor Stang,' Eleanor interjected.

'That's right,' Bates replied. 'I read Stang's obituary in *The Times* a while back. The submarine was a new class they were testing when its reactor failed. They were trapped down there for nearly two weeks or so.'

'Sixteen days. And it was the prototype of the new Virginia Class submarine currently in production,' Eleanor corrected. 'There was a skeleton crew of twenty-seven men on board, but in the end only Pearl and Stang made it out alive.'

There was silence as Bates imagined being trapped a mile

104

under the ocean with a dwindling supply of oxygen. The waiting, the desperation, then the horror of watching the entire crew slowly suffocate. Stang and Pearl would have had to witness each man's death, never knowing that their own rescue was just at hand.

Bates could remember the disbelief among the world's media when one of the submersibles had finally reached the stricken vessel. No one had expected there to be anything on board but corpses as the scientists on the surface had done their calculations and there just wasn't enough air to sustain the crew. But somehow two men had survived.

Now that Bates thought back to it, he could remember an image of Fedor Stang from his obituary. The picture was of him being helped off the rescue boat by two young marines. Fedor had broken both legs when the submarine had first become stricken and was being carted off to hospital in a wheelchair. But even sitting, it was clear that he was a giant of a man. He also looked far from American with his white-blond hair and classic Scandinavian looks, but reading further down the page Bates had discovered that, although born in Norway, Fedor had been raised in America from an early age.

He had been the ranking officer on board the submarine and, after surviving such an ordeal, had become something of a legend in the US navy. His celebrity status helped to secure his next promotion, and from then on he had achieved a meteoric ascent through the ranks. Two years ago he had become a full Vice Admiral before suddenly falling prey to a particularly virulent form of stomach cancer. He had died only two months after his discharge.

Eleanor retrieved the glasses from her forehead and carefully studied them.

'Richard Pearl was only a petty officer during the submarine incident,' she said. 'According to our reports, he dropped out soon afterwards and suffered nearly three years of depression. Somehow he managed to pull himself out of it and successfully reinvent himself. He went on to found a voice-recognition tech company back in 2006, which made him very wealthy, very quickly. Then he founded a few other companies before running for Senate last year in what was a very slick campaign.'

'Isn't he the senator who won't travel to any city with certain levels of air pollution?' Bates added, an incredulous smile appearing on his lips. 'Didn't he turn down the chance to go on a trade mission to Shanghai recently because of the smog there?'

Eleanor nodded. 'Pearl believes he has chronic asthma as a direct result of oxygen depletion suffered during the submarine incident. He uses an inhaler almost constantly, and even has oxygen pumped into his residence in San Diego. But according to our sources there is no physical basis for this. His condition is purely psychosomatic.'

Bates shook his head, then grunted. 'Guess I'd have a few foibles if I had seen my entire crew suffocate in front of me. But what is his connection to this project exactly?'

'Pearl is the one who's going to start the ball rolling. It's all in the file. I just wanted to give you some background on the man, as . . . well, let's just say, he is complicated.'

Pushing the inch-thick file across the desk, Eleanor raised herself to her feet, slipping her cashmere overcoat across her shoulders.

Bates looked up at her. 'Before you go, I wanted to clarify something. Parker has gone a long way down the line on this and for obvious reasons. The British will get a slice of Antarctica and that's something we have been after for a long time. But we're essentially working blind here and, I think you'll agree, the risk is significant.'

Eleanor remained silent, to all intents and purposes waiting for him to continue while inwardly her mind had suddenly filled with unspeakable doubts. 'Significant' didn't even come close. If word of this got out it would tear apart US foreign policy for the next decade.

'Why is all this happening now?' Bates continued. 'The Antarctic Treaty has been in effect since the sixties, with the US never recognising a single land claim. No one owns the land down there and you've been happy in that knowledge for nearly fifty years. What's suddenly changed? I'm only asking because what we are planning is seriously going to upset the apple cart.'

A brief smile passed across Eleanor's lips at the Englishman's turn of phrase, then it faded and she suddenly looked very tired. What they were attempting was the greatest land grab of the last two centuries, which if successful would ensure the continuation of the US as the world's leading superpower. If not, it would undoubtedly start them on a downward trajectory from which they would probably never recover. It took several seconds for her to regain her composure. Then, tilting her head to one side, she fixed Bates with a coy smile. 'All in good time,' she purred. 'Now, why don't you order me a car?'

Chapter 8

The convoy of tractors ground on.

Luca sat in the back seat of one, trying to ignore the stench of diesel fumes and clouds of cigarette smoke wafting back from the driver. The lingering taste of vodka had finally gone; but with it went the heady self-confidence he had felt on first leaving GARI. As the hours had passed, new doubts had risen like bile in his throat, while his mouth had gone so dry that he was finding it hard to swallow.

Luca knew that he had to compartmentalise his feelings and trust that something of his old self remained, but his mind kept circling back to the fact that it had been three years since he had last stood on the side of a mountain. Three years.

Unclipping his rucksack, he began checking through the quickdraws and carabiners, counting them out as he clipped them on to the back of his climbing harness. As he opened the screw-gate of the second one, the carabiner suddenly slipped from his grasp, spinning down into the metal footwell of the tractor. It clattered so loudly that even the drunken Russian sitting opposite was roused from his stupor.

Luca looked up, straight into the man's eyes. It felt as if the Russian could see right through him; see the fear inside. But just as Luca went to blurt out an apology, the man's head lolled backwards, cracking against the side glass of the window. He was so drunk that he didn't even notice.

Luca exhaled slowly, trying to blank out what had just happened. But the fact remained that he had clipped and unclipped thousands of carabiners before and couldn't remember the last time he had dropped one. What had once been instinctual was now clumsy and unfamiliar. He knew that the incident itself could easily be brushed aside, yet deep down it sharpened everything into focus. The truth was obvious: he was in no shape to take on this job.

His thoughts turned to Bear and for the briefest moment he allowed himself the fantasy that he could confide in her and that she would make it all go away. But deep down he knew that she would have done nothing but admonish him for being so pathetic. It wasn't that she didn't understand, more that she just didn't tolerate any sort of procrastination and would always delve straight to the core of the problem. Bear did what needed to be done. It was just how she was wired.

God, he missed that about her; missed the strength of her convictions and the way it always seemed to rub off on him.

Luca heard a shout and then the sound of the tractor's gearing grinding down. With a final lurch, the convoy drew to a standstill directly under the jagged peaks of the mountain range. Long shadows stretched down from the highest summits as if beckoning them closer, but to Luca, they only reinforced his own sense of foreboding.

Stepping out into the deep snow, he stared up at the nearest cliff face. It rose like a monolith from an open desert and would definitely require some technical climbing. Why the hell had Dedov chosen this place? In the long range of mountains, surely there was an easier route than this across to the lake. Luca wondered if this wasn't some part of a deliberate plan to test his climbing prowess.

Turning back the way they had come, he looked across the snow and ice, endlessly shimmering under a low sun. The landscape was inert, desolate.

'English!'

He turned to see Dedov's bulbous head hanging out of the window of a tractor just in front.

'Take this,' he shouted, handing across a small parcel wrapped in fleece cloth. 'It's a satellite phone.'

'Already have one,' Luca replied, patting his rucksack.

'Then have two.'

Luca nodded, staring along the line of tractors as the other Englishmen began to pile their rucksacks and equipment on the snow. None of the Russians were helping. Instead, they glowered from behind closed windows, the previous bonhomie at the base drained by the hours of travel and the endless rumbling road.

'We have dropped you on eastern side and now you follow the route I marked,' Dedov said, his watery gaze fixed on Luca. 'And report *everything* you see.'

The driver next to him stabbed a finger towards the high

peaks. A new wind was blowing across the summits, dusting off the snow and causing a trail to reach out across the sky like the wash of a plane's jet engine. The weather was already starting to turn.

'Dedov,' Luca called up. 'You make sure the tractors are here in time.'

The Russian smiled. 'They'll be here. And if you make it back safe, you get to call me Poet!' He then slapped his driver on the shoulder, signalling for them to leave.

Luca only nodded as he watched the snow kick up behind the massive tracks of the vehicles as the convoy pulled off. Thirty yards behind him the other Englishmen instinctively grouped together as the landscape seemed to expand around them. No one spoke; all eyes watched the vehicles gradually recede, until finally they dipped out of sight behind a low rise.

Everyone was waiting, desperate for someone to break the silence of the mountains.

'Luca!'

He turned in response and saw Joel approach, followed by two other men. As they drew closer, Luca pulled his sunglasses down to conceal the hesitancy in his own eyes.

'This is Andy McBride,' Joel said, gesturing towards the heavy-set man standing closest to him. He was wearing reflective orange goggles and a thick fur hat that wrapped right across his chin so that the only visible part of his face was a pair of rouged lips, blistered by the sun.

'All right, mate?' Andy offered with a quick wave of his hand.

'And this is Katz.'

Jonathan Katz walked around the pile of rucksacks, taking off his right glove before shaking Luca's hand.

'So you're the new guide,' he said, tilting his head forward and peering over the top of his sunglasses as if inspecting the fine print of a book. 'Hope you do a better job than the last one we had.'

'For fuck's sake,' Andy muttered.

'It's true, isn't it?' Katz snapped over his shoulder. He was a big man in his early-fifties with receding blond hair that accentuated an already high forehead. His eyes were pale blue and lacked any trace of empathy. Instead they seemed to shimmer with untapped annoyance. 'Idiot led them straight over a crevasse field. What did he expect?'

'That could've happened to any one of us,' Andy retorted, clearly happy to rekindle an old argument.

'Well, you can be damn sure of one thing – it's not going to happen to me. Isn't that right, Matthews? We heard a lot about you on the drive over. Apparently, you're the "real deal".' He said the last words with a faux-American accent, drawing them out.

Luca looked from one man to the next, quickly realising that he was somehow going to have to stop their incessant bickering and unite them as a team.

'Save your energy,' he said, keeping his voice low to bring them in close. 'We have seventy-two hours, maybe less if the weather hits early. So I'm going to make this really simple – you do exactly as I say on the mountain. And I mean exactly.' He then turned specifically to Katz. 'From now on, the past is exactly that. Antarctica won't give a shit about your petty crap. Give her the chance and she'll swallow us whole. All of us.'

Turning back towards the pile of kit, he pulled his rucksack on to his shoulders. 'Get ready. We're going to move fast and get the job done. Together.'

Luca led through the snowfield. The four men were roped together, moving with the same lurching gait as convicts in a chain gang. Every few minutes, the rope would tug at Luca's harness as Katz, positioned directly behind, struggled to keep pace through the deep snow. He had already taken off his hat and unzipped his Gore-Tex jacket all the way down to his waist in an effort to cool himself down, but sweat still beaded across his forehead. Luca could see it glistening in the sun, plastering his thinning hair to the brow of his head.

The rope pulled tight again, bringing them to a standstill. Katz took off his sunglasses, mopping at the sweat welling into his eyes. He began to tuck them into his jacket pocket when Luca called out: 'Put them back on. You'll go snow blind.'

'But they steam up!' Katz protested, squinting in the glare. Luca didn't respond, waiting for him to comply. Katz made a show of cleaning the lenses, holding the smeary glass up to the light.

'Put 'em on, Katz!' Andy shouted from twenty feet further down the snow slope. He was doubled over, hands resting on his knees, but obviously keen to keep moving.

Katz's body visibly flinched at the command, his exhaustion quickly turning to anger at being given an order by anyone other than their guide. Luca could see him muttering a string of invective as he jammed the glasses back on and the lenses immediately fogged up once again. He fussed some more with his clothing, deliberately keeping everyone waiting.

Luca stared down at his watch. Even pushing them like this, the pace was slow. He didn't want them to sweat like they were doing because he knew the moisture would be trapped in their thermal layers and make them cold. But, by the same token, they had to keep ahead of the storm. The problem wasn't with Joel or Andy, they were moving relatively well, but Katz was seriously out of shape. Luca could hear the rasping in his lungs, the sick wheeze of a body working beyond its limit. He must have been a smoker at some stage in the past, or, more likely, still was.

Luca turned back towards the mountain. They were nearing the top of the saddle. From here, a wall of rock thrust up from the ground, rising maybe a hundred feet in the air before it tapered back into the main body of the mountain. There was no other option – they were going to have to climb up the main face before they could look for an easier route across to the other side. Given what he had already seen of the team on a simple snow slope, he was going to have to keep them on a tight leash.

Luca reached the base of the cliff and, throwing down his rucksack, waited for the others to arrive. He unfurled a hundred-metre rope and pulled out the rest of the climbing hardware before craning his neck back towards the summit. The rock loomed over him like the buttress of an immense castle. Already he could feel the pads of his hands dampen in anticipation.

Bringing his fingertips up to his mouth, he slowly blew on the ends. In the old days, he wouldn't even have thought twice about a route like this. It was a simple pitch, following a long running crack with good handholds. All he had to do was remember how to do it.

After a moment more he heard the laboured breathing of Katz approaching. Then, one by one, the others coalesced into a group.

'I'm going to anchor this line along the route,' Luca said, slow and clear. 'It's static – meaning it doesn't stretch. So you can hold on to it, just like you're going up a flight of stairs.'

He then paid out a long stretch of slack from the original climbing rope they had been using.

'I'll shout down for you to start,' he said. 'Move slowly and help each other.'

As he turned back towards the cliff, Andy reached across to him, taking hold of his shoulder.

'Wait,' he whispered, wrenching the goggles from his face. As the mirrored lens lifted, Luca saw that he had a chubby face, ringed by stubble. Sweat prickled under his eyes and, as Luca looked more closely, he noticed there was something wrong with Andy's left eye. The iris looked duller somehow, while the eye itself didn't quite keep pace with the other.

Andy hesitated, having been trying to tell Luca something since they had first left the tractors.

'I'm not that good with this kind of thing . . .' he began.

'You'll be fine,' Luca reassured him. 'I'll have you on the rope the whole time.'

'No, you don't get it. I can't judge perspective so well, which gets worse with heights.'

Luca stared at him, the words jarring in his mind. Before he could respond there was a slow clap from behind them. The noise echoed across the rock as Katz stepped closer.

'We're climbing a mountain and you didn't think to tell anyone that you suffer from vertigo,' he said, an unpleasant smile forming on his lips. 'Now that's what I call teamwork.'

'It ain't vertigo!' Andy protested. 'It's all about the perspective. It's not easy on cliffs and that.'

'How precious,' Katz taunted. 'Did you expect anything different, seeing as we're crossing a mountain?'

Andy squared off his shoulders. With a jerk of his wrists, he threw down his gloves. Although shorter, he was younger and stockier, with the assurance of someone who'd spent a large part of their early childhood brawling in the streets of east London.

'Back off, Katz. I'm warning you.'

Katz paused for a second, but then couldn't help himself.

'Fucking deadweight,' he whispered.

Andy's body listed forward as he suddenly charged. From somewhere deep within him the frustration of weeks of confinement exploded. He rushed through the deep snow with his arms flailing widely. There was the sound of Joel shouting for him to stop, but Andy was deaf to the warning. Katz's taunts had finally proved too much.

At first Luca watched Andy clamber past, assuming this was little more than bravado. But as the man's hands instinctively clenched into fists, Luca realised the anger was real. And a fight was the last thing they needed on the mountain. Quickly reaching forward with his left hand, Luca grabbed on to the webbing straps of Andy's rucksack, sending him spinning round to one side. Andy tripped, losing his balance, and crashed headlong into the base of the cliff. As his forehead cracked against the cold granite, he staggered back a pace with his legs threatening to give way. He stood like that for several seconds, before raising his hand to his forehead and feeling for the inevitable swelling.

He didn't speak. Instead, he just glowered at Luca.

'I always knew . . .' Katz began, but Luca snapped round to face him.

'And you,' he hissed, 'say another word and I'll do the same fucking thing to you.'

Katz stared back defiantly, but there was something unnerving about the way Luca was staring at him. It was entirely removed from the easily taunted McBride, who ran hot and cold with equal measure. This was different. There was a coldness to Luca's stare that was unsettling even to someone as self-absorbed as Katz. Luca looked as if he would follow through with his threat, and more.

There was a moment's silence before Luca broke the

deadlock. Reaching down to the ground, he picked up the dropped gloves and shoved them against Andy's chest.

'We don't have time for this bullshit,' he said. 'Any more arguments and I swear I will cut you both off the rope. We clear?'

Neither man moved.

'Joel, you're going to be second on the rope,' Luca ordered, trying to get back to the job in hand. 'Andy – you're in the middle. Stay close to the man in front and keep your hands working up the static line. That's all you have to do.' He then pointed a finger towards Katz. 'You bring up the rear. And I don't want to hear a single word.'

Tying both the static and climbing rope to the front loop of his harness, Luca moved towards the cliff. Joel watched him step up on to the first foothold. 'Wait,' he said. 'What about you? Don't you need to be secured?'

Luca paused, but didn't turn back. 'All you'd do is pull me off the wall.'

With that, he stepped higher, pressing his body flat against the cliff. As his fingers dragged across the surface, searching for the first of the handholds, the rock felt smooth and hardened by the cold. His hands grasped on to one crack, then another, but none felt secure enough to take his weight. It seemed as though his fingers would just slip clean off.

Luca could sense the others watching his every move. He forced himself on, the anger still burning within and helping to mask his own fear. Jerking his body higher, he fought every inch. Movements that had once been so fluid and natural now became robotic, with his legs doing little more than drag up the wall behind him.

On he went, gaining a few feet with each move. Luca stared down between his legs and, despite it all, found he was already twenty feet off the ground. He could see the tops of the others' heads as they stood in abject silence, refusing even to acknowledge each other's presence. Babysitting – that's how Bates had described it, forgetting to mention that the group Luca had been given was a bunch of fucking lames. They were almost as bad as each other.

Luca reached behind him, pulling a cam from the back of his harness, and released the spring-loaded mechanism into the crack in front. The teeth bit in, locking tight. Still cursing his luck, he threaded both ropes through, tying off the static line so it was fixed in position. He then moved higher, his fingers spreading out across the rock before the tips instinctively crimped around a tiny indent in the surface and he dragged his body higher.

He climbed, his mind reeling from the implausibility of the situation he now found himself in. It had all happened so quickly; the foreman, the helicopter, then being bundled on to the Ilyushin plane to Antarctica with barely anything more than a sketchily marked map as briefing. If this was so important to the Polar Division, why hadn't they sent an entire team of climbers in?

Luca paused again, this time another ten feet higher. He jammed a second cam into the cliff in front, jerking it down with a rough pull of his hand. As he fumed with anger, the crippling doubts he had experienced in the tractor became lost in the general fog of his frustration. His progress became quicker, more fluid, as climbing techniques that had been hardwired into his brain began to return. As he shifted his balance from one side to the next, with his boots expertly swivelling on their points, he smoothed his body higher, gaining height with each minute that passed.

On he went, fixing anchor points every ten feet and running the ropes through. He could feel the drag on his harness, the weight of the ropes pulling him back towards earth as if loath to let him go. But it was something he was well used to from the oil rig. Blanking it from his mind, he forced himself on.

The top of the cliff was just ahead now, only a couple more moves to go. Swinging his right leg up, he hooked his heel over an outcrop of rock and used the momentum to heave the rest of his body higher. The move was flawless, as if staged for a climbing magazine, and with it Luca reached over the summit and pulled himself on to the flat ground beyond. He could feel his heart beating in his chest and his eyes were wide with sheer exhilaration. Old muscles that hadn't ached in many years were now brimming with lactic acid, while his forearms felt pumped to bursting.

He straightened his back, staring out across the view. For that single moment a sense of freedom returned to Luca that had been lost somewhere inside his brooding self for so very long. He could feel the wind tugging at his hair and, as he stared out over the panorama of massive mountains, he smiled.

Maybe he could still do it after all.

Chapter 9

Almost an hour later, the three other Englishmen arrived at the summit. They were breathless and tired, but had done as Luca said and climbed slowly and in silence. With the static rope running the length of the cliff, they had felt secure enough, with even Andy making reasonable progress. As they piled over the summit and lay exhausted against their rucksacks, the silence continued. Only Joel seemed willing to voice his excitement.

'Now this is what I came to Antarctica for!' he proclaimed, a full set of teeth visible in his smile. 'Been cooped up behind a computer screen for so long, I forgot what it's like out here. Man, that climb was good.' He reached a hand across to Andy, offering to hoist him to his feet. 'Wasn't so bad, was it, mate?'

Andy ignored the proffered hand and only nodded vaguely. He didn't want to say anything out loud in case it betrayed his real feelings. He had been petrified the whole way up, but had forced himself on, desperate to prevent Katz from deriving any sense of satisfaction from his failure. Despite

the safety rope ahead of him and Luca's occasional assurances shouted down the cliff face, he had found it one of
the hardest things he had ever done. His lazy right eye made
it hard for him to judge perspective at certain angles, and
the sensation was always compounded as soon as he moved
any distance off the ground.

Now he lay still, clenching and unclenching his hands.
The joints in his fingers ached from where he had been
desperately gripping on to the static line. As he slowly began
to recover his breath, he found his eyes boring into the back
of Luca's head.

Joel was determined to share his enthusiasm and even
cast a glance towards Katz, resting a few metres away, dabbing
the sweat from his brow with a small square of towelling
pulled from his Gore-Tex trousers. Far from looking pleased
with himself, the natural sneer on his face had only hardened.
It made whatever encouragement Joel was about to offer
suddenly seem redundant.

For want of any other option, Joel zeroed in on Luca.

'How much farther do you think it is to the drill site?' he
asked.

Luca stared out towards the far side of the mountain.
They'd been lucky. The route ahead looked comparatively
easy, with a wide snow slope funnelling across to the other
side. Beyond it they could see the flat pan of the lake, but
they were still too far away to discern anything of the actual
drill site. In the distance, he could see the faint outline of
the 'barrier' and the beginnings of the mighty Southern
Ocean, littered with icebergs.

'If we can get down to the lake easy enough, it should be about four hours more,' he replied, eyes switching between the view ahead and the map in his hands.

'Great!'

Joel moved closer still, glancing over Luca's shoulder at the map. As they stood side by side, he reached up to reposition the same sweatband he had been wearing at the base, tugging a few strands of hair back under its elastic. Luca briefly turned towards him, registering a long line of zinc that Joel had smeared under his eyes to protect his skin against the sun. The tacky cream left a streak of brilliant white across his long nose and cheeks, making him look like a mime who had only half-finished his makeup.

'You reckon we'll get to the lake today?' he asked.

'Depends on us,' Luca answered. 'We've got twenty-four-hour daylight, so we can keep going as long as we want.'

'We've got plenty left in us, haven't we, lads?' Joel declared, but there was little by way of response. 'And once we get to the site, it's going to be quick. That main winch system shouldn't take too long to get up and running.' He turned to his left. 'What do you think, Katzy? The tube extraction is your deal.'

Katz shut his eyes at this bastardisation of his name. There was a pause, leaving the others unsure as to whether he was considering an answer or simply too irritated to try.

'If everything is still set up,' he finally replied in a monotone, 'it'll be a couple of hours to get the first sample out. I just hope the rest of you don't screw up your jobs.'

As he spoke his eyes flicked towards Andy, still slumped

against his rucksack and brooding. He had returned the goggles to his face, masking his expression once more.

'I'll get the job done,' he muttered.

Luca stepped a few paces away from the group, unable to stomach the constant bickering. He cast his eyes up to the neighbouring mountain. The wind they had seen earlier on the high peaks was now being funnelled down towards the lower valleys. It kicked up the ground snow, swirling it across the ice so that it looked as if the entire surface was covered in ankle-deep cloud, streaming in a constant flow. Luca knew that once the wind passed a certain speed, the 'cloud' would build, drawing more and more snow up from the ground until it became a full-blown blizzard scorching across the open lake.

It was still too early to tell, but it looked like Dedov might have been wrong. The storm was steadily building, coming in more quickly than any of them had suspected.

'Get ready. We keep moving,' Luca called over his shoulder.

'What difference is five minutes going to make?' Katz asked, slumping back against the hard rock.

'Have it your way,' Luca replied. 'But I wouldn't want to be caught in the middle of that lake when the storm hits. Doesn't look like there's too much shelter out there.'

Katz craned his neck a little higher as his eyes turned towards the route ahead. Despite the exhaustion he felt, he knew that Luca was right.

Joel smiled awkwardly, feeling partly responsible for his team mates.

'How long do you think we have before the weather changes?' he asked.

Luca shrugged, knowing it was better to tell them what they wanted to hear. 'We'll have enough time if we push hard. Come on, everyone up.'

The descent along the back of the mountain led them through a deep valley, strewn with open crevasses. Here, the immovable rock was slowing the glacier, stretching it to breaking point and ripping open the surface ice. Crevasses were everywhere, some interlocking at angles, while others radiated out in symmetrical lines as if part of some elaborate design.

Roped up and led by Luca, they twisted around the gaping holes, barely daring to stare down into the depths as they passed. The edges of the crevasses had wind-blown snow stacked up in twisted heaps like tombstones besides open graves. The landscape itself looked timeless and unchanged.

As they passed through the icefall each man followed Luca's footsteps exactly. No one spoke. The danger was so palpable that nothing seemed important enough for them to break the silence. The only noise came from Katz's rasping cough that had worsened over the last couple of hours, with the dry air catching in his lungs.

At last they came on to the flat ground by the lake. Time had passed quickly, but now that the obvious danger was gone, the final march to the drill site felt like a bitter slog.

With his Global Positioning System in hand, Luca led them on, hour after hour, tracking ever closer to their goal. The ground snow swirled at their feet, with spindrift curling up and freezing against their bare cheeks and stubble. The vapour from their breath condensed against the collars of their jackets, soon turning to solid lumps of ice and making it look as if the tops of their clothing had been dipped in frost. All of them had their shoulders hunched, bodies tilted into the wind as they pressed on and on.

Luca kept them to a strict routine: walking for an hour, with five-minute breaks in between. Their reward was a glug of sweet tea from his thermos and an energy bar, whose chocolate-plastered oats were frozen solid, snapping off in their mouths and threatening to crack their back teeth with each bite. During the breaks they all sat in silence, perched on their rucksacks with their backs to the wind.

Just as they finished their last mouthful, Luca would force them on to their feet once more. He knew this tactic would only last so long, and Katz was already starting to stumble when he was pulled back up.

As the sun passed midway through the sky it ducked behind one of the adjacent peaks, casting an immense shadow across the lake. Only a watered-down twilight remained, immediately making everything feel colder, more hostile. Luca could feel a little more pull on the rope. The rest of the team were slowing and he doubted they were going to make it to the next break.

Tilting his head back, he peered across the swirling snow. The GPS was telling him that the drill site was now less than a kilometre away. As he stared into the distance, he suddenly saw it. Dead ahead was the top half of the drilling platform, with the main scaffolding tower jutting high into the sky. He shook his head, almost unable to believe he had missed it for so long.

'That's it!' he bellowed, raising his voice above the wind. 'Keep going and we'll be there in less than thirty minutes.'

The news was greeted by resigned nods, with only Joel mustering a tired smile. As Luca unclipped from the rope and watched them file past, Joel pulled the fleece neck gaiter down from his face to speak.

'We made it!' he said, stumbling past.

Luca returned his smile, but silently repeated the old climbing maxim to himself: reaching the summit is only halfway. He knew well enough that they would only have made it once they had returned to GARI and were safely inside.

Chapter 10

A single scaffolding tower dominated the drill site, rising over sixty feet in the air. It stood alone, like a monument to some long-forgotten dynasty, with two custom-built shipping containers positioned either side. They were encased in drift snow with only a single side and the roof visible, the colour of which had long-since been turned an indeterminate grey by the sandblasting effect of the wind.

The sides of the containers opened with a hydraulic winch to reveal miles of yellow piping turned around a central reel. A massive generator had been built into the side of the nearest one, its component parts protected by a heavy-duty storm blanket. Luca stared from one piece of machinery to the next, amazed by how basic the whole site was. But then again, it had to be one of the most remote drill sites on the planet.

Luca led them to the leeward shelter of the first container and they all collapsed back on to their rucksacks, enjoying the respite from the wind. Andy and Joel looked tired but they were more or less alert, already starting to look towards the drill equipment and deciding where to start. Katz, however, moved like a drunk, sheer exhaustion buckling his legs. Ice particles covered his cheeks, while his eyes looked glazed as if recently having borne witness to some unspeakable tragedy.

'All of you,' Luca called, 'get your down jackets and trousers on now.'

'We haven't got trousers,' Joel replied, rummaging in his rucksack. 'Only these.'

He pulled out a crumpled jacket, the fabric already covered in a layer of wet snow. Luca could immediately see it was made by one of the cheaper brands, with only a thin fill of protective down feathers.

'Jesus Christ,' he muttered, taking it from Joel's grasp and dusting off some of the snow. He knew that as their guide it was his responsibility to have checked their clothing before leaving, but thanks to Dedov's urging it had all happened in such a chaotic stampede. He cursed, already wondering what else he had overlooked.

'So this is it? Your only insulation layer?' he asked. Joel nodded.

'OK, put 'em on. But for Christ's sake, keep moving. You have to keep your core temperature up.'

As Luca spoke, Katz nodded vaguely as if the instructions were for the benefit of someone else. After a moment more he clumsily moved towards his rucksack and begun fumbling with the clips. Each took him twice as long as normal to open, and Luca could already see how close to hypothermia the man was.

Moving nearer, Luca saw that all the venom had drained from Katz's expression, to be replaced by a kind of lost bewilderment. His eyelids were half-closed as he desperately fought wave after wave of tiredness. All he wanted to do was lie down and sleep for a moment, but if he did it would be a sleep from which he would never awaken.

Taking his own down jacket and trousers out of his rucksack, Luca zipped them over Katz's frame, sealing the Velcro flaps tight. He had used both on Everest years before and knew how warm and restorative the down was, trapping every last trace of body heat beneath its thick layers. The only drawback was that the clothing was so bulky it made it almost impossible to do anything while wearing it. But, as Luca looked across at Katz and watched him slowly sway from side to side, he realised that the scientist was long past doing anything meaningful anyway.

Finally turning to survey the rest of the drill site, Luca saw the two Ski-Doos Joel had mentioned parked a little way off. Both had had their windshields snapped off during a previous storm, while the nearest one had been rolled on to its side by the wind. It lay with its tracks up, the snow around it stained yellow by the fuel leaking from its tanks.

'We need to check that those are working,' he shouted.

'Andy's the man,' Joel replied, causing him to glance up. He was sitting a few feet away with his body curled up into itself, arms wrapped around his knees.

'We have to get the gen-set working first,' he managed, glancing towards the generator. 'Then I'll take a look.'

'OK,' Luca said. 'Come on, everyone. Keep moving.'

With an audible groan, Andy pulled himself on to his feet and set off towards the neighbouring container, while Joel and Luca swung Katz's arms over their shoulders and moved off towards the drill tower. As they staggered forward they passed scores of empty kerosene barrels, half-concealed beneath the blowing snow. Now that he was aware of them, Luca could see more barrels littered over the entire site in vague and dirty piles. The Russians had simply drained their contents then discarded them without further thought. To them, the prize was the pristine water hidden within the lake. The surface surrounding it was just another part of Antarctica, and to be treated as such.

'Animals,' Joel said, kicking the nearest barrel as he passed. It gave a hollow clang.

'Fuel for the generator?' Luca asked.

'No, they use it to lubricate the borehole and stop the ice from re-freezing. Just wish they didn't leave the site like a complete shithole.' He paused, straining under the weight of Katz on his arm. 'Guess the main thing is that they didn't contaminate the lake itself.'

Luca moved closer, his face tilting sideways against the wind.

'So how do you stop the kerosene going back down the pipe and into the lake?'

'They plug the bottom with an inert liquid called Freon then do the last section with a heated drill bit,' Joel shouted. 'They may be a bunch of complete piss heads, but when it comes to this kind of stuff, the Russians are the best in the world.'

Reaching the main tower, he helped Katz sit down on one of the scaffolding supports, where he was part-sheltered from the wind.

'I'm all right,' Katz breathed, the extra warmth of the down clothing already starting to restore him a little. He then nodded towards the seal plate covering the borehole.

'Come on, Joel. Get it open.'

As Joel began hooking up the main winch cables from the tower, Luca stared into Katz's face, amazed to see the change in him. A spark had returned to his eyes and instead of the usual contempt, the prospect of completing years of scientific research had given rise to a new emotion – excitement.

'Three years,' Katz said, his voice just cutting above the wind. 'Three years of research and only now do we get to see what's down there.'

He leant forward as if trying to peer down the borehole and catch sight of the water within.

'This is like exploring another planet,' he said, 'except this one's our own. If we find life down there, it'll be over twenty million years old.'

It was all the affirmation Joel needed. As he connected the last of the steel cables, he gave a loud whoop.

'What do you think twenty-million-year-old water tastes like, Katzy?' he joked as he engaged the gearing in the tower and the seal was raised from the ground with a low hiss. Luca stared from Joel's excited face to the very ordinary-looking five-inch borehole he had just exposed, marvelling at how abstract a scientist's emotions could be.

Katz gave a thin smile, his chin just visible above the fold of his jacket. 'At the amount this extraction cost, that'd be an expensive glass of water.'

Joel's smile widened. As excited as he himself was, he was amazed to see the change in his team mate's attitude. While he continued working there was a low rumble from behind them, and Joel turned to see that Andy had got one of the Ski-Doos working. They heard the engine rev a few times before he drove over to join them at the tower.

'Does the other one run?' Luca called across to Andy as he pulled to a halt.

'Got to refuel it, but it doesn't look too bad.'

Before going back to work, Andy came and joined the others for a moment. Standing side by side, they stared at the top of the borehole. Each of them could sense a new energy in the group. It was palpable, as if they had all been given another chance to start their relationships afresh.

Twenty minutes later, the first of the yellow piping had been fed through the main calibres on the tower and was being lowered into the ice. It slowly unravelled, descending metre after metre into the depths of the glacier like the body of a giant snake.

Andy, Joel and Katz went about their tasks in near silence, only shouting above the wind to give a quick order or to instruct each other in some way. They were all entirely focused on the job in hand, ignoring the steadily building wind and the fog of blowing snow. They all knew that this was it – the culmination of years of research – and worked with the exactitude of professionals.

Joel had taken a Panasonic Tough Book laptop from his rucksack and plugged it into the sensor panel by the main generator housing. He crouched in the shadow of the wind, every once in a while using the thumb of his gloves to wipe the screen free from the blowing snow. He had pushed his goggles up on to his forehead, wedging them over his sweatband as he peered at the raw data being fed back from the pipe's nozzle sensors.

As they worked, Luca suddenly remembered to check his watch. He cursed, realising that he was twenty minutes late for his scheduled call. He pulled the battery from a breast pocket of his warm thermal layer and quickly clipped it in place at the back of the satellite phone. He could just hear the electronic dial tone above the howl of the wind. As soon as it connected to GARI, he shouted down their coordinates. Sergei the radio operator barely had enough time to note them down before Luca signed off and cut the line again. His fingers were too cold for him to waste time on relaying anything other than the most vital information.

Another hour went by before Joel shouted across to Andy to slow the pipe's descent. The sound of the generator lowered a pitch as, a few seconds later, Andy shut off the reel and the massive pipe wheel clunked to a halt. Joel craned his neck, face only an inch from the blurry screen as he double-checked that they had passed the Freon barrier and that the end filter was now in the waters of the lake.

'Watch the pressure!' Katz barked. 'Don't let it spike.'

Far from annoyed at being given such an order, Andy only nodded. Any pressure surge, even a minor one, could blast the Freon liquid back up the pipe and contaminate their samples.

'Ready?' Katz shouted, holding his arm up as if about to start a race. He had already taken from his rucksack three stainless-steel cylinders about a foot long and laid them by the side of the piping container. These were the sterile collection tubes, and screwing the first on to a custom-built tap on the end of the flow pipe, Katz turned to Joel for confirmation.

'Wait,' Joel shouted. He wiped the screen again, obviously hesitant to give such an order.

Katz didn't hurry him. They all just stared across the driving snow, knowing that everything depended on the next few seconds.

'OK!' Joel said, finally nodding his head. 'Go!'

Andy increased the pressure and the generator gave a low rumble. The minutes passed as they waited for the first of the water to rise through the pipe. Katz hovered by the sample tubes, eyes switching between the dials on the extraction board and the pipe running into the ice. Luca watched the absolute concentration on his face. His gloves were off as he double- then triple-checked the freezing metal cylinders, but he was anaesthetised to the cold. Everything depended on the next few seconds.

'Hundred feet,' Joel shouted, watching the rising liquid displayed on his laptop. 'Ready?'

'Set,' Katz shouted over his shoulder.

'Twenty. Ten,' Joel counted down. 'Watch that pressure, Andy.'

A red light lit up on the extraction board as the first sample of liquid was transferred into the cylinder. There was a pause, then the light switched to green. With well-practised dexterity, Katz carefully unscrewed the first cylinder and replaced it with the second. As he held it in his grasp, there was a wistful smile on his lips as his arms silently registered the new weight of the cylinder as if unable to believe that the lake water was truly within. The second cylinder was filled, then the third, before Katz signalled to Andy to lower the pressure once again.

Katz swivelled the last cylinder in his hand, checking the thermostat and the quantity gauge. Eight hundred and seven millilitres of lake water was contained within, holding at an ambient temperature of 1.7 degrees Centigrade.

'It's stable!' he beamed, clutching the cylinder in his hands as if it were a trophy. Beside him, Andy opened a foam-packed Pelican case and, one by one, they placed the samples inside.

'OK,' Luca shouted. 'Get the pipe out of the ground and let's start sealing it off.'

Andy quickly scurried back to the main reel and, a few seconds later, the process was reversed and the pipe began to rise once more. Each man watched the ascent with arms clamped against their bodies for warmth, while the reel turned and turned. It was tortuous, the machine working at the same unhurried pace, oblivious to the rising wind that surged all around them now. Each gust was stronger than the last, making them stagger forward a few paces just to regain their balance.

Luca stared at his watch. The storm had advanced far more quickly than any of the forecasts had suggested and already they were dangerously behind schedule. He thought back to Dedov's assurance that he would never risk one of his own men out in such weather and cursed the hollowness of the words. Why had Luca allowed himself to be seduced by the base commander's shallow praise and empty reassurances?

The ground snow was rising higher now, almost to chest height, and as Luca looked down towards his feet, he could see only a swirling outline through the maelstrom. It was as if his lower body were little more than an apparition. The storm was advancing rapidly. One more hour and they'd be right in its teeth.

Then came a squall that seemed to last longer than the others. The noise rose louder, shrieking suddenly as the full impact of the wind sent them all collapsing forward, on to their knees. The main drill tower swayed, the reinforced steel resisting the wind with every nut and bolt, but it was not enough. The running calibres became misaligned, dragging the piping against the sidewall of the borehole.

'Shut it down!' Katz bellowed, wagging his arm towards Andy. The generator lowered in pitch as Andy stepped closer to the tower to inspect the damage.

'Shit!' he shouted, stepping up on to the first of the steel girders.

'Can you fix it?' Katz asked desperately.

Andy pulled himself closer and, dragging his goggles up

from his head, stared hard for several seconds before turning back. 'Yeah, but it's going to take time.'

He jumped down and turned to Luca. 'It'll take a couple of hours at least.'

Luca shook his head. 'We don't have that long. Will it still work even if you just drag it up?'

'Yeah, but we're going to knacker the entire gearing.'

Luca stepped towards him. 'Gearing?' he shouted. 'You've got to understand something. The storm is on us. Right now! And even with the Ski-Doos working properly, we're going to struggle to make shelter.'

Checking his watch, he pointed towards the tower. 'You've got thirty minutes, then I'm pulling the plug.'

Katz's objections were drowned out by the howling wind as Andy ran across to the generator housing. With a low, graunching sound the reel began trailing upwards once more. He then moved back to the tower, standing almost directly above the pipes, and watched every inch move through the calibres. As he gripped on to the freezing metal of the drill tower for support, he was exposed to the full force of the wind.

It lasted twelve minutes. Then the pipe caught again and the gearing faltered, causing the generator to rev high for several seconds before it automatically cut out.

'Shit!' Andy screamed, clambering down from the tower, but Luca stepped in front of him.

'This isn't going to work,' he said, grabbing on to the other man's forearm. Andy seemed to hesitate, the certain knowledge that Luca was correct contrary to everything he felt inside.

'We can't leave the pipe down there!' This time it was Katz. He had moved out to join them by the tower, with Joel standing just by his shoulder. 'We leave it now and the pipe will freeze inside.'

'What do you not understand?' Luca bellowed. 'It's us or the lake now!'

'But we have to seal the borehole!' Katz thundered. He turned towards Andy for support, but there was no response. Above his neck gaiter, Luca could see Andy's teeth chattering convulsively.

Luca stared from one man to the next. 'We have the samples. Your job is done. Now get on to the Ski-Doos.'

Andy gave a hesitant nod, followed by Joel. Luca quickly bustled the two of them on to the nearest vehicle, pushing their rucksacks down into the luggage tray at the back.

'You stay right behind me. And keep close,' he ordered.

He then clambered on to the remaining snow machine and started it up. The engine turned over several times before he felt the steady rumble through the padded seat. As he turned to collect Katz, only his silhouette was visible through the storm.

'Get on!' Luca screamed.

Katz didn't respond, staring back towards the drill tower. Luca waited a moment longer before he swung his leg off the saddle and, reaching across, grabbed hold of Katz's thick down jacket and manhandled him back towards the machine. 'Wait!' Katz screamed, his big frame twisting against Luca's grip. 'We can't leave it open!'

Luca didn't answer, instead shoving him with both

palms so hard that Katz's head snapped back against the rear seat.

'Shut up,' Luca shouted. 'Your job's done.'

The borehole was the least of their problems. Now it was only a matter of survival.

Chapter 11

Two days after her conversation with Kieran Bates, Bear found herself standing at Cape Town International Airport, staring into the face of an overweight immigration officer. The man dragged his tired gaze away from the grimy counter before him, slowly surveying the length of her body. He paused, for no other reason than to suggest he could keep her waiting there as long as he chose, before his gaze finally came to rest on her face. He then seemed to register the fleck of white in Bear's left eye. She had always had it – a sharp streak of pure white running across the otherwise deep brown of her pupils. It made it appear as though some unseen light was constantly reflecting in her eyes.

The man sniffed loudly, dredging the phlegm into the back of his throat as Bear tried to expedite the process by flashing him a smile. He ignored it, his expression unchanged as if observing her from behind the tint of a two-way mirror. Then, with a flick of his wrist, he waved her through.

Stalking across the main foyer, Bear bypassed the

multitude of taxi drivers idling around, waiting to prey on the new arrivals. As she went by they gawked at her suggestively, part business, part pleasure, but Bear kept up her stride. She knew the airport well, having been a private pilot for the last twelve years and often taking off in her little bush plane, a Cessna 206, from Cape Town International. But despite being well used to the jolts and bumps of turbulence, their descent earlier that morning had made her feel horrendously sick. Now, all she could think about was getting some fresh air.

It was six-thirty in the morning. Already smokers had grouped together outside the terminal building, clutching oversized cups of coffee and talking loudly. Over the last few days her sense of smell had heightened to such a degree that it was as if she could distinguish every one of the rancid cigarette butts in the overflowing ashtrays. She pushed past, holding her breath through the smoke and desperately trying not to be sick. A hundred yards farther on she spotted a bench and stopped to sit down, feeling too light-headed to continue.

Bear sat for several minutes, letting her eyes drift towards the view of Table Mountain. Cloud was pouring over the summit like a ceaseless waterfall, but only a few hundred feet lower down it dissolved into thin air, leaving the most expensive properties in the city basking in the morning sun. Here the whites had grouped together, their estates rimmed by electric fences and razor wire, while only a couple of miles further out from the mountain, life had an entirely different meaning.

Bear's focus pulled back to an expanse of land called the Cape Flats. The area was hazy from the smoke of burning tyres, and the morning light glinted off thousands of corrugated-iron rooftops. The shantytowns sprawled for miles in every direction, bloated to bursting by the daily arrival of foreigners searching for a better life. But there was none to be found, only the varying shades of violence and poverty that typified each community. From the immigrants in Nyanga to the coloured gangs of Mitchell's Plain, each district was fenced off behind broken concrete walls, as if the city itself were desperate to conceal its wounds.

Bear had travelled her entire life, and even now was amazed by Cape Town's fusion of natural beauty and raw, unchecked violence. But it was a combination that was all too familiar to her. It was the very hallmark of her native Congo.

Feeling her phone vibrating in her handbag, Bear covered her ear against the distant sound of a plane landing before connecting through to her researcher, Louis, back in the Paris office. Since her conversation with Bates, she and Louis had worked for two days straight, delving into the background of the Antarctic science base, GARI.

For all that time, Bear had sat in her office in Paris, reading file after file dug up by Louis and his team. It was as if all the passion and decisiveness that had been so lacking in her choice of du Val's assignments had been poured into this new venture. The old Bear was back and the whole research team had seemed renewed by her energy.

Unable to voice the real reason for the enquiry, Bear had

given the researchers a wide remit. As they trawled through the background of the science base and the drilling project in general, a single name kept recurring: Richard Pearl. He had personally invested over fourteen million dollars towards the drilling project and seemed integral to almost every facet of life at the base.

Bear had heard his name before in connection with the submarine incident, but knew little more than that. Louis worked to fill in the gaps, compiling a huge dossier on the man, covering everything from his political career to recent aspects of his private life.

Aside from his position as a US senator, Pearl also owned a consortium of companies, and through one of these, called Global Change, had invested the fourteen million dollars for the Antarctic drilling project. At first glance Global Change's mission statement seemed highly worthy, with their stated aim being 'to restore eco-systems and reverse the process of climate change', but as Bear and Louis delved deeper into each project, they soon realised that nearly all were only at a nascent stage or, worse, had already been decommissioned.

Every scrap of marketing information about Global Change featured photographs of Pearl. An athletic man in his early-fifties, he had light reddish hair, now greying and combed back from his tanned, but freckled face. His square jaw and perfect smile adorned nearly every page of the company brochures, with a raft of politicians and celebrities crowbarred in, just in case there was any doubt as to his social standing.

The official biography listed Pearl as an ex-naval officer and father of four children, all girls. There were personal quotations in his own handwriting, citing the cure-all of 'positivity' and how the 'power of now' had been the backbone to his success. But as interesting as Pearl was, none of the information seemed to substantiate the feeling of unease Bear had had while on the phone with Kieran Bates. The Antarctic base seemed innocuous enough and Pearl himself, although a little delusional in the scope of his ambition, appeared to be investing in projects that were at least *trying* to do some good.

Midway through the second day of research, Bear was about to call a halt to the whole investigation. She had been replaying the call with Bates in her mind and had come to the conclusion that she must have misjudged his tone, or simply read too much into the situation. Luca was probably just fine and had overcome his aversion to the mountains for the sake of a healthy paycheck. She'd intended to call a halt to the whole line of enquiry when Louis had suddenly burst into her office.

He had discovered that two of Global Change's leading microbiologists had suffered untimely deaths. The first drowned while on holiday in the Maldives; the second was killed in a car crash eight months later. These two incidents could have been explained by the vagaries of fate, but not when combined with the fact that the company's latest head microbiologist, a woman called Charlotte Bukovsky, had disappeared only two months ago. A missing persons report was still officially open with San Diego's police department, but after some desultory enquiries the case officer there had evidently filed the report with the singular intent of letting it gather dust.

Bear had given Louis free rein in trying to track down Bukovsky, and he in turn had called in some favours with the Direction Générale de la Sécurité Extérieure. The DGSE had some new and highly impressive phone-tracking software and his contact had agreed to sift through the phone records of all of Bukovsky's immediate family. A day passed before the contact came back with an anomaly – two calls had been made to Bukovsky's younger sister from Nairobi, Kenya. After some more digging, Louis was convinced he had a lead. As Bear had flown to Cape Town that night, he had continued trying to get through and, on the sixth attempt, actually connected to a hotel room in downtown Nairobi and Charlotte Bukovsky herself.

Now he was calling to relay the basics of that conversation. Bear remained silent while he made his report. Finally she stood up.

'I want to meet this woman.'

'I knew you'd say that,' Louis replied. 'That's why she's booked on a flight via Joburg and arriving in Cape Town tonight.'

'Tonight? She's been off the grid for two months. How the hell did you persuade her to get on a plane?'

'I told her you're a journalist for Reuters. And, believe me, this woman has got a serious axe to grind.'

Bear nodded to herself. They had used the same cover several times before, but it still seemed incredible that

Bukovsky would come out of hiding so readily, even to meet a journalist.

'What's the flight number?' Bear grabbed the Biro pinning up her hair and scrawled the number on a ticket stub. 'And email me anything new you've found.'

'What about du Val? He was asking how your visit to Cape Town is in any way connected to the new assignments.'

'You let me worry about him,' Bear replied. 'Just don't advertise what you're doing.'

There was a pause while Louis weighed up the trouble he would be getting into by covering her tracks, but Bear already knew what he was going to say next.

'Leave it with me,' came the response, and for the first time in days a smile crept across Bear's lips.

'Thank you, Louis. I owe you.'

'Yeah, yeah.' And with that, he hung up.

Bear returned the phone to her handbag then made for the taxi rank. Now that she had time to think about it, she still couldn't quite believe what she had done. Just walking out of the Paris office and on to the flight last night had been audacious, even for her. Already she was wondering how she would justify it when she got back, but fortunately last-minute travel was part of her job description and, for the moment, du Val shouldn't be asking too many questions.

Ever since her call with Bates, she had been thinking about Cape Town almost constantly and been fighting the desperate urge to be there. Seeing her son, Nathan, plus the chance to inform Luca of her pregnancy constituted two fundamentals in her life, if not the *only* two fundamentals right now. And the more she had thought about this, the more she had realised that she just had to leave, no matter how unprofessional it seemed or what the cost to her future career.

As the taxi driver followed the N2 towards the City Bowl, Bear went back over the files Louis had prepared on the Antarctic base, GARI. The drilling project itself had been going for nearly three years when it looked set to stall. The Russians had been going over budget almost continually and, by the third year, the Japanese were already proposing a 'review' period when, suddenly, Richard Pearl stepped in.

To the delight of the scientific community, he had simply written an open-ended cheque. No matter what the cost, he declared, they must break through to the lake in the name of science. The British government had been the first to accept the donation, quickly followed by the other countries involved in the project.

In return for his contribution Pearl had already received certain 'dispensations'. His Bombardier Global Express private jet had landed four times on the ice runway of Droning Maud Land, the only private plane to be granted permission to do so, and one scientist had even posted online a photo of the Robinson 44 helicopter that Pearl was being allowed to garage inside one of the GARI's hangar units.

Like the politician he was, Pearl toured the Antarctic base with fanfare. He would shake everyone's hand, from the base commander to the lowliest cook, as though he were canvassing for votes. And the tactic seemed to be working. The latest edition of *Scientific Weekly* had practically described him as a twenty-first-century Messiah.

But with Louis's discovery of the microbiologists' deaths, Bear was certain that there was a great deal more to Richard Pearl than met the eye. Whatever it was, Bukovsky would certainly have a take on it, and she was scheduled to arrive in Cape Town in under six hours' time.

After checking in at the Cape Grace Hotel, Bear decided to go for a walk along the sea front. She still felt a little nauseous from the flight and was sure that the sea air would do her good. As she ambled along the main quayside, she watched the profusion of Cape Coloured workers blasting at the underside of the mighty ships with high-pressure hoses. The spray drifted high into the air, catching in the hot morning sun, while further along the harbour she could make out the beginnings of the V&A waterfront. The shopping mall was brimming with street entertainers, from human statues and gumboot dancers, to street merchants and touts selling dolphin-watching trips. They were all there, vying for the easy buck of the half-bored tourists as they walked laps around the canals and interlocking waterways.

As Bear passed one of the larger boats she noticed it was flying an American flag. Then, a minute later, she passed another with the Stars and Stripes gently flapping in the breeze. She stood still, eyes scanning the gun-metal grey of the vessel's hull before tracing back up to the stern deck. Huge coils of towlines were visible above the guard rail, while neatly stacked to one side was a row of hydrophones. Bear recognised them from an offshore mining job she had done a few years back. The devices were used in seismic surveys when boats were prospecting for oil or gas.

Out on the rear deck, a sunburnt man with a black beard and balding head moved from one hydrophone to the next, checking each one meticulously. As he came close to the quay, Bear called up to him.

'Where are you headed?'

For a moment the man didn't realise he was being hailed, but then he craned his neck over the edge to peer down at her.

'I said, where's your boat headed?' Bear shouted, remembering to flash him a smile, but the man only stared at her for a couple of seconds before returning to his work. She watched him for a moment longer, guessing that they were probably heading up to the Niger Delta. There had been another find up there last week and now all the big oil boys were throwing everything they had at it.

Glancing down at her watch, Bear realised that there were only another eight minutes to go before the scheduled call with Luca. For the last two days she had rung at precisely 18.00 GMT as Bates had suggested, but there had only been a blank tone. If only she could somehow get a message to Luca, asking him to call her instead.

Another five minutes' walk took her to the front steps of her hotel. After the bustle and commotion of the docks, the cool interior was a welcome respite and Bear smiled gratefully at a waiter.

'A double espresso,' she said, before checking herself. 'No, wait. Make that a glass of sparkling water, please.'

'And your room number, madam?'

Bear opened her purse to check the card key and paused as her eyes settled on a picture of Nathan in the inner pouch.

'Two hundred and four,' she heard herself saying, while her eyes passed over every line and contour of her son's face. He was laughing in the picture, eyes shining with pure joy. His curly brown hair was wild and unkempt. Despite her ex-husband Jamie's continual protests, Bear had refused to keep it short. She loved her son's hair like that; the smell of it and the soft tickle as Nathan would curl up against her chest.

Bear looked up and out towards the bank of windows. The situation with her ex-husband had to change. She had rung him from the back of the taxi that morning and been tersely informed that Nathan was still with his grandparents. Jamie had hung up, not even telling her when her son would be back.

It had been like that for several months now, with Jamie spurning her every attempt at compromise. He just couldn't get over the residual anger. Bear knew that if this had been any other part of her life, she would have hit back, and hard, but when it came to Nathan, she found herself instinctively backing down. Her own guilt at leaving him, even for six months, had given her ex-husband the upper hand and now it played out in their every conversation.

During the long, sleepless nights of the last few months, Bear had even fantasised about kidnapping her son. She had plotted routes and imagined the paper trails she would leave to throw the police off her scent. After spending so many hours staring into the dawn skies, her plotting had become ever more sophisticated, with the web of lies growing until her own head spun from the mindboggling detail. But Nathan? Could she really rip him away from Cape Town and everything he had grown up with?

The sparkling water arrived and Bear slugged it down, still desperate for a coffee.

Screw this. If Jamie didn't get Nathan back to Cape Town by the time her flight was scheduled to leave, she would act. He had five days, although he would never know the clock was ticking.

The decision made, she signalled to the waiter again.

'Can you get me that espresso after all?' she asked. 'I've got a feeling, it's going to be a long night.'

She then dialled Luca's satellite phone number and waited, the minute hand on her watch just having clicked on the hour. Once again the call didn't connect, only adding to her mounting sense of frustration. The desperate need to speak to Luca was growing with each day, and with it, her need for answers.

Chapter 12

Charlotte Bukovsky had the look of a woman scorned. She walked with her shoulders hunched, accentuating her already wary body language, while her arms were kept crossed in front of her as if attempting to shield herself from some as yet unseen danger. Moving out on to the hotel veranda, her eyes darted furtively from one table to the next as she searched for the woman she was supposed to be meeting.

Bear remained still, observing her approach. Bukovsky was in her mid-forties and relatively tall, with sun-kissed blonde hair that had been scraped back from her face and secured in a tight ponytail. It pinched the skin either side of her eyes, giving her a slightly startled look. Around her tanned neck she wore a green silk scarf tied in a knot. The scarf was the only touch of colour in her otherwise drab ensemble. Bear watched her draw nearer, realising that Bukovsky must once have been quite pretty. Now, however, her looks had faded and instead, she radiated a mixture of wounded scepticism and impatience.

From Louis's brief Bear had discovered that Bukovsky had swiftly become one of the pre-eminent microbiologists in the US despite her relatively young age. She had graduated from Princeton with a near-flawless grade average before being recruited into an advanced division of GlaxoSmithKline's exalted R&D department. One success followed another, each accompanied by career advancement until she was heading up the entire division. All this before she had celebrated her thirtieth birthday.

The unprecedented speed of her ascent was matched only by the equally unheard of financial package offered by Richard Pearl to persuade her to work for him. She had tendered her resignation the same day.

Bear signalled across the sea of tables, standing up to shake hands. Despite the heat of the day, Bukovsky's hand felt cold, with long and slender fingers that would have been the envy of any pianist.

'Nice to meet you, Charlotte. It's good of you to come at such short notice,' Bear began.

'The name's Lotta,' Bukovsky replied, dispensing with any pleasantries.

Bear gave a conciliatory smile. 'Sorry, Lotta.'

Perching on her chair with a small overnight bag resting on her lap, Lotta stared at Bear without speaking for a few moments. There was something discomfiting about that stare, something aggrieved and agitated. Without even realising it, she was clenching her hands into fists so that her fingernails bit into the soft pads of her palms.

'Your accent,' she asked. 'That French?'

Bear nodded. 'From the Congo.'

'So how long have you worked for Reuters?'

'Four years,' Bear answered casually. 'On and off. Sometimes freelance.' She reached into her bag and slid a business card across the table. A printer in town had made them up for her that afternoon.

'These feel new,' Lotta said, bending the stiff card between her thumb and forefinger.

'They are. A new batch arrived two days ago. Got a promotion to cover the whole of Southern Africa, and for some reason the pen-pushers in head office always like to have our titles correct.'

'Congratulations. So where is your head office nowadays?'

Bear smiled thinly. 'I thought it was supposed to be me asking the questions?'

Lotta didn't flinch, waiting for a response.

'Three Times Square, New York. Do you want my press ID as well?'

Lotta looked as though she might and there was an awkward pause. Bear remained motionless, not giving away anything. She had been stupid to blurt that out, knowing full well that she hadn't had time to get a fake ID made as yet. After a moment more, Lotta bent forward, placing the bag on the ground at her feet.

'He always used to say he could tell when we were lying,' she said in a soft voice. 'Used to do this thing where he'd fire questions at you, totally unrelated questions, saying that truth could only come from within.'

'He? You mean Pearl, right?'

Lotta flinched visibly at the mention of his name. 'You have to understand who you are dealing with here. Pearl is utterly mercurial. He's not classically intelligent, but he has this ability to be totally different things to different people.'

'For example?'

Lotta's eyes moved skywards as she tried to articulate her feelings. It was obviously something she did not enjoy doing.

'He's like . . . this thing . . . this controlling thing that knows everything about you. He's there *all* the time – sometimes generous and charming, almost spoiling you. Then, without warning, he flips. It's like living with a schizophrenic. I worked for him for all that time and only now that I am finally away from him, do I realise how manipulative he was. He played us right from the start but we went along with it anyway, like lambs to the fucking slaughter.'

She looked weary, eaten up by the strength of her own feelings. 'After a while, that was the norm. *Pearl* made it all seem normal.'

Bear studied Lotta's expression every time she mentioned his name. The revulsion she felt was palpable. 'Was Pearl ever more to you than just your boss? Anything . . .'

'Go on, say it,' Lotta dared her. 'You goddamn journalists are always looking for the dirt. You mean anything sexual, don't you?'

'Yes, I mean sexual,' Bear countered.

Lotta remained silent. Then her hostility seemed to fade, replaced by a kind of dulled introspection.

'He was my lover for nearly a year. And the whole time, it seemed like he shared everything with me. But actually, it was only ever what he wanted me to know.'

'So what happened between you?'

'I didn't suspect anything until about three months ago. We were staying at a hotel in New York and it was early in the morning. I was working on my laptop while he was still asleep in bed. I noticed him wake up and go into the bathroom. A few minutes later I went over to turn off the main bedroom lights and somehow I managed to trip all the fuses in the suite.'

Lotta hesitated as the memory came flooding back. 'He just went mad, absolutely mad. He started throwing himself against the bathroom door, trying to break it open. The whole time, he was screaming. It was this horrible, blood-curdling scream that went on and on.' She bit down on her lip, trying to keep her voice steady. 'Eventually, he broke through the door and then came at me, strangling me with his bare hands. I could feel his grip around my neck, getting tighter and tighter, while his face hung over mine, so close that we were almost touching.'

Raising her hand to her neck, Lotta ran a finger across the smooth silk of the scarf. Pearl's wedding ring had left a deep, raking cut on the left side of her throat, but after three months, the scar was just beginning to fade.

'It was only after I passed out that he finally stopped,' she whispered. 'He was trapped, you see. Trapped in the dark. Since his ordeal in the submarine . . .' Lotta shook her head slowly, drifting into silence. Several seconds passed before she managed to regain her composure enough to continue. 'But him hurting me like that made me re-evaluate everything. Right from the start. I began going back over everything and doing my own research. One of the things I discovered was that there is a lot more to the submarine incident than the press ever reported.'

Bear raised one eyebrow. 'How do you mean?'

'Pearl and Fedor Stang weren't *lucky* to survive. They did so for a reason.'

'I thought it was just a case of the rescue team arriving in the nick of time.'

A sneer appeared on Lotta's lips, curling the edges upwards. 'There was never going to be enough air for twenty-seven men. Fedor Stang was the ranking officer, while Pearl was one of his juniors. Only a couple of days into the whole thing, they ordered the rest of the crew into the bulkhead under the pretext it would help with the rescue. Then they locked them all inside, sealing the flood doors.'

Bear's mouth widened in disbelief.

'They guessed how long it would take for the submersibles to make it down to that depth and link on to the hull,' Lotta continued. 'So they decided to take control of ninety per cent of the air supply.'

'You're saying they actually murdered twenty-five other men?' Bear asked incredulously. 'If that's true then surely someone else would have done the maths and figured out that only two men were breathing down there.'

'After they got out, they explained everything away, saying they had used the air tanks in the ballast and part of the diving equipment. At the time, they were heroes. No one was going to start looking for an explanation that didn't need to be found.'

Bear jotted a few notes on her pad, but inwardly she wondered how much of this she could take at face value. Lotta looked every inch the jilted ex-girlfriend prepared to go to any lengths to get her revenge. Mind you, Bear could hardly blame her. If someone had tried to strangle her, she would undoubtedly have done the same.

'You have proof of all this, right?'

Lotta shook her head. 'Not enough to re-open the matter officially. It was over a decade ago and there's nothing concrete that would stand up in an enquiry. But I found a full copy of the forensic report hidden in Pearl's private office. He'd even annotated certain sections. The rest I figured out for myself.'

Staring across the table, Lotta seemed to pick up on Bear's hesitancy.

'What?' she asked. 'You don't think he has blood on his hands?'

'Look, as a journalist, I can't pin an entire article . . .'

'What about the two other microbiologists?' Lotta challenged, cutting her off mid-sentence. 'Their deaths were no accidents.'

Bear moved back in her seat, eyeing Lotta carefully. 'You can substantiate that?'

She nodded, eyes turning towards her overnight bag. 'I have it right here.'

Bear followed her gaze, but resisted the temptation to ask

to see the proof. 'So that's why you ran?' she said. 'Because you thought you were next?'

'I *was* going to be next,' Lotta replied flatly. 'That's exactly what Pearl had planned.'

A waiter approached the table and both women stopped speaking, leaving the sentence hanging in the air. Ordering a glass of water, Bear looked towards Lotta who simply shook her head. But just as the waiter went to leave, she suddenly called him back.

'Actually, make that a tequila on the rocks. A double.'

As soon as he had gone, Bear picked up her notepad once more. 'I want to step back a bit and start from the beginning. Tell me about the work you were doing at Global Change. I've read some of the reports on the website, but it's all pretty vague.'

Lotta seemed a little deflated by the change in tack, but then nodded. 'The projects are vague because so is the science. We switched from one project to the next, drifting really, until earlier this year Pearl got it into his head that algae was the future of bio-fuel. He was going to revolutionise the fuel industry and ploughed millions into the project. A few months later, we had vast growing chambers set up brimming with hexane solvents, but of course we could never make the fuel stable enough for production on a large scale. We failed again and again, with Pearl refusing to accept that the science just wasn't there yet. Instead, he would simply blame us for not working hard enough.'

Lotta exhaled deeply. 'Then he had us switch to something else. Have you ever heard of the term "iron fertilisation"?'

'Vaguely,' Bear replied with a shrug. In reality she had read several papers on the subject.

'The theory has been around for a while,' Lotta explained. 'You take iron sulphate particles and spread them into the ocean. The iron causes plankton to bloom and, as the plankton grows and completes its life cycle, it sucks carbon dioxide out of the surrounding air. When the plankton dies it sinks down to the bottom of the ocean, thereby locking in all that carbon on to the seabed. People were looking at it as a solution to climate change.'

'And Pearl was one of these people?'

'Yeah, he was. Last summer he had me fronting a team that dumped over a hundred tons of iron sulphate off the islands of Haida Gwaii on the west coast of Canada. Initially, the experiment reacted well and there were traces of huge phytoplankton blooms all around the boat. But then, things started to go wrong . . .'

Lotta's lips pursed in disdain, causing her cheeks to pinch a little tighter. 'We didn't realise it at the time, but under certain conditions iron sulphate can cause the nitrous oxide level to spike. It sucked the oxygen out of the water and we managed to kill every living organism within a hundred-and-eighty-square-mile radius. We literally created a desert in the blink of an eye.'

She shook her head, eyes glowing with a mixture of anger and contrition. Over the ensuing months, she had obviously been eaten alive by guilt.

'You know, I grew up by the sea,' she said in a quiet voice. 'I spent almost my entire childhood there, and now . . .'

'Did you know the iron sulphate could react like that?' Bear interjected, trying to bring her back on topic.

'The initial tests were inconclusive. No one had ever tried it on such a large scale,' Lotta answered, then paused, gently shaking her head. 'Shit. I'm talking like him now. The answer is yes – we knew there was a chance it could happen, and instead of postponing for further testing, we just streamroll-ered ahead.'

'But it's over, right? After what happened, Pearl can't be looking to bleach out any more of the Pacific.'

'You don't get it. This is not a rational mind we are dealing with here. Pearl is *only* interested in the quality of the air and the levels of carbon dioxide in the atmosphere. It all stems from the days he spent in the submarine. I mean, just look at the man – he uses an inhaler when he doesn't even have asthma and hooks himself up to an oxygen mask when he sleeps.'

She paused, cheeks flushing a deep red. 'And the one thing he doesn't give a shit about is the sea. In fact, it's the reverse. He actively despises anything to do with it. Pearl believes that if his experiments to combat climate change damage the oceans, well, that's just collateral damage.'

Their drinks arrived and Lotta sipped her tequila, wincing slightly at the bite of the spirit.

'After Haida Gwaii, Pearl said the scale wasn't big enough and everything had to be refocused on finding an alternative to iron sulphate. Something bigger. He then hit on the idea that it wasn't to do with quantity. When we looked at the numbers, we realised that they were just too big. Essentially, we were never going to be able to dump enough iron sulphate into the oceans to make a difference. Instead, we needed a chain reaction.'

Bear froze. 'A what?'

Lotta seemed to crumple in front of her. She no longer bristled with anger and recrimination. Instead, she looked desperate.

'You don't understand what it was like. Day in, day out, we were being told we were going to find a solution to climate change – the great ill of the twenty-first century. It was like working on the Manhattan Project, trying to split the atom. Only a handful of us knew the whole picture and we became so engrossed with trying to *create* the substance that we lost sight of what it would actually *do*.'

She ran her fingers through her hair, scraping her nails against the skin of her scalp. The horror of what she had been carrying finally releasing.

'In November we managed to modify a type of irradiated radical that would chain react in saltwater. We created Tetramethylsilane.'

Bear remained silent, waiting for her to elaborate.

'Tetramethylsilane was specifically designed to trigger a non-reversible event. In the lab we used to call it the "seed".'

Bear's forehead creased as she tried to grasp what had been said. 'You're telling me that this seed will trigger plankton to bloom all over the ocean. And that the plankton will suck up the carbon in the atmosphere.'

Lotta nodded, her eyes locked on Bear's. 'That's exactly what I am saying. The seed could be the panacea for the twenty-first century's ills, lowering carbon levels by anything up to twenty per cent on a *global* scale. Or there's a chance that it could do the same as at Haida Gwaii and decimate an entire ocean.'

'Chance? What kind of a chance?'

Lotta shrugged, blankness filling her eyes. 'It's complicated. Like, really fucking complicated. Do you have any idea how many variables have to go into the modelling?'

Bear didn't speak but her eyes pressed for an answer.

'OK . . . you want an answer? The last model I worked on put the probability at somewhere between forty and fifty-five per cent. Maybe they've got that narrowed down some more, but right now, all I can tell you for certain is that Pearl is prepared to take that chance.'

'*Mon Dieu,*' Bear whispered, shaking her head. 'What if he is wrong?'

'Then we are not talking about a few dead fish here. We're talking about an entire eco-system being shut down *overnight*. It would mean the desertification of one of the richest maritime systems on earth. Just like that. Everything dies.' Lotta clicked her fingers to emphasise the point. 'No one can predict the knock-on effects if this thing goes bad, but one thing's for sure: it'll be on a *planetary* scale.'

Bear stared across the table in shock. 'But I don't understand. Why didn't you go to someone?' she asked, voice laden with recrimination despite her best efforts. 'Why didn't you inform one of the agencies and get them to stop him? Wouldn't the DHS have oversight on something like that?'

'Homeland Security! They're nothing but trumped up beat cops. I went all the way to the goddamn FBI!'

Bear signalled for her to lower her voice. Despite her flushed cheeks, Lotta slowly seemed to take stock of her surroundings and did as she was asked.

'In December I sent an anonymous email to the FBI. I detailed it all: the dumping off Haida Gwaii, the blueprint structure for the seed, everything they needed to close us – and more importantly, Pearl – down. But there was no response.' She stared across at Bear, eyes begging her to believe the story. 'Three weeks later I saw a car parked opposite my house for two nights in a row and I just knew that Pearl was coming for me. But after New York and all that had happened, I'd already planned my exit. I was following it too, until your man tracked me down.'

Bear didn't respond. She was still trying to guess the reason why no one in the FBI had reacted to the evidence Lotta had sent them. Did they think it was so improbable it didn't warrant investigation or had Pearl somehow managed to quash it at source?

'So why did you come out of hiding?' Bear asked, her mind rapidly switching tack. 'If you knew Pearl was looking for you, why did you risk everything by coming to see me?'

'Because Pearl is *here*! Right here in Cape Town. And in only a few days' time, he is going to try and fly into Antarctica to test the seed.'

Bear leant forward in her seat. 'What do you mean . . . Antarctica? I don't see the connection.'

'Why else do you think he has invested all that money in

the GARI science base? Pearl needs to test the seed, and the subterranean lake they've been drilling into is the perfect place. It's the one site on earth with saltwater encased in ice – a real-life Petri dish where he can gauge how the chain reaction will work before launching it into the Southern Ocean.'

Bear shut her eyes, feeling like the air had just been driven from her lungs. It seemed as though all the misgivings she had been harbouring for the last few days were now leaching out through the pores of her skin. The lake – that was exactly where Luca was now.

'That's why I came to see you,' Bear heard Lotta say, but her mind was still locked on Luca and the danger he was in. Opposite her Lotta continuing talking using her long fingers to emphasise each point. 'When I left for Nairobi, I thought it would take Pearl at least six months to create a transportable prototype of the seed. I knew that Antarctica would be shutting down at the end of February and so, if he missed that deadline, Pearl would have to wait a whole other year to perform the test. But then I found out that his private jet was in Cape Town and that could only mean one thing – somehow he's found a way to transport the seed. I decided then that I had to try and stop him, and when Louis called I realised that perhaps the best way to do it was to go to the press.'

Lotta stared across at Bear and, for the first time, registered the look of deep concern on her face. Not aware of Bear's personal interest in the story, she took it for general apprehension about what had been said.

'Not everything's lost,' Lotta soothed. 'There's still a reasonable chance that the ice surrounding the lake will contain the reaction.'

Bear blinked several times before registering that Lotta was addressing her once again. Dragging her mind away from thoughts of Luca, she jerked forward in her seat.

'The ice,' she said, her voice taking on a harsh, impersonal tone. 'You said that's why Pearl had chosen the lake in the first place. That it was like a Petri dish. So, even if he does launch the seed in the next few days, what does it matter? None of it will get into open water.'

'That's the theory, but as in everything he does, Pearl bent the facts to fit his own agenda. We knew from the beginning that ice dramatically slows the reaction and, over a certain distance, could even stop it. So the lake *was* the perfect place. When we did our original research, the ice mapping over the last fifteen years suggested that there would be an average of at least five kilometres of ice between the lake and open water.'

'Is that enough?'

'It would have been, but things have been changing down there over the last couple of years, and I mean radically. When I was in Nairobi, I started tapping into the latest data from the German base of Neumeyer. Two years ago, the ice was down to two point seven kilometres. Last year, it was under two. This year, the distance is already only point eight of a kilometre. That's just eight hundred metres of ice separating the lake water from open sea, and there may be places where it's even thinner.'

'Is that enough?' Bear pressed her.

Lotta shook her head, eyes brimming with desperate uncertainty. 'I don't know. I just don't. But one thing is for sure, it stacks the odds further in favour of some of the seed reaching open water.'

Lotta then seemed to snap out of her own nightmare and bent down to the bag at her feet. Emerging with a digital camera, she pulled a slim 64GB flashcard from its side with the tips of her nails and placed it on the napkin in front of her.

'This has everything you need to blow the story wide open. There's a full schematic of the seed, and enough of a trail to prove that Pearl was the one heading up the entire project.'

Folding over the edges of the napkin, she pushed it across the table. 'But you must hurry,' she added. 'He'll be leaving in the next few days for sure.'

Bear didn't reach for the napkin, ignoring the urgency in the other woman's voice.

'I need to know more about the actual lake,' she insisted. 'Is there anything dangerous there?'

Lotta's forehead wrinkled in confusion. 'I was talking about the seed and . . .'

Bear reached forward, grabbing hold of Lotta's cold hands. The sudden physical contact made her flinch and stare at Bear in alarm. 'The lake,' she repeated, speaking slowly as if to a child. 'Is it dangerous?'

Lotta nodded hesitantly. 'There's a man . . . I only heard Pearl mention him once. He was sent out to Antarctica over a year ago.'

'Go on.'

'He was told to wait for Pearl's arrival and to protect the lake. That's all I know about him, I swear. But given the fact that Pearl has already had two of my work colleagues killed, I can only imagine what this man will do to protect the place. Whenever anyone gets too close, they are silenced. That's how it works with Pearl.'

Bear slowly unclenched her fist, letting Lotta's hand fall from her grasp. Everything hinged on the lake and now, more than ever, she felt a desperate need to speak to Luca. As the past had amply proved, he had a talent for putting himself in harm's way. If this man Lotta was talking about had been sent to protect the lake, then Bear felt sure it would only be a matter of time before his path crossed Luca's.

Rising from her chair, she took the napkin and pressed the flashcard into the small side pocket of her skirt.

'Stay hidden, Lotta,' she said. 'Well hidden. No phone calls to anyone.'

'What are you going to do?'

'I don't know yet,' Bear replied, turning to leave, 'but somehow I'm going to stop Pearl getting on to that plane.'

Chapter 13

Vidar Stang swung the hunting rifle off his shoulder and brought the muzzle round in a slow sweep while he surveyed the mountains. His left eye was clamped shut against the wind while his right was magnified by the telescopic lens of the rifle, monstrously distorting his eyeball.

'Stang.'

The Norwegian heard his name again, whispered on the air across the expanse of ice. Having been alone in Antarctica for so long he was well used to the tricks of solitude, but this time it felt different. He stood motionless, forefinger curled tight against the trigger, drawing up the slack. Despite his gloves he could feel the metal begin to drain the heat from his fingertip, but knew that he could hold out a few minutes more before the first signs of frostbite would appear.

He brought the rifle left then slowly arced back across the mountain ridge, searching for the source of the sound. Another few seconds passed. Nothing.

Stang remained still, staring up from the lake at the

towering façades of the mountains. They ran in a tight semi-circle around him, shielding him from the worst of the wind like a bay in an ocean storm. He watched as trails of snow streamed over the tops of the peaks before dipping down towards him through the cold, lifeless gullies.

The storm was getting worse. At first, he had heard nothing more than a low hiss as wind channelled through the surface cracks in the rocks. But now it funnelled into the deep mountain caves, creating a hollow, rasping noise that reminded him of the sick wheeze his father had made on this deathbed.

'Stang.'

There it was again, this time clearer. Somebody was calling for him, but as soon as he tried to zero in on the sound, it seemed to fade back into the landscape. Stang waited another whole minute before finally letting his finger uncurl from the trigger and lowering his rifle.

Pearl. It had to be him. Stang wondered whether it could be just another of his tricks, but how could he have got here so fast? He had only received the satellite message three days ago informing him that Pearl was coming to Antarctica and that everything should be made ready for his arrival.

Upon hearing the news, Stang had spent hours staring at the single photograph he had stuck to the wall above his bed. Hours passed, maybe even days, and the whole time he'd revelled in the strength of his feelings. Finally, the time had come.

Clenching his hand tighter around the rifle butt, Stang felt the smooth, hard wood beneath his grip. It gave him a sense of reassurance and purpose. He was tired, he knew that, and should try to get some sleep. A constant headache had settled across his forehead, splitting his skull whenever he moved too quickly, but he fought the desire just to lie still for a moment and let his eyes close. There was still too much to do. Pearl's imminent arrival had overturned every constant in his life. Now he must keep pushing himself to the limit.

Stang knew he was in good shape. The winter months of conditioning had seen to that. Now he could make the climb up from the lake to his base in thirty-nine minutes flat. Thirty-nine! The same distance had taken him over two hours when he had first arrived in Antarctica.

There was a whistle of wind and Stang's gaze turned towards the mountains once again. Maybe it was his imagination, maybe not. But he needed to be sure. Straightening his back, he raised himself to his full height.

'I see you, Pearl!' he shouted, propelling each word towards the mountains like a prophet from the Old Testament. If Pearl wanted to play games then so could he.

Stang waited for an answer, but none came. A smile crept across his face. It was a thin smile, brimming with deadly intent. Let Pearl play his games. He would find a very different Vidar Stang waiting for him in Antarctica. The snow blindness had drained away the last of his naivety and misplaced trust, just as much as it had robbed him of the colour of his eyes.

Gathering his faded Bergen rucksack off the snow, he swung it over his shoulders and fastened the buckles. Despite his being in the lee of the wind, it was getting dangerously cold and he needed to be back inside. He started jogging across the deep snow of the lake, before reaching a narrow, zigzagging path that ran up towards his base.

Stang ran faster. He could feel his breath quicken, the cold air burning his throat as he pushed himself harder and harder. Sweat beaded down his lower back, welling out from under the shoulder straps of his Bergen. Normally, he would never have allowed it to happen as the moisture would make him far more susceptible to the cold the moment he stopped moving. But today was different.

Screw Pearl and his games. Today Stang was the master of his own environment, not a slave to it. Nobody could best him out here. Nobody was as fit or strong as he.

His thighs burnt as he rounded the last bend in the path and caught sight of the huge slab of rock that stood like a gateway to his base. Passing to the left of it, he came to a halt and glanced down at his stopwatch. Thirty-eight minutes flat. A full minute off his record!

Although now exposed to the full force of the wind, Stang swaggered the last few yards, moving deliberately slowly. His core temperature was still up, making him feel impervious to the elements, but it was more than that. It was the fact that he was Vidar Stang – a Norwegian hunter, forged from Viking stock – and nothing on this entire continent could stop him.

As he entered the base, he sealed off the dilapidated wooden door and moved further into the adjacent rooms. Ditching his Bergen and outer Gore-Tex jacket, he hurried along the corridor of stacked equipment, arriving at his metal chest. Quickly propping up his hunting rifle next to it, he stood and stared, picturing the cover of the magazine within.

Why not use up the very last of the perfume? His time in Antarctica was done. Soon, he would be back in Europe and able to realise every one of the fantasies he had played out in those dark winter months. It would be an orgy of long-denied pleasure and Stang vowed once more that he would give himself over to it fully. While he relished the thought, he felt a bead of sweat run down behind his ear and through the stubble of his shaved neck.

Yanking the key from the leather strap at his neck, Stang lunged forward, nostrils flaring greedily. Just as his hands took hold of the chest, his rifle, resting nearby, slowly toppled over on to the floor. There was a crack of gunfire, the report deafeningly loud at such close range, before the bullet rico-cheted off one of the base's metal supports, sending shock waves across the room.

Stang reeled back in surprise. Instinctively, he covered his ears with his hands, but it seemed as if the sound itself was still echoing within him. Then the full realisation of what had happened dawned on him – he had fired his weapon accidentally!

The implications were too shocking to contemplate. It was the one absolute in weapons handling that had been drilled into him, right from the start. In the past, he had always been fastidious about his rifle. He had prided himself on having perfect control. Now, all that was gone.

Tears of confusion began to well up in the corners of his

eyes, before flowing freely down his face. Stang could taste the salty liquid in his mouth as his entire frame began to shake. He gasped, feeling as though the air was sticking to his windpipe, while his vision blurred. Shadows stretched across the room, merging like the blots of a Rorschach test.

How could he have made such a stupid mistake? The ill discipline was unforgivable!

Emotion wracked him, intensifying with each moment that passed until he could take it no more.

'The circle,' he managed to say in a cracked voice.

Stang crawled there on his hands and knees, bashing against the corner of the metal chest as he raced forward with one purpose in mind – he had to reach the circle.

In one corner of the room a neat ring of rocks had been placed. Each had been painted white, while lying dead centre was a small paper bag of the type used for airsickness. Scraping his massive thighs as he crawled over the stones, Stang curled into a ball and jammed the open end of the bag over his mouth and nose. The bag inflated and deflated as he tried to regulate his breathing and slow the onset of the panic attack.

'I'm inside. I'm inside . . .' he repeated, the words bubbling out in a continuous mantra from somewhere past the back of his throat. The circle was his one place of sanctuary. Once he was inside, nowhere else existed for him. It was as if the stones themselves were able to blot out the world all around. His father had taught him to do this when they had crossed the wild expanses of northern Norway together.

Several minutes went by with just the soft crinkling of the

paper bag before Stang shifted his weight. His massive body twisted awkwardly within the confines of the ring as he dragged himself on to his knees and finally raised himself higher.

Things were getting worse. He could feel it. Grinding his fingers into his temples, he tried to relieve the pressure but it still felt as if a vice were ratcheting tighter and tighter around his mind. With each turn it seemed to wring out the very last of his sanity.

He needed to see Pearl again. To confront him once and for all.

Chapter 14

The two Ski-Doos powered on through the blizzard, the buzz of their engines lost to the howling wind. All around them snow rushed past in an unending flow, with each gust threatening to topple the men from their saddles.

Luca sat in the first Ski-Doo with Katz directly behind. His body took the brunt of the wind, shoulders hunched as he tried to stave off the incredible cold. As he drove, his left arm was crooked upwards holding the Global Positioning System beneath his goggles. He didn't bother to look up. Beyond the buckled windscreen of the machine, there was nothing to see but white.

Every few minutes, Luca would signal to Katz to check that the others were still behind. Swivelling in his seat, he could just make out the murky headlights of the second Ski-Doo and the dark smudge of Joel and Andy's silhouettes. They were driving only inches behind, so close that he could have leant back and touched the front skids had he wanted to.

Nearly thirty minutes had passed since they had left the

drill site and now the wind came in terrifying squalls. They hit every few seconds, rocking the Ski-Doos from side to side. But worse than the wind was the snow that came with it. Heavy and wet, it slapped against the hoods of their jackets and clung to the fabric of their outer clothing.

The snow was unstoppable, working its way into their mouths and noses while the ice-cold particles clung to any exposed flesh. They had each pulled their neck gaiters high over their cheeks, but almost immediately the fabric was encrusted in a thick layer of snow that threatened to suffocate them. They would raise their hands, quickly brushing off the worst of it, but more snow soon took its place, like sand draining back across a hole in the beach.

Without warning, there was a shunt from behind as Andy's Ski-Doo smashed into theirs. Both Katz and Luca were thrown forward in their seats, jarring against the handlebars and causing them to swerve wildly to the left. Luca only just managed to keep the vehicle upright, leaning over with his whole body to correct their balance. Then, only a few minutes later, it happened again. It was obvious that Andy was getting too cold to continue driving.

Luca cursed, bringing the screen of his GPS even closer. They were only another kilometre from the old Russian base that Dedov had told him about. They had to make it there. It was their only chance.

Already, he could feel the numbing effects of the cold. No matter how hard he tried to focus everything seemed to have slowed, becoming abstract and unimportant. He knew that his mind was trying to retreat from the terrifying reality all around and that soon he would simply slip into unconsciousness. Soon there would only be the endless white of the storm.

There was a sudden dip in the snow, then another, making them almost bounce out of their seats. The ground then began a sharp incline, bringing them up towards the top of the storm. As they continued climbing visibility started to break through in places, revealing the peaks of the high mountains.

There was a roar from the tracks as they passed from the edge of the snowline on to exposed rock. The jolt sent Katz crashing forward into Luca, with his massive bodyweight pitching them both on to the ground. A second later Andy's machine slammed into the back of theirs, engine revving high before it spluttered and stalled.

Luca slowly kicked off Katz's deadweight and staggered to his feet. The right side of his face had smashed down on to a rock, bruising his cheek. As he stood up he swayed, almost unable to keep his balance. He could see Joel and Andy still seated on the snow machine directly behind, the one hunched into the other for warmth. They were both just sitting, waiting.

Andy wasn't moving. His arms had slipped off the handlebars and now lay limply at his sides. As Luca approached Joel attempted to say something, but the words fell from his mouth in an unintelligible slur. His entire lower jaw was numb, the cold freezing it like a powerful anaesthetic. He tried again, but with no better result.

'Stay here,' Luca shouted. He turned away and began

staggering up the hill just in front. Katz was still on his hands and knees as Luca passed him. He weakly raised one arm, pleading for help, but his fingers only curled around the outline of Luca's disappearing form.

Away from the others now, he slowly rounded a low outcrop of rock about forty yards further on. He checked his GPS and stopped. He should be right on top of the old Soviet base by now. Where the hell was it? He was just about to curse Dedov's name again when, to his left, he saw the beginnings of a structure rise out of the gloom.

Luca stared in disbelief. He had been expecting something broken-down, but nothing quite so ruinous. Most of the base was little more than a pile of twisted metal and half-standing, pre-fabricated walls. It looked like it had never been completed, even in its heyday, and as Luca staggered back a pace, he was suddenly overcome by a sense of absolute hopelessness. For so long, he had built up the idea of the old base as their salvation. Now the very last of his faith drained away in bitter disappointment.

Slowly, his eyes passed across the entire complex. It was a pitiful collection of three modules, connected in sequence and running nearly sixty feet in length. A central tower, maybe thirty feet high, was the only part still intact, but over the years sections of metal panelling had been stripped away by the wind, exposing the plasterboard beneath like a half-picked skeleton.

Luca staggered closer, searching for anything resembling a door. He clambered over discarded wooden beams and around solitary metal poles jutting up from the ground like spears from a battlefield. Almost directly ahead of him was a dilapidated door leading into the central tower. It was still slightly ajar, with a long trail of hard-packed snow rimming its outer edge.

Using his shoulder, Luca slammed his body weight against it. The wood budged a few inches, but was frozen solid. Luca shunted again, then stepped back and kicked; once, twice, then again, and again. With each blow, the door creaked a little further open, but didn't relent. Luca could feel his heart thumping in his chest. With each kick he knew that he was getting weaker and weaker.

'Come on!' he screamed, stepping back a pace and making one last surge at the door. He crashed forward, with his shoulder then his face impacting on the raw wood at almost the same time. Finally it buckled, sending him sprawling into the room beyond with arms outstretched. He lay flat on the frozen ground for several minutes, the exhaustion too much for him to do anything other than let his eyes slowly pass over the piles of snowdrift that filled every corner of the room. He could see another door to the inside of the base. It was no more than ten feet away.

The sudden quiet here made the storm outside seem all the more terrifying. He could see his breath condensing in the air around him. It hung there momentarily before sinking back down to the icy ground. For the longest time he just stared at it, the fear of going back outside too much for him to bear.

Every instinct screamed at him to force the door closed again and shut out the wind. The entire situation had gone beyond anything that could be expected of a client-guide relationship. This was now a matter of survival. If the others made it up here then so be it, but it was for *them* to get here, not for him to go out and rescue them. This was Antarctica. Here you had to fend for yourself.

Luca reached towards the door, his gloved fingers curling around the rickety frame. He stared at his hand for several seconds, willing it into action to seal out the storm.

'Shit!' he screamed, the sound of his voice quickly dying against the icy walls.

A second later, he yanked the door back on its hinges and stepped outside once more.

He returned to the Ski-Doos to find Katz and Joel still there. They were sitting on the hard ground, sheltering in the lee of the machine's tracks. Snow had already started to drift over their legs and neither man was making any attempt to move.

'Where's Andy?' Luca shouted, half-squatting to be level with them. Only Joel raised his head.

'You said stay,' he slurred. 'Stay.'

'Andy?' Luca asked again, but already knew that he wouldn't get any intelligible response. As he looked closer, he could see where the cold had stripped the skin from Joel's cheeks in two neat lines beneath where his goggles had been. It looked almost surgical; the raw flesh peeling back towards his ears like a dissection from an anatomy class.

'You two, get up!' Luca ordered, pulling them by the straps of their rucksacks and on to their feet. They stood, swaying with bewilderment, until finally he pushed them forward in the direction of the base.

The going was slow. Joel's and Katz's boots scraped across the rock, their every movement dogged by uncertainty. Minutes passed with Luca man-handling them forward, screaming at them to continue when they drifted to a stand-still, and physically dragging them up the steeper incline of the slope. Finally, he managed to push them through the door and into the base.

Luca remained by the door, panting from the effort. He knew that if he went back down and started looking for Andy he would be seriously endangering his own life. Again, his mind rationalised everything so clearly, pleading with him not to go back outside. He had done enough already, done everything he could possibly be expected to do.

But something deep within already knew that he would go back one last time. Reason had nothing to do with it. It was just something that had to be done and had there been anyone else capable of doing it, Luca would gladly have deferred to them. This wasn't heroics. It was absence of choice.

'There's an MSR in my rucksack,' Luca called across to Katz and Joel, but neither of them was listening. They just lay against the broken wall, unable to muster the strength to do anything other than breathe.

Luca dropped to his knees, fumbling with the top of his rucksack, and pulled out a small gas stove. Even out of the wind, Katz's and Joel's core heat would already be critical. If he didn't do something to raise it right now, by the time he got back from finding Andy, all that would be left were two huddled corpses.

A few minutes later Luca had them grouped around a low, roaring flame in the neighbouring room of the base, with their damp sleeping bags draped across their thighs. The sudden warmth was so alluring, the blue flame acting like a beacon, drawing him further into the room. It took the very last of his will-power to straighten his stiff legs and move back out into the storm.

Andy . . . Why the hell had he left the Ski-Doo in the first place? Luca stumbled back down the hill, yanking the hood of his jacket a little lower on his face in a vain attempt to combat the wind. Slowly working his way across to the Ski-Doos, he then turned in a circle, trying to decipher which way the missing man might have gone. They were surrounded by gullies on both sides with a huge tabular rock lying to the right. It was immense, like some kind of ancient, sacrificial altar.

Luca moved closer to it. Just past the leading edge of the rock, he suddenly spotted the top half of a figure seated on the far side. It looked almost serene, with its face turned into the wind and arms lying gently by its sides. Luca moved closer still, not trusting himself to believe what he was seeing.

It was Andy. He had taken off his jacket and thermal layers and now sat bare-chested against the storm. His fleece hat and goggles were also gone, allowing his hair to flow horizontally behind him, tugged by each gust of wind. He seemed to be just sitting there, staring out into the middle distance.

'Jesus,' Luca whispered, clambering towards him and

quickly stripping off his own gloves. As he touched Andy's shoulders, he could feel the ice-cold temperature of his skin, but the other man didn't react. Instead his eyes continued staring into the void. Then Luca realised what had happened. His left eye had already frozen open. The lashes were fixed, while the eyeball itself had been robbed of its natural moisture, becoming waxy and lifeless.

'Andy!' Luca shouted, so close to him now that their faces were almost touching. Slowly, he turned towards him.

'Yes?' he said simply, as if confused by the urgency in Luca's voice.

'Your clothes! What the hell did you do with them?' As Luca spoke, he desperately looked behind Andy, but all that remained was a single glove lying trapped underneath a rock a few yards distant. The rest had been taken by the wind.

Luca began stripping his own jacket off his back, pulling open the zip and twisting his body out of the protective fabric, but then he stopped. Andy had raised a hand in protest.

'Hot,' he managed to say. 'Too hot.'

Luca suddenly felt tears welling up in his eyes, clouding his vision. He sniffed, zipping up his jacket again before reaching out with both arms and gripping Andy tight. His skin felt inhumanly cold and the last residue of colour had drained from his face, making him look more like a cadaver than anything living. This was the final stage of hypothermia, where extreme vasodilation could make a person experience illusory sensations of heat. Luca had only read about it before in mountaineering textbooks, but he knew that once a person was this far gone the result was always the same. Andy would be dead within minutes.

'You got any family?' Luca asked him.

For the longest time Andy didn't react, then his right hand slowly moved across to his trouser pocket, resting on top of it as if comforted by the thought of what lay within. Luca fumbled with the zip, his own fingers now stiff with cold. He pulled out the crumpled photograph that Andy had been keeping safe. Holding it tight against the strength of the wind, Luca caught sight of the image. An attractive, dark-haired woman was posing with a boy of about four years old, the pair of them staring towards the camera with heartfelt smiles.

Luca held it up in front of Andy's face and watched as the pupil of his good eye dilated for the briefest of seconds in recognition. Then he let out a shallow breath and started to lie down. As Luca reached forward to steady him, the photograph slipped from his grasp, twisting away on a current of air before bouncing across the rocks behind and becoming lost to the swirling grey storm.

'Think of your family,' Luca said, gently lowering the dying man down on to the rock. 'Just rest for a moment and everything will be OK.'

Andy seemed to hear the words and nodded vaguely, as if grateful to be tucked up to sleep in such a place. Luca stepped back, watching as the last embers of life finally drained from the good eye. Then all that had been Andy was gone. There was no earthquake or roll of thunder. No momentous natural event to signify his passing. There was only the cruel indifference of the wind.

Luca stared at the dead man's face, at the pale features and frozen skin. It would be like that for them all, he thought – a silent death in a landscape that could absorb a million others within the blink of an eye. They were alone out here. Utterly alone, and Luca had failed. He had let a man for whom he was responsible die.

The inevitability of their fate became so clear to him. They were all destined to die the same death – it was now only a question of who would last the longest.

But then, as he stood over Andy and stared down into his lifeless features, something else was triggered within Luca. He suddenly felt disdain. It was a kind of innate derision, like a mother pushing out the weakest from the litter. He wanted to get away from Andy, from all the failure and weakness that his dead body represented. Luca staggered back a pace, the impulse to survive steadily mounting with each beat of his living heart.

He would not be the one to die out here like that. Not the one to have his eyes frozen open.

Whatever happened, he was going to survive this storm.

Chapter 15

The two men from the South African State Security Agency stood side by side staring out of the window. Dark wooden shutters shielded them from Cape Town's harsh morning light. They waited in silence as the minutes passed. The shorter of the two had his arms folded across the bulge of his stomach, while the other had his fists firmly jammed into his trouser pockets. They were standing in Interjet's private jet lounge. Although their drab suits and scuffed shoes looked decidedly incongruous against its plush décor, this was not the source of their angst.

All around them deep, inviting sofas had been interspersed with contemporary glass tables. The entire setting had been designed to cater to the serious work ethic of the high-flying businessman, while also appealing to the families of the über-rich as they passed through on their latest summer jaunt.

The smaller man was named Eugene de Toit. He let his gaze wander over to the right-hand side of the room where the owners had built their pièce de résistance – a twenty-foot brass plaque emblazoned by the sketches of Leonardo da Vinci's flying-machines. Just below it stood a bank of refrigerators filled with soft drinks, while perched on top of the farthest one was a cylindrical-shaped SodaStream. One of the jet owner's children had expressed their preference for the old-fashioned drink dispenser in passing, and only the next day it had been purchased and installed.

'*Fokken windgatte*,' Eugene muttered, lightly tapping the toe of his leather boot on the coffee table. *Fucking snobs.*

He had grown up a farmer in the Eastern Cape and loathed such overt displays of opulence. It was something that had been hardwired into him from a very young age when he had witnessed the forced sale of his family's farm. A lawyer from Transvaal had tied them up in court until his parents' savings had been bled dry and they could no longer afford to fight. They had divorced a couple of months later, broken by it all, leaving Eugene to realise that, in the wrong hands, the law could be bent to only serve the rich.

His taller colleague moved back from the window and turned to face him. He had a lived-in face, with pale blue eyes the same shade as the sky outside. The skin of his cheeks sagged a little, still bearing the pockmarks of adolescent acne, and as he stepped out from the shadow of the blinds, an unhealthy smudge of yellow became visible at the corners of his mouth. Years of heavy smoking had taken their toll.

The two men stood facing each other. They had said very little on the plane down from Pretoria that morning, both absorbed in the file that a mining investigator called Beatrice Makuru had sent them late the previous evening.

'You do realise, Frankie,' Eugene said, breaking the deadlock, 'that if this *kaffir houdkop* is right, we're going to be in a whole heap of *kak*. You don't just go around arresting a man like Richard Pearl. And you know who it'll come round to bite? You and me, *boet*.'

Frankie nodded, his watery eyes fixed on the entrance to the room, double-checking that no one else was within earshot.

'Think about it,' Eugene continued. 'What's a man like Pearl doing smuggling diamonds anyhow? I've read his profile. It doesn't make sense.'

Frankie shrugged, suggesting that the rich had to get that way somehow. 'You read what the Makuru woman said. Pearl's working with old Bob up in the Marange mines, using his plane to ferry the diamonds into Namibia and then on to Antwerp. That way, they keep their Kimberley certification.'

'Come on. Mugabe and Pearl?' Eugene hissed. '*Wat die fok?*'

'I know how it sounds, but you're wrong about her. She's not just some *kaffir*. You know that blast up in Bloem a few years back?' Eugene nodded vaguely. 'She was the one who figured out it was an inside job.'

Eugene grunted, still far from convinced. '*Ja*, well, I had them check through the plane logs, and the closest Pearl's jet has been to Harare is here in *fokken* Cape Town.'

Frankie shrugged again, much to the annoyance of his

colleague. 'We have to hear her out. And if Makuru gives us any *kak*, then I'll be the first one to kick her back under the rock she came from.'

They both fell silent as Bear entered the room. She wore a tailored grey suit and two-inch heels, while her long, jet black hair was neatly brushed back from her face and secured in a ponytail. Aside from a slight puffiness around her eyes, she bore no other signs of the terrible night's sleep she had endured. With a work file pressed against her chest, she walked towards them, hand outstretched.

'Pleasure,' Eugene croaked, with a thin smile.

With a gracious sweep of his hand, Frankie gestured for Bear to be seated. She perched sideways on a luxurious white sofa, knees clamping together as the skirt she was wearing hitched a little higher than she would have liked.

'Now, my dear,' Frankie began, his voice cool like water, 'I am sure we don't have to tell you that these are some very serious accusations to be making.' He paused, feeling the impatience radiating off Eugene beside him. Half turning in his seat, he saw his colleague staring unblinkingly at Bear across the low coffee table. He knew how hot-headed Eugene could be, but they had to treat this Makuru woman with respect. As far as Frankie could tell from a few well-placed calls made earlier that morning, she was connected to just about every single person on the South African mining scene.

'Mr Richard Pearl is a very prominent American who . . .' Frankie hesitated, looking skywards as he struggled to find the right word. 'Well, let's just put it this way. If you want us to move on this, you are going to have to show us *irrefutable* evidence.'

He dragged the word out as if the number of syllables alone would be a sufficient deterrent.

'I have everything right here,' Bear countered, placing the folder on the table in front of her. She wedged its corner under the bronze statue of a Cessna Sovereign private jet that stood between them, wingtips tilted upwards as if soaring across the open skies.

Eugene angled forward, his eyes drawn to the folder.

'You'd better be right,' he said, his smile shifting slightly until it resembled a snarl. 'Because he is going to be arriving in a couple of minutes and I for one am not going to sit here with my thumb up my *gat* just on your say-so.'

Bear didn't flinch. 'Like I said, it's all in there.'

As Eugene stretched forward towards the file, Bear raised her hand.

'Wait,' she commanded, making him turn a shade redder at being addressed in such a way. 'I want Pearl's plane immediately impounded and every inch of it searched. Tear the damn thing to pieces if you need to, but my sources say there are over four million dollars' worth of uncut diamonds cached inside.'

She said the words with as much confidence as she could muster. She knew only too well that the State Security Agency would never have believed her if she'd said Pearl was trying to introduce some kind of exotic compound into Antarctica, with all the consequences that Lotta had described. They would have kept her bouncing between agencies as they tried to figure out what it was, and more importantly whose juris-diction it fell under. And while they procrastinated, Pearl would simply have climbed on board his jet and gone. Better to keep it simple.

It would take them days to search such a massive jet for something as easily concealed as diamonds. Then there would be the endless paperwork needed to get the plane re-certified for flight. When they finally discovered the truth, the SSA would never trust her as a contact again, but that was just something she'd have to live with.

Ever since she had left Lotta the previous evening, Bear had been trying to think of a way to detain Pearl yet keep herself out of harm's way. She was pregnant now and, however reckless she had been in the past, had to be mindful of that fact. By contacting the SSA she had found a way out. All she needed to do was to get them to detain Pearl on reason-able suspicion. 'Sources?' Eugene repeated. 'I want to see backgrounds on everyone you spoke to. I want to . . .'

His demands trailed off as behind them the glass door swung open and a smartly dressed Indian man presented himself. Despite the cut of his immaculate blue suit, it was obvious that he was wire-thin. His dark hair was oiled and parted dead centre, framing the red smudge of a *bindi* on his forehead. He was holding a black leather briefcase and with the slightest hint of a bow, let his keen brown eyes pass from one person to the next.

Behind him, on the far side of the glass door, they could see another four men. They had the build and bearing of a security detail. Each had military-style haircuts, and as Bear looked closer she could see the coiled wire of earpieces running down into the collars of their starched shirts.

'My name is Hara Predesh,' the Indian man said softly. 'I am the personal assistant to Mr Pearl and have been instructed to assist you with these quite . . . disconcerting allegations.'

Frankie was the first to get to his feet. 'Mr Predesh, I believe that our office was very clear on this matter. We need to talk to Mr Pearl himself.'

Predesh gave a conciliatory smile, raising the palms of his hands slightly as if to imply that he was nothing but a humble servant.

'My employer has a demanding schedule, so perhaps I might offer some details prior to his arrival. He will be here soon and is looking forward to clearing his name most swiftly.'

The news that Pearl would be arriving in person seemed to appease Frankie. He sat back down, gesturing for Predesh to do likewise. With the briefest of nods to the security detail outside, he placed the briefcase next to the coffee table and sat down on the same sofa as Bear. A smile tinged with boredom played on his lips, as if this were just another meeting for him in a day filled with far more significant matters.

'First things first. I must make it clear that we are not pressing any charges or making any accusations at this stage,' Frankie began by way of a disclaimer. 'It is purely a routine investigation in light of an official complaint.'

'I understand,' Predesh replied magnanimously.

'Quite. Quite.' Frankie's eyes flicked towards Bear. 'We

just have some informal questions about the whereabouts of Mr Pearl, relating to his travels to Zimbabwe late last year.'

Predesh's fingers gently touched the top of his briefcase. 'I have already taken the liberty of printing out the itinerary of Mr Pearl's plane on each occasion it entered African airspace. As you will see, it went nowhere near Zimbabwe at any time.'

Eugene nodded in agreement, glaring at Bear as he did so.

'My office is genuinely bemused by these allegations,' Predesh continued, 'and welcomes any chance to refute them.'

As he spoke, the low rumbling of a jet's engine started up. Parked on the apron outside the lounge were a profusion of planes, ranging in size from the small Pilatus PC-12s to the heavier jets of Gulfstream and Bombardier. These were all private planes held in a different location to the massive Boeings and Airbuses of the commercial operators.

Bear listened as the sound of the engines mounted. She knew the difference between one of the smaller jets doing its pre-flight checks and the roar of a fifty-million-dollar Bombardier. The turbofans of the BMW Rolls-Royce engines were deeper, with a smoother, heavier rotation. For years her own Cessna 206 had been parked only a few hundred feet away in one of the cheaper hangars, and she had often passed the heavy jets coming out on to the taxiway.

Bear stared at Predesh. For the briefest of moments, his eyes flicked towards the window before quickly re-engaging with Frankie. Then, like a lantern being switched on, his faint smile glowed a little brighter.

Bear studied him closely. The allegations she had made were nothing less than outrageous. In all truthfulness, she was amazed that the SSA had not simply dismissed them out of hand. So why was Predesh being so conciliatory? Any normal person confronted like this would have shown signs of indignation, or at the very least confusion, but Predesh was displaying neither. He had another agenda. She was sure of it.

Frankie was about to speak again when Bear suddenly stood up.

'Given that I'm the one making the allegations, perhaps I might say a couple of words.'

Frankie seemed to hesitate for a second, then with an air of resignation he gestured for Bear to continue. Instead of immediately addressing the room she strode towards the long bank of windows, looking every bit the barrister cross-examining a defendant in the dock.

'Mr Predesh, tell me – how many times has Richard Pearl flown to South Africa in the last three months?'

'Four.'

'He must have some pressing work commitments to travel such long distances, or does he come here for pleasure?'

As she spoke, Bear came to a standstill in front of the windows. She poked her finger into the blind distractedly, as if Predesh's answers were all part of an inevitable stream of logic, but while she waited for a response, her eyes scanned the runway's apron, searching for the jet that was starting up. Could it be Pearl's Bombardier?

Unlike the international airport with its security fences

and restrictions, the private lounge of Interjet opened directly on to the tarmac where the jets were parked and Bear could clearly see all the way to the runway. As her eyes passed from one plane to the next, she caught sight of the N-registered tailfin of an American aircraft. It was fifth in line amongst the row of parked planes. Pearl's was the biggest, dwarfing the others in width and height, and as she stared more intently she could see the faint wash of exhaust fumes in the air behind it. Her instincts had been right. The plane was getting ready to depart.

Suddenly, she spotted two figures hurrying across the tarmac. One was definitely male, while the other ran in his shadow, half-concealed, as they ducked under the wing of the neighbouring jet. As the two heads re-emerged, Bear caught the slightest hint of red in the man's hair. It was Pearl! It had to be, and he was running towards the open entrance of his plane.

Suddenly it all made sense. Predesh was only here to distract them. In just a few minutes, Pearl would be airborne.

Bear turned back towards the men. 'So tell me, Mr Predesh. Were the journeys for business or pleasure?'

She moved her hands to her hips and stared down at Predesh as if arriving at the crux of her argument. She desperately needed time to think and had to keep up this pretence. Eugene snorted at the clichéd courtroom antics, before his eyes switched back to Frankie, imploring him to take charge.

'It is no secret that my employer is a major benefactor of an Antarctic scientific base,' Predesh answered. He spoke slowly as if the words might somehow need to be translated for Bear's benefit. 'We access the base from right here in Cape Town, which adequately explains his previous visits. Now, I think it is time for us to see some evidence rather than continuing *ad infinitum* with Ms Makuru's conjecturing.'

Eugene murmured in agreement, while Frankie gave Bear a look that suggested she'd better know what she was doing. Bear remained still, her mind reeling. She had to act, had to do something, or Pearl would be gone. Something was triggered within her at the thought of Pearl landing in Antarctica – that would put him right next to the lake and, by extension, Luca. As the thought began to crystallise in her mind, an impulse surged through her. It was the same impulse that had seen her charge into the crippled mineshaft in Chile all those years ago; a realisation that if *she* didn't do something about the situation, no one else would.

Her eyes settled on a small item sitting on top of the bank of refrigerators.

'With your permission,' she said, turning back to address Predesh, 'we should close the door. Some of the documents I have brought within this file are *extremely* sensitive.'

Predesh shrugged as if it were a matter of no importance, but inwardly he knew that his security detail just outside had been carefully briefed as to their mission. Whether it was by force, or by Predesh himself managing to spin out the meeting until Pearl was safely in the air, they had to contain the two SSA operatives and the Makuru woman. By locking the door, all she was doing was playing into their hands.

Eugene got up to close the door, turning the key in the lock.

'The blinds too,' Bear commanded.

Muttering under his breath, he found the dangling cord and clattered them down.

'Gentlemen,' she began, 'what you are about to witness is something that cannot pass beyond these four walls.'

She gave them all a look of the utmost severity as she placed the folder down on the table. Predesh stayed still, seemingly content for Eugene to reach forward and open it. The first page consisted of a long and rambling history to the background of the Marange Mines in Zimbabwe. Eugene scanned through it, quickly realising that this was little more than information pulled from the internet.

His eyes narrowed in confusion as he flipped to the next page, then the next. There was nothing but generalities that would be accessible to pretty much anyone with a computer. He looked up, questioning how any of this was related to the case in hand, and noticed Bear backing off towards the bank of refrigerators while pulling the leather strap of her handbag tight across her shoulder. He then watched as she clicked open the back of the SodaStream and slid out the smooth gas cylinder contained within. In the drawer directly beneath she found two spare cylinders and, pulling the elasticated hair tie from her ponytail, she wound it around all three, securing them together in a bunch.

Eugene watched for a moment longer before a snarl appeared on his lips.

'*Wat di fok* are you playing at?' he hissed, raising himself to his full height. He was slightly overweight with a paunch that stretched the mid-section of his shirt, but still had quick reflexes, and knew it. His neck muscles twitched in anticipation.

Bear hesitated for a split-second more, torn between the need for action and an innate sense of self-preservation. Then her reflexes seemed to take charge and on pure impulse she swung round, throwing open the double-glazed window of the lounge. She stared out. The drop could be no more than ten feet.

Stretching up her arms, she grabbed hold of the dark-wood blinds and wrenched them off their fittings. Now both Frankie and Predesh had got to their feet and were staring in absolute bewilderment, as if witnessing the antics of a lunatic. Eugene was the first to react; but just as he took a step towards Bear she kicked off her shoes and hitched her skirt up past her hips. Confronted by the sight of her long thighs and a pair of black lace knickers, Eugene faltered. He tried to speak, but confusion momentarily paralysed him.

Without looking back, Bear planted her right foot on the windowsill then levered the rest of her body on to the ledge. Only then did the others fully understand what she was about to do, and both Eugene and Frankie pushed past Predesh, sending him flying back on to the sofa.

Bear dropped down on the tarmac outside, knees jarring from the impact. With the gas cylinders from the SodaStream clamped in her right hand, she ran as fast as she could, while somewhere behind her she heard shouts as both SSA men craned their necks out of the window, screaming at her to stop. She half turned, catching sight of Eugene trying to push past Frankie, but he was leaning so far out of the window that he couldn't manoeuvre his way back for several precious seconds.

Eugene grabbed the collar of Frankie's shirt and heaved his colleague back into the room. He himself then surged forward, jumping with both feet on to the windowsill, but as he pushed himself on, his right boot caught in what remained of the rope for the blinds. His body pivoted downward so that he fell head first, with the side of his face smacking against the tarmac with a grim slap. He groaned, briefly dragging his head off the ground before it slumped back down again. He passed out before his eyes had managed to close.

Ahead of him Bear ran barefoot over tarmac that was scalding hot from the midday sun. Passing the parked jets one by one, she quickly drew nearer to Pearl's. There in the cockpit was the pilot. She could see him through the armoured glass windscreen, talking into the radio as he completed the last of the pre-flight checks.

Just as she drew level with the wingtips, the plane's engines roared with deafening power. They slowly pulled the standing weight of the plane into a roll and Bear watched as the porthole windows lining the fuselage passed by her in sequence. Then, suddenly, she saw him.

The sheen from the glass obscured the lower part of his face, but she recognised Pearl's slicked back hair and steel-grey eyes. His face moved closer, nose almost pressing into the glass as he returned her stare. His eyes hardened with absolute focus as if he were attempting to stop her by force of will alone. Then he twisted back towards the cockpit and she saw him yell something to the pilots. A second later the plane lurched forward as the captain quickly shunted in the power.

There was a great whooshing sound as the jet engines sucked the air through the fan intakes, followed by the roar of vaporising fuel. It was deafening, shaking the ground all around her, and Bear had to fight every instinct not to drop the cylinders and run in the opposite direction.

With eyes narrowed against the rush of air, she watched as the massive plane began its inexorable roll towards the runway, gaining speed with every passing second.

Almost tripping as she forced herself on, Bear ran beside the wings. She wasn't thinking, only reacting. With her back arched, she ducked beneath the expanse of riveted metal to get closer to the engines underneath. Now she could feel the heat; the intense, searing heat of the exhaust fumes. Shielding herself as best she could, she raised the cylinders with one hand and lobbed them in a low arc into the open intakes of the jet engine.

There was a sudden clash of spinning metal, followed by a small explosion. Splinters of broken metal spun off into the air like shrapnel, while the exhaust flame spluttered, then, a second later, went out.

The plane continued rolling towards the runway, seemingly impervious to the damage, but then it jerked to a standstill. There was a moment's pause before an explosion broke out across the open expanse of the airport. The force of the blast lifted the entire portside of the plane off the ground, wrenching it over to one side and buckling the length of one wing. Everything went quiet. The only movement was a smudge of acrid smoke clawing its way up from the broken engine and into the clear Cape Town sky.

Bear lay flat on the ground, dimly aware of a pain in her side. There was an intense ringing in her ears that seemed to block out all her other senses. The shockwave from the explosion had burst her right eardrum. As she lay on her side on the hot tarmac, a thin trickle of blood oozed out of her ear, running down the side of her jawline.

She stared in shock at the grazed palms of her hands before her eyes regained their focus and gradually settled on a group of four figures running around the corner of the Interjet building. She blinked, trying to see more clearly, but the silhouettes looked hazy and unthreatening. As she raised her head, her skull felt like it had just fractured across her temples and she let out a low groan before dropping it back down.

Seconds passed, with only the heavy thud of her heart pounding in her chest. Black spots blurred across her vision and she could feel herself slipping into unconsciousness.

Then something deep inside her commanded her to move. Bear groaned in protest, trying to ignore it, but the feeling rose within her, surging through the crippling apathy. The impulse was primordial, flooding new energy into each tired muscle. The baby. She had to save the baby.

Rolling on to her stomach, Bear pushed up from her palms, trying to wrench herself clear of the ground. She felt so heavy, as if a massive weight were pressing down on her back. Scraping her knees up underneath her torso, she struggled on to all fours and lifted her head. Through strands of black hair, she could see her pursuers clearly now, rounding the first of the planes.

'Move!' she whispered to herself as she struggled to get onto her feet. As soon as she stood vertical, her right ear seemed to explode with pain, making her stagger backwards and almost collapse. She swayed for several seconds, her knees threatening to give out from under her, as her gaze slowly settled on the airport fence line directly behind her. It was no more than three hundred metres away.

Swivelling her whole body round, she could see that beyond the airport and the motorway which served it was a brief stretch of scrubland before the first of the corrugated-iron shacks of Nyanga shantytown began.

Bear started moving forward, half stumbling, half running. Her legs dragged one after the other, while her whole body seemed to list to one side. She forced herself to keep moving, concentrating on pumping her arms and raising her knees high. Ten metres. Then twenty. With each step, the movement began to normalise and slowly her momentum built.

There was the crack of a pistol shot. Then another. The noise seemed tinny and innocuous in such a vast open space. Checking behind her, Bear saw two of the men had stopped, their shoulders hunched as they levelled their pistols. Another crack. But even as she ran, she knew that the distance was far too great for a pistol to be aimed accurately.

Further to the right, Bear caught sight of Frankie's tall,

spidery frame. He had managed to get down from the window and give chase, but the years of heavy smoking were taking their toll. He trotted forward as fast as he could, feet shuffling over the ground while his pistol hung limply from his right hand. He was trying to make up the ground between them, but even he knew the futility of his pursuit. The threat was from Predesh's personal security team and Bear knew it. Her only chance was to outrun them.

She pushed on, the countless morning runs making her body respond automatically. As she crossed the furthest tip of the runway and reached the sandy ground of the outer perimeter she saw the fence line directly ahead of her. It was maybe ten foot high, with a single coil of razor wire running its length. Bear sprinted towards it, raising her hands, fingers outstretched in anticipation. Checking her stride, she sprang upwards, nearly reaching the top of the fence in a single bound. Her body smashed into the metal links, sending a reverberation along its length as she grabbed on to the razor wire and pulled herself higher.

The wire bit deep into her palms and Bear cried out in pain as she bundled herself on to the top. Teetering at the apex with her back arched like a cat, she tried to pause for a split second and catch her balance, but instead, simply toppled over, landing flat on her back with a heavy thud. She groaned, her hand reaching up to the back of her head to where a fist-sized chunk of hair had been ripped out by the wire.

Just ahead of her now was the busy N2 motorway, beyond that the first shacks of Nyanga shantytown. Crude corrugated iron sheets had been nailed together, barely big enough to shelter a single bed, while old shopping bags and scraps of tarpaulin were patched together to form roofs. These stretched on for mile after mile, a sickening mass of poverty and human suffering.

Nyanga – the single most violent place in the Cape Flats. It was a place ungoverned by law, where violence ran unchecked through the streets, like the streams brimming with rotting plastic and human effluent.

Bear dragged herself to her feet. Dodging the line of cars hammering down the motorway, she stumbled into the open arms of the shantytown. She passed one shack, then another, venturing deeper into the sea of corrugated-iron sheeting until it stretched around her in every direction like an apocalyptic city of ruined metal.

For all its horror, Nyanga had one saving grace – it was the one place where white men feared to tread.

Chapter 16

From the far south of False Bay, a thunderstorm rolled in across the Cape Flats. The skies grew dark, bruising to a deep purple as a wall of rain steadily moved in from the sea and on to the parched land. Soon, the entire city became breathless and charged with electricity, everyone waiting for the release of the first strike of lightning.

As the rain began to fall in earnest, Bear forced herself to a halt. Her chest heaved from such a prolonged sprint, while her forehead and neck glistened with sweat. She looked one way, then the next, already feeling disorientated by the endless labyrinth of shacks.

Her clothes . . . She had to get rid of her office suit or they would immediately peg her as an outsider despite the colour of her skin. Leaning over a ramshackle wooden fence just to her right, she saw two rows of laundry still hanging on the spider's web of electricity lines that spread out across the shanty-town. The clothes flapped like prayer flags in the new breeze – the single burst of colour in an otherwise drab landscape.

Bear hopped over the fence, suddenly noticing a woman lying on her side by the back entrance to the shack. She was rounded and porcine, with a band of indelible fat stretching across her buttocks and stomach, while her weather-beaten face was of indeterminate age. She was slumped on the ground, snoring, inches from the smouldering remains of a cooking fire, while flies buzzed from one part of her body to the next.

Pulling a bright purple sarong off the line, Bear swapped it for her charcoal grey skirt. She then went to take off her shirt, but as soon as she raised her arms above her head there was a stabbing pain in her side. She stared in confusion, gently dabbing her fingers across the line of her ribs until she noticed a small puncture wound, no bigger than a pencil nib. It ran right through her, from just under her right breast to where it exited from her side. A piece of shrapnel from the jet engine must have hit her, and as soon as she pressed her fingers lightly against the wound, a trickle of blood oozed out and ran down her side. She stared at it for several seconds, thanking God that it hadn't been a few inches lower and nearer to the baby.

After a couple more gentle dabs with her forefinger, Bear decided that there was nothing she could do about the wound right now. It was just going to have to wait.

Moving further down the line of shacks, she found a low-cut, black T-shirt that was greyed from age, followed by a short length of orange fabric to tie around her hair. The flashcard Lotta had given her was still wrapped in a paper napkin. Pulling it from the pocket of her skirt, Bear stuffed it into her bra. She then stared at her mobile phone, knowing that they would soon be tracking her on it. But she had to try and get hold of Luca one more time. Just once. For now, she told herself, it was worth the risk.

Sliding two credit cards from her purse, she quickly counted out what cash she had been carrying. She had nearly four hundred euros, but the crisp notes were as good as useless out in a place like Nyanga. No one here would even have heard of the currency. Other than that, there was some change in South African rand, only two hundred bucks at most. It'd be enough for a taxi ride back to the City Bowl, but that was it.

Just as she was about to leave, she crouched next to the old woman's fire and dug her fingers into the burnt-out ash. She then rubbed it across her cheeks, greying out her clean, freshly moisturised skin and dulling the last of her lipstick. Emptying the remaining contents of her purse into the embers, she watched as the various receipts flared up in a quick orange flame and then, with a flick of her wrist, tossed the handbag into the interior of the shack. Bear only hoped that the old woman would figure out what the thing was worth. It'd buy nearly a year's worth of groceries in this neighbourhood.

There was a yellow jerry can, stained and old, sitting on the ground nearby. Bear swung it up. She clambered back over the fence, and balanced the can on the crown of her head as she had done as a little girl in the Congo. Arching her back, she continued down the line of shacks with the ubiquitous gait of an African woman performing her daily chores.

A white Toyota Land Cruiser turned left out of the airport, its engine revving as it powered along the open road towards Nyanga. Inside were the four men from Hara Predesh's security detail.

The driver, Johan Botha, was the only South African in the group. He had joined Pearl's usual security team as a local 'fixer' and to help orient them on their arrival in Cape Town. But as he had soon discovered, the Americans were a tight bunch. They were all former US marines, two of them having completed a tour of Laghman Province in Afghanistan together before discharge when they turned to close protection. Johan had learnt a great deal about them in the last two days, with the Americans talking almost as much as they fidgeted with their weapons.

As they reached the outskirts of Nyanga, all four passengers stared out of the Land Cruiser's windows, craning their necks to look down each street.

'Shit!' shouted the American in the passenger seat. His name was Darin Perez, a former sergeant in the US Marines and leader of the security detail. He was slimmer than the other two, with a pointed, rat-like face and pallid skin. His right knee bounced up and down with impatience as his eyes moved from one person to the next in the crowded streets, never settling for more than a second on each figure.

'We've got to get closer to the airport fence line,' he said, jabbing a finger against the window. 'Take a left.'

Johan hesitated, not wanting to leave the busy flow of taxicabs on the main Terminus Road.

'Come on! Left!' Darin repeated, this time banging his fist against the glass.

'Take it easy,' Johan retorted, dragging the steering wheel round and turning them into the first of the side streets. Only a few hundred yards on the brick houses disappeared and the streets grew narrower, riddled with potholes.

'You guys need to understand something,' Johan explained as the rain began to drum against the front windscreen. 'We stay in the vehicle at all times.'

He switched on the wipers, causing a smear of red dirt to stretch across the windscreen. Behind him, the two Americans on the back seat exchanged glances with one of them mouthing the words 'Chicken shit' to the other. They had seen nothing but women and schoolchildren out on the streets, with the only potential danger coming from the erratic driving of the local taxis.

The car drove on, bouncing slowly across the potholes as a group of about ten teenagers appeared, hanging out on the corner of the next intersection. They leant against a low wall smoking old cigarette butts and wearing a ragtag collection of school uniforms and hooded tops.

There was an air of listlessness over the entire group, all of them seemingly oblivious to the onset of rain. Their movements were slow and apathetic, heads bent low, chins almost touching their bony chests as if engaged in some kind of protracted prayer. Only two of the group were standing up straight, with the nearest teenager to the road openly holding a *panga* in his right hand. He waved the machete lazily from side to side, illustrating some point to his friend like a professor with a marker pen.

'Kids,' Darin muttered dismissively.

'Yeah, they're kids. But those are the Vatos gang from Zwelitsha.'

'So? They got a couple of machetes. Big deal.'

'There'll be another twenty or thirty kids like that close by in the neighbourhood. And these have just scored a hit. That's why they're doped out like that. The *tik* makes them feel dizzy.'

The American shrugged, not knowing the local term for crystal meth on the Cape Flats, but it seemed to him that a drugged-out gang like this could only be to the visitors' advantage. They needed to get in and find the girl. If they had to step around some doped up kids, then what the hell.

Johan jammed the gear lever into first as the front wheels of the Land Cruiser dipped into a muddy pothole.

'But that'll only last for twenty or thirty minutes,' he continued ominously. 'Then they'll be fired up and awake for days. The *tik* makes them invincible.'

Darin raised an eyebrow.

'I'm serious,' Johan continued. 'It took three of us to hold down a fifteen-year-old boy jacked up on that stuff a few months back. Fucking animal sank his teeth into my arm.' He raised a hand, gently massaging the old injury. 'Had to have a rabies shot and everything.'

Darin gave a snort, then half-turned towards his companions in the back seat.

'Eyes open,' he ordered. 'She'll have changed out of her clothes if she's got any sense, but she's tall and slim, and it looked like her balance was shot by the explosion.'

The car trundled on, pausing by the narrow opening to each shack. There were few occupants visible. Women sat by weak, smouldering fires, sheltering from the rain, while grubby children with lines of snot running from their noses stared from behind their grandmothers' backs, surprised to see such a plush vehicle pass by.

The air felt close, the approaching thunder making the men's shirts cling to their backs with sweat. The sky became darker still, turning the sea of metal houses into a uniform block of colour, while all around them the streets of Nyanga stretched on and on. Johan reached forward, cranking the air conditioning. Seconds later he sighed as the flow of cool air washed over him.

They followed the same narrow track until it led out on to an open area in the middle of Nyanga where they drew to a halt. A small crowd had gathered there. Judging by the brightly coloured clothing, most of them were women. They huddled around open barrel fires cooking meat in the *Tshisa* stands, sheltering under old tarpaulin that had been stretched across crooked wooden frames. A few of the taxicabs had stopped en route to allow their clients the chance of a quick meal.

The Americans stared out of the window, watching the locals go about their business. As the rain began to fall from the sky, some had raised umbrellas above their heads as they moved from one side of the square to the other, while others simply tried to shield themselves with plastic shopping bags. Along one side of the square was a line of small shops with adverts for Coca-Cola and MTN cell phones hand painted on their wooden walls. Behind the small hatches lay the shop's entire inventory, with the shelving half bare.

'This is where I'd come if I had to blend in,' Johan said. Then, seeming to check himself, added, 'If I were black, that is.'

'What do you think the chances are she even came this way?' Darin asked impatiently.

'Fifty-fifty, but we've more chance of finding her here than going door to door. It's a fucking rat's maze out there.'

'Why the hell can't they just triangulate her cell phone?'

'They're working on it,' Johan said, checking his own phone to see if any message had come through. 'But you got to remember something, my China. This is Africa. Things don't exactly run like clockwork round here.'

Darin snorted, his disapproval a broad stroke that usually encompassed anything not American. As the minutes passed he became more and more agitated, his knee bouncing in constant spasm, while an unintelligible mutter came from somewhere between his clamped jaws. Unable to bear it any longer, he threw open the side door and stood against the vehicle's wide bonnet while he lit a cigarette. Ignoring the weather, he breathed out a cloud of smoke directly above him, expelling it high into the air as if trying to combat the falling rain.

Two schoolchildren hurried past the car, one boy sheltering another with the open fold of a newspaper. As they drew level, they suddenly stood still. Darin's arm had crooked upwards as he raised the cigarette to his mouth and the younger of the two had seen the American's sidearm under the flap of his flannel jacket. Darin spotted their expressions and, tilting his hips round a little more, held his arm aloft, allowing them a good look at his pistol. It was a Beretta M9A1, the trusted 9mm of the US military, and a weapon he had carried almost every single day since his discharge. He gave a self-assured smile, knowing how such firearms had impressed him as a child.

The two boys didn't react, only scurrying on under the pouring rain. They rounded the side of the nearest *Tshisa* stand, waving away the plumes of meaty smoke. The elder of the two saw one of his uncles in a parked taxicab, passengers already crammed into the back seat waiting to be off. The child ran over to the open driver's window and whispered something.

The uncle's broad face remained impassive behind his fake Armani sunglasses. He listened to the boy before swatting him away with a flick of his wrist and letting his eyes slowly drag across to the other side of the square and the parked Land Cruiser.

Shifting in his seat, the man pulled at the front of the dirty brown singlet he was wearing, releasing the fabric from a patch of sweat that had collected at his midriff. He always wore a singlet and it was little to do with the heat. It made sure his upper arm was visible, in particular the number 28 crudely tattooed on it in dirty blue ink. The numbers related to his time spent at Pollsmoor prison, and signified that he had either been arrested for rape or murder. In fact, he had done both, but only been convicted of the latter offence.

The news that the *wazungu* were carrying pistols changed everything. A lot of the charities and NGOs used the same kind of white Toyotas and would occasionally pass through Nyanga, especially during the day. But invariably they had nothing to steal. Pistols on the other hand . . . they were more prized than drugs or money.

Picking up his cell phone from the well by the handbrake, the man quickly dialled a number. It connected through to another 28 from the neighbouring township of Khayelitsha and the taxi driver spoke to him quickly in his native Xhosa, telling him to bring the guns they had stashed away after a break-in, plus as many of their crew as were on hand. As the line went dead he stared enviously across at the *mzungo* standing outside the car smoking a cigarette.

A crooked smile appeared on the taxi driver's lips, revealing the gap where his two front teeth should have been. He wanted that pistol. Pistols gave a man *power*. Then, as the side door of the taxicab slid open and a middle-aged woman peered in, the smile faded.

'You going to Philipi?' she asked, stepping halfway into the vehicle.

'*Voetsek*,' the driver replied, not bothering to turn round. *Get lost*.

Without a murmur of complaint, the other passengers already waiting inside the taxicab slowly got up from their seats and dispersed into the crowd in search of alternative transport. Something was about to go down and they knew enough to be as far away from it as possible.

Bear stared through the haze of smoke rising up from the barrel barbecues. The Toyota had been waiting on the edge of the square for the last twenty minutes and she felt she was becoming more and more exposed. Predesh's security team must somehow have found out where she was and were waiting for her to make the first move.

She had already bought a skewer of beef from the nearby stand. Holding it in her hand, she sheltered from the rain under some patchy tarpaulin. After chewing half-heartedly for a couple of minutes, she placed the dirty-looking metal spike on a nearby table and retreated a pace further back into the stand. She lowered her head, willing herself not to stare at the ratty-looking man who had just got out of the Land Cruiser and was now smoking a cigarette.

Bear took the mobile phone from inside her bra and, flipping it open, redialled Luca's satellite phone number. It wasn't the scheduled time for the call, but given the fact that she hadn't got through on any of those occasions either, perhaps it was worth a try. There was a long pause as the networks searched for such a distant connection, then a monotone. The sound made her feel even more desperate. She tucked the phone back, telling herself she'd make just one more try at 18.00 GMT tonight. After that, she would ditch the phone altogether.

Bear then stared down at the yellow jerry can beside her. She knew that she should just balance it on her head and stride calmly over to one of the back streets and disappear, but each time she bent down to pick it up, she froze halfway. Her hands were trembling and she knew it was nothing to do with the effects of fading adrenalin. She was scared. And the more she looked at the Toyota, the more she felt that the men inside it knew exactly where she was. Like hunters, they were waiting for her to separate from the crowd.

Hunching her shoulders against a dribble of rain coming through a gap in the tarpaulin, she raised her arm, gently pressing her fingers against her side. The ache in her ribs was getting worse, while the thumping pain in her right ear had spread to her forehead and temples. She felt faint, clinging to the rickety shelter for support as she tried to figure out what the hell she was going to do next. She could wait for cover of darkness, but that was nearly five hours away and Bear doubted she would last another ten minutes without needing to sit down.

She shook her head, cursing her own stupidity. Her mind reeled at the speed with which her situation had changed. Because she had followed her intuition and simply reacted, she now found herself right in the middle of one of the most hostile townships in the whole of Southern Africa, while being pursued by a professional security detail. Why didn't she step back once in a while and rationalise her situation? She was pregnant, for Christ's sake, and yet she had done the same thing she always did – leapt in first and thought later.

While she was desperately trying to make sense of her situation, a face appeared through the smoke. A woman was staring at her. She was slender, bordering on malnourished, with thick black hair that had been woven with bird's feathers and crude, fake-gold earrings that gave her a gypsy-like air. As the woman raised her hand Bear saw that her fingers were covered in tattoos, with the ink lacing all the way back to her wrists. She was staring at Bear with a smile that was more knowing than pleasant. 'Malawian?' she asked. 'Zimbabwean?'

Bear didn't respond, watching closely as the woman stepped around the fire and came closer, seemingly unperturbed by Bear's recalcitrant body language. She was younger than Bear had first supposed, with a light brown complexion and unhurried eyes.

'Non,' the woman guessed, switching to French. 'You are from the Congo.'

'Oui,' Bear replied curtly.

Her eyes turned towards the Toyota, wondering if this newcomer could be in any way connected to her pursuers.

'Me too. I grew up in Kinshasa.'

Bear nodded vaguely at this open attempt to claim common ground. The woman took her time looking Bear up and down. The T-shirt she had stolen was a size too small, and the rain was making it cling to her back and sides. Its low neckline revealed too much of her cleavage, and as the woman's eyes traced along each part of her body Bear shifted uncomfortably, suddenly suspecting that there was something far more sinister to her attention than she had first supposed.

'Got family here in Nyanga?' the woman asked.

Bear shook her head, already moving over to the table to put extra space between them.

'You must be alone then?'

'No. My friends are just over there buying some food,' Bear answered automatically, directing her eyes to the shops on the edge of the square. 'They'll be out any second.'

The woman lazily followed her gaze.

'I don't think they're there at all,' she whispered, nostrils flaring as if savouring something sweet. 'You're alone. And you have a secret, don't you?'

'Go screw yourself,' Bear retorted, moving to push past her, but the woman grabbed hold of her wrist.

'You're rich,' she breathed. 'Only rich bitches have nails like that.'

She cast her eyes down to Bear's long fingers and the professional manicure with its brown nail polish.

'They'll like your face,' the woman continued, obviously pleased with her find. 'I'll get an extra two hundred just for that.'

Bear hesitated, having seen such women before in the markets of Kinshasa. They patrolled the local hangouts, searching for any young female who looked out of place or lost. They would cajole or threaten the women, or more often girls, into the shadows of the back streets, where the gangs would rape the victims over and over again. They'd do it until bored, before leaving them to rot in one of the shacks, or, if they were attractive, doping them up and selling them into one of the local whorehouses.

'This is what's going to happen,' the woman continued,

her voice suddenly taking on a rasping, vicious tone. 'You're going to get on board the taxi behind us. And you're going to do it quietly or I'll tell the twenty-eights exactly what you really are. They love to cut up rich bitches like you.'

Her eyes swivelled down to between Bear's legs as if that were the first place the knives would go. She then reached out, the tips of her fingers trailing down Bear's stomach towards her crotch.

'Don't you fucking touch me,' Bear growled.

'Shhhh,' the woman breathed, her eyes still lowered. 'Don't make it any harder on yourself.'

Out of the corner of her eye, Bear could see that a taxi had quietly drawn up on the other side of the *Tshisa* stand. The woman raised her eyes and was about to signal to the driver when Bear grabbed hold of her forearm and pulled her in so close that their bodies touched at the hip.

'Signal to them and these manicured nails won't be the only things sticking into you,' she hissed.

As she spoke, she grabbed the discarded skewer off the table beside her, bringing the metal point round so that it dug into the soft flesh of the woman's stomach.

'Even if the taxi guys jump me, I'll still have time to stick you with this,' she spat as her eyes bored into the woman's. 'That's the thing about puncturing the stomach lining. All the acid leaks out. Makes it real messy.'

The woman's smile faded, replaced by a dreadful uncertainty. She had been watching Bear for the last fifteen minutes and had seen only a lone, scared woman sheltering from the rain. All that had changed in an instant. Now the same woman seemed to have grown in size, with eyes that blazed with hostility and self-assurance.

Bear inched closer, realising that she could use this situation for her own ends. There was a better chance of passing undetected if they moved together.

'Now, you're going to signal your guys to pick me up on the other side of the square. Right near the back.'

The woman didn't respond for a second, eyes narrowing in confusion.

'But . . .'

'Do as I say.'

Bear twisted the skewer round to reinforce her point, causing the woman to double over in pain. Then, gripping her tight, Bear waited for her to signal to the taxi before they moved off together through the crowd. They walked side by side, like sisters clinging to each other for support, but the whole time Bear's skewer never once left the madam's side. She could see the taxi slowly shadowing them, the occupants hidden by mirrored film that had been crudely glued to the inside of the windows.

Bear tried to control her pace, resisting the temptation to hurry across the open ground. She clung to the woman, using her to steady herself as balance seemed to desert her once again and she listed to one side. The woman immediately sensed something was wrong and was about to try and flee when Bear dug the skewer a full inch into her flesh. As she cried out, Bear pulled her in closer.

'Don't even think about it,' she hissed.

Passing the last of the *Tshisa* stands, they saw the Land

Cruiser away to their left, no more than fifty feet at most, with the same man still standing outside, finishing up the last of his cigarette.

Bear watched him exhale a plume of smoke into the air before throwing the butt into a muddy puddle at his feet. Just a little further, she told herself, then they would be into the maze of shacks. If the gypsy woman gave Bear any trouble she would stick her right there and then, but after the last warning she was dragging her feet, the fight drained out of her. After that, all Bear needed was thirty seconds' head start on the gang.

The taxi wouldn't be able to follow her into the narrow streets, so they would have to chase her on foot. Bear planned to run straight ahead for a couple of hundred yards, then double back to the main road. There were crowds of people there and, more importantly, the Golden Arrow buses that connected Nyanga to the city centre.

She breathed in deeply, then again, steeling herself for what was about to happen. Her legs had felt leaden and tired, but now that she was on the move again a jolt of adrenalin had begun to limber her up, like oil on a machine. The pain at her temples seemed to subside as she focused only on the next two minutes. She would have to move fast if she were to have any chance of getting clear.

As they drew level with the first of the shacks, she turned to see two jeeps that had been crudely converted into tow trucks arrive in the square. Both had blackened glass and lowered suspension. Although Bear did not know it, they had driven at full speed across the potholed roads of

Khayelitsha to get there so quickly. Now they slowed, gliding smoothly round, one following the other as if part of a funeral procession, and circling wide so as to come up behind Johan's Land Cruiser.

As they approached, the American was still outside. He stood with his arms folded across his chest, moodily surveying the crowd, and was just about to get back inside the car when the first of the tow trucks drew level. Tapping on the glass of his own vehicle, he stared at Johan.

'You call these guys?' he asked.

Johan's eyes flicked to his side mirror. He had been concentrating so hard on the crowd, and wondering whether to voice his suspicions about the taller of the two women who had just passed by, that he had entirely missed what was happening behind them. Now the image of the trucks filled his side mirror.

'Get down!' he screamed, twisting the key in the ignition and ducking his head low.

'What the . . .' Darin raged, reaching for his Beretta, but before he had time to pull it from its holster, a hail of gunfire rang out across the crowded square.

Chapter 17

The news of Andy's death hit the others hard. For the longest time Katz said nothing, only curling deeper into his sleeping bag, while beside him Joel openly wept.

After delivering the news, Luca had slumped down on the floor of the deserted base, unable to muster the strength even to strip off his outer clothing. Every inch of him was plastered with wet snow and his hands were balled into fists by his sides as he tried to control the terrible shaking that racked his body.

'I should have seen him walk past me,' Joel said, before sniffing loudly. He was sitting up in his sleeping bag with his dripping wet hair clinging to the sides of his face. The zinc suntan cream he had smeared over his nose had now smudged across his entire face, giving him an almost ghoulish pallor, while the two strips of exposed flesh looked raw and painful.

'Andy was right next to me,' he continued mournfully. 'I should have stopped him from going.'

There was a pause before Katz's voice emerged from the folds of his sleeping bag.

'We were all just trying to survive out there. There's nothing more to say.'

He poked his head out of the sleeping bag. His lips were swollen and split, a trace of dried blood running down his chin. He settled his gaze on Luca and for several seconds just watched him shake.

Then, pulling himself on to his knees, Katz shuffled across the room. He reached forward, dusting the snow off Luca's chest, and then helped unzip his outer jacket. Guiding him closer to the flame of the MSR stove, Katz carefully took some of the water they had boiled and mixed it with a sachet of hot chocolate pulled from his rucksack. He handed it across, nursing the plastic cup beneath Luca's chin and letting the steam waft up over his frozen cheeks.

'We wouldn't have made it out there without you,' Katz said suddenly. 'None of us would.'

He then seemed uncomfortable with his own admission and nodded hesitantly before returning to his sleeping bag. Luca didn't respond. He lay with both hands clasped around the cup as he tried to take a few more sips. Dribbles of hot chocolate escaped his numb lips, running into his neckline, before he let the cup fall from his grasp as his eyes gently closed.

Luca woke to the sound of the stove spluttering and then going out. There was darkness, with only the howl of the wind and occasional clatter of the broken-down walls flexing in the worst of the gusts. As he pulled himself up his head pounded from dehydration. He groaned loudly, raising a hand to his forehead in pain. It took several seconds for him to steady himself enough to be able to reach over to his own rucksack and find a replacement fuel bottle for the stove.

Pulling an old metal lighter from the top pocket of his Gore-Tex trousers, Luca worked the flint over and over again with his thumb. It cast flash images across the room, revealing the bunched up body of Katz just next to him, snoring loudly. On the far side, he could see Joel's dim silhouette. He had fallen asleep while still sitting upright and now his hunched body seemed to consist entirely of angular joints and long, folded limbs.

As the stove's flame burnt orange and then settled back to a low, roaring blue, Luca stood up. He winced, thigh muscles threatening to cramp as he scooped up the plastic cup he had been using and drained the very last dregs of hot chocolate. The liquid was viscous and cold, with ice beginning to crystallise across its surface, but he knew the sugar would do him good.

Reaching into the top of his rucksack, Luca carefully unwrapped the satellite phone that Dedov had given him. He wiped away the moisture clinging to the small yellow screen and extended the antenna, watching as the signal strength oscillated between zero and a single bar. The number for GARI's main communication room had been neatly stencilled in white marker pen on the back. After five beeps the line connected.

'GARI science base,' came a voice laced with a thick Russian accent.

'Sergei, this is Luca Matthews. We are caught in the storm. Sheltering at old Soviet base. Lat: 71.37.58. Easting: 11.16.38. Impossible to move.'

Luca could hear the line fading in and out. He waited, hoping that Sergei would be able to piece together all that he had said.

'Copy. You at old Soviet base. Have co-ordinates. Everyone OK?'

'Negative. One man down.'

'Say again.'

Luca went to speak, but found the words stuck in his throat. His jaw clenched several times before he finally managed to shout, 'McBride is dead.' There was static before he repeated, 'Andy's dead,' several more times into the handset.

Luca heard the phone bleep once more, signalling that the satellite had dropped out. That was always the frustration of satellite phones – sometimes you had a flawless connection, while at others it felt like it would be quicker to tap out Morse code. Just as Luca was about to give up on the call, Sergei's voice flooded back on to the line.

'. . . cannot send assistance. Stay in location . . . copy?'

'How long will the storm last?' Luca shouted.

'Storm dying. Expect drop in wind speed in next four to six hours. We have notified . . .'

But then the line went dead once more. Luca stared at the dull glow of the screen. Despite the brevity of the contact, he felt a sudden sense of reassurance. The sound of another human voice seemed to dispel the claustrophobia of the freezing room; it was a relief that somewhere beyond the swirling maelstrom, someone else now knew where they were.

From behind him Luca could feel a draft circulating up through the crooked wooden planks of the floor. The stove could only do so much. Despite having it on full blast, it was still biting cold inside the little room. Perhaps there was somewhere more protected further inside the base?

The internal door was just to the left of Joel. After trying the handle several times, Luca stepped back to kick it open. His heavy climbing boots thudded against the old wood only a few inches from where Joel slept, but it was not enough to rouse him. Both he and Katz were too exhausted. Another kick and the dilapidated door splintered open, revealing a much larger room beyond.

Luca stepped cautiously inside, turning his eyes up to where a murky half-light filtered down from a single bank of skylights. The room was huge, far bigger than he would ever have supposed from the outside. Looking closer, he saw heavy steel girders interspersed at regular intervals to reinforce the main walls. Someone had taken great pains to seal this room away from the worst of the Antarctic weather.

Luca ventured further inside, passing hundreds of sections of metal piping, each about eight inches in diameter and all meticulously stacked. A pathway snaked in between, leading him towards the centre of the room. There were more piles, again perfectly assembled, but this time containing climbing equipment and an odd assortment of polar clothing.

'What the hell?' Luca whispered, brushing his hand over a row of dehydrated food packets at his feet. He picked one up at random, tilting the label to catch the light. It was written in a language he didn't recognise at first. The o's were struck through diagonally, and there were small circular marks above the a's. It looked Dutch maybe, or on closer reflection, one of the Scandinavian languages. Below the text was a picture of mashed potato, photographed in a perfect imitation of a fresh meal, just served.

Luca pulled out another. It was exactly the same. There were hundreds and hundreds of the same meal. It just didn't make any sense. Why on earth would the Russians have left all this equipment after abandoning the base?

Turning the glossy plastic over in his hands, he read the sell-by-date. It was last year. Luca frowned, recalling that Dedov had told him they had abandoned the base nearly ten years ago and that no one had returned to it since. Yet this food had been bought just before the last winter had set in, and, by the quantity of it, someone had been planning on staying a long time.

There was a low metallic snap, like the sound of a padlock unlocking, and Luca swivelled round. He waited for several seconds, peering through the gloom and wondering where the noise had come from. It had sounded close by. He continued waiting, just listening in the silence, before supposing that it must have come from one of the loose cables outside, flapping in the wind.

A gust whistled over the top of the skylights and Luca looked up, suddenly realising that the bank of windows would mean a better satellite reception. Twisting round the antenna on the phone, he was about to ring GARI once more when he stopped. What was the point? Sergei knew where they were and there was nothing more to do but wait until the storm had passed.

Standing alone in the half-light, an image came to him. It was of Andy and that final flicker of recognition when presented with the image of his wife and child. In that single moment he had connected to something outside the storm, to something he loved. Now, Luca felt an overriding urge to do the same. He exhaled heavily, leaning back against a nearby shelf for support.

His thoughts turned to Bear. God, how he missed her. It was like a physical ache, a loss that seemed to resurface in every quiet moment of his life. Looking back over the last few months, he just couldn't understand how he had spent so much time running from her, arguing with her, doing everything except being with her. What had he been thinking? His own deliverance from the storm suddenly made every argument they had ever had seem trivial and petty. They had cut so deep at the time but now they paled into insignificance, leaving him to question how things had got so bent out of shape in the first place.

For the first time in his life, he suddenly realised that Bear was the *only* person he wanted to see. That she was all that mattered.

Dialling her number, he waited impatiently for the line to connect, his mind brimming with a confused mix of apologies and assurances of love.

'*Allo? C'est qui?*' came Bear's voice. Her tone was quiet and suspicious.

'Bear! It's Luca! Damn, it's good to hear your voice!'

'*Mon Dieu!*' she whispered. 'I was about to give up on you. Are you all right? Where are you?'

A huge grin spread across Luca's face. He felt heady with the relief of just being able to speak to her. He pictured her smouldering brown eyes and the curve of her lips as she spoke. The image was such a welcome relief after everything he had been through in Antarctica. 'I'm OK. We're holed up in this broken-down base waiting out a storm. But, Bear, listen . . .'

'Are you safe?' she interrupted.

'Yes. I am safe,' Luca confirmed, the words suddenly consigning to the past everything that he had been through in the last few days. He was safe and that was all there was to it. The future was now something to be considered, and Luca felt an overwhelming need to tell her how he really felt. He wanted to peel it all back. To start again. 'Can we talk? About us, I mean . . .'

'Wait, *mon chéri*,' Bear urged. 'Please, wait. I have so much I need to tell you, but I want to do it face to face. You need to get back here as soon as you can.'

'Believe me, Bear, that's all I want to do. But why not tell me now? Over the phone.'

There was a moment's pause as she deliberated. When her voice eventually came back on the line, it was filled with a sense of urgency that Luca had rarely heard in it before. 'Before that, I need to tell you what's happening. I spoke to

233

Kieran Bates and things are *not* what they seem.' She paused again, wondering how to articulate all that she had learnt. 'It's to do with the lake, Luca, and a man named Richard Pearl.'

'Pearl?' Luca repeated. 'I've heard his name from one of the scientists. What's he got to do with anything?'

'Richard Pearl is some kind of deluded vigilante. He's developed this compound, this "seed", which he's planning on dumping in the oceans. But it's the lake, Luca. He's using the lake to test it on first.'

'Slow down, Bear. I don't understand. If Pearl had been at GARI when I arrived then one of the scientists would have told me. And anyway, no one has mentioned anything about any seed.'

'No, it's nothing to do with the scientists. They all think that Pearl invested in the project to get the water samples, but he doesn't give a damn about any of that. The lake's encased in ice, so he wants to drop the seed down the drill pipe and use it as a testing ground before releasing it . . .'

Her voice trailed off.

'Bear? Are you there?'

There was silence.

'Come on, talk to me, Bear!' Luca replied, his voice rising in concern. 'Are you OK?'

'I'm all right,' she whispered, her voice so low that he could only just hear her.

'Are you hurt? Please, Bear, I can tell something is wrong.'

'Luca, I'm OK. I just have to talk quietly. I'll explain everything later. I promise, *chéri*.'

The word '*chéri*' seemed to cut right through him. Old emotions that had been buried deep suddenly resurfaced. Luca felt his shoulders sag, realising that it had been so long a time since either of them had spoken to each other with any degree of tenderness. Without even realising it he found himself pressing the handset hard against his ear, feeling every one of the thousands of kilometres that stretched between them. 'Are you still at your office in Paris?' he asked. 'You're safe, right?'

Bear ignored the question. 'Richard Pearl is trying to get to Antarctica and he'll be bringing the seed with him. It could be carried in something as small as a suitcase or rucksack.'

'How do you know all this?'

'Let's just say that I kind of ran into the man this morning.'

Luca raised his hand to his forehead, eyes passing blankly over the contents of the room as he tried to gasp what Bear was saying.

'Well, Pearl isn't getting back into the lake any time soon. We've just returned from the drill site and we couldn't get the pipes out in time before the storm hit. The borehole will be frozen solid by now, so no one's getting into the lake without re-drilling.'

'So you're telling me there is no way he can get back into it?'

'Not that . . .' Luca began then paused. The base, the equipment, the food – somebody had taken great pains to be concealed from the rest of Antarctica and they had

235

positioned themselves in a location that gave ideal access to the lake.

'Hold on,' he whispered, picking his way across the room. On the way in, he hadn't paid any attention to the piping he had passed, but already he felt sure it was the same kind as the ones he'd seen at the drill site, only bigger. 'I mentioned we were at this broken-down base. Well, the Russians told me it was deserted, but from all the equipment I'm seeing, it's anything but.'

He dragged his fingers across the first line of stacked piping. It was drill casing for sure.

'And someone's definitely been drilling another hole,' he said.

'Shit,' Bear hissed, remembering Lotta's warning. 'You need to get the hell out of that base, and I mean now. There's a man that Pearl sent . . .'

Luca pulled the handset from his ear mid-sentence, cutting the sound of her voice. He was suddenly aware of his own heart beating faster in his chest. The muscles of his shoulders were locked tight, tensed in reflex, as a single realisation filtered through to his conscious mind.

Someone was standing just behind him.

He turned, mouth opening to speak, to see a man only a foot away. He must have moved with absolute stealth to have got so close and now, his broad shoulders seemed to block out what remained of the natural light. Luca's eyes ran up the side of his bulging neck and into his white-blond hair, but the face itself was lost to the shadows.

'Who . . .' Luca began, but then the man stepped even

closer and into the light. The skin of his face was charred black, burnt by horrific exposure to the sun, while a long, weeping sore extended from below his chin to past his right cheekbone. Despite all this, Luca still found his gaze drawn upward to the man's grey, lifeless eyes. They were bleached of colour, devoid of any natural sense of animation or empathy. They were just blank. Without a word, the man raised his hands and smashed the butt of a hunting rifle into the side of Luca's head, sending him spinning across the floor.

Blackness fanned out across Luca's vision. On the floor beside him he could see the satellite phone that had fallen from his grasp. It was close, only a few inches away. He was dimly aware of Bear's voice continuing as she tried to tell him something, then the blackness merged, becoming one, until finally unconsciousness took him.

Chapter 18

Kieran Bates left his office on Whitehall, turning right along the busy street before cutting back through a small alley into St James's Park. His pace was brisk. Swinging his tan leather briefcase purposefully in his left hand and pulling up the collar of his suit jacket against the cold morning air, he approached the edge of the manicured parkland and stopped.

The temperature had been dipping below zero for the last week, causing ice to collect on the outer rim of the lake. Swans kept their dizzying vigil, turning in unending circles across the deeper waters in an effort to keep the lake from freezing altogether. They swam with necks arched, feathers plumped against the cold.

The park was empty, a weak morning haze hanging in the air. It faded the natural colours of the trees and grass, giving the whole scene a rare sense of calm. Normally Bates would have relished such a morning, but the black S600 Mercedes parked at the edge of Horse Guards Parade had dispelled any chance of that. Despite the dark tint of its windows, he knew exactly who was seated within. Eleanor Page was waiting for him.

Bates came to a halt by the exit to the alley. Undetected by the car's occupants, he studied the vehicle for a moment, watching as the monoxide cloud from the exhaust slowly sank to the tarmac. Despite her playful manner, Bates was starting to suspect that Eleanor Page was every bit as noxious as the car fumes. In the last few days, he had begun to feel a needle of doubt, which was becoming stronger and stronger with each new piece of information he acquired. Something wasn't right about the whole operation. The more he thought about it, the more convinced he became that he was being set up.

On a practical level, he was the *only* operative in MI6 to be involved. That alone was cause for concern. He reported directly to Parker, and only him, while everything else was handled by the Americans. Bates understood the need for secrecy well enough, but this smacked of something else. By being removed from any team or department he was effectively being isolated, which would make him the obvious scapegoat should anything go wrong.

As he stood watching the car, Bates' hand moved to the breast pocket of his suit jacket, feeling for his passport. He had been specifically requested to bring it, but without any further information as to where they were going. God, he hated the Yanks and their overblown sense of 'need to know' bullshit.

He could feel the situation slipping from his grasp. Every day there seemed to be some new snippet of information that only served to obscure the big picture rather than reveal it. The last time he had met Eleanor, he had posed a simple question – why now? Why were the Americans doing everything in their power to dismantle the Antarctic Treaty after nearly sixty years of inertia? It didn't make any sense. What had shifted that could be so fundamental as to precipitate one of the greatest land grabs the world had ever seen?

Nine days had passed since he had been to see Luca on the oil rig, and since then his old school friend had evidently done as asked and inserted the spyware into GARI's main satellite system. Bates had been able to access all the email traffic coming in and out of the base and his primary objective had been fulfilled. Everything was going according to plan. Then Beatrice Makuru turned up on the scene.

He had known of her reputation for tenacity, but would never have suspected that she would have been able to connect the dots so readily, nor actually get to Richard Pearl. And the wake of destruction that followed read like something from a war zone; a fifty-million-dollar jet destroyed, a South African SSA operative hospitalised with a splintered jaw, and a private security detail gunned down in Nyanga township. Bates had barely believed the reports when they had come filtering back. One thing was for certain – he had grossly underestimated Bear, which was not an error he was about to repeat. It was also something that wouldn't have escaped the notice of Eleanor Page.

Exhaling deeply, Bates smoothed back his hair and cut across the gravel expanse of the parade ground towards the waiting car. As he settled into one of the sumptuous leather seats, Eleanor smiled amiably, pulling her glasses up on to the crown of her head.

'Glad you could come,' she said, shifting forward in her seat to signal to the driver. The car immediately sped off, turning left on to Pall Mall and powering along the wide, red tarmacked road towards the towering edifice of Buckingham Palace. Despite the obvious hurry they were in, Eleanor took her time in addressing Bates.

'It seems that your contact's ex-girlfriend has been busy. And I thought we'd agreed you were going to handle that situation.'

Bates was about to respond when he realised that Eleanor was speaking rhetorically. He watched as she tucked a long strand of hair behind her ear, then smiled as if about to introduce him to an acquaintance at a dinner party.

'In the end, this Makuru woman only managed to delay Pearl by twenty-two hours. He had to scramble another of his planes from San Diego just to get to Antarctica in time. Not that his people would have realised it, but we had to pull quite a few strings to expedite the whole process.'

Sliding the glasses from the top of her head, Eleanor inspected one of the tortoiseshell arms thoughtfully.

'But Pearl is now in Antarctica and, for the time being, safely ensconced at GARI.'

'So he's finally in play,' Bates offered.

'He is,' Eleanor conceded, 'but it was a close-run thing. We believe that Makuru was just trying to prevent him from reaching Antarctica. That's it. But Pearl himself didn't see it that way. When they pulled him from the wreckage of the plane, he was convinced it had been some kind of assassination attempt and was this close to backing off from the whole project.'

A single tut escaped her lips.

'And he used to be a naval officer,' Eleanor continued. 'You'd have thought he'd have shown a little more backbone. Fortunately, a mutual friend persuaded him to get back on board the new plane. So, after all that, he now has the seed and is within striking distance.'

'And what about getting to the drill site?'

'Pearl has his personal helicopter pilot with him, an Italian woman by the name of Helena Coroni. There is an R-44 helicopter stored in the hangar units of GARI, so if the weather continues to improve they should be at the second drill site in the next three to four hours.'

There was a pause before Bates shifted expectantly in his seat.

'So what do you want from me?'

'What I have always wanted,' Eleanor replied, tilting her head sideways to catch his eye. 'For you to do your job and contain this Makuru woman. We've triangulated her cell phone and it would seem she is still using it inside the township.'

'My understanding was that you were waiting for the right assets to be in place,' he replied, but something in the way Eleanor had spoken the last sentence made him feel that this information was directly for his benefit.

'I think we need someone to take charge *personally*, don't you?' Eleanor suggested. 'Someone to manage the whole situation and ensure we don't suffer any repeat of the security detail disaster. It's a dangerous place, Nyanga. Or so I hear.'

'But if Pearl is already in Antarctica, why are we continuing to pursue Makuru? Surely she missed and that's all there is to it.'

'Not quite. We picked up the microbiologist, Bukovsky, late last night and it seems she gave Makuru a flashcard that links Pearl to the seed.'

As she said the last words Eleanor's smile dimmed, almost imperceptibly. The thought of the ripple effect if the seed were in any way traced back to an American national had made her throat go dry. Turning to the car window to mask her expression, she stared out as the Mercedes powered along Bayswater Road before turning right at the Shepherds Bush roundabout and out towards the A40. Ahead of them the piercing blue lights of a police motorcade reflected off the car bonnet as they cleared the traffic.

Bates followed her gaze, already guessing their destination.

'Northolt?' he asked.

'A plane is waiting for you. You'll be in Cape Town in under eleven hours.'

'At the risk of sounding ungracious, wouldn't your embassy be better placed to do this?' he asked. 'They're already on the ground in South Africa and, from what I hear, I've got the wrong complexion to be going door to door in Nyanga.'

'After all the places you've been assigned, I would have thought this would be child's play for you,' Eleanor replied, while sliding a file across the empty seat between them. 'You are being redirected to a contact in the South African mobile infantry and all orders will come directly from you. As far as they're concerned, it's purely a British operation. It keeps us out of it. And besides, our embassy has its work cut out ensuring that the clean-up boats are ready in time. Four are already in dry dock in Cape Town's harbour, while another seven are in transit over the Atlantic. They'll all converge on Cape Town in the next two days to take on fuel and supplies before heading south to Antarctica.'

'And how long after Pearl launches the seed do you expect to see any results?'

'We're not sure, but soon. We already have an independent boat in place that should be able to spot the environmental damage almost immediately.'

'That's something I wanted to clear up with you. How bad do you anticipate it will be? What are we talking about here?'

'Modest damage to the coastline. Nothing too extravagant,' Eleanor said, with a slight shrug. 'But it will be enough to trigger an emergency session of the permanent members of the Antarctic Treaty. From that point on, our boats will have the green light to go in and clean it up.'

Bates nodded. 'And have you considered that, after all this, Pearl's seed might actually work?'

Eleanor didn't reply for a moment, only watching as the driver slowed the car before pulling into the private jet airfield of Northolt. A Falcon 900EX jet stood on the tarmac just beyond the fence line, its engines already turning over.

'In its original form, the seed had a chance,' she conceded. 'But something that unknown has the potential to change everything. Imagine it – carbon reduction on a global scale? It could disrupt the entire US energy strategy, and the bottom line is we're not prepared to take that risk.'

'You mean, you've tampered with the seed?'

Eleanor gave him a chiding look. 'Why don't you concentrate on finding me that woman instead?'

'And what happens when I find her?' asked Bates, stepping out of the car.

'Full rendition protocol. And do make sure you get the flashcard. Find that and the wheels keep spinning.'

She nodded to the driver and the car pulled off, leaving Bates staring at the bruised winter sky. As the sound of the plane's jet engines gradually rose in pitch, he stood motionless. Perhaps being sent to Cape Town was a blessing after all. With her acquisition of the flashcard Bear had become central to the whole operation. If he were able to take charge of the manhunt personally, then at least he could try and shield her from the worst of the Americans.

He had not meant this to be anything more than a minor betrayal of his old friend. Luca would never have discovered the real reason why he had been sent to Antarctica. Instead, he would have taken the money and gone back to his normal life. But Bear had changed all that, and the situation was fast turning ugly. If she were pulled into the American rendition programme, there would be no going back.

When he had first started all this, Kieran Bates had not intended for anyone to get hurt. But now there was a very real prospect of that happening, unless he could find Bear and somehow broker a deal with the Americans.

Turning towards the open door of the plane, he climbed on board. Eight minutes later they were airborne and heading south for Cape Town.

Chapter 19

Luca woke. His eyelids flickered, then again, before finally pulling open to reveal a murky light filtering down from the skylights. He lay on the rough wooden floor of the deserted base, a half-empty rucksack under his head to serve as a makeshift pillow. He tried to move, but a stabbing pain lanced through his temples.

Raising his right hand, Luca brushed his fingertips across the side of his face. The butt of the rifle had smashed hard into his cheek and temple, creating a nasty swelling and turning the skin a deep purple, laced with yellow. The bruising felt puffy and unfamiliar, as if he were somehow touching another person's face.

For a moment Luca let his eyes drift. He was dimly aware that he had been searching for something, though the whole notion felt abstract and unimportant.

'Bear,' he called out, but his voice was nothing more than a dry croak.

There was a banging noise a little way off, the thump,

thump of metal striking against wood. The reverberations seemed to penetrate right through his skull and Luca winced as the noise continued, over and over again. Each thump echoed just long enough to be replaced by the next, magnifying the pain in his head.

'Bear!' he cried out.

The banging stopped.

'He's awake! Katz, quickly.'

A moment later Joel's face swam into view. He was close, his long, hawk-like nose only inches from Luca's.

'Shit, mate, you were out a long time,' he breathed, then the concern gave way to a broad smile. He'd started to help Luca into a sitting position when Katz's voice rang out.

'Move him slowly,' he warned. 'Otherwise he'll pass out again.'

A moment later, Luca was slumped against the pile of drill pipes with Katz and Joel crouched in front of him.

'So? What happened to you?' Katz demanded.

'Water,' Luca gasped. Joel moved his hands across to a saucepan sitting on the floor nearby. He moved with almost exaggerated care, fingers feeling across the rough flooring. After watching him for a moment, Katz cut in.

'For Christ's sake,' he muttered. 'I'll do it.'

Taking the saucepan from his grasp, Katz raised the cold metal rim to Luca's chapped lips. He poured in a tiny trickle of water, careful not to let any spill.

'More.'

Katz hesitated, but Joel urged him on. Reluctantly, he raised the saucepan once again, draining the last of it.

'You've been out for nearly four hours,' Joel said. 'We woke up and found you like this. How are you feeling? You must have one hell of a headache.'

Luca didn't get a chance to respond. Katz had other priorities.

'First things first,' he said. 'You tell us what's going on. And I mean now.'

'There was a man . . .' Luca managed '. . . standing right here. He was just standing . . . then everything went black.'

He glanced away, remembering that monstrous silhouette with its broad neck and hair cropped so short as to be little more than stubble. But it was the eyes that came back to him now; the grey, spent eyes. The man had moved as silently as a ghost, managing to get within a couple of inches of Luca without so much as a sound.

He exhaled deeply, trying to blot out the image. It didn't feel real and if it weren't for the swelling on his face, he might have doubted it had even happened. But then he remembered what he had been searching for – the satellite phone. He had been on the sat phone to Bear.

He tried to recall the details of their conversation but all he could remember was the desperation in her voice. Then it became clear to him. She had been in danger, and for some reason had decided to hide that fact from him.

'The sat phone,' he whispered. 'Give it to me.'

'It's gone,' Joel replied flatly.

'There's another that Dedov gave me. In the top of my rucksack.'

'Gone too. We've checked through everything. Whoever

your man was, he took the lot; sat phones, the cooking stove, everything.'

'The son of a bitch!' Katz roared, slamming his fist down on the stack of piping.

'Must have done it while we slept,' Joel added, shaking his head slowly. In the silence that followed, he raised his right hand, rubbing the skin under his eyes where his glasses would have been. He had woken earlier to find them smashed on the floor beside him. Now, anything further away than a couple of metres was a blur. He blinked, a flicker of doubt passing across his face.

'Look, I need to speak to . . .' Luca began, trying to pull himself a little higher, but Katz pressed him backwards.

'Didn't you hear what he said? The sat phones are gone. And if you're going to do any talking, then you talk to us. I want to know what the hell is going on around here.'

Katz drew closer, his pale blue eyes sharp and venomous.

'We're trapped,' he said. 'You realise that, don't you? We woke up to find the main entrance has been deliberately sealed off from the outside. Do you hear me? Someone has *deliberately* trapped us in here!'

Luca stared at him blankly, trying to keep up.

'And whoever it was, he's made damn sure we aren't getting out. Everything's been stripped from this place – no tools, no ropes.' Katz paused, his eyes turning down to the empty saucepan at Luca's feet. 'And we've only got half a litre of water left in my bottle. That's it. Without the stoves, we can't melt any more snow. So, you tell me, Luca, what the fuck is going on?'

Joel turned towards Katz. 'Come on, mate, give him a minute. He's only just woken up.'

'A minute? What the hell do you mean, a minute? Without water, we'll be dead in two days!'

As he spoke, he looked down at the hundreds of packets of dehydrated food stacked just beside them.

'Shit!' he screamed, kicking the one nearest to him. 'Even the food hasn't got any damn water in it.'

They all watched the packet skid across the floor, before coming to rest against a sidewall. Directly above was a pathetic collection of dents and scratches running in a vague semi-circle. They were the sum total of three hours' hard work during which he and Joel had been trying to break through the wall using the aluminium drill casings. Despite the base's derelict exterior, someone had taken great pains to reinforce the interior and all they had to show for their efforts were superficial marks. If breaking through the sidewall was going to be their means of escape, it would take a lot longer than two days.

'Listen,' Luca said, raising a hand to try and calm him. 'This base is old and broken-down. There must be a way out.'

'There isn't,' Joel replied flatly, eyes tilting up towards Katz for affirmation. 'We've been through every part of this module and there's only one way in and out. The rest was sealed off long ago. And the really creepy bit is that whoever did it was living alone here.'

A couple of hours earlier they had come across a bizarre enclave tucked away from the main part of the room, where a single bed had been bolted to the wall. Around it were hundreds of little images drawn with the point of a compass. They were of simple things, like rain and trees, flames and an open hearth, but they told of an absolute removal from normal life. There was something haunting about them, each image wracked by the desperate desire to remember, a human being trying to crystallise and hold on to memories of a life outside Antarctica.

Enshrined by them all was a single photograph. It was fixed dead centre and showed a man with slicked back red hair, now greying from age, and a square, wholesome jaw. The rest was difficult to discern because someone had repeatedly jabbed the point of a compass or knife into the man's eyes, perforating the photographic paper until only two gaping holes remained. They stared out blindly from the image, imparting a lingering sense of disquiet, as if he were still somehow observing their every move. Joel looked up. 'I mean, who the hell are we dealing with here, Luca? Who would want to trap us inside this place?'

'I don't know,' he replied. 'The guy came out of nowhere and didn't utter a word.'

As he desperately tried to make sense of the situation, Luca's gaze turned towards the skylights. He pictured Bates sitting in an armchair on the oil rig, then Dedov with his vodka-laced smile and underlying hint of menace. Finally, an image of Bear came to him and his eyes narrowed in concentration as he tried to piece together the fragments of their last conversation. Raising a hand to his temples, he pressed down on them in an effort to shut out the constant pounding. The pain was unbearable.

'He said . . .' Katz began.

'Shut up,' Luca breathed. 'Just shut up.' He closed his eyes momentarily, mustering his strength. 'I don't know much. But while you were sleeping I spoke to GARI, telling them we were holed up in here during the storm. Then I got through to a contact of mine on the outside.'

Over the next ten minutes, he recounted as much of his conversation with Bear as he could remember. Every few seconds Katz would punctuate his narrative, firing questions at Luca about the technical composition of the seed or how Pearl was even planning on getting to Antarctica so late in the season. But Luca was steadfast, telling them what he knew and simply shrugging when he didn't. He had soon realised that there were huge gaps in what he had been told or could figure out for himself, and made no effort to disguise the fact. Katz, however, remained convinced that Luca was holding something back. With each new question, his tone became more and more accusatory.

'This is such bullshit!' he shouted, stabbing his finger towards Luca. 'I've met Pearl and he's invested millions in the lake. He's not going to wipe all that out by using it as a goddamn Petri dish.'

'Hold on, Katz,' Joel interjected, raising his hands in an effort to placate him. 'Let's just stick with what we know. Someone's been out here for a very long time, and from all the casings we've seen, they've obviously been drilling. Whichever way you slice it, those two facts alone mean that there's got to be some truth in what Luca said.'

There was a moment's pause before Joel added, 'And

whatever they're up to, it's obviously secret. Secret enough for them to want to stop us leaving here and telling anyone about it?'

Katz shook his head, his mind plagued by doubts. 'But why didn't they just open up our drill site and throw the seed down there? Why go to all the effort of constructing a totally new borehole?'

Joel turned towards the drill casings. 'Maybe it's got something to do with the fact that those are eight-inch casings. We used five. They must need a larger-diameter borehole for some reason.'

Just as the room went quiet, there was a low electronic beep and it took Luca several seconds to realise that it was coming from his own watch. Staring down at the luminous dial, he shook his head slowly. It was set to trigger one hour before they were due to meet Dedov's tractors at the rendez-vous point. The simple fact was that time was running out for them. With each hour that passed, they were getting closer and closer to the departure of the last flight of the season.

'Look, we need to concentrate,' he told the others. 'The lake, Pearl – all that is secondary. Right now, we need to figure out how the hell we are going to get out of this place and back to GARI. The last flight arrives in fourteen hours' time. And they aren't going to keep it waiting on the runway just for us.'

'But they *have* to wait,' Joel said, his eyes switching between the other two men. 'It's the last one. They'll wait while Dedov puts together a Search and Rescue team. You said yourself, they know we're here at the base.'

Luca slowly shook his head. 'E.A.P.,' he said.

'What the hell's that?' Joel asked desperately.

'Emergency Antarctic Protocol,' Katz explained, dragging the words out as if they were somehow unholy. 'The plane will wait a *maximum* of twelve hours, if the pilots think it's safe. They can't risk the entire plane being trapped for the winter with everyone on board. As soon as the light starts to fade, everything changes.'

'But they can't just fucking leave,' Joel protested. 'We'd be trapped.'

'Any more than we are already?' Katz taunted.

'I'm serious, Katz!' Joel countered. 'So why doesn't the plane fly back again? Just drop off everyone else and then come back and get us a few days later?'

'Think about it!' snapped Katz. 'All the bulldozers and snow ploughs get garaged for winter, so who's going to clear the snow from the runway? With these storms, it'd be metres deep within a couple of days.'

Joel shook his head, standing up and looking towards the door to the base. 'We've got to get another message out. Tell them they *have* to wait for us. For Christ's sake, all we need is a few more hours.'

Luca raised a hand to silence him. 'A few more hours? Even *if* – and it's a big if, by the way – Dedov has already put together a Search and Rescue team, they are going to have to find a way over the mountains. Then they'll have to break through the door of this base and after that they'll have to get us back to the runway. All that within twenty-six hours.'

There was a long pause. 'Sorry, Joel,' Luca continued,

'but it ain't going to happen. Best case, Dedov leaves behind a wintering team which actually tries to come and get us. If we did all make it back to GARI, we'd still have to wait until the following summer to go back home.'

'But that's not going to happen either,' Katz added, his top lip pulling into a foul sneer. 'Because we're going to run out of water long before a rescue team can get to us!'

Reaching down, he picked up the empty saucepan and flung it across the room with all his might. It struck one of the base's internal supports before clattering to the ground. There was silence.

A full minute passed before Joel slowly slid down to sit beside Luca, a look of utter bewilderment on his face. Katz stood with hands on hips, while his jaw clenched in seething fury. His gaze switched between them as if he were unable to decide where the blame belonged.

Luca let out a long sigh and let his head fall back against the stack of drill casings. The pounding at his temples had receded a little, but already he felt thirsty. His lips were chapped and dry, the skin cracked by the sheer absence of moisture in the Antarctic air.

He let his eyes drift across the room, blankly passing from one object to the next, as the sheer futility of their situation began to sink in. Whichever way he looked at it, they were out of time. Their only chance was to try to break out of the base and make it back over the mountain, but with only half a litre of water between them, they'd die of thirst in less than a day. Just a couple more litres and maybe they'd stand a chance.

His eyes continued to drift before finally settling on the handle of a Pelican case standing upright no more than ten feet away. It looked battered from exposure to the elements; smatterings of ice still clung to the black plastic ridges. Katz had brought it into the main room upon waking and discovering that everything else was gone. The lake samples had been the first thing he had looked for in all the confusion.

'Looks like we've got another couple of litres after all,' Luca said, nodding towards the case.

Both Joel and Katz followed his gaze, taking several seconds to grasp what he was referring to.

'Not a fucking chance!' Katz blurted, staggering forward to guard the case. 'It's taken three years of work to get these and you're not going anywhere near them.'

Luca stood up, wincing from the effort.

'I'm serious,' Katz growled. 'No one is going to start drinking the fucking lake samples!'

'Let's see how you feel about that twenty-four hours from now,' Luca replied, gingerly rubbing the side of his head. 'Just hope you can drink the stuff after twenty million years.'

As he spoke, they each became aware of a low vibration. It was distant, a soft mechanical thud that steadily grew louder. Several seconds passed before they realised it was the sound of a helicopter coming directly towards them. The noise grew and grew, becoming impossibly loud, until the dark underbelly of the machine suddenly passed directly over the skylights.

'It's a rescue mission!' Joel shouted, hopping up and down as he tried to see further out.

'But we were told Pearl's helicopter was completely unserviceable,' Katz replied. 'All the ski planes had already flown back and so the chopper was the first thing we looked at to get us here. We were told it was completely knackered.'

'Who cares?' Joel replied, his mood already lifting. 'Somebody got the damn thing working and now they're here for us.'

'That's Pearl's helicopter, right?' Luca asked.

Katz nodded. 'Yeah. It came in by container ship and he flew it once or twice at the beginning of summer, visiting some of the other science bases. Then it broke somehow and it's been sitting in the hangar at GARI ever since.'

Luca nodded, processing the information. Eventually he shook his head.

'What is it?' Katz asked, watching his every move.

'If that's Pearl's helicopter and he needs to launch the seed,' Luca said, following the direction of Joel's gaze, 'then I don't think it's here for any rescue.'

He turned towards Joel, who was still staring up at the skylights expectantly.

'Don't get too excited,' Luca warned. 'We're not out of this yet.'

Chapter 20

In the station chief's office at GARI, Vladimir Dedov pulled a small black-and-white photograph off the wall, revealing a neat square of unblemished paint underneath. He held the print up to the light, tilting the grainy image to one side, and smiled. Despite his reputation as a poet, he was not a man prone to nostalgia, but, in the last few days, he had arrived at the inescapable conclusion that all he had left of any real worth were his memories.

The image had been taken almost forty years ago and showed seven men dressed in Soviet-style polar clothing and posing in front of an old Antonov-2 bi-plane. It had been 1974 and the beginning of his first winter in Antarctica. As he stared from person to person, his eyes settled on his own slender face from all those years ago. His beard had been shorter back then, and untouched by grey, while his eyes were a deep, brooding brown. They stared unflinchingly into the camera, filled with the self-assurance only the young possess.

Dedov shook his head, almost unable to believe how

confident and energetic he had looked back then. His pose spoke of a man with his whole life ahead of him, a man destined for great things.

Turning the photograph over in his hands, he saw his late wife's handwriting scrawled across the back. His eyes narrowed as he tried to decipher the deep slanting letters and flamboyant loops. He heard himself tut affectionately, remembering how they had always joked that her handwriting was so bad it could have been used for military codes.

Together always. Stay warm, my poet.

Dedov sniffed as a flood of emotion caught him by surprise. His eyes misted up. Normally he would have been quick to fight any such sentimentality, but he was too old and too ill to pretend any longer. Instead he squeezed his eyes shut, forcing out a single tear which rolled down his cheek and quickly became lost in the thick hair of his beard. Katerina. His late wife had been so beautiful back then and they had laughed, even when times were so tough that they barely had enough food on the table.

'My dear Katya,' Dedov whispered. After so many years, his pet name for her felt so familiar on his lips. She had been killed outright in a car accident on the Nevsky Prospekt in Saint Petersburg. It had been a Tuesday, a totally unremarkable Tuesday.

'Perhaps I will be seeing you sooner than I thought.'

Placing the photograph in the shoebox in front of him, Dedov reached for a cigarette. He lit it with his father's gas lighter, snapping the lid shut with the same click he had heard every day as a child.

The seizures were happening regularly now. The last had left him feeling utterly drained, with barely the strength to lift himself off the ground. He had woken on the floor of his office with the back of his head damp with blood. Somehow, he had hit the corner of the desk on his way down. Although the cut wasn't deep, with head wounds there was always so much blood.

Dabbing at the mat of dried hair, Dedov glanced at the wall clock directly above him. After all this time, it seemed bizarre to be suddenly rushing.

Outside his room, he could hear the clamour as the rest of the base readied themselves to leave. They had been working throughout the night, garaging the heavy machinery and battening down the external window hatches. Everything had to be sealed before the light faded and winter was upon them. The last plane of the season would be touching down in only a few hours' time.

There was the sound of heavy, clomping boots as one of his men sprinted down the narrow corridor just outside his room. Dedov listened, waiting for the sound to fade gradually. As much as he tried to be part of the whole process, he felt detached from it all, choosing instead to spend the last three hours alone in his room.

Leaning back in his armchair, he watched the smoke drift up to the ceiling before settling into a faint haze. One thing was for certain – it wouldn't be the cigarettes that got him, nor the drink as Katya had always warned. It was the seizures that would hasten his end.

Before coming to Antarctica he had spent nearly six

months feeling unwell before finally taking himself off to a hospital. A CAT scan had revealed that he had three metastases growing on the frontal lobe of his brain. The small carcinogenic tumours would most likely grow and multiply, said the doctor, but as for how fast and the exact timing of events, he couldn't say.

After some deliberation, Dedov had arrived at the conclusion that these kinds of things usually took months, if not years, to fully develop and as such, he could see out the Antarctic summer before returning home and actually doing something about it.

But in the last two weeks all that had changed.

He could feel the tumours growing. And fast. As millimetre followed millimetre they put inexorable pressure on his brain, squeezing it against the hard bone of his skull. Side effects followed. First to go was his sense of taste, then his sense of smell. As the tumours pressed ever harder on the outer cortex of his brain, he knew that the next side effect would be even worse. His personality would disappear.

The certainty of this was worse than anything he could imagine. What else was a person apart from their *personality*?

He knew that he should return home to Saint Petersburg and immediately go under the knife, spend his life's savings to line up one of the best brain surgeons in the whole of Russia to perform the operation. In one fell swoop, he would rid himself of the cancer and continue life as before. But as he sat in his office, watching the smoke curl against the ceiling, all that seemed like a distant promise. Circumstances were fast spiralling out of control and he needed to make a choice.

Swivelling round in his chair, he broke the seal on a small 75cl bottle of Stolichnaya. With the stubby forefinger of his left hand, he dragged a nearby shot glass across the desk and dribbled in a measure of the vodka. But as he raised it to his lips, he suddenly stopped.

What was the point? He couldn't even taste the stuff anyway. He was drinking out of force of habit rather than any real enjoyment. All he could feel was a slight burn as the liquid passed down his throat. For the same effect, he might as well sip hot water. With a swipe of his hand, he sent the shot glass spinning off the desk and watched as it rolled in an arc across the floor, before coming to a halt somewhere beneath the nearby filing cabinet.

'What have I done?' Dedov whispered, clamping his eyes shut.

He was not accustomed to feelings of guilt or self-loathing, but now the two emotions seemed to spread through him almost as fast as the cancer. He had been going over and over the same sequence of events in his mind and, whichever way he looked at it, Pearl had outplayed him at every turn.

The American had arrived on his private jet three hours ago on what was ostensibly a 'base inspection'. As one of the main investors in the drilling programme, he had the right to come and check that everything was sealed for winter, given that it would be GARI's first test of the incredible winds and cold. But from the start, Dedov had known it was nothing more than a pretext to launch the seed.

Pearl had arrived and, using Dedov's own men, had got the Robinson 44 helicopter carried out of the garaging unit.

In less than an hour, the female pilot travelling with him had fixed the machine and got the rotors spinning. All the while, Dedov simply stood and stared, the sheer powerlessness of his situation making him tremble with rage.

Just as the helicopter was about to lift off, he had seen Pearl through the Perspex window and their eyes had met. A smile was plastered across Pearl's face, a smug smile laced with venomous contempt and self-congratulation. Pearl knew that he had won. He had known it right from the start.

Dedov had watched them fly away, almost unable to believe the train of events that had brought him here, or how quickly they had developed. In the beginning, it had been so simple – just a single request.

A contact at the Polar Academy in Saint Petersburg had told him that a man named Richard Pearl needed his help to build a second drill site on the lake, but this time it was to be done in secret. He was told that the secrecy stemmed from the need to have a control experiment with which to compare samples extracted by the British. It didn't make sense to Dedov, but given the fact that Pearl had just handed over a cheque for fourteen million dollars to the GARI programme, he didn't feel he was able to question the man's motives too deeply.

For his trouble, Dedov was to receive a 'personal expense account'. Nothing too extravagant, but in hindsight he realised that it had put him on Pearl's payroll – and from there the slope was far more slippery than he could ever have imagined.

All Dedov had been asked to do was to conceal the extra

shipping containers coming off the boat. They were filled with sections of piping and drill equipment, and, he was told, would be collected by a man named Vidar Stang. That was to be the sum total of his responsibility and for the first few weeks, things had run their course.

Then he had been out on the ice barrier one day and actually met Vidar Stang.

The Norwegian was preparing to convoy back some supplies and almost immediately Dedov had found something deeply unnerving about the man. It wasn't just his reclusive nature, nor even his grey, blank eyes that had been so badly burnt by the sun. There was something entirely unhealthy about his devotion to Pearl. He barely spoke, but when he did, it always seemed to be about Pearl.

The more Dedov listened, the more he realised how unwholesome it was, like a son's love for a father that had somehow been corrupted. There was something tragic about it too, mixed with an undercurrent of menace and fanaticism that Dedov found hard to take in, let alone understand.

As they had stood together on the ice barrier and prepared to move the supplies, a storm had come up that had forced them both to shelter inside one of the tractors. For nearly three hours they had sat side by side with the cabin heaters on full blast, and it was then that Dedov had begun to understand the true depths of Pearl's intent. For all Stang's natural reticence and suspicion, on an emotional level he was little more than a child. Once he seemed to accept that Dedov was involved with the project and, more importantly, connected to the American, he opened up to him wholeheartedly.

Dedov soon learnt of the seed's existence and what it might do to the Southern Ocean. It was like a living nightmare. He had unwittingly become involved with a plan that could decimate his beloved Antarctica, a place that had been his passion and home for nearly forty years.

Even now, Dedov could remember the sheer relief he had felt as he had climbed down from the cabin and got away from the Norwegian. In all his years of being cooped up with strangers at science bases, Dedov had never met anyone who had made him feel quite so uncomfortable.

Almost immediately after the encounter, he had tried to detach himself from the whole scheme, even refusing Pearl's offers of extra money. It was then that he caught his first glimpse of Pearl's true nature. Somehow, he had found out about Dedov's uranium-smuggling days and immediately threatened to expose him. But the smuggling had all happened such a long time ago and now no longer held any great threat for the Russian. Its significance, like the majority of the evidence, had long since faded into obscurity.

Just as Dedov had been preparing to send a team round to the old Soviet base to finally put a stop to the whole nefarious project, an image had arrived on GARI's main computer. It showed Dedov's son, Nicolai Vladimirovich, sitting in a coffee shop in San Diego with a disbelieving smile on his face. He was staring across the table at a man mostly out of shot, but Dedov had instantly recognised him as Pearl. He could well imagine the fantastic job offer he was putting to Dedov's unsuspecting son, drawing him in close. The inference was clear. His family was no longer safe.

In that single moment, Dedov had realised that he would do nothing to endanger his own son's life, not even to save his beloved Antarctica.

But then Sommers had died in the crevasse and the British had informed him that they were sending out a new guide. Dedov had seized the opportunity, seeing it as his last-ditch attempt to blow the whistle on Pearl. He deliberately plotted a route close to the second drill site, feeling sure that the British would see it and, in turn, question its existence. He had even given a second satellite phone to the new guide, Matthews, and told him to report anything out of the ordinary.

The spotlight would then have fallen on Pearl's clandestine drilling without dragging Dedov himself, and by extension his son, into the affair.

But it hadn't happened. The British had only called once to report their position and, tragically, to say that one of their number had died in the terrible weather. Dedov slowly shook his head, regretting that he had pushed them so hard to leave ahead of the storm. Some of the responsibility for the man's death would be on his conscience, but then again, perhaps there was more to it than just weather. Perhaps Stang was somehow involved.

His eyes moved across to the double-glazed window and the clearing skies beyond. The British must have driven right past the second drill site but not seen it in the storm. Now, his only hope was that they would spot it when they emerged from the base and tried to make their way back to GARI.

It had been seven hours since their last communication. Seven hours and Dedov was starting to get worried. Their satellite phones would be working fine in this weather, so why hadn't they checked in to say they were on the move? It would be the most logical thing to do. They would then be able to establish a new rendezvous time for the tractors and coordinate a proper rescue.

As much as Dedov asked the question, deep down he already knew the answer. Stang. He knew that the man would protect the secret of the lake at all costs and, if he had half a chance, would prevent the British from getting back to GARI.

Dedov exhaled heavily. He lit a cigarette, expelling a cloud of smoke against the wall in front. That was another point to consider. Someone was going to have to stay behind and man the station throughout the winter months. Without any direct contact with the British, he couldn't just write them off. What if one of them did make it back alive? By sealing shut the base and sending everyone home, he might as well be signing their death warrants.

Dedov's eyes moved skywards as he trawled through the list of names of his work crew. Every one of them was desperate to return home. For him suddenly to propose they spend another ten months in the long dark of winter might well incite a mutiny. He loved his men, just as they loved him, but from hard-won experience he knew that there was only so far he could push them.

With a slow bow of his head, Dedov sighed, feeling the weight of the decision pressing down upon him. For the first time in as long as he could remember, he felt totally unsure of what to do. On the one hand he had to get back to Saint

Petersburg for his own cancer treatment; on the other he couldn't leave men in the field like that, even if they were British.

Dedov turned towards the calendar hanging on the wall beside him. Flicking through the pages to the correct date, he stared at the handwritten entry he had placed there nearly six months ago when they had first arrived. In two days' time, the cargo ship the *Akademia Federov* was due to dock alongside the barrier to unload. It would only be for a few hours as they dropped off some containers, but anyone left at the base would still be able to clamber on board and get back to Cape Town by sea. It bought them an extra forty-eight hours. But even now, he wondered if that would be enough.

Dedov was about to stand up when he suddenly heard a high-pitched scream echo out from somewhere nearby. The sound was muted, but filled with deep-rooted terror. Swinging open his office door, he stood stock-still, listening.

It came again. This time it was a longer, shriller note. Pacing down the corridor in his slippers, he arrived at the central atrium of Module Four. Up on the main stairwell, two of his men were trying to force open the top hatch.

'What's happening here?' he barked.

The two Russians immediately turned, a mixture of exasperation and annoyance in their eyes.

'She stabbed me with a fork!' the nearest man protested, raising an arm to display his wound.

It took Dedov several seconds to attribute the offence to Hiroko, the Japanese scientist who had been living in solitude ever since her husband had died in the crevasse. He had known about her agoraphobia and, on one of the rare occasions when she had left to get some food, even seen the little area she had been living in.

It was bizarre, like a bird's nest. Hundreds upon hundreds of plastic bags tied up with string surrounded a meticulously folded mattress dead centre. She must have used up an entire year's worth of food bags from the kitchen, filling each with a random assortment of treasures. From screws to shredded paper, children's sweets to discarded pens, her surroundings spoke of a mind that had long since lost its grip on reality.

After weeks of this seclusion and secrecy, Hiroko had become so removed from daily life at the base that Dedov had almost entirely forgotten about her. Now he stared at the hatch, wondering what on earth to do.

'She won't come out and the flight's coming in early,' said the injured man, gesticulating to the hatch. 'We've got to get moving if we're going to make it up to the runway on time.'

He banged his fist on the hatch. 'You hear, Hiroko?' he shouted, switching to his limited English. 'Or you want . . . stay all winter?'

Dedov was about to tell him to be quiet when he suddenly stopped. 'What do you mean, the flight's coming in early?'

The man paled, looking to his companion to share the blame.

'Just now I was running through the radio room, sir, and heard the message come through. Sergei was finishing something up before coming to tell you.'

'How early?'

'Two hours, sir . . . I think,' the man added as if to distance himself from the information.

Dedov shook his head in annoyance. On top of everything else, he now had to contend with a genius-level Japanese woman who was too afraid of open spaces to climb down a flight of stairs. As if to reinforce the point, the wailing started up again, the sound even louder at such close range.

'Tell Sergei to radio the tractor at the RV site and get the men back here immediately. We can't wait for the British any longer.'

Then Dedov's eyes turned towards the hatch. 'And get that open. Cut your way in if need be, but that woman's coming with us whether she likes it or not.'

'Yes, sir.'

The base commander shook his head. By pulling back the tractor from the RV site, he couldn't help but feel he had just condemned the Englishmen to their fate. Now they were truly on their own.

Chapter 21

Police cars reversed in sequence, peeling back from the roadblock to make way for the three Mamba Armoured Personnel Carriers to pass, followed by a single Range Rover 4x4. The vehicles trundled along towards Nyanga township in tight convoy, the six chest-high wheels of the Mambas making short shrift of the potholed road. Through the narrow windows of toughened glass, soldiers could be seen sitting side by side. There were ten men per vehicle, each one anticipating the moment when the back doors would be flung open and they would be ordered out into the red-dust streets.

Kieran Bates stood at the rear of the last Mamba, awkwardly hunched in the low cabin. As he clung on to the guardrail for balance, his right arm was raised, revealing a large sweat patch fanning out from under his armpit. A faded bulletproof jacket covered the rest of his midsection, but it was at least a size too large and the padded collar ran high across his neck, making it difficult for him to tilt his head sideways.

Bates had his eyes narrowed and his jaw clenched, trying to suppress the motion sickness that had started almost the moment he had clambered on board the vehicle.

Forty-five minutes into the journey, the claustrophobic heat of the cabin seemed to exacerbate every bounce and bump in the road. His already pale skin had turned a sickly white, and Bates knew that the other men in the vehicle would be confusing this with fear. It was entirely the wrong message to give out to a bunch of South African squaddies who, at best, were indifferent to his presence and, at worst, openly resentful.

The private seated just next to him looked up and straight into Bates' eyes. He was young, maybe only nineteen, with a soft complexion and a thin, reedy moustache. He looked barely old enough to be out of school, let alone clutching a 5.56mm R4 assault rifle. Bates tried to smile encouragingly, but only received a look of ill-concealed contempt in return. Fair enough, he thought. He was an *Engelsman* and the reason why their unit was venturing into one of the most inflammable districts in the whole of the Cape Flats. If he had been sitting in that seat, he'd probably have felt the same.

'This is a straight man-hunt,' shouted the sergeant from the front passenger seat. He briefly swivelled back towards the cabin to hand around a stack of coloured photographs. 'Alpha and Delta teams will set up a perimeter across the market square. Our job's to give cover to the grab team chasing down her cell phone. But if necessary, we go door to door.'

There was a murmur of consent, but the prospect of kicking down doors in Nyanga was not something that any of them relished. Everyone knew the residents had a pathological hatred of the police and, by extension, the military. Only two weeks ago, the usual undercurrent of animosity had become supercharged after news broke that sixty miners had been gunned down by the police at the Lonmin platinum mine, north-west of Johannesburg. Some of the residents had family at the mines and as the massacre played out again and again on the local TV networks, the simmering hatred had boiled over into unchecked rage. Now, anything vaguely resembling an official vehicle was being instantly attacked.

Efforts had been made to restore calm, but recently police had simply declared the whole of Nyanga a 'no go' zone. When two of their number had somehow got separated from the main squad two days ago, they had found their bodies dumped in one of the filth-ridden streams that criss-crossed the neighbourhood. They had been stoned to death just by virtue of being there.

On board the Mamba, each soldier steeled himself for what he was about to face. They stared at the glossy image of Bear, committing it to memory, while Bates ostensibly did the same. But it wasn't out of necessity. He knew every line of the image.

He had taken the photograph himself when he had been staying with Bear and Luca in Paris a few years ago. It had been winter, with snow on the ground, and the image showed Bear turned three-quarters towards the camera, with her long black hair spilling out across a soft cream jacket.

She was smiling but her gaze was distant, eyes blurring on some unseen object beyond the frame of the camera. There was something knowing about her smile, something enigmatic, and on the flight over from London he had spent hour after hour just staring at the image, sensing something familiar about it but unable to put his finger on what exactly it was.

With the image, memories had come flooding back of his time in Paris. He had only been there for a couple of days, but he remembered every detail. The three of them had strolled from café to café, chatting freely and laughing. Life had seemed light and carefree, so much so that he hadn't even bothered to question why. Then he had realised.

It was because of Bear and Luca. They were so clearly in love. It was in everything they did; the way they glanced at each other, the way they stood close, just touching, whenever the occasion arose. Around them, life seemed that little bit lighter.

At first he had been genuinely happy for them both, but as time passed in their company, his happiness had cooled, to be replaced by an undercurrent of jealousy. He had realised that the look Bear gave to Luca with such ease and regularity was a look that he would never know. He wasn't made to love or be loved like that. And the realisation seemed to throw the realities of his own marriage into focus. It all suddenly felt so bland, so mind-numbingly ordinary.

Bates had left Paris vowing to banish any thoughts of Bear from his mind and, after some time, had managed to do just that. But then that same photograph had flashed across his computer, and with it a sense of familiarity had resurfaced that seemed to stir something deep within him. There was something about Bear that kept on coming back to him.

As the sergeant handed out the last of the prints, Bates watched a couple of the soldiers grin and nudge each other like hormonal adolescents.

'Don't know whether to find her or fuck her,' the nearest joked, before rubbing the picture on to his crotch and moaning in a high-pitched falsetto, much to the amusement of the rest of his unit.

'*Fokken* joker,' murmured the sergeant, ignoring him and turning back to the front of the Mamba.

Bates watched as the same soldier then raised the creased photo and stared more closely at it. His nicotine-stained fingers itched at the dark ring of stubble across his neck, while his eyes sparkled with libidinous glee. Bates could well imagine what grubby fantasy was being played out in his mind.

'No one touches her,' Bates suddenly ordered. Every soldier looked up, surprised by the conviction in his voice. It was the first time that they had heard the 'civvy' speak.

'She's an SSA priority 1,' he continued, checking himself, 'and wanted in connection with multiple bombings. She could be carrying any number of devices. If you spot her, you don't get clever. You call it in and wait for the grab team.'

The order was greeted by silence. Bates glowered from one man to the next, his eyes eventually settling on the joker.

'We clear?' he shouted.

'Yes, sir!' came the chorus.

Bates nodded, more to himself than anyone else, and went back to willing the journey to end. Through the rear windscreen, he could see the Range Rover following a few feet behind, its sleek black bonnet dwarfed in size by the height of the Mamba. Inside was a specialist team he had met briefly at the American Embassy. All of them were professionals with at least two years' experience in the field and Bates had been impressed by their resumés. But now, as they entered the outskirts of Nyanga, he wondered how they would fare in an environment as fluid and mercurial as an African township.

As the four vehicles passed into the sea of corrugated-iron shacks, Bates slowly shook his head. He had never seen anything like this. It was immense; an endless warren of dead-ends and potential traps. No wonder Pearl's four-man security team had been taken to pieces. If his own team were going to get in and out before the locals realised what was happening, they would have to hit hard and fast.

From the front seats, Bates could hear the sergeant on the radio. He was being talked on to the location of Bear's cell phone, and every so often his hand would jab right or left to direct the driver. The hulking frame of the Mamba turned into one of the narrow back streets, the gap so tight that its wheel rims scraped along the side of a low barbed-wire fence. For a brief moment the middle wheels spun, trying to gain traction, before the massive machine lurched forward, ripping the fence posts from the ground and dragging them a few hundred yards further down the alley.

The sergeant raised his hand. The signal was coming from the faded blue shack dead ahead. It looked identical to the ones either side, with a crooked frame and patchy tarpaulin roof held down by rocks.

The soldiers jumped from the vehicle with impressive order, grouping around the shack with rifles raised to cover the perimeter. The grab team then rushed forward with a heavy metal ram, splintering the door of the shack as easily as driftwood before streaming inside with their pistols at the ready.

As the last man entered, Bates caught sight of a syringe pen being held behind his back, while in his other hand he held a video camera with a live feed back to Langley. There was a clattering of pots, then a scream, before a woman was led out into the open street. Bates leant forward, pressing his nose against the windscreen as he tried to see whether it was Bear or not. She was hunched over with her face thrust down towards the ground, while her arms were pinned behind her back, bound by cable ties.

The woman was the right build, but her long black hair made it impossible to see her face. Bates could hear her screaming; a shrill, desperate note that was putting all the soldiers on edge. They clenched the butts of their R4 rifles tight into their shoulders, all of them aware that the noise was attracting far too much attention.

The woman let out another scream, this time louder. A second later the syringe was jabbed into her neck somewhere close to her carotid artery. Almost immediately, her legs buckled. Her limp body was then dragged round to the back of the Mamba and presented to Bates like some kind of hunter's trophy.

He paused, so much of him not wanting it to be Bear. But all around him now he could feel the expectant stares of the soldiers. He knew how they would treat a suspect, female or not, and so put on a display of yanking back her hair roughly.

It wasn't Bear. This woman was younger, with faux-gold earrings and tattoos lacing across her hands and wrists.

'Shit,' he cursed, staring down at the woman's face. 'It's not Makuru, but load her up. I want to see what she knows.'

One of the soldiers emerged with the woman's scant possessions, bundling them into large plastic bags and placing them in the back of the Mamba. He passed over Bear's cell phone that they had been tracking and Bates immediately started scrolling through the call history. There was an incoming call from a satellite phone that lasted six minutes. Luca had obviously made contact.

Without another word, Bates climbed into the back seat of the Range Rover, pushing the legs of the unconscious woman over to one side to make space. He knew if he wasn't here in person, the soldiers would have gladly taken this woman as enough of a prize and made any excuse to leave the township. But the fact remained that if he wanted to find Bear, they were going to have to stay a little longer.

'We regroup with Alpha and Delta teams,' he shouted towards the sergeant. 'We'll hold position there.'

The sergeant nodded, then glanced down at his watch. They'd been in Nyanga too long already.

The effects of the anti-serum were almost immediate. As soon as the syringe was pulled from her neck, the woman's eyes flickered open.

Before she had time to utter a word, the agent seated next to her grabbed her face in his hands. The plastic of his surgical gloves clung to her cheeks as he shone a pencil torch straight into her left eye. The beam flashed across her dilated pupil and the woman moaned in discomfort, raising her hands in a pitiful effort to ward him off.

'*Qui êtes-vous . . .*' she managed to say, but her speech was slow and groggy. A trail of saliva ran down her chin and on to her neck as the agent roughly jerked her head round so that she was facing the picture of Bear held directly in front of her.

'When did you last see this woman?' Bates asked, enunciating each word slowly.

'*Je ne . . . comprends pas,*' the woman panted, still blinking unsteadily. 'No . . . English.'

'I think you understand just fine,' Bates retorted. On the drive over to the market square, he had sifted through her possessions and discovered that the second mobile phone she had been carrying, which was presumably hers, was set to English as the primary language. He'd also found her Congolese passport.

'You speak good English, don't you, Inés?'

Hearing her name, the woman raised her soft brown eyes

to meet his. Bates stared into her face, realising that, despite her young age, her looks had already begun to fade. Crystal meth had etched premature lines around her eyes, while the attention of the street gangs had long-since robbed her of any trace of innocence. Bates was sure that she would be well used to physical abuse and getting information out of her that way might take some time. Better to try other means.

Holding the image a little higher, he moved closer to her. 'I'll give you a thousand rand if you tell me everything you know about this woman.'

Inés' eyes widened at the mention of money. It was less than eighty pounds, but to her it was food for a month. For that much she would have betrayed anyone she could think of, let alone that bitch of a woman who had stuck her with a skewer. As Bates reached into his jeans, pulling out a wad of sweaty notes, her hand went to her side involuntarily, feeling for the wound that Bear had inflicted. It still hurt like hell whenever she moved.

Counting out the blue one-hundred-rand notes, Bates watched her fear slowly turn to suspicion. Her eyes followed his every move, as if the slightest distraction might in some way annul the offer.

'Yours if you tell me,' he said, pressing the notes into her open hand.

Inés hesitated a moment longer, then she started to speak.

'I met her in the market place. By the *Tshisa* stand,' she said, her voice surprisingly soft and melodious. 'We got talking because she's from the Congo – like me. But then this gang came along and wanted to catch her. I tried to warn her, but the twenty-eights were too fast.'

She paused, lowering her eyes dolefully. Bates followed her every move, already suspecting he was only hearing half-truths. 'So what happened then?'

'There was gunfire and everybody started running from the market. The white men got taken down. Just like that.'

'To the woman. What happened to the woman?'

'In all the confusion, she ran and managed to make it a little way down one of the back streets and hide.'

'And?'

'They found her,' Inés answered matter-of-factly. Her gaze lowered as she remembered the sound of the taxicab's door sliding back, then the rush of the gang members as they charged past her towards the ramshackle hut where their quarry had been hiding. The tall woman had been so close to getting away, but by chance one of their men on the street had heard her whispering into her mobile phone and had kicked open the door.

Inés had watched as they set upon their prize like dogs, pulling, dragging, kicking her back towards the vehicle. She remembered how viciously the woman had fought, lashing out with the skewer she had been holding and jabbing it straight into the neck of the first assailant. There was a bright spray of blood, before the man made a horrible gurgling sound and collapsed on to his knees. As the others in the gang tried to pin her down, the woman had scratched, bitten and screamed like a wild animal.

In the last few seconds, Inés had seen the woman

desperately search for help. Her eyes had switched from side to side along the alleyway, but nobody was about to risk their own skin by intervening. In the end, they had bundled her into the waiting taxi, leaving only the mobile phone she had been using, lying in the mud.

Inés looked up, but this time a cocky smile edged at the corner of her lips.

'Give me another thousand and I'll tell you where she is.'

Bates didn't appear to have heard. Then, with a sudden crack, he smashed his elbow into the top of her chest. The blow drove all the wind out of Inés' lungs and she reeled forward, gasping in shock. He waited without speaking while the other agents in the car simply stared ahead impassively, the stick and carrot routine all too familiar.

Checking his watch, Bates waited for the prisoner to recover enough to be able to hear him. Then he addressed her again.

'You were going to tell me where she'd been taken.'

Inés nodded hesitantly, her whole body curling in on itself.

'Just up ahead,' she stammered, still wheezing for air. 'There's a . . . big house on the edge of the square. Everyone knows it. That's where . . . the gang keep the women before shipping them on.'

Bates nodded, signalling to the driver of the Range Rover to continue. Just as they were about to move off, the Mamba drew level and the sergeant poked his head out of the window.

'Delta team reports a crowd gathering in the north-east corner, sir,' he said.

Bates turned in his seat. Not too far away he could see trails of acrid smoke rising into the air. The inhabitants were starting to burn tyres, sealing them in with a ring of fire and smoke.

'Check our exits and get Delta and Alpha teams to hold them off until we're ready to move,' he ordered. 'We've got one more call to make.'

Chapter 22

Thick, choking smoke wafted across Nyanga's market square. Through the gaps in it, Bates could see movement as hundreds of people prepared themselves for battle. There was chanting and weapons were brandished high in the air. These ranged from simple *pangas* and gardening knives to fully automatic AK-47s.

Behind the seething ebb and flow of people, taxicabs arrived from the neighbouring townships. As the news had spread that the military were out in force on the streets, they had raced across town, packed with an assortment of pistols and ammunition. As the vehicles drew to a halt, the contents were quickly handed out to the children, who in turn ferried them to their elder siblings and fathers on the front line.

The chanting grew louder, becoming more unified and coherent. For the briefest of moments, the various tribes inhabiting Nyanga had put aside their festering animosities and now stood side by side in the face of this sudden attack. Excitement grew, stoked to fever pitch by the elders. Already rocks were being hurled through the wall of smoke in the vague direction of the soldiers. They rolled out across no-man's-land, as if preparing the ground for the onset of blood.

Bates watched as Alpha and Delta teams took up positions on the opposite side to the crowd. He needed them to hold off the mob for at least another twenty minutes while he focused on finding Bear. But with each minute that passed, he could see the crowd's confidence growing. Already they vastly outnumbered the soldiers and now they edged closer, step by step.

Turning his attention to his own men, Bates watched them shuffle along the road using the Mamba's rear cabin for cover. As they came within fifty metres of the house that Inés had mentioned, a long, raking burst of machine-gun fire suddenly rose to greet them. The bullets thudded into the muddy street before tracing left and finding their target. They ricocheted off the high bull bars of the Mamba before smacking into the front windscreen and splintering the toughened glass.

'Contact front!' shouted the sergeant. Instantly the lead soldiers widened their stance and opened up with their R4 rifles in response.

'Shit!' Bates screamed, grabbing the radio from the dashboard of the car. 'Sergeant, do *not* return fire! Repeat: do *not* return fire. I want the suspect alive. Only fire once inside the building and in line of sight.'

There was a silence, the sergeant clearly bemused by such a command.

'Do you copy, Sergeant?' Bates barked. It was the first time the others inside the car had seen him so animated. They watched as he craned his whole body through the gap between the front seats, fighting against the restrictive padding of his bulletproof vest.

'Drive the Mamba through the front wall of the house,' he ordered. 'Then go room by room.'

'Yes, sir.'

He watched as the order was relayed and a plume of diesel smoke belched out from the Mamba's exhausts as it changed gear and sped forward. Behind it the soldiers broke into a full sprint as they tried to keep under cover and follow in its wake. There was another burst of gunfire from inside the house, but this time it was panicked and sporadic. The occupants had already guessed the vehicle's intent and were running for cover as it surged towards them like the prow of a mighty ship.

The Mamba ploughed into the rickety wall of the house, reducing the doorway to rubble and dragging down the entire front section of the roof. Bates cursed again, the driver having come in too hard, and wondered whether they would soon be digging Bear's body out from the wreckage. There was a brief lull while the sergeant ordered two-man fire teams to take position on either side of the house in case anyone tried to escape.

Towards the rear of the building a chair was tossed through a window, sending fragments of glass bursting into the sunlight. Two skinny men followed, but only managed to get two or three paces clear before they were cut down in a storm of gunfire. At such close range, their bodies jerked and twitched as chunks of flesh were ripped from their torsos. The macabre dance continued for several seconds before they collapsed lifeless to the ground in a pile of broken limbs.

The Mamba then reversed, allowing the rest of the unit to swarm inside the house.

'I want her alive!' Bates screamed into the radio, but there was no response. They heard the muffled clatter of gunfire, then an interminable silence. The seconds dragged on and on, with Bates trying to see through the sweat running into his eyes. Finally, the sergeant's voice drifted over the radio signalling the all clear.

Bates leapt out of the Range Rover, so close behind the grab team he was almost tripping on their heels. They stepped through the gaping hole in the front wall to find the inner rooms clogged with masonry dust and the smell of cordite. Moving further, Bates could see a television in the far corner of the room. It was still on, with a half-drunk can of Coke lying spilt to one side.

They were funnelled upstairs and on to a narrow landing where a figure was sitting upright, slumped against the wall and clutching its stomach. It took Bates several seconds to realise that the man was already dead. He then noticed the sergeant gesticulating towards one of the rear bedrooms. As Bates moved past him he stared into the man's face, desperately hoping for a hint of what he would find, but the layer of dust had made the sergeant's expression entirely unreadable.

Bates stumbled on, his momentum bringing him deep

inside the room. Rubbish bags had been taped against the single window, blotting out all but a thin sliver of light, but still he could see a woman lying naked on a bed. Her wrists had been bound to the metal bedposts with cheap gardening wire which had cut deep into her skin, leaving small circular stains of blood on the filthy mattress underneath. She was lying twisted to one side with her short-cut hair clinging to her face.

Bates inched closer but, from the woman's short hair, realised almost immediately that this wasn't Bear.

'Found her like that,' the sergeant said, hovering just behind him. 'God knows what those bastards did to her before she died. Fucking animals.'

Bates stared into the lifeless brown eyes of the woman on the bed. She was young, little more than a teenager.

'Shit,' he whispered, shaking his head. He stood up and moved towards the door. 'Cut her free and get her out of here.'

The sergeant nodded grimly, when from somewhere further along the corridor, they heard a shout.

'Got another one!'

Bates stumbled forward, barely daring to hope. He pressed down the corridor towards the front of the house, where the soldier was clearing bricks away from a door. As soon as Bates entered the room, he recognised Bear. Again the gang had used wire, this time to tie her to a chair. Her body was hunched over in the seat, with her hair spilling into her eyes.

Bates stood still, feeling as though his feet were rooted to the floor. He finally understood what it was about the image of Bear that had so unsettled him on the flight over. It was that hair. The long black hair spilling over her face looked exactly the same as an operative he had lost in the Yemen all those years ago. Bear and she had been different in almost every other way, but each of them had long jet black hair that always seemed to fall in strands across their cheeks. He had been the one to find his agent in a backstreet in Sana'a, a single bullet through her throat.

He shook his head, trying to drive the terrible image from his mind. A second passed before he managed to regain his breath enough to speak.

'Out,' he said. Still coughing from the hanging dust, the soldier stepped outside the room. Bates crouched lower, moving slowly so as not to startle her.

'Bear,' he whispered, 'it's over. We've come to get you out.'

She didn't respond. Only her eyes moved as they scanned his face. She looked wired from adrenalin and fear, and it took several seconds before a spark of recognition passed across her face. 'Kieran?'

'Yeah,' he said, reaching past the pistol on his belt to a small leather pouch. Taking a Leatherman multi-tool inside and jamming the pliers over the wire coiled into her wrists, he freed her arms. The wounds looked to be weeping and sore, but there was nothing else to be done until they got safely back to the military base.

As he helped Bear to her feet, a strange sense of relief washed over him. Although her clothes were ripped and dusty, they hadn't been stripped from her. There was a chance the gang hadn't got that far with her.

With him gently leading her across the loose bricks and

broken timbers of the house, they reached what remained of the front room. A halo of light poured in from outside. As they drew closer, he felt Bear's head lift from his chest and her eyes fix on the light as if it were some kind of epiphany. Tears streamed down her face, the prospect of being released from the nightmare almost too much for her to take.

Together they walked the last few steps out into the open and got in the back of the Mamba. Bates could see the other members of the grab team eyeing her suspiciously. They had cable ties, Tasers and syringe pens at the ready, and were obviously confused by Bates' sudden break from protocol.

'Leave it,' he warned, raising a finger towards the nearest of them. He sat Bear down, feeling her whole body tremble. She immediately pulled her feet up to her chest and began gently rocking back and forwards, eyes darting from one thing to the next in the cabin as she tried to piece together everything that was happening.

'Please,' she whispered, turning to face him, 'get me out of here.'

'Two more minutes,' Bates replied. 'Then we'll be out of this hellhole for good.'

But just as the words left his mouth, gunfire erupted like a roll of thunder across the market square. They both turned towards a gap in the far row of houses to see a mass of screaming people suddenly burst through the wall of smoke.

The battle for Nyanga had begun.

The first wave of the attack ran into a hail of machine-gun fire. The soldiers of Alpha and Delta teams were dug in and ready. They fired at knee-height into the sea of advancing people and soon a mass of men and teenagers lay twisted and writhing on the ground. They clutched splintered bone and shattered kneecaps while behind them their comrades tripped over the tangle of limbs, only adding to the carnage and confusion.

The soldiers reloaded, clipping in new magazines and steadying their grip, but just as they were about to recommence firing men suddenly appeared on either side of their position, leaping down from rooftops or bounding over the low, corrugated fences. Concealed by smoke, they had crept up through the maze of alleyways and now ran out into the open, firing wildly. But what they lacked in accuracy they made up for in numbers. Soon the soldiers found themselves turning from one side to the next, desperately trying to fend off attacks from every direction.

From deep within the crowd a bottle was suddenly hurled through the air; then another, and another. As the glass smashed on the ground it ignited the petrol within, sending a pool of yellow and blue flames licking into the air. The last was a direct hit, landing in the midst of three soldiers taking cover behind an abandoned car. They leapt up, running heedlessly as their clothes went up in sheets of flame. Two of them managed to stumble towards their neighbouring unit and as they dived to the ground, their comrades frantically tried to pat out the flames, even burning the palms of their own hands in the process.

But for the third man it was too late. He staggered out into the centre of no-man's-land, visible to both sides through the haze of drifting smoke. There was a strange hiatus, the shouting suddenly fading to near-silence as hundreds of people took in the terrifying spectacle. The flames rose higher, consuming hair, skin and flesh as he stood, swaying slightly, as if caught in a current. Finally, almost to their relief, he dropped to his knees and fell face-first into the dust.

The sense of horror turned to one of victory and the crowd roared in triumph, screaming with wide eyes and even wider mouths. As the soldiers smelt the stench of burning flesh mingled with the smoke from the mob's tyres, they realised the dead man's fate could easily be theirs.

They fired again, but no longer in the controlled bursts of trained professionals. This firing was panicked and random. The first few rounds would hit their targets, but then the soldiers would keep their fingers locked down on full automatic, spraying wildly into the sky. Magazines ran dry in just a few seconds, leaving them to stumble through the process of re-loading, every movement dogged by fear. Above the din of the crowd, the sergeant's voice could be heard as he barked orders and tried to instil some discipline in them, but to little avail. Fear gripped them all.

By the time the second wave of the attack struck, Delta team was already running. They sprinted with arms wide, some firing wildly over their shoulders as they made a desperate bid to reach the safety of the vehicles. The rout continued, soldier following soldier without order or sequence. They piled into the waiting vehicles, some clutching wounded colleagues while others did nothing more than throw themselves behind the seating and implore the driver to leave.

As the first of the Mambas lurched forward, its rear door still swinging back on its hinges, Bates watched the crowd surge towards it like a tide. They were almost on top of the vehicle, their victory now beyond doubt.

Bates cursed. He had been caught unawares, expecting the teams to be able to hold off the crowd for at least another five minutes. But if he didn't act now, there would be a full-scale massacre.

'For Christ's sake, get closer!' he shouted to the sergeant of his own Mamba. 'They need covering fire.'

The sergeant turned back in his seat, eyes wide.

'But, sir, shouldn't we set up a defensive perimeter here and wait?'

'We do that, there'll be no one left to wait for. Now move!'

As their own vehicle trundled towards the fray the soldiers within nervously checked their weapons, eyes continuously switching back to the chaos unfolding only a few hundred yards away.

'I want a quick deployment,' Bates shouted, struggling to be heard above the clamour. 'Lay down covering fire. Controlled bursts. We stay until the others get clear.'

None of the men made eye contact, desperate to conceal their own fear. The sickening prospect of being out in the open was almost too much for them to bear. Around the cabin soldiers could be seen trying to remember fragments of their training, while others recited prayers and openly crossed themselves.

Turning back towards Bear, Bates whispered, 'Stay down,'

just as the first of the escaping Mambas passed in the opposite direction, accelerating hard. He caught a flash image of the confusion and blood inside the rear cabin and felt a familiar sense of dread wash over him. It was the same on every mission. But through experience, he had learnt that the only way to deal with it was by taking action. Pulling his own Glock 17 pistol from his belt, he chambered the first round and tried to slow his own breathing.

The stricken profile of the second Mamba was just ahead. People from the crowd clung to its bonnet and roof, while others smashed stones into the side windows. The rear door had been entirely wrenched off its hinges and, as he watched, one of the soldiers was dragged feet first from within. Bates saw him kick and twist, but arm after arm rose up from the crowd, yanking him clear of the machine. He appeared briefly once more, transported over the heads of the crowd as if floating on a heaving wave, before he suddenly disappeared, lost to a fate that was as frenzied as it was short-lived.

As their own Mamba drew to a halt, Bates screamed at the soldiers to get out. They rose to their feet but hesitated. For a brief moment there was a bottleneck of men and rifles. Ramming his shoulder into the man in front, Bates pushed them forward until they spilled out on to the street. They stood in an unsteady group, staring in bewildered awe at the sheer rage and hostility of the crowd.

'Form up!' he ordered, grabbing them by their webbing straps and forcing them into some kind of order. As they moved, more petrol bombs arced over from the crowd but this time fell short, exploding in circular pools of flame just metres ahead of them.

'Fire!' Bates screamed, raising his own pistol. After a second, the others followed suit. Soon, there was a steady thud from the R4 rifles. Bullets smacked into the crowd with pitiless force, dropping one figure then the next, as a constant stream of empty shell casings hit the ground around the soldiers' feet. This sudden semblance of military order caused the crowd to falter. Almost as one they pulled back, leaving the dead and dying to litter the ground like a vision from hell. There were so many of them, lying on top of each other, connected by trails of gut and bone, the ground itself was awash with pools of still-warm blood.

'Move! Move!' Bates shouted, shuffling forward. As they advanced, the soldiers of Delta team saw their salvation and jumped down from the carcass of the trapped Mamba. They ran headlong towards their rescuers, hurling themselves and their rifles inside the cabin without looking back. Bates counted them in, noting that only four remained from the original ten-man unit. He could still see the outline of at least two others inside the APC, but they sat with their heads slumped forward, arms resting by their sides, already dead.

His own men climbed on board their Mamba. The engine roared as the driver sent them swinging round in a tight circle away from the crowd. Bates stood by the open rear door, watching with pistol raised. He didn't attempt to fire, realising there had been enough bloodshed for one day. Instead he watched, eyes switching from face to face in the crowd as the distance between them widened with each passing second. Soon, the Mamba had crossed to the far side of the market place and was powering up towards the open ramp of the motorway.

Just ahead of them a barricade had been hastily erected, but it was little match for the speed and momentum of the Mamba. It crashed through the meagre collection of rubbish bins and old chairs, scattering them like leaves, before swerving on to the open road.

Bates continued to stare as the township melted into the distance. He shook his head, almost unable to believe the sheer level of destruction he had witnessed in such a short time. He had never seen anything so incendiary. If there was one thing he now knew – Nyanga deserved its reputation.

He switched his gaze inside the cabin to the mess of wounded soldiers. They filled every inch of the Mamba, lying across the bench seats and on the floor. Right at the back, he could see Bear ripping open a medical pack she had found and jamming a wad of gauze into the wound in a soldier's neck. Her hands and wrists were covered in his blood and she was struggling to keep her balance amongst the slew of discarded weaponry and empty shell casings.

Bates watched her for a moment longer, his eyes following every move. He had got her out of Nyanga, but now he was going to have to deal with the Americans.

Chapter 23

'It'll never work,' murmured Katz, craning his neck back to stare towards the ceiling of the old Soviet base.

After the bitter realisation that the helicopter's arrival did not signal a rescue attempt, Joel, Katz and Luca had spent nearly an hour discussing their fate. Eventually, they had arrived at a single solution. Luca was going to have to climb up to the skylights and attempt to smash his way through. But at over thirty feet above their heads, the task seemed virtually impossible.

'Even if you do make it up there, how are you going to break the glass?' continued Katz, his forehead furrowing in doubt.

'Look, if you've got any better ideas, then let me know,' Luca retorted. He moved across to one of the room's steel girders and gently placed his right hand on the cold metal. His fingers brushed across the line of rivets, assessing the extent of the grip. It was barely wider than his fingernails.

In the old days, the years of climbing had conditioned his

hands into vices. He could dangle his entire weight from nothing more than two fingers, while the skin on each finger had been worn down so many times that it had become as tough as leather. But things were different now. He just wasn't like that any more.

Clenching his hands into fists, he cracked the knuckles of each finger in sequence. The other side effect of so much climbing was that it had triggered the early onset of arthritis. Now his joints ached more than ever. His hands felt brittle and inflexible, while a nervous sweat had already started to dampen his palms. Luca rubbed them against his thighs, drying them off, then slowly shook his head. What was he even thinking? The climb would have been daunting when he was an over-confident adolescent, let alone now.

His eyes gradually followed the line of the main girder as it ran vertical for about twenty feet before angling back towards the skylights. The entire top section was an overhang and, once committed, there would be no place for him to rest. His only option would be to keep going.

Luca's eyes narrowed as he stared up towards the apex of the room. A fall from that height wouldn't kill him, it would just break a leg, or, if he landed badly, be enough to snap one of his lower vertebrae. It was the worst kind of distance – not enough to kill him, but just enough to leave him crippled.

'You can do it, mate,' Joel said encouragingly, but as Luca turned to face him, he could see the lack of conviction in the other man's eyes. To Joel, the climb looked simply impossible. When the idea had first been mooted, he had walked over to the sidewall and tried to hang off the girder himself out of sheer curiosity. After only a couple of seconds, he had slipped off and crumpled to the floor.

Impossible or not, they all knew that it was the only option they had left. Everything rested on Luca now.

'Just so you know, I'm not going to be the one scraping you off the floor if you fall from there,' said Katz unhelpfully, raising an arm skyward as if in premonition.

'Christ's sake, Katz!' Joel snapped. 'That's not what he needs to hear right now.'

Joel turned towards Luca by way of an apology, but realised that he hadn't even heard. He was entirely focused on what lay before him, his eyes narrowed on the drab grey metal of the girder.

'Take this,' Joel offered, handing across a squared metal pole. He had managed to unscrew it from the leg of a low table and thought it might be useful for smashing skylights. Luca nodded distractedly as he tied it on to his belt.

'You'll do just fine,' Joel added, but his words fell on deaf ears. Luca had already stepped up on to the girder.

Carefully positioning the tip of his right boot against one of the rivets, he arched his heel as if attempting a ballet position. He then smoothed the rest of his body upwards with his hips pressed flat against the raw metal, before finally reaching up and crimping his fingertips tight. His body was suspended a foot off the ground, like a chameleon attached to a tree branch, with the slightest loss of balance threatening to keel him over.

Steadily raising his other boot, he repeated the process, using the nub of the rivets as footholds. From such close range, both Joel and Katz could see the muscles of his abdomen trembling with strain as he gradually uncurled and reached higher. All the while, his fingers remained clamped to the minuscule ledge, with his knuckles whitening from the effort.

The seconds passed, one after the other, in the dead silence of the room. Luca made short work of the vertical section, but now the girder angled out behind him in a long, sloping overhang towards the skylights. As he reached back on to it, his body naturally swung out, trailing into the open air. It left only his fingertips and the edge of one of his boots still attached to the metal.

'Holy shit,' Joel breathed, expecting Luca to slide off with each passing second. Both he and Katz watched in amazement as the climber's back arched and his shoulders contorted outwards, almost unnaturally, as he shifted his weight higher. It didn't seem physically possible.

Even from that distance they could hear Luca's laboured breath, while droplets of sweat beaded his hairline and fell on to the hard surface of the floor thirty feet below. But he was making progress. The first of the skylights was only a few feet away now.

Joel winced, neck painful from being crooked at such an angle, but his eyes stayed locked on Luca's every move. He was higher now, almost touching the glass.

'What's he doing?' Joel whispered as he saw Luca pause

then retreat back a few hard-won inches. Without his glasses, Joel could only see the hazy outline of what was going on.

'He's stuck,' Katz blurted. 'He's trying to climb back down again.'

They both watched as Luca's right leg slowly lowered into the open air beneath him, dragging the rest of his body with it.

'He's going to fall!' Katz warned. Joel looked towards Luca, wondering if they should attempt to catch him, but Katz was already retreating towards the edge of the room.

But Luca didn't fall. Instead, he adjusted his grip, then reached back to his belt with his left hand. He swung the metal pipe up towards the ceiling, jabbing it into the sealant around the windowpane as opposed to attempting to smash the glass as originally planned. On the third attempt, the rod pierced though and Luca twisted the end sideways, locking it tight against the wooden frame and giving himself a chance to rest his full weight on one arm.

'It's all rotten,' he managed to tell them, shouting down between his legs. Although he had a better hold, he was at a loss as to what to do next. The glass was too thick to smash with the rod.

Luca grunted, trying to resist the tremor in his forearms. He knew that he only had a few more seconds before they would give out completely. His abdominal muscles were cramping with the effort of holding his body in such an unnatural position, while sweat ran down his forehead and into his eyes. He shook his head, trying to clear his vision, but it only seemed to make it worse as strands of hair clung to his face and open mouth.

Seconds. He had seconds before his strength would desert him completely and his fingers would slowly uncurl from the bar as if someone were deliberately trying to peel them back. He had to act now or it would be too late.

'Shit!' he panted, trying to swing his body round and kick the glass with his boot, but he barely had enough momentum to touch it, let alone smash through. With his whole body hanging now, he reached forward, digging the fingers of his free hand into the thick smudge of sealant surrounding the glass. His fingernails scraped and bent, forcing their way through the rotten substance with frenzied determination. He could feel his other hand start to slip. It was only a millimetre, but it sent a terrible wave of panic running through him.

Twisting his whole hand round, his fingers finally broke through the window seal and he curled them up and over the edge of the glass. It wasn't much of a grip, but at least now he could spread his weight on to two arms. He waited, swinging in the open with his body stretched out. His core strength had wilted to such a degree that it felt as if the weight of his legs would pull his whole torso in two. He hung for a few more seconds, unsure if he had the strength to do anything else.

Shifting his weight slightly, Luca heard a crack and watched as a splinter stretched right across the pane of glass. That was it! He could use his body weight to try and snap off a section of the skylight. Jerking his body up and down, he heard another crack, then another, before a huge slice of glass suddenly carved off. He swung back on one arm as it cut through the air, slewing sideways, before smashing down on to the ground and narrowly missing Joel.

There was a shout from somewhere below, but Luca was only aware of the sudden whoosh of air as the cold came streaming in from outside. Particles of snow flurried in all around him, plastering his face and eyelashes as he desperately swung his right leg up into the gap. Finally, he was able to rest his leg on top of what remained of the skylight.

Levering his hips up and through the gap, Luca pushed out on to the topside of the frame. As his full weight pressed down on the structure, the glass in the other skylights began to break, sending cracks out in a semi-circle like the web of a giant spider. Then another large triangle of glass broke off, spinning down into the darkness below. Spreading his arms wide, Luca inched back across the skylight and on to the relative safety of the plasterboard roof.

He lay still, arms outstretched. The exhaustion was just too much. His forearms and shoulders felt as if the muscles had been slowly peeled back from the bones. This wasn't just fatigue. It felt as though he had torn every last muscle in his arms and shoulders.

An entire minute went by. He was dimly aware of shouts from below, but they were muffled by the breeze. Already, the cold had begun to freeze the sweat on his forehead and neck, with the moisture crystallising in large patches. Luca shivered, the sudden transition from panicked sweat to freezing cold taking him completely by surprise.

With a low moan, he pulled himself up and began clambering across the roof on his hands and knees. It sagged under his weight, threatening to send him tumbling back into the base. Half sliding, half crawling, he made his way to the edge and rested once more.

From the vantage point of the roof, he could see that the skies had finally cleared and, instead of the terrible wind, there was now only a light breeze gently curling around the mountain ridges. He could see the Ski-Doos still parked where they had left them. Whoever it was that had trapped them inside had obviously just abandoned them, thinking that there was no chance of escape.

As Luca's feet finally touched the ground, he allowed his legs to buckle and dropped on to all fours. He leant forward as if in prayer and let his head rest on the freezing cold rock in front. It suddenly felt strange to be free. The open skies and distant mountains felt limitless, instantly dispelling the feeling of hopelessness that had settled over him like a shroud back inside the base.

He sat up, already feeling his thirst return. His mouth was bone dry and he knew that he must have lost a lot of moisture from sweating so much. Reaching forward, he grabbed a fistful of snow from the drift in front and bit deep. It was so cold as to freeze his teeth and send a bolt of pain through the front of his skull, but then the moisture fanned out across his lips and he sucked it back, drinking in every last drop.

He turned towards the entrance of the base and the pile of rocks barring the door. With arms hanging limp at his sides, he shuffled closer, pulling the nearest rock with a clatter. It would take him an hour or so to move enough of them to free the door.

Then there was another, more pressing issue. They still had to figure out a way to get back to GARI before the last flight. Luca glanced at his watch and shook his head. Only four hours remained.

Katz and Joel emerged from the base, blinking in the daylight. Their eyes passed over the circle of mountains, staring in wonderment at the wide, open scenery.

'I can't believe it,' Joel murmured, before reaching across with his long, angular arms and enveloping Luca in a hug. 'You did it, mate. You actually did it!'

Behind him, Katz nodded with appreciation. His eyes were still narrowed, but this time there was something almost contrite about his expression. Finally, the suspicion was gone. He stared across and was about to say something when he noticed that Luca was shivering. On the climb up, he had ditched his heavy clothing. Now only a thin fleece protected him from the cold.

'Take this,' Katz offered, returning Luca's own down jacket that he had borrowed at the drill site. Without a word, Luca jammed his arms into the sleeves and zipped it tight, grateful for the thick insulation.

'This is all very well,' Katz said, 'but we've still got to figure out a way to get back to the RV point in time. And that's if the old bastard Dedov has even left a tractor there for us at all.'

No one answered. Behind him, the joy in Joel's eyes slowly dimmed and for a long time there was silence. They each stared out across the expanse of the lake, knowing that they didn't have enough water to make the trek to GARI. Even if they did make it back across the mountains, without vehicles, it would take another three to four days to reach the base on foot and they barely had enough water for one. Eating snow would only buy them so many hours. It wouldn't be enough to sustain them.

It felt so unfair to have broken out of the base only to be trapped by the infinite space of Antarctica.

'I could handle the winter,' Katz added suddenly. 'I could handle getting back to an empty base and waiting it out. I'm practical like that. I would just take each day as it comes, and count them down one by one. It's a pity, really. I could have done it.'

He turned towards Joel. 'We've waited three years to get these samples. What would another few months matter, eh?'

Joel shook his head, unwilling to resign himself to his fate. 'We have to ration the water, stretch it out for as long as possible. There's no way Dedov would just abandon us out here. I bet you a search team's already on its way. I'm right, aren't I, Luca?'

But he didn't respond, still staring out across the lake.

'We break it down into days,' Joel continued, trying to muster some consensus. 'Assign an amount of water per person. We supplement it with snow . . .'

Luca suddenly turned towards them, silencing Joel.

'I say we take the Ski-Doos and drive them back across the lake. We then follow the base's original route over the mountains to GARI. At the speed we'll be travelling we should make it in under a day. That's if we have enough fuel of course.'

'But there's a crevasse field,' Joel replied, forehead knotting in confusion. 'Akira and Sommers died there, for Christ's sake.'

'The last storm blew a lot of snow over the surface and there's a good chance that most of the openings are filled up.'

'Most?'

Luca nodded. 'Yeah, most. And the Ski-Doos are a hell of a lot lighter than a tractor. If we drive fast enough, we shouldn't break too far into the snow's crust.'

Both Joel and Katz remained silent, trying to imagine driving Ski-Doos at breakneck speed over the thin layer of snow that covered a crevasse field. Both of them had seen Sommers' body and the stripped fingernails after he had tried to claw his way out.

Eventually, Joel looked up.

'There's got to be another way,' he said meekly. 'That's just suicide.'

Luca nodded slowly. 'Maybe. But it's either that or we go back inside the base and wait it out.'

Behind him, Katz spat a thick globule of saliva on to the ground in pure disgust. 'Great. We either die of thirst or freeze to death in a crevasse. Nice choice.'

Still shaking his head, he moved away from them both,

venturing across to the cliff edge where a long sloping valley fed down towards the lake. Katz shuffled forward aimlessly, still muttering in anger, but as he came closer to the edge, he saw the unmistakable outline of a helicopter parked on the lake bed below.

'Hey! Look at this!' he shouted. Luca and Joel came to stand next to him, peering down at the scene unfolding below.

'What's going on?' Joel asked, squinting into the distance. Down on the lake floor, three figures were just visible beside the helicopter. Behind them stood the elusive tower of the second drill site, a near-exact replica of their own.

'You think that's Pearl?' Joel asked.

'Who else?' Luca replied grimly. 'And I bet the guy who hit me is down there too, showing them where to drop in the capsule.'

Beside him, Katz was already shaking his head. 'We've got to do something. If they launch that thing, the whole lake will be lost.'

'And what the hell do you suggest we do?' Luca snapped. His eyes were tracking from one tiny silhouette to the next, before enviously settling on the helicopter. While Luca's party would have to risk the crevasse field and desperately race back before their water ran out, Pearl would be able to climb aboard and take off. He'd be back at the runway within minutes.

Eventually, Luca dragged himself away from the cliff edge. 'There's nothing we can do except get the hell back to GARI and blow the whistle on the whole thing.'

'Luca, this idea of going back with the Ski-Doos . . .' Joel began, but Luca didn't wait. Instead, he continued walking. Swinging his leg over the saddle of the nearest machine, he yanked the starter cord. On the fifth attempt, the engine gurgled into life. Wiping the layer of snow off the display screen, he brought the machine round until it was facing back down towards the lake.

'Come on,' he shouted. 'Let's get it over with.'

The others watched for a moment, still unsure. Several seconds passed before Katz, then Joel, stepped forward and, without a word, clambered up on to the remaining Ski-Doo. Both of them knew that Luca was right – the crevasse field was now their only hope.

Chapter 24

Richard Pearl pulled off his sunglasses, squinting in the bright Antarctic sun. He smoothed back his light red hair before tilting his head a little closer towards Vidar Stang and staring directly into his ghostly pale eyes. He could see so much of the father in the son. A fact that greatly pleased him.

A second passed before Pearl's forehead creased in a calculated display of regret.

'I never meant to leave you alone like that,' he said. 'The other pilots had to leave and I wasn't able to get anyone back to you. You know me, Vidar, I would never have abandoned you.'

Stang shifted from one foot to the other in the snow, still doubting Pearl's sincerity. He was dressed in snow-camouflage fatigues with a black balaclava rolled up over his head to serve as a hat, while his hunting rifle was slung lengthways across his colossal back. Towering a full head higher than Pearl, he stared down at him for a moment more, upper lip curled into a disbelieving sneer.

'But . . . you left me blind . . .' he managed to accuse the other man.

Stang had practised what he was going to say for nearly ten months, but now that Pearl was finally before him, all he could do was stammer half-baked recriminations. Nothing was going according to script, and with each failed attempt his frustration mounted.

'I swear I knew nothing about the missing goggles,' Pearl countered, quick to continue. 'I couldn't have known that you would go snow blind.'

He stepped forward, reaching out one hand and gently cupping Stang's chin in his fingers. When he had left Antarctica over a year ago he had calculated everything to ensure that Stang suffered but survived. He wanted the Norwegian's existence out on the ice to be nothing short of a living hell and knew how much the petty torments would sap his morale. By changing the ration order to consist of only a single meal and removing all the books Stang had planned to read, he was condemning him to months of misery. Stealing his sunglasses had been a last-minute idea but one that had evidently cost Stang the most.

As Pearl stared into the Norwegian's burnt eyes, the corners of his lips slanted upwards in satisfaction. But he had to tread carefully. He could see the simmering rage inside the man and knew how easily Stang could snap. The childlike uncertainty had gone, replaced by a new and assertive Vidar Stang. It was a side to him Pearl had never seen before.

'Vidar, you have to understand something. Since your father died, you've been like the son I never had. And you know me, I'd never do anything to hurt family.'

Stang stared into his eyes, desperate to refute him, but equally desperate to believe. How many times had he pictured this scene? How many hours had he spent in fantasy, revelling in the thought of crushing Pearl's skull between his bare hands? He had laughed in pure joy at the thought of pressing his thumbs into Pearl's eyeballs and feeling the soft orbs pop into liquid mulch. Each night, he had used the compass to gouge out a little more of Pearl's eyeballs from the photograph above his bed. It had acted like an antidote to all his suffering. He had revelled in the knowledge that one day he would blind Pearl and watch *him* fumble and panic, just as he had done in those first few days after arriving in Antarctica.

But now, everything seemed to have changed and he felt so confused. Pearl had described him as a 'son'. The thought was incredible, magical even. A son! Since Fedor had died so suddenly, Vidar had wanted nothing more than another father in his life, someone he could trust and depend on. Pearl's words instantly filled him with a glow that he hadn't experienced in as long as he could remember. It was the glow of requited love.

As Stang's slablike face glanced shyly towards the ground, Pearl looked back towards Helena Coroni, the helicopter pilot, standing a few feet away. He signalled to the back seat of the helicopter to where a sealed metal case still lay, motioning for her to retrieve it. In that one moment, Pearl knew he had won Stang over, but it had taken him nearly an hour to do so.

Coroni turned, not bothering to hide the alacrity with which she bounded back to the machine. She had to get away from that monster, if only for a few minutes. Ever since they had first landed, she had been utterly mesmerised by Stang, watching him with the same fascinated revulsion as she might a car crash being played out in slow motion.

Stang's gigantic frame and barrel chest gave him an imposing demeanour, but what really appalled her was his face. The black skin and chunks of peeling flesh made him look demonic, as if he had just passed through the gates of hell. For the entire hour they had been there, Stang hadn't once registered her presence. All he seemed to see was Pearl, those blank eyes never leaving the man for a second. There was something insatiable about his behaviour, as if Pearl's attention were the only thing Stang craved.

Now Pearl had won him over. He had deflected every accusation, and in return drip-fed Stang his own particular brand of 'love'. Following Pearl around day after day in her role as his personal pilot, Coroni had seen the same performance many times before, but never had she felt such a desperate yearning for him to succeed. She could only imagine what the Norwegian would have done to them if things had gone awry.

Over the last few years she had occasionally heard Pearl mention Stang's name, but always with derision and anger in the way he did it. It was one of the few times his veneer cracked and she got a glimpse into the real man. One thing was for certain: his relationship with Stang wasn't just about the lake. She saw elements of fear in Pearl's hatred, as if he were trying to fulfil some kind of long-standing vendetta, but was too afraid to see it through.

'Helena!'

She turned at the sound of Pearl's voice. He was standing next to Stang with his fist lightly pressed against the Norwegian's brawny arm. The pose was casual, ingratiating even, but she could see the faintest look of uncertainty in Pearl's eyes. She knew that he was not a brave man by nature and suspected he was actually terrified of the monster he had created in Stang.

Just as Coroni approached, holding the briefcase in her right hand, Stang looked up and into Pearl's eyes.

'I want to go with you,' he said. This time the anger was gone, replaced by something desperate, almost pitiful.

'We've been through all this, Vidar,' Pearl replied, flashing him a reassuring smile. 'You have to stay to ensure the monitoring equipment is working. It's only another two days.'

'But I want to go now.'

Pearl shook his finger at him as if scolding a child. 'Be reasonable. After so many months and so many accomplishments, why would you want to throw it all away now?'

He gently patted his fist against Stang's arm. 'You're our man, Vidar. You're the only one who can get it done. And don't worry. All the arrangements have been made. The container ship will dock off the barrier in two days' time to unload and you'll be able to get onboard then. Everything's been planned to the last detail.'

Stang stayed motionless, expression entirely unreadable behind his blank eyes.

'After we launch the seed, Helena and I need to fly back. But we'll be seeing you in under a week. You mustn't worry. We'll be together again soon.'

Stang could feel his breath quicken at the thought of them leaving. A surge of panic washed over him and he reached out, grabbing Pearl's shoulder. The sheer weight of his arm made the older man stagger back a pace.

'You can't go,' panted Stang. 'You can't leave me again.'

Pearl steadied himself, swallowing several times to regain his composure.

'Vidar, you do this for me and, I promise, you'll want for nothing when you're back in the real world. There's so much you've had to endure, so many sacrifices you've had to make. Together, we're going to right all that.'

As he spoke, he slowly released himself from Stang's grip and moved over to Coroni. She stared at him in confusion, eyes following his every move as he came around behind her and gently, but forcefully, gripped her by the shoulders.

'Look what you've been missing,' he whispered across to the Norwegian. Raising his gloved hand, Pearl pulled back a few strands of her long dark hair, revealing her high cheekbones and classic, Italian looks. Coroni flinched, her jaw clenching with revulsion as Stang's eyes slowly changed direction across to her, taking stock of her for the first time.

Unabashed, his pale eyes followed the line of her forehead and down past her nose, until finally they settled on her full, red lips.

'Think about it,' Pearl whispered, trailing his hand down her face and slowly pulling at the top of her jacket to reveal her neck. As a small square of tanned flesh became exposed, Stang's head tilted to one side, eyes transfixed by it as if he were savouring something sweet.

'Just two more days . . .' Pearl whispered.

'Now,' Stang countered, his voice rising like an imperious child. 'I want her now!'

Coroni stared wide-eyed as Stang stepped forward, his hand outstretched. She pushed back against Pearl for protection, but only felt the grip of his hand holding her tight.

'Wait, Vidar,' said Pearl, his voice breathing across her ear. 'You only get this at the end. You do your job and complete the mission. Then it's time for your reward.'

Stang paused, the decision held in the balance. Coroni struggled once more but Pearl dug his fingers viciously into her shoulder blade, making her groan in pain. Stang didn't seem to register the emotion, his eyes still locked on her lips, while his imagination took hold. He stepped closer.

'Please,' Coroni whimpered, eyes trailing across the charred skin of his face with pure disgust. As Stang reached out a hand towards her, Pearl slapped it away. 'Only at the end!' he shouted. 'Otherwise you get nothing!'

There was a moment of absolute silence. Then, slowly, Stang's massive head tilted down in frustration. Pearl released his grip on Coroni. Throwing off his arm, she half-ran, half-stumbled back to the helicopter.

'Come on, Vidar, she's just a distraction,' Pearl soothed him. 'Let's do what we came here to do. Let's launch the seed.'

It took Stang another thirty minutes to open the borehole and get everything ready. He moved with utter confidence, having practised the assembly over and over again throughout the early-spring months. Soon, the cradle for Pearl's capsule was ready and winched high above the borehole, pointing directly down into the ice.

Pearl watched, breathing deeply the whole time. He sucked in air through his nose, filling his lungs almost to bursting point. Inside his pocket, his left hand curled around the L-shape of his inhaler, marvelling at how long it had been since he had last used it. Usually, his chest felt unbearably tight and every few minutes he would squirt the cool gas deep into his lungs. But out in Antarctica, things were different. Out here the air was pure and crisp, utterly devoid of the sickness of the world's cities. It was how air was supposed to be, and the seed was the very first step towards redressing the balance.

Unclipping the sides of the briefcase, he removed an aluminium cylinder. It was smooth and almost entirely unremarkable, except for a vertical slither of glass that ran through its centre. Holding it up to the light, Pearl's eyes narrowed in on the single dot of red fluid contained within. It was tiny, like the faintest pinprick of blood in suspension. He shook his head, marvelling at how something so small and innocuous could herald nothing less than the dawning of a new era. From such small beginnings he would change the world.

If the tests on the lake went to plan, they would launch the seed in the Pacific in under three months. As the largest and most significant of all the world's oceans, it would be the perfect place to start.

Pearl carried the capsule across to the borehole, all the while muttering something under his breath. His eyes were wide as he loaded it into the metal casing of the cradle and locked it tight.

'History,' he said, resting his fingers lightly on the surface. 'That's what this is, history.'

Stang didn't respond, only pressing the button to activate the winch. A massive roll of steel cable began to uncoil behind them. A few seconds later, the capsule was immersed in the borehole and began to be lowered into the ice. Stang stood stock still, eyes following every metre.

'How long before it reaches the water?' asked Pearl.

'Forty-three minutes.'

Pearl nodded, instinctively checking his own watch. 'Good. You've done well.'

Just as he said the words, they heard the sound of an engine starting. They both turned towards the helicopter but the sound was much further away, echoing across the cliffs towards the old base. Stang immediately swung his rifle off his shoulder and, without averting his eyes, slid back the bolt action and chambered the first round. Stepping past

Pearl and shielding him with his own body, he searched for the exact source of the sound, but already he'd guessed it was the whine of the Ski-Doos' two-stroke engines.

The Englishmen must have somehow escaped.

'What is it?' Pearl asked.

Stang's expression hardened. He didn't want to admit to any of the previous day's events. 'Nothing I can't handle.'

Pearl's eyes switched across to the winch and the running cable. 'What if they go for the seed?'

'Even if they did, it'd take them more than thirty minutes to drive around the side of the mountain and get here. And then they'd have to get past me.'

'And if they talk?'

Stang slowly raised his rifle in his hand.

'There's nowhere for them to go,' he said with an air of finality. 'Trust me, no one will ever know that you were here.'

Pearl looked at him and smiled. Stang was right. There was no way that anyone could interfere with the seed's launch now and he needed to get back to the runway. The pilots had already contacted him on the helicopter flight over, complaining that the cloud level was dropping fast and they needed to take off as soon as possible. Besides, his visit was officially nothing more than a quick site inspection of GARI, and already so much time had been spent dealing with Stang.

'I don't want any mistakes,' Pearl said. 'You make certain that no one talks.'

Stang nodded, knuckles tightening on the rifle grip.

Pearl signalled to Coroni to start the engines and both men watched as she flicked the switches in her pre-flight check. Seconds later the rotors began to turn. Pearl then turned to Stang one last time.

'Like a son,' he repeated with a glowing smile.

Stang didn't reply. He felt his chest swell slightly with pride at the thought of being close to a man like Richard Pearl. He simply watched as Pearl turned and climbed on board the helicopter. As the rotors spun faster, kicking up the ground snow and whipping it across the whole drill site, Stang made no effort to shield his eyes or turn away. He stared, trying to savour every last detail of Pearl's presence.

Inside the cabin Coroni pulled on the collective, sending them pitching forward fast and low. The ground streamed past, soon blurring into a continuous flow of white as they accelerated towards the flanks of the mountains. Shadowing the line of a ridge, Coroni expertly twisted the aircraft right then left, flying only a few feet clear of the ground. Normally, Pearl would have objected to such aggressive manoeuvres, but he knew that she was still smarting from the incident with Stang. He had presumed that she would remain silent for the whole flight back and so was surprised to hear her voice crackle to life across the headset.

'Are you really going to have the boat wait for him in two days' time?' she asked, curiosity outweighing her indignation.

Pearl swivelled in his seat. He was smiling, eyes sparkling with undisguised glee. After so many years, he was finally about to get his revenge on Vidar's father, Fedor Stang. It had been Fedor, as ranking officer on board the stricken submarine, who had ordered Pearl to seal the doors closed on the rest of the crew. With two broken legs, Fedor had been unable to do it himself and had spent hours persuading, cajoling, and eventually threatening him. Pearl had been only a young man at the time, too lacking in confidence to challenge such a senior officer's command.

So he had done it. He had screwed shut the doors and sealed the other twenty-five men inside, leaving them to their fate. For hours they had heard their muffled screams, their pleas, and then their silence. All the while Pearl had implored Fedor to let him open the doors and release them. He had sobbed and begged, tried to reason with him and change his mind, but the Norwegian had been steadfast. In the end, Fedor had been right about how long the rescue teams would take to reach them, but it did nothing to change the fact that Pearl had been the one to murder all those men.

For years afterwards, he had wished he had been able to die in there with them and so be released from his guilt. Each night as he went to bed he could feel his chest constrict. He would gasp for air. It was as if he was right there with them, with the weight of water that surrounded the submarine pressing against his body, squeezing the life from him.

For three long years he had languished in the most pitiful depression. Then something inside him had snapped. It was like a release, finally allowing him to float to the surface, and he had immediately set about becoming the man he wanted to be. Finally, he was free to fulfil his own destiny.

'I gave Stang false coordinates for the ship,' he said. 'And he doesn't have enough fuel to last the winter.'

He paused for a moment, letting his gaze roam across the endless ice and deciding that it was a fitting tomb for the man they had just left behind. For the first time in years, Pearl's chest felt light and unencumbered.

Fedor Stang had died too soon. Only now, through his son, could he finally gain his revenge.

Chapter 25

The two Mamba APC vehicles stood in the far corner of the army barracks' hangar. Both were crippled by the scars of battle, a mess of dents and shattered glass. The soldiers had long-since departed, leaving pools of blood and empty shell casings spilling out across the concrete floor.

Bear Makuru sat in the shadow of the vehicles, slumped against an old ammunition box with a coarse grey blanket wrapped across her lap. Kneeling at her side was a young army doctor with a fresh face and light blond hair, who was busy administering a local anaesthetic. He had already cleaned the wire cuts at her wrists and bandaged them up, and was now trying to figure out how best to deal with the puncture wound running across her ribs.

'Looks like shrapnel as you thought,' he said, squinting closer. 'I can suture it now, but you'll still need to get it checked out properly. Could be fragments of clothing in there that'll cause an infection.'

'Thanks,' Bear said, as her eyes switched across to Kieran

Bates. He was standing only a few feet away, hovering impatiently. They stared at each other for a moment, but neither of them spoke. The deadlock was only broken when Bear felt the needle jab into her side and the pressure of the anaesthetic being forced in.

The doctor stood up then paused, his attention drawn to the line of dried blood trailing down from her ear.

'You got any loss of hearing?' he asked.

'Yeah. My right ear is pounding.'

'And your balance?'

'All over the place,' Bear replied.

The doctor shrugged. 'I'd need to do some tests, but you've probably ruptured the eardrum. We get that from time to time around here when the guys work with heavy ordnance.' He frowned, tilting his head a little closer. 'Looks like a bad one, though. I'll need to book you in for a scan.'

Bates stepped forward. 'Just stitch the damn wound,' he snapped. 'The rest can wait.'

Bear glowered at him, but remained silent as the doctor nodded hesitantly then hurried through his work. Using a pair of metal callipers, he clamped together the flesh to either side of the wound, causing blood to ooze out and dribble down Bear's ribs and back. She groaned in pain, but forced herself to remain still as he ran the thread through in neat surgical stitches.

Finally, the doctor straightened up to admire his handiwork but Bates had had enough.

'You're done,' he said, motioning for the doctor to gather

his instruments. They both watched as he scurried off, foot-steps fading away over the vast expanse of the hangar.

Bear expected Bates to say something then. Instead, he shifted from foot to foot with a strange, almost pained expression on his face.

'Did they hurt you?' he managed to say finally. Bear glanced down at her wrists, suggesting the answer was only too obvious.

'I mean, *hurt* you,' he repeated, but this time his eyes dropped the length of her body.

'No,' she whispered. 'Not like that.'

Raising the blanket over her shoulders, she retreated into the rough fabric. Her memory of the ordeal was still so rushed and confused. She could remember the hard pressure of a knife at her throat, tilting her head back, and then the hands, shoving, pushing and beating her, as they forced her on to the chair and tied her down.

She didn't remember screaming, but must have done so because her throat felt raw. At some point they had stuffed a filthy rag down her throat, almost choking her completely. It had been covered in some kind of cleaning agent, making her eyes water and mouth burn from the chemicals.

Bear had been expecting the worst, but once the gang had tied her down they had just left. Seconds had passed, each filled with the horrific certainty that they would be back at any moment and then it would begin. But nothing had happened. Instead, all she could do was listen to the sound of their voices through the gaps in the floorboards.

There was shouting, but it was in their native Xhosa and

she couldn't understand much of what was being said. It seemed as if one of the older gang members was warning the others, ordering them to wait, why she couldn't tell. Then there was the sound of a chair being pushed over, before finally the low hum of a TV. As the SABC news presenter droned the latest headlines of the day, it felt bitterly unfair and incongruous that outside the horror she was being subjected to, life was somehow continuing as normal.

Minutes turned to hours, and still no one came. Alone in the tiny room she had tried to escape, but with each movement of her wrists, the wire only bit deeper into her skin, until she had been unable to take the pain any longer. It was then that hopelessness overcame her. The inevitability of her fate seemed so clear she stared wide-eyed into the darkness, too despondent even to cry.

She was going to be raped. Not by one man, but by them all.

Time had passed in a kind of twilight, where she tried to detach herself from the reality of her situation. She fought hard to picture her son, to her the very essence of purity and love, but each time the image only stayed for a few seconds before the shadows in the room seemed to overwhelm it. Then she had tried to picture Luca, hoping that this time the image would last. She imagined him striding towards her through the crystal-clear snow of Antarctica, hand outstretched, that knowing smile of his playing across his lips. Then there was another shout from the room below and the dream seemed to slip from her grasp once more.

The truth was she couldn't detach herself, nor project her

mind to any other time or place. There was only now. And the realisation had made a cold sweat prickle across her neck. She was going to have to experience every moment of what was to come; to feel it in its most vile intimacy.

But then she had heard the sound of a truck's engine, and a few seconds later the roof had collapsed in a volley of loose bricks and timber. The next thing she remembered was seeing Bates.

Bear looked up into those same eyes.

'I got a report that a man name Loheso D'hala was killed in the fighting today,' he said.

'And?'

'The gang that took you . . . he's their main man. Apparently he got caught up in the fighting when he was coming back from a drinking shebeen. Looks like they were waiting for him to arrive before deciding what to do with you.'

Bear nodded slowly. 'Guess I was lucky,' she said, without any show of feeling. She decided to change the subject. 'Tell me, Kieran. Why did you come and get me?'

'I had a call from Luca out in Antarctica. He said you were in trouble and I was able to help. That's all.'

'So you just happened to fly ten thousand miles from London and then be able to mobilise half of SANDF? I don't suppose the South African military hand out vehicles and soldiers just like that. You must be some kind of guardian angel to pull that off.'

'Look, Luca is an old friend and . . .'

'*Assez!*' Bear shouted, raising her hands in protest. 'I never even told Luca I was in Nyanga. You've been feeding me bullshit ever since we first spoke. Now, I know you are up to your neck in it with Pearl and the seed, but right now that doesn't concern me.' She paused, levelling her gaze on him. 'I want to know what you've got Luca into. And no more lies, Kieran. If your friendship with him ever meant anything to you, you'll tell me what the hell is going on.'

Bates didn't answer for a moment. Instead, he let his gaze fix on the shard of light shining through the gap in the hangar doors. The truth was that they had lost all communication with Luca and the British team since they had first gone for the drill site. With all the predictions of bad weather, Bates had simply assumed that the attempt would be abandoned and all Luca would have to do was sit around in GARI for a few more days. But evidently that had not happened.

'We lost comms after the storm hit,' he said eventually. 'Honestly, that's the last we've heard from him. But Luca's a born survivor, Bear. If anyone will make it through this shit, it will be him.'

She remained silent, remembering the last conversation she had had with him on the satellite phone. He had suddenly stopped talking and then she had heard someone else on the line, just listening, before it went dead.

'You know,' Bates continued, 'Luca's not the one you should be worrying about right now.'

'Is that a threat?'

He shook his head. 'Threat? Six men are dead and most of the others are queuing up outside the infirmary. All because I ordered them to come and get you. So why don't you take stock of the situation? Haven't I already proved that I'm on your side?'

'My side? You're only on one side – Pearl's.'

'Look . . .'

'Stop the games!' Bear exploded, throwing off the blanket and standing up to face him. 'Pearl was scared that I'd blow the whistle on the whole project and he got you to do his dirty work. You came into Nyanga to try and silence me. Period.'

She stared at him, eyes burning with resolve. 'Understand this – I am going to expose Pearl for all his sordid bullshit. So, if I were you, Kieran, I'd stay the hell out of my way.'

Bates' voice took on an edge that Bear had never heard before.

'Who the hell do you think you are?' he hissed. 'You steamroll into a situation you can't possibly understand and then start issuing warnings. If it weren't so damn pathetic, Bear, it'd be laughable. This is so much bigger than Richard Pearl. But right now you have to understand something – I am the only person left on your side.' He paused then, seemingly to check his anger, before finally continuing. 'But I can only protect you from them for so long.'

'Them?'

Bates nodded as he glanced down at his watch. When he looked up again, Bear could see real concern in his eyes.

'Tell me what you know and I give you my word that I'll do everything I can to get you transferred to the British. That way I can protect you. But please, Bear, speak to me. We don't have much time left.'

The sincerity in his eyes scared her, but not enough to make her give it all up.

'What do you want from me?' she sighed, feigning dejection. 'I tried to stop Pearl and failed. That's it.'

'And the flashcard that Bukovsky gave you?'

Bear didn't avert her gaze. Bates could only have found out about that if they had already brought in Lotta and questioned her. They must have been on to her, right from the start.

'I don't have it . . .' she began, but he stepped forward and gripped her forearm.

'You can't beat these people,' he whispered. 'And you can't just leak this kind of information and expect to get away with it. They will come after you, your son, Luca – anyone who so much as touches that flashcard will be crushed. We're not talking about one man here. We're talking about the entire American government and trust me, they will *not* give up.'

Bear froze, a trail of dots suddenly connecting in her mind. The Americans couldn't have the flashcard out in the open because it implicated Pearl, who in turn was an American citizen. They must have known that the seed could cause one of the biggest environmental disasters the world had ever seen and yet were still content for it to be launched. So why would they deliberately try to trigger such an event?

The American boats . . . She had seen them lined up in dry dock in Cape Town harbour. There had been the tow cables on the stern with the coils of hydrophones attached. Bear had presumed they were heading up to the Niger Delta, but now she realised the boats weren't heading north at all. They were at the southernmost tip of Africa because it was the closest refuelling point to Antarctica.

This was all about America, all about oil.

If the US triggered a massive environmental disaster in the international waters of Antarctica and somehow managed to shift the blame on to another nation, that would put the entire Antarctic Treaty in jeopardy. The Americans could claim that the tenets of the treaty had been violated and that it was no longer binding. The entire continent would then be opened up for the taking, and the first nations on the scene would plant their flags and stake their claims.

Bear's expression went blank as she considered the ramifications. It would be the biggest land grab of the century, and if Bates was involved, then it followed the British government was too.

'*Putain*,' she breathed, as she wondered how many others were complicit.

Bates looked on, confusing her introspection with fear. He watched as she blinked several times before focusing on him once more.

'Now you listen to me,' she said. 'This *is* going to leak to the press, and you bastards are not getting away with it. So why don't you run away and hide? Go cover your tracks. And if governments fall, then so be it.'

Bates shook his head. 'You're wounded, weak, and taking on this whole thing like it's a personal vendetta. Do what's right for little Nathan, Bear, hand over the flashcard. It's the only play you have left.'

She glowered at him, the mention of her son's name making her eyes flash venomously.

'Don't you ever fucking talk about my son again!' she hissed.

'Give me the card,' Bates continued, 'or there is nothing more I can do to save you.'

'I don't have it. I mailed it to myself.'

'No, I don't think you did. There was no time to do anything else apart from run when you left Interjet.'

As he spoke, his grip tightened on her forearm. There was an urgency to the way he spoke that couldn't be faked.

'Once you're out of my hands,' he told her, 'there's no going back. It's the system, Bear. Even I can't change that. Please, do what's right for everybody.'

From the other side of the hangar they heard the sound of military boots. A team of eight men, dressed in black with M4 assault rifles at the ready, had rushed though the opening and was rapidly covering the distance between them. They fanned out in quick order, blocking the only other exit from the hangar.

'Back away, sir,' the lead soldier shouted, but instead of moving Bates stared into Bear's eyes. There was a sadness in his that suddenly made him look incredibly tired.

'I need you to back away, sir,' came the soldier's voice once more. 'Now!'

'You're on your own,' Bates whispered, before slowly moving to one side.

Bear stared from one face to the next as the soldiers advanced towards her.

'Don't you fucking touch me!' she shouted, retreating a pace. 'I am a French citizen. I have rights . . .'

The two leading soldiers rushed towards her. Bear lashed out with her arms, flailing them towards the closest man's face, but they bounced off his forearms as he easily defended himself. In a single movement he pivoted her whole body round, while the second soldier darted forward and jabbed a syringe pen into her neck. Almost immediately, Bear's legs gave way. Without another word, she went limp in his arms.

'You're early,' Bates said to the soldier in command.

The man only shrugged in response as Bear's body was dragged across the hangar floor and hauled in to the side of a waiting truck.

Chapter 26

Kieran Bates pulled open the iron door and stumbled out into the centre of the old farmyard. He felt sick and needed some fresh air, but it was already past midday and outside the searing hot sun of the Karoo Desert beat down upon the tin roofs and mud-stained, breezeblock walls with stifling intensity.

Pulling open the pack of cigarettes he had swiped off the counter, he jammed one into the corner of his mouth and lit up. He sucked back the thick, oaky taste of the American tobacco – his first cigarette in over eight years. He knew that he had a highly addictive personality and it had cost him a lot to quit. But today he just didn't give a shit.

He let his eyes survey one building and the next, feeling more tired than he could ever remember. The farm was one of the CIA's main interrogation centres for Southern Africa and comprised six outbuildings set about a central farmhouse, long-since defunct. The site was intentionally remote, with no phone lines or landing strips within a fifty-mile radius.

A dirt track was the single route into the whole complex, as dusty as it was interminable. It cut through the Karoo's boundless landscape with nothing but a solitary fence running to its left-hand side. Beyond there were no other signs of human inhabitation, only an occasional cluster of sheep chewing on dry cud.

Bates raised the cigarette to his mouth, then coughed violently. It was a vile habit and was only making him feel worse, but there was something self-destructive about the whole process. In some small way he felt it help ease the burden of what he had just seen.

Eleanor Page's contact out on the ice had informed her that Pearl had launched the seed. Over the ensuing twenty-four hours, Bates had watched events unfold with a mounting sense of disquiet.

At first everyone had waited, wondering if the seed would indeed chain react as it was supposed to do. From the Americans' point of view, another vital element was that it should penetrate the ice surrounding the lake and, in so doing, leach out into the open ocean. Although Pearl had discounted the possibility in his haste to succeed, the Americans had the original report that Lotta Bukovsky had sent to the FBI, and like her knew the ice to be much thinner than anyone had at first supposed.

But nothing about this was predictable. Throughout the entire waiting period, Eleanor Page had thrown herself into almost every other aspect of the operation, demanding updates when there weren't any, and insisting on progress when little or none could be made.

Already, she had positioned a boat called the *Sea Shepherd* off the coast of Droning Maud Land, having surreptitiously persuaded the famous environmentalist skipper, Dougie Hayward, that the Japanese were whaling in the area. The *Sea Shepherd* had charged off at once, her crew chosen specifically for their love of direct action and their incorruptible consciences. But they had been chasing phantom radar bleeps, with Eleanor keeping them close to the coastline so that they would be the first to see the fallout from Pearl's experiment.

Time passed, the uncertainty of it all making her second-guess every part of the operation. But then, the first effects of the seed had registered on the satellite imagery. It was out past the lake ice, spreading into the black waters of the Southern Ocean.

At first it looked innocent enough, with barely anything to report, but all that changed with time. From the lake's epicentre it spread out for one mile, then for two. On it went, the reaction defusing quicker and quicker, until it passed the edge of the floating icebergs and into the ocean proper.

Bates had stared at the satellite imagery, refreshing the page every few minutes as he watched Pearl's original dream of vast phytoplankton blooms become a holocaust of spiking nitrous oxide. The de-oxygenation of the water was complete, killing every living organism in its path. In less than a day, an immense desert had been created in one of the richest marine environments on earth.

Then came the emergency reports from Hayward and

the crew of the *Sea Shepherd*. Right on cue, the non-governmental charity had begun beaming back imagery via satellite to the news agencies, who were barely bothering to check its authenticity before splurging it on every channel and broadsheet.

And Hayward's imagery wasn't the dry abstract of a satellite photograph. It was stark and graphic. It showed the grim reality of millions of dead fish and krill floating on the surface of the water. They littered the ocean as far as the eye could see, just bobbing to and fro in the icy current, the only break in the apocalyptic scene coming in the form of the icebergs jutting up through the surface of the water.

But the headline grabber came in the form of a pod of orca whales that had been swimming near the port side of the vessel. Hayward had photographed their perfect white bellies as they lay upended, their hulking frames lapping up against the steel hull of the boat. Amongst the family unit was the smaller dorsal fin of a young adolescent. The tip was framed to the right of the picture, as it seemed to reach out, grasping for its dead mother. The composition was flawless, a Pulitzer by anyone's reckoning.

Bates had sifted through the imagery being fed back, his stomach turning at the sheer scale of the destruction. Eleanor Page had told him that the damage would be 'modest' and 'confined to the coastline', and he had gone along with the whole project believing that to be true. Instead, the despoliation was cataclysmic. What he was witnessing was nothing less than the death of an ocean.

Already calls had been made for the entire assembly of

Antarctic nations to meet in emergency session. Amongst the murky details and panicked reports, the question of who was to blame was starting to be asked and Eleanor was playing her contacts to the full. The culprit would be sought out, official channels stated, and punitive action taken, but behind each admonishment came a secondary message – if others had so blatantly violated the treaty, then why should any nation be forced to abide by its terms?

Bates shook his head in disgust and was about to throw what remained of the cigarette to the ground when there was a noise from the building just in front. He turned as a figure emerged, followed by a trail of thrash metal music. The sudden explosion of angry, screeching sound echoed around the farmyard before the figure mercifully slammed shut the sound-proof doors. Bates knew the interrogators often used loud music to keep subjects awake in the final hours of sleep deprivation.

The figure paced across the yard towards the main building, then spotted Bates and his cigarette. He paused, patting the breast pocket of his shirt looking for his own pack, before switching direction and approaching.

'Mind if I steal one of those?' he asked, stretching out his hand.

'Sure.'

Bates offered up the pack as the man tilted his head. One eye scrunched up as he peered closer at the security tag hanging around Bates' neck from a beaded chain. He seemed to relax after reading it and hoisted his white shirtsleeves a little higher, revealing pale, wiry arms. Bates guessed him to be about forty years old, but it was hard to tell given that the skin around his eyes was dark and mottled from lack of exposure to the sun.

'Name's Devin,' he said, his voice thick with an American drawl. 'You part of the programme? Because I haven't seen you around.'

'Just a drop off.'

'Right,' said the other man, stretching the word out. 'You're that English fella. I heard about it from some of the other guys. Got real nasty down in that township. Nanya or some shit.'

'Nyanga,' Bates corrected.

'Right.'

The man's squint narrowed as he sucked on the cigarette. He shifted round so that his back was to the sun, his face now masked by shadow.

'Well, I'll tell you something. I'm looking forward to getting the hell out of this place. Been cooking my ass off here for an age and thought I was about to be rotated out.' He took another deep suck on the cigarette, with the paper crackling slightly. 'No such luck. Fucking whole world's on fire right now, and I guess we gotta get to it.' He nodded. 'Thanks for the cigarette, though. Appreciate it.'

'Any time.'

Bates watched the man work his way back across the yard before scanning his pass through the side of the metal security door. The automatic lock buzzed open and he disappeared from view.

Devin must be one of the interrogators. His slow, affable

manner ran contrary to everything Bates would have anticipated from a man employed by the American rendition
programme. He shook his head at the thought. He had seen
the apparatus evolve from one or two exceptions that were
surreptitiously granted post 9/11, to a monstrous machine
that swallowed people whole. Rendition meant no lawyers
and no appeal, just hundreds of detainees lost to the 'system'.
For them, the days would blur one into the next, in a process
with only one stated aim – to break them.

First, new arrivals would strip for a medical and to be
photographed. Then they would be dressed in hospital gowns
and tied to the back wall of the cell. Sometimes just that
was enough to make them talk. Having to suffer the indignity
of shitting and pissing where you stood was a powerful
motivator.

Others, however, took more persuasion, and dehuman-
ising the subject and depriving them of any sense of time
or routine was the next step. Interrogations would be sporadic
and vary in length. The subjects would be moved from one
cell to the next in a ceaseless and seemingly pointless rotation. It gave them nothing to cling on to, no sense of order
or control. Combined with continual sleep deprivation, few
of the detainees lasted more than a week.

The concept of rendition was something that didn't sit
well with Bates. He liked things to have an end, closure
even, and while he had no issue with taking down the enemy,
he did have one with a rapidly expanding population of
detainees languishing indefinitely. Instead of a viable solution, rendition offered only a grey halfway house, where the

CIA put people that it couldn't quite convict in a trial. Invariably, the detainees ended up staying on a permanent basis.

That's why the situation with Bear filled him with such unease. Eleanor Page had insisted that she be taken to the 'farm' for questioning until the whereabouts of the flashcard were known. Bates had insisted Bear should stay under his control and, although that request had officially been granted, he suspected that, for the Americans, this was just the start of the whole process. Soon, they would transfer her from the site and he would be fobbed off with some technicality. Then she would be lost for good. Already he was starting to hear platitudes instead of real answers from the base commander.

All last night Bates had stayed awake, wondering what Luca would do when he found out that Bear was missing. Bates knew enough to realise that his friend wouldn't go quietly and wondered just how much wreckage would be involved along the way. He was going to have to find a way to control Luca, or at least deflect the blame from himself, but right now he didn't have the faintest clue how to go about it.

Finally turning back towards the main building, Bates stared at the drab breezeblock walls. It was too hot outside and he needed to get under some air conditioning. Just as he took his first pace forward, the door of the main building was flung open and two men clutching medical kits burst through. They sprinted across the yard, prising back the door of one of the adjacent buildings. Briefly the sound of grim thrash music filled the air before being mercifully silenced by the closing door.

A few seconds later Devin emerged. This time his pale cheeks were flushed with anger and he stalked across the open ground, swearing in a continual stream. His hands stabbed at the air as if admonishing some kind of invisible companion, before he followed the medics into the building and everything went quiet.

Bates waited, the minutes turning slowly. Nearly ten minutes passed, but still he stayed outside in the baking heat, his concern deepening with each one.

Suddenly the interrogator burst through the door once more, blinking in the daylight. The first thing Bates noticed was that his hands were dripping wet with blood. The palms had been stained a deep crimson and he had hitched up his shirtsleeves until they were nearly past his bicep.

'What's going on?' Bates asked. But Devin was so preoccupied that he hadn't even heard him speak. Instead, he immediately set off towards the main building.

'The stupid mother—' he muttered, quickening his pace.

'Hey, what's happening here?' Bates repeated, grabbing on to the crook of his arm and spinning him round.

Devin glowered at him. His eyes, once so languid and heavy, were blazing and small flecks of spittle had collected at the corners of his mouth.

'Fucking medics didn't do their job,' he seethed. 'I tell you, man, I am *not* going down for this one.'

'What happened?'

The man looked doubtful for a moment. Bates tugged at his arm.

'I have NSA clearance on this. Now answer me!' he growled.

'The woman's fucking haemorrhaging all over the floor. The idiots didn't spot it in the medical.'

'Haemorrhaging?'

'Yeah, she was pregnant.' The interrogator raised his arms skywards in sheer disbelief. 'Everyone has a medical when they arrive. Everyone! And now I've got a pregnant woman dying on me after only twenty-two hours of detention.'

Bates felt his hand slide off the interrogator's arm.

'Dying?'

The man shook his head slowly. 'Jesus. I've never seen so much goddamn blood.'

As he said the words, the last of the colour seemed to drain from Bates' face and he felt a terrible dryness creep into the back of his throat. He knew in that instant that he would never be forgiven, that something terrible and unmentionable would forever haunt him. He had played his part in causing Bear to miscarry, and now she was bleeding to death only a few yards from where he stood.

He shut his eyes, the nightmare closing in around him. He didn't make any attempt to go to her, knowing full well that the medics would never let him into the cell. But more than that, there was an overarching sense of shame; that he was so despicable he shouldn't even taint the same room with his presence. He had caused the death of Bear's unborn child and now it looked like her life was being thrown into the balance as well.

'I never meant anyone to get hurt . . .' he mumbled.

'Yeah, well. That's not really why we're here, is it?' Devin retorted, eyeing the Englishman with vague suspicion. He then waved a bloodied hand towards the main building. 'Look, I gotta get cleaned up and call this in. Christ knows how this shit is going to go down if she doesn't pull through.'

Bates nodded, vaguely aware of Devin moving away from him.

After all that had happened in the township, it seemed incredible that Bear should be dying now. Bates knew that he had to *do* something. He had to act. But how could he save her?

Chapter 27

The two Ski-Doos powered up the gradient, leaving fresh tracks in the otherwise unblemished snow. As they reached the top of the saddle, Luca pulled to a halt and jammed his fist down on the kill switch, cutting the engine. Behind him Joel and Katz did the same. For the first time in six hours there was silence.

They had traversed all the way across the lake on the original tractor route back to GARI. Now they looked straight ahead, eyes scanning the sloping expanse of snow. For hours they had built up the crevasse field in their minds, fear and anticipation creating a sea of monstrous séracs and sheer, precipitous walls of ice. But the route ahead showed nothing more than a few gentle undulations covered by a dusting of snow. It looked tranquil and inviting; the very antithesis of the danger that lay beneath.

They all knew that Sommers and Akira had frozen to death only metres from where they now stood. The crevasses were out there, waiting.

Dragging his leg over the saddle, Luca brought himself to his full height with a groan. He had been hunched behind the broken windshield of the Ski-Doo for so long that his back felt rigid, while his entire right hand was numb from holding in the throttle. As painful as his body was, it paled in comparison to his thirst. It had been nearly eight hours since his last sip of water in the old Soviet base. Now, his lips were swollen and sore. A thumping headache had settled over the middle of his forehead like a thundercloud. Luca knew that it wouldn't be long before dehydration really started to take its toll. Soon, the effects would become far more insidious.

Staggering across to the other Ski-Doo, he held the black Pelican case in his right hand and threw it down on the snow in front of Joel and Katz. Both men watched his every move, having battled their own thirst for the entire duration of the journey. Now, it was all they could think of.

Sliding the first of the three aluminium cylinders out of the protective foam, Luca was about to unscrew it when Katz suddenly cut in.

'If anyone's going to do it,' he said, 'I will.'

Luca stared at him for a moment, watching as Katz's tongue poked out to the edge of his lips in anticipation and wondering whether he might have some ulterior motive. But then he looked deeper into the scientist's eyes and even behind the reflective sheen of his glasses, could see the conflict within him. To men like Katz the lake water was the ultimate prize and, by extension, what they were about to do, the ultimate sacrilege.

'One canister. Eight hundred and seventeen millilitres split three ways,' Katz whispered, using his bare hands to carefully unscrew the lid. There was a low hiss as the pressure escaped before he raised the flask to his lips and poured.

The water felt ice cold, almost burning the back of his throat. As it slipped down he could taste a peculiar lightness to it, caused by the sheer absence of any chemical or mineral taint. It was unbelievable. He was drinking twenty-million-year-old water that had first existed at the beginning of the Miocene era.

The cylinder was handed across to Luca, who took his share before passing it to Joel. None of them spoke, each silently policing the amount the others were drinking, until finally Joel raised the cylinder and drained the very last drop. Silence continued, the same thought repeating across all their minds. It wasn't nearly enough. Just over two hundred and fifty millilitres had barely revived their parched throats, let alone quenched any real thirst. As Joel slowly placed the empty cylinder back in the case, they all looked at the remaining two with envious eyes.

Katz was the first to act, sliding off the Ski-Doo and slamming shut the lid of the Pelican case. The click of each lock signified that, for now, the matter was closed.

Luca then turned his gaze to the route ahead. He could only make out vague dips and slight variations in the colour of the snow; nothing that resembled the classic shape of a crevasse. The storms had blanketed snow over everything, making speed their only chance. All they could hope was that if they hit a crevasse, they would be travelling fast enough to glance across it.

Letting his eyes blur against the glare of the sun, he tried to shut out the thought of the previous guide, Harry Sommers. His fingernails worn away . . . That's what Bates had said, and instinctively Luca found himself balling his hands into fists as if to protect himself from the same fate. There was something terrifying about crevasses. Out of all the deaths that could befall a climber, a crevasse was the most feared. Unlike the others that led to mercifully swift ends, once inside a crevasse there was nothing else to do except die slowly.

There was a cough from behind him and Luca turned, realising that he had been staring blankly into the middle distance for some time.

'What do you think?' Joel asked.

'I'll go first,' Luca replied, trying to mask the uncertainty in his voice. 'I'll be lighter and can test the route. Just make sure you follow my tracks – and I mean exactly – and, for God's sake, keep your speed up.'

He paused, finding only one thing left to say.

'Good luck.'

As Luca moved towards his Ski-Doo, Joel suddenly raised his hand.

'Wait,' he pleaded. 'Just wait a couple more minutes. We need to talk about all this. You know, make a plan.'

Luca turned back, seeing the fear in his eyes.

'This is the plan, Joel,' he said softly. 'This has always been the plan. We're going to be out of water in a few hours and so, if we don't go now, that'll be it.' Then, as an after-thought, he added, 'I'm sorry.'

Joel shook his head in disbelief, before looking to Katz for support.

'Come on, Katzy, you're off-the-scale smart. There must be something we can do here? What we need is a strategy. A way round . . .'

He trailed off as he looked closer and saw Katz's expression. This was the first time he had actually looked terrified. The sight drained the very last of the fight out of Joel and he staggered back a pace, just managing to prop his wiry frame up against the side of the Ski-Doo.

'Come on, kid,' Katz said eventually. 'Don't make it any harder than it is.'

As he spoke, he reached forward and gently pulled Joel back on to the seat. Ahead of them, Luca revved the engine several times before jamming down the throttle.

He drove flat out down the slope, with the rev counter spiking into red with each jolt of the throttle. His whole body was pressed forward over the handlebars as he strained to see, while cold air rushed past his face with stinging intensity. Up ahead he could make out some of the bigger, more obvious crevasses, but knew that many more were out there, just inches below the surface.

The Ski-Doo powered along for nearly a kilometre, its tracks leaving a narrow, snaking trail. Just as he was daring to hope that he was past the worst of the field, the whole machine dipped down suddenly, almost causing him to lose his balance and roll over the handlebars. There was the sound of the tracks spinning, then, before he had time to realise what was happening, the machine lurched forward again, up on to the other side of a snow bank, tugging him back into his seat.

Luca glanced over his shoulder. There was a dark tear in the snow from where his Ski-Doo tracks had momentarily broken through the surface. But this time he'd been lucky and his momentum had carried him across. Signalling widely with his spare arm, he then looked ahead towards a low bank of twisting ice.

The disturbance was no more than a few feet high, looking as if a bubbling undercurrent of air had somehow broken through to the surface and frozen on contact. He powered towards it, trying to decide whether he should crash right over it or veer to one side. At the very last second, he jammed the handlebars sideways, throwing the machine to the right in a long, drifting arc.

As he passed around the side of the disturbance, he could see the colossal crevasse that had been lurking just behind. The opening was inky black against the brilliant white snow, and no less than twenty feet wide. He shook his head in disbelief. He had been moments away from being swallowed whole.

On Luca went, twisting the Ski-Doo around a series of huge crevasses that lay in jagged lines across his route. These were old, too ancient and established to be covered by the storms, but they were easy to spot and wide tracks of snow ran in between. He drove past them, trying to keep his eyes locked forward and resist the mesmeric pull of the dark interiors.

Finally, the convex shape of the slope changed, dipping into a compression. That meant no more crevasses. Slowly, Luca eased back on the throttle, before turning the machine round so that he was facing back up the slope.

It took him several seconds to spot Katz and Joel against the mounds and bulges of ice, but suddenly he saw their Ski-Doo no more than three hundred feet away. Even from a distance, he could see that Katz could barely keep control of the machine. He was trying to follow Luca's tracks but overcompensating with each turn, violently shifting their balance from right to left. With each swerve, the opposite track nearly lifted clear of the ground, threatening to topple them over and send them sprawling.

Luca watched, his lips moving in silent prayer. Then, just as they were rounding out on to the flatter area, he saw the whole front end of their Ski-Doo dip, catapulting them over the handlebars. For the briefest of moments, their dark silhouettes seemed to hang in the air before they were thrown forward and bounced down across the ground. Behind them, the machine spun lengthways, kicking up a hazy cloud of snow with each turn, until it finally came to rest with a resounding thud and a splintering of bodywork.

Luca stared at the destruction. Before he even realised what he was doing, he had begun to retrace his steps and head back up the slope.

Both Katz and Joel were on the ground when he arrived, limbs spread wide on the snow, while just to one side, only inches away from Katz's head, lay the Ski-Doo itself. It was a mess of broken parts and hanging tracks. The engine had already cut out, while a black stain of oil fanned across the snow like blood from a mortal wound.

Katz was the first to raise his head. His entire face was plastered in snow and he stared wide-eyed at Luca, still unclear as to what had actually happened. With a heavy groan he rolled on to his back and seemed to do an internal inventory of his body parts, twitching each muscle in turn before slowly coming to the conclusion that he was remarkably unscathed.

Joel, on the other hand, was not. When Luca rushed over and hoisted his head on to his lap, there wasn't the slightest flicker of reaction. 'Joel?' he shouted. 'Come on, Joel!'

Luca shook him slightly, then slapped him hard across the cheek. Nothing. He could see a long, raking wound across the top of Joel's forehead from where he had slid across the snow, but knew that it was only superficial. The real damage could be to his neck or spine as an impact like that could easily have snapped one of his vertebrae.

Katz stared across at Luca, trying to muster the strength to stand. He managed to pull himself up into a kneeling position, but then paused, gasping from the effort.

'Is he . . . breathing?' he panted.

Luca twisted his head to listen. 'Yeah. But he's out cold.'

'Has he broken anything?'

Running his fingers behind Joel's neck, Luca urgently kneaded the flesh for any sign of a break. After a couple of seconds, he looked up desperately.

'Shit! I don't even know what I'm doing. I'm not a bloody doctor.'

'If it's not obvious,' Katz managed, 'then it can wait.'

With that, he slumped over and lay on his back in the snow. He stared up at the clear sky, watching as his breath condensed in a cloud in front of him.

'You win,' he muttered, as if addressing the entire continent. 'You win, you bitch. I give up.'

'Give up?' Luca called. 'What the hell do you mean, give up? We've got to get Joel back to GARI. So get up and help me move him.'

Katz gave a scornful laugh. It came out as little more than a gurgle.

'Just admit it – we're fucked.'

'For Christ's sake, Katz,' Luca seethed, surprised by the rage in his own voice. 'The end of the crevasse field is two hundred yards away! Get up and help me.'

Katz barely seemed to register that he was being spoken to. Instead, he glanced down at his watch as if he had all the time in the world, before letting his shoulders slump back against the snow.

'The Emergency Antarctic Protocol runs out in two hours' time and then the plane's gone,' he said. 'We're over four hours away from GARI. So tell me, Luca – what's the goddamn point?'

Luca stared at him, still trying to ignore the reality of their situation. For so long he had been pressing on, turning a blind eye to any sense of logic or reason. Now Katz's words seemed to cut right through him. The man was right. They were never going to make it back before the plane took off. There was now only one prospect for them – they were going to have to wait out the winter in Antarctica.

Ten months. Luca tried to consider such a huge amount of time. It would be like the worst kind of prison sentence; each day an endless tedium with nothing to do but pace the cold corridors and wait for the season to change. He knew that he would go stir crazy inside that base, passing each hour and day without once having the opportunity to see Bear.

'We won't have enough fuel either,' Katz offered unhelpfully. 'I checked. The tanks were less than a quarter full. And now we only have one Ski-Doo.'

Luca looked up towards the horizon. The sun was just skirting across the far mountain peaks, threatening to set for the first time in five months. The darkness would give Antarctica another, more terrifying aspect, and the prospect made him absolutely desperate. He had never experienced such an absolute dread of a place. He just had to be free from it.

Forcing himself to his feet, he gently laid Joel's head back down on the snow before moving across to the Ski-Doo and flipping open the saddle. Inside was an assortment of old spanners and long-forgotten spares for the engine, but tucked right at the back amongst some sections of frayed rope was a thin piece of black rubber tubing.

'We'll siphon the fuel out of your Ski-Doo and combine the tanks,' he said triumphantly, raising the tubing. 'Come on! Get up and help me. That plane could be delayed by a few hours and, whatever happens, we've still got to get Joel inside.'

Katz looked on, too tired to refute this, but still made no effort to get up. 'Come on, Katz! What the hell else are you going to do?'

'Lie here,' he retorted, but already he knew that Luca was offering the only hope that remained. After a moment more he finally rocked his body forward and got to his feet.

Nearly an hour passed before they were ready. While Luca had been siphoning off the last of the fuel, Katz had spent the time searching for the black Pelican case with the water samples. Luca had looked on, astounded that he could let Joel lie unconscious on the freezing snow while he searched for his prize. After nearly twenty minutes Katz had found it dug into a section of soft snow a little further down the slope. Inside, the two remaining cylinders were intact.

As he returned triumphantly, Luca made no effort to hide his contempt.

'Glad you got what you were looking for,' he snapped. 'Now help me get Joel off the snow.'

They carried his deadweight over to the Ski-Doo and stacked him against the backrest. In all the time they had been working, he hadn't regained consciousness. Now, his skin felt deathly cold to the touch. The clock was ticking and both of them knew that they wouldn't have the strength to carry him to GARI if their single remaining Ski-Doo broke down.

Luca stared at the machine on which all their hopes were pinned. It was covered in dents and cracks, while an oily plume of unhealthy exhaust wafted out from behind. As he climbed on board, pressing up against Katz and Joel on the narrow seat, the Ski-Doo's suspension buckled under their combined weight. The underside of the seat was pressing right into the rubber tracks, and as he revved the throttle it began to grate with a horrible, lurching rattle. There was the stench of burning rubber and they both knew that it wouldn't be long before the track wore through completely and snapped.

'Hurry,' Katz said, as Luca jammed it in gear and, with a rattle of the exhaust, sent them forging off towards GARI.

Chapter 28

Vladimir Dedov stood outside on the metal gangplank at GARI. His eyes were narrowed as he watched the sun dip below the horizon for the first time in as many months as he could remember. Long shadows stretched out, bleeding into a uniform grey, before a pale, chilling darkness passed across the land.

Dedov inhaled on a cigarette before blowing out a cloud of smoke in the direction of the runway. It was seven kilometres away, but still he could hear the low rumble of the Ilyushin-76 jet. It was holding on the brakes at the start of the runway, powering up just before take-off.

Everyone from the base was on board, even little Hiroko. They had dragged the Japanese women from her nest in the top hatch before force-feeding her a powerful sedative. She had looked ghostly pale, with eyes wide and mistrustful. For so long her world had been little more than a few square feet of insulated attic. Now she was on her way home. Dedov shook his head, hoping that the psychiatrists back in Japan could mend such a broken mind.

The distant rumble grew louder as the plane careered along the runway. He spotted the first flash of a navigation light skirting low across the dark skyline. For the first time in many months, his eyes tried to adjust to the darkness and it took him a full minute to discern the outline of the plane flying towards him. A second later its huge fuselage scorched directly overhead and Dedov looked on as the pilots dipped their wings to say goodbye for the last time.

Finally, he was alone. Even the monstrous Ilyushin plane had fled before the onset of winter. The dawning realisation that he was hundreds of miles from the nearest science base made him feel as though he was the very last human being on earth and, instinctively, Dedov hunched his shoulders against the cold. He was well used to the sub-zero temperatures, but the darkness somehow made it feel all the more threatening, as if the cold were seeping in all around. He shivered, zipping up the collar of his jacket until it pressed right up against his chin.

Dedov had overwintered once before back in the 1990s and experienced the same deep-rooted sense of separation, as if marooned in the middle of the ocean. But that time he had been part of a skeleton crew of nineteen men. This was different. He could have another seizure at any minute and there would be no one around to help. If he fell down the stairs or choked on his own tongue, no one would even know that he was dead.

Dedov forced himself to shut out such fears and instead

try to be pragmatic. The ship was docking in only two days' time and he needed to get a message to the captain if he was to have any chance of getting on board. He had already tried to contact them via radio, but had yet to elicit a response. He knew that they would only be skirting alongside the barrier for a few hours while they unloaded the containers. It wouldn't give him much time.

Dedov sucked the air deep into his lungs until it almost burnt, caught between a sense of duty and his own need for self-preservation. If the British didn't arrive in two days' time, he could either leave them to their fate and attempt to reach the ship alone, or he could elect to stay the winter at GARI and wait for their eventual return, if they made it back at all. Although he knew the latter choice would all but guarantee his own death, there had been an element of martyrdom in his decision to stay from the very beginning. The truth was that he had failed to stop Pearl. More than that, he had been actively complicit in the whole diabolical scheme.

Dedov hung his head, remorse weighing heavily on his shoulders.

'If I was afraid of the wolf,' he said eventually, 'I should not have gone into the woods.'

He was about to move back inside when he heard a faint noise. It was some kind of vibration, just cutting above the silence of the landscape. He listened, wondering if perhaps it was still the aftermath of the hulking Ilyushin plane, but then the noise grew louder. As he stared out into the gloom, he saw a light winking in the darkness.

Dedov sprinted down the metal steps, the heavy clang of

his boots reverberating across the base. Striding out through the snow, he waited until the outline of a Ski-Doo appeared in its entirety. Three figures were slumped on top of it, so close as to be leaning into one another, while the machine itself rattled in the final stages of its death throes. Dedov stared in amazement before raising his hands in welcome.

'You made it!' he thundered, beaming with joy, then his expression dimmed as he realised the condition the men were in. He was just able to recognise Luca, slumped over the handlebars and shivering uncontrollably from cold. Frost had iced against his collar and jawline, and he stared at Dedov with hollow eyes.

'The plane . . .' he managed to say.

Dedov's gaze switched briefly up to the sky, where only a few minutes ago the Ilyushin had thundered overhead. The British were in no state to handle the truth. First, he had to get them inside.

'Everything will be OK,' he said, grabbing Luca under his arms and manhandling him off the Ski-Doo. As Luca was dragged clear, Katz slumped forward in the seat, too weak to keep himself upright with the weight of Joel's body pressing down behind him.

Hoisting Luca's body across to the hangar entrance, Dedov bundled him in before staggering back outside for the others. By the time he had them all lying inside the main base next to the heating vents, rivulets of sweat were running down his face. He stood staring at them and wondering what on earth they had been through since they had last met.

'Water.'

Dedov turned to see Luca's head raised an inch off the ground.

'I have put kettle on for tea,' he replied. 'Just one minute.'

'Please . . .'

'Of course,' Dedov said, suddenly realising just how thirsty they all were. Rushing out of the room, he returned a few seconds later with three coffee-stained mugs brimming with tap water. Luca reached up, but his hands were trembling too much for him to be able to drink unaided. Instead, Dedov knelt at his side, gently helping him. He watched as the excess spilt across Luca's chin but he didn't stop drinking for a second, his throat bulging as he gulped down as much as he could.

'Careful,' Dedov warned, slowly pulling the mug away. 'Too fast will make you sick.'

Luca nodded, then looked towards Katz and Joel. Katz had immediately fallen asleep, while Joel still had not regained consciousness. His face was sheet white in the harsh neon lighting, while his breathing was shallow and weak.

'Give the others water,' Luca said, before his head dropped back down on to the floor. A second later he was asleep.

Nearly six hours passed before Joel stirred.

He cried out in panic as he came to, screaming a stream of unintelligible words. His eyes were wide, but there was a blankness to them, as though he wasn't able to recognise anything he was seeing. Luca was sleeping right next to him and soon woke with all the commotion. It took several seconds for him to understand what was happening, before he reached across and tried to pin Joel down. By now his arms and legs were flailing widely and he had rolled off the couch where he had been laid and on to the hard floor.

'Dedov!' Luca shouted. 'Help me!'

The Russian arrived, panting from having sprinted down the corridor.

'What is wrong with him?'

'He was like that when I woke,' Luca replied before turning his gaze back to Joel. 'You're safe,' he said, repeating the words several times. 'You're back at GARI. Just take it easy.'

Joel's gaze fixed on him, but before he had time to speak his eyelids drifted closed and his body went limp again. Then there was only the sound of his snoring. Luca pulled away, slumping back against the side of the couch.

'Jesus,' he whispered, still trying to collect himself after such an abrupt awakening. 'He needs to be in a proper medical facility. He has to get out of here.'

Dedov stared at him for a moment before reaching across and hoisting Luca to his feet.

'We have much to discuss,' he said, leading him out towards the kitchenette and away from the others.

After three cups of tea and nearly a loaf of toasted bread, Luca had successfully recounted the details of their journey. Throughout his entire monologue Dedov's expression had remained set, his gaze only averted from Luca's so that he could light the next in a near-continual stream of cigarettes. As Luca spoke, Dedov stared deep into his eyes, searching for the slightest tell that he might be inventing parts of the story, or indeed omitting others.

The only time Dedov showed any emotion was when Luca recounted the story of Andy McBride's death. Then he had slowly shut his eyes, repeating twice that it was such a senseless waste of a human life. For a long time afterwards both men remained silent, with only the sound of the kettle filament sizzling from lack of water filling the room.

Eventually, Luca leant back in his chair.

'So with the plane gone, there's nothing to do but wait,' he said. As he spoke, his eyes passed over the room, already finding it depressingly small.

Dedov shook his bulbous head. 'Plane is gone, but there is container ship. The *Akademia Federov* will be arriving in two days off the coast of Droning Maud Land. Now that you are here, we will catch this boat together.'

Luca's eyes suddenly filled with energy. 'A boat? Why the hell didn't you tell me that in the beginning?'

'I wanted to hear what you had to say first.'

Luca ignored him, too excited to deal with the Russian's idiosyncrasies.

'You're sure there's a boat coming? Like, a hundred per cent?'

'I have already tried to reach them by radio, but am not yet successful.'

Luca stood up, a disbelieving smile appearing on his face. Dedov's news changed everything. For so long, he had been steeling himself to accept the reality that they would have to spend months in the darkness of Antarctica. Now it felt as if a crippling weight had just been lifted from him. They could be back in Cape Town in under a week!

'This is amazing news,' he whispered. 'Amazing!'

He looked around the room. 'But we've got to get packed up. Get everything ready.'

'We have time to prepare,' Dedov assured him, seeing his excitement. 'We can drive tractor or even Ski-Doo to ice barrier. We have four machines in garaging unit and journey is no more than five hours. Maximum.'

Luca's smile widened. In just a few seconds everything seemed to be back on an even keel. As he stared at the Russian, he thought over the sequence of events in the last few days.

'Would you have stayed?' Luca asked eventually. 'I mean, if we hadn't got back here in time, would you have waited out the winter?'

'I could lie to you and say yes, but the truth is that I had not decided.'

Luca raised an eyebrow, appreciating the Russian's honesty. For so long, he had harboured a multitude of suspicions about Dedov and yet, as on the first occasion they had met, he found himself wanting to believe everything this man said. Maybe it was just his manner, but it always seemed as if Dedov were telling the truth.

'I want you to tell me something,' Luca said finally. 'Did you know what Pearl was planning? With the whole second drill site and the seed.'

'Yes,' Dedov replied evenly.

'So why are you helping us? The last guy we met did everything he could to stop us from getting out and telling anyone about it.'

'The man you met is called Vidar Stang,' Dedov explained. 'He is a very dangerous and troubled man. But all the same – he is devoted to this project.'

He paused, fingers stroking his thick beard. 'Whether you believe me or not, I am not such man. I work for Pearl because I am forced to. He holds my son hostage in America.'

Luca stared at him sceptically, but found only a sad sincerity in Dedov's eyes. They glazed over as the Russian's thoughts turned to his only child.

'He holds my son captive and I am not a strong enough man to sacrifice my family. For me, this is only thing left.' He paused, sniffing loudly as he tried to shake off the image he had been sent of his son with Pearl in San Diego. 'This is why I told you to go a different way across mountain and gave you satellite phone. I wanted you to find the second drill site and tell to the British government. I needed you to do it, because I cannot.'

He puffed out his chest, accepting his own culpability. 'But I made a mistake and forced you to shelter at Stang's base. For this, you have my apology. I deceived you.'

Luca remained silent. Every instinct told him that Dedov was telling the truth. He thought back to Bates and all that he had said about 'the poet' and his smuggling operation. None of that seemed to be connected to Pearl.

'There's something else,' Luca said. 'I need to ask you a question.' The Russian nodded, signalling his acquiescence. 'Did you smuggle uranium through this base?'

Dedov recoiled in shock. 'How did you hear about such things?'

'Just answer the damn question.'

Dedov thought for a moment, then reached forward and lit another cigarette. He blew the smoke up into the haze already there.

'Regrettably, the answer is yes,' he replied. 'Nearly fifteen years ago, when I worked as a radio operator at Novolazarevskaya Station, my brother-in-law approached me. He was a big military man and proposed a way for us to make a fast buck. We did four shipments, but it was a long time ago and now, I assure you, this part of my life is over.'

'When was the last shipment?'

'I have already told you!' Dedov snapped, slamming his fist down on the table. 'Last one was fifteen years ago, after the collapse of the Soviet Union. Now, everything is different. With Putin in charge, there is no smuggling, no uranium.'

Luca thought back to Bates and the urgency with which he'd needed the spyware inserted in GARI's main communication room. It seemed improbable that this had anything to do with Dedov's smuggling days. It had to be connected to Pearl and the seed.

Luca stared across the table. The time for secrets was over.

'I asked the question because I was sent here for two reasons,' he said. 'The first was to get the scientists to the drill site. The second was to plug a certain type of spyware into the main computer here at GARI.'

'Spyware?'

Luca shrugged. 'I don't know much about it, but a contact

of mine in the British government gave me this job. He wanted to monitor all satellite communication coming out of this base and told me it was all to do with your smuggling.'

Dedov paused for a moment, trying to process the information. 'So, Snow Leopard. We deceived each other.'

'Yeah. It looks that way.'

'Then let us see what this spyware does on our computer.'

Dragging back his chair and standing up, Dedov signalled for Luca to follow, leading him back along the narrow corridor to the base's main communication room.

It was small, with floor-to-ceiling shelving crammed with heavy radio transmission sets and wiring. It looked as though a physics professor had taken issue with most of the devices as almost all of them had their front faces stripped off, revealing the raw components and circuitry behind. Silver wire and the occasional crocodile clip ran in between, while to one side a large computer screen stood on top of an old-fashioned writing desk.

Dedov heaved himself down on to the swivel chair. As he took hold of the mouse and opened up the email system, Luca peered closer. The writing was all in Russian Cyrillic.

'You plugged in a memory stick?' Dedov asked.

'They said the programme would run itself and that it would help to crack the encrypted messages you were sending out.'

Dedov shook his head at such fanciful notions. 'I send no encryption, just normal email for normal Antarctica matters. Weather and such like.'

He fell silent, leaning closer towards the dull glow of the

screen as he scanned for any irregularities. His left hand hovered over the keyboard, occasionally holding down a command, while his right moved the mouse with surprising dexterity. Luca saw that he was scan reading all the emails in and out of the base, and the process continued for nearly fifteen minutes.

All the while Luca stared blankly, unable to read the dense lines of text. The close heat of the room was starting to make him feel woozy and it was all he could do to stop his eyelids from drifting closed. He had slept so little in the last few days that as soon as he wasn't actively focused on something, his body seemed to shut off. He felt his head gradually tilt down to his chest and his breathing start to slow. Just as he was slipping into a deep, comfortable sleep, he heard Dedov creak forward in his chair.

'Mother of God,' he hissed, prodding his finger on to the screen and leaving a circular grease mark.

'What is it?' Luca managed to say, widening his eyes.

'I never sent this email,' the Russian said, before scrolling through the sent items and stopping once again. 'Nor this one.'

'What do they say?'

For a moment he didn't respond. Instead he re-read the emails several times over. Finally he turned away from the screen. 'They talk of extra drilling equipment and certain logistics. In short, they say that I am responsible for launching seed. That I am one who planned it all.'

'But why would the British want people to believe that it was you?'

Dedov stared at him. 'I was hoping you could tell me that.'

As he spoke the electricity suddenly flickered then cut out. There was a whir as the computers shut down and then only a faint ambient light reaching in through the double-glazed window. It was eerily calm and the sudden darkness made both men feel disorientated.

'Don't worry,' Dedov said. 'We have back-up generator. It will start directly.'

As if on cue, the lights flickered back on and suddenly everything returned to normal. With a sigh of relief, Luca was about to continue when the same thing happened again and the lights went out.

Both of them waited once more, but this time nothing else happened. The darkness only deepened.

'Don't concern yourself,' Dedov said. 'This happens from time to time. Generators are still running in properly. But, in any case, we have plenty of spare parts.'

Luca ignored him. 'How many people got off Pearl's helicopter?' he asked suddenly.

Dedov thought for a second, having briefly caught sight of the helicopter as it came into land.

'Two. There was only Pearl and the woman pilot.'

Even in the dim light, Luca could see the realisation dawn on his face.

'You mean, Stang is here?' Dedov asked in alarm.

Luca stood up, feeling the same sense of dread wash over him that he had experienced in the old Soviet base. In the darkness Stang had crept up on him without a sound. Now

Luca felt as though the man were standing right behind him again. Turning in his seat, he checked the door as if expecting to see those grey, merciless eyes once more.

'He must be going for the generators,' Luca blurted out. Jumping up from his seat, he sprinted down the corridor, ricocheting against the sidewalls in the gloom. He heard Dedov bellow behind him, but kept running until he slammed into the storm-sealed door at the end. Heaving it back on its hinges, he felt the cold rush in, tensing every muscle in his body.

There, on the other end of the gangplank in the second module, was the generator house. At first Luca just stared, but then he saw a flicker of orange and the first flames come creeping round the seals in the door. Just as he was about to venture out on to the gangplank, there was a loud crack as the window in the generator house suddenly shattered from heat. Inside, a fire was raging.

Dedov arrived next to him, staring at the same scene.

'If we miss that boat,' Luca said, 'we're dead men. We can't survive the winter now.'

Dedov grabbed hold of his shoulder, pulling him away from the entrance and sealing the door.

'Get back inside,' he hissed. 'He'll be coming for us.'

Chapter 29

Over one hundred and twenty delegates from the combined signatories of the Antarctic Treaty sat around a colossal U-shaped table in the ballroom of the Dorchester Hotel in London. The unprecedented events occurring in the Southern Ocean had forced every nation to send a representative and now, a long line of placards with their names neatly stencilled in black ink ran the length of the table. They had been printed with such haste that two were spelt incorrectly, while another was missing altogether.

Behind the seated men and women was a small army of underlings positioned on faux-gilt and red velvet stacking chairs from the ballroom stock. They lined the periphery with their laptops balanced awkwardly on their knees, rising every few minutes to shuttle messages forward to the official representatives or talk on the sidelines in hurried whispers on their cell phones.

Normally, a general malaise of tedium and political

manoeuvring typified such gatherings, but today was different. There was a fervoured sense of purpose among the group, made worse by the stream of outright accusations that flowed across the table as the two main players attempted to absolve themselves from any blame.

As the delegates' shouts echoed against the intricately corniced ceiling, an American with silver hair and a heavily lined face stared out from the low stage at the front of the room. His slow, penetrating eyes took in the array of emotions that were reflected on the delegates' faces. There was anger and disbelief, sadness and outright indignation; the scale of the environmental disaster they faced was greater than any of them could ever have imagined.

Eventually his gaze turned a full ninety degrees and settled on Eleanor Page, sitting just out of sight at one side of the stage. She had been watching quietly for the last two hours. With a nod of her head, she signalled for him to proceed with the prepared statement.

Tapping the microphone several times, the American managed to restore a semblance of order.

'After due consideration, the United States of America concurs with the Chilean proposal,' he said. Sensing what was coming, silence gripped the room. 'We support their motion that the Antarctic Treaty be suspended in its entirety pending a review.'

The announcement was greeted by shock. When the Chileans had tabled the motion nearly an hour ago, it had been met with incredulity and all but dismissed out of hand. But now the Americans had just added their weight to it, and in so doing had made it all but certain that it would be passed.

In just a few hours a treaty that had remained in effect for over sixty years would be dismantled. It had survived the pressures of the Cold War when Russia and America had skirted the continent, building science bases in lieu of military ones, and had competed in every indirect way imaginable. But always they had respected the ban on the commercialisation and militarisation of the seventh continent. And by extension the same adherence had rippled out across all the other nations vying for position in their wake. Against all odds, the Antarctic Treaty had worked.

'In light of the unprecedented environmental damage we have seen,' the American continued, switching his focus to the Russian delegation seated opposite, 'we propose to send our fleet immediately to the Southern Ocean, to make an initial assessment and begin doing what we can to reverse this terrible tragedy.'

As if to remind the assembly what he was referring to, he glanced behind him at an enormous projector screen. A satellite image depicted the Southern Ocean and a basic outline of the Antarctic coastline. A rough boundary line had been overlaid depicting the extent of the de-oxygenated water. It covered thousands of square miles of ocean, spreading out like a great stain on the face of the planet.

The single piece of positive news was that the reaction had been slowing over the last forty-eight hours, and at three o'clock that morning they had received an unconfirmed report that it had actually stopped.

'The United States of America has the capability to perform this task and she will do so, the best she can.'

He stopped on a patriotic note, gaze still fixed on the three men fronting the Russian delegation as if daring them to retort. They remained silent, faces still flushed at the sheer extent of their vilification.

For them the emergency meeting had started in a whirlwind of partial information and unconfirmed reports as everyone fought to understand the extent of the crisis. As one of the two major players in Antarctica, Russia had an interest in almost every facet of life on the continent and had never been shy of voicing her opinion. But then things had shifted. Slowly but surely, it had been implied that responsibility for the calamity lay with them.

At first it had been only muttered accusations, which the Russians had hotly denied, but then a consensus seemed to build and so-called evidence was circulated. Only after it had passed through the hands of almost every other nation around the table were the Russians finally shown the damning report, leaving them reeling. How could it have come to this?

As the long-standing head of the prestigious Antarctic Research Institute on Bering Street in Saint Petersburg, Sergei Lukinski had at first refuted the report in a fury. Little over an hour later he slumped back in his chair, steeped in shame and disbelief. What was there left to say?

He had been a colleague of Vladimir Dedov's for the last thirty years and, while Lukinski had always found the man to be a headstrong maverick with little regard for the rule book, he just couldn't believe Dedov capable of an ecological crime on this scale. If there was one thing Lukinski was sure of, Dedov had always loved Antarctica. He would never knowingly have tried to harm it.

But somehow the British had irrefutable evidence of his involvement. Lukinski's mind boggled as to how they had procured it so quickly, but he had had little time to dwell on that. As the news spread that a member of the Russian Polar Academy was responsible for such unimaginable destruction, the other delegates had distanced themselves as though the disgrace had suddenly become contagious. Nations that would never have dared so much as to voice a word of dissent, now stared with brazen hostility across the table. It was as if the Russian shame was shining like a spotlight on their placard.

Lukinski was an intelligent man, well suited to politics, but in the face of such united condemnation he could only look on as the Americans took centre-stage. As the motion was officially tabled for a dismantling of the Antarctic Treaty under Part 12, Protocol 7, he lowered his gaze to the floor. Cloaked in the most impenetrable legal language, he knew that the underlying message was actually very simple. Antarctica was up for grabs. And once the land claims started, every nation would be forced to follow suit or risk being left with nothing.

Once it was done, it could never be undone. No one would ever willingly give back land. Finally, the last unclaimed chunk of the planet was to be carved up. Lines would be drawn and argued over, the true nature of ownership made all the more surreal by the sheer absence of natural features in the vast, frozen expanse.

Lukinski only half-listened to the translation echoing in his earpiece. By controlling the clean-up operation, the Americans would make themselves 'responsible' for almost the entire eastern ice shelf of Antarctica. With three thousand summer workers already stationed at McMurdo, plus their showcase station at the Geographical South Pole, they would soon control the lion's share of the continent.

Lukinski knew that under any other circumstances he would have insisted that Russia play an equal role in the clean-up operation and mobilise their winter fleet. But no one would accept their involvement. Not now. Not after such absolute disgrace.

As the American turned to walk off the stage, head bowed with grievous duty, Lukinski eyed him warily. It did seem as if the Americans were remarkably well placed to be able to action the clean-up so soon. They were driving things forward at an unstoppable pace, and by coincidence, seemed to have the right assets in place to back up each move.

Lukinski's eyes darkened. To him this stank of a set up, but as suspicious as he was, he knew that once the memorandum was passed and the Treaty dismantled, the world would forget the details. In the confusion only two points would be remembered – Russia had caused the disaster, while the US had cleaned it up.

The American seemed to pause at the edge of the stage, eyes briefly connecting with someone hidden in the wings. He then took his place at the great table and, with all the gravitas of a man charged with saving the fate of the Southern Ocean, began issuing orders to the tide of underlings already massing behind his chair.

Fifty feet away, Eleanor Page exited the room through an unseen service entrance towards the back of the mighty ballroom. She moved at a brisk pace down the whitewashed, utilitarian corridor, heading for a car parked just outside. As she walked her eyes stayed locked on the small screen of her mobile phone, waiting for the signal to register.

On the face of it, she had much to be pleased about. All but two of the fleet were already heading south from Cape Town, while the other boats were in the final stage of preparation and would be clear of the harbour by the end of the day. Her other main concern had been the Russians at the emergency meeting, but they had been far less vocal in their defence than she had anticipated. She shook her head, amazed even now by how proud the Russians were, and how easy it was to manipulate that pride. Once they had been publicly shamed they had stared like sullen schoolchildren, reeling from the injustice of it all.

It had been remarkably easy to persuade the rest of the world that Vladimir Dedov was to blame, and as long as she managed to quash any evidence to the contrary, she now felt certain that things would run their course.

One of her security detail was standing by the exit, holding the heavy door to the street ajar. Passing through into the daylight, she immediately pressed the redial button on her phone as the waiting car started its engines. There was a

PATRICK WOODHEAD

frustrating pause, during which Eleanor felt the muscles of her cheek twinge several times, before the line finally connected.

'Get me Kieran Bates,' she said.

The only thing that remained undone was to find the flashcard Beatrice Makuru had hidden. It was all that linked Pearl, and by extension America, to the seed.

Chapter 30

A flurry of sand swirled into the room as Bear opened her eyes. She watched it settle across the meagre furnishings before there was the sound of the barn doors being slammed shut against the wind. Outside, a storm was raging across the Karoo Desert.

Her gaze slowly drifted from one item to the next in the room. She could see the underside of two faded plastic chairs only a few feet away; further back along the side of the breezeblock wall coils of rope hung on nails. Closer up, she could see a thin plastic pipe running down into her own forearm, the end lost to a gauze bandage that ran tight across the muscle. Bear stared at it for several seconds, trying to work out what it was. She had been unconscious for so long that everything felt abstract and new. Eventually, she realised what she was looking at – they were giving her a blood transfusion.

Bear shifted her weight on the mattress. Immediately, an intense cramping pain shot up through her stomach. She gasped, waiting for the throbbing to subside, when from somewhere deep within her subconscious, a sudden panic took hold. Delving her hands between her thighs, she started to tremble as the memories came flooding back.

'No, no, no,' she groaned, raising her hands and tilting them towards the light. There on her palms was a weak stain of blood and for the longest time she stared at it, transfixed by the sight. Then, suddenly, she begun pawing at the hospital gown she was wearing, dragging her palms across the fabric as she tried to wipe the stain away. But with each attempt, the blood only seemed to smear further up her wrists. She started to scream, thrashing from side to side on the mattress, until two arms shot out, pinning her down.

Bear looked up and into the face of a man with a dishevelled black beard and a pursed slit of a mouth. He was regarding her with a look of utter dispassion, like a butcher might a carcass on a meat hook. With a heave of his brawny arms, he wrenched her off the mattress and on to a stretcher set on a gurney standing just to one side. At the sudden movement the IV line whipped round, nearly detaching itself from Bear's arm.

'Careful!' shouted a voice from somewhere behind. 'Do it slowly!'

Concealed in the shadows at the back of the room, Kieran Bates looked on. He wore a light blue T-shirt and desert-style camouflage trousers, and stood with arms folded tight across his chest. His expression was fixed, masking a virulent contempt for the American brute in front of him, now securing Bear's body to the stretcher with thin cargo straps, ratcheting them tight as if he were packing boxes.

'Get her into the van,' Bates ordered, trying to keep his tone level, before he turned and vanished into the sandstorm outside.

Bates walked across the windswept courtyard with his body tilted forward. His eyes were narrowed almost to closing as the visibility had dropped to only a few metres. Several seconds passed before he was even able to find the security door in the neighbouring building. He ran his card down through the slot and heard a low buzz as the lock clicked open.

Once inside he dusted down his shirt before running his fingers across his face, trying to get the worst of the grit out of his eyes. When he finally looked up, the base commander of the interrogation site was staring at him across the makeshift office.

'We still haven't been able to reach Langley,' he said, tilting back in his chair. 'Satellites are down in this goddamn storm.'

Bates shrugged as if disappointed. 'Storm or not,' he said, 'we've got to get her moving. You heard what the medic said.'

The commander nodded, having no intention of letting one of the detainees croak on his watch. With the British agent volunteering to escort her out, he wouldn't even need to sacrifice some of his already overstretched team. There were only fourteen of them on the entire site and, with the wind as it was, he was going to need every available man just to secure the farm's dilapidated roofing. Already a chunk had been ripped off one of the smaller, outlying buildings.

Although the British agent was ostensibly in charge of the new detainee, he knew well enough that any transfer off the base had to have the prior consent of Langley, even in a medical emergency. The commander had been trying to reach them for the last three hours, but so far all communication had been severed by the dust clouds and swirling storm outside. It had happened once before and lasted nearly two days.

'Sure you don't want to wait till this clears up? We can get a chopper in as soon as the wind drops a little. Looks like it's rough out there.'

Bates sucked in air through his teeth, as if deliberating. In fact, he had spent nearly an hour speaking with the medic, plaguing him with doubts as to the seriousness of Bear's condition. Previously the medic had been content simply to monitor the situation and see how things went. Now he was advocating an immediate evacuation, such was the power of persuasion and the desire of most people to cover their own back.

After a moment's pause, Bates shook his head. 'Used to drive the Land Rover 110s in Iraq so I'm used to this kind of storm. And truth be told, I could do with getting out of here myself. Got a touch of cabin fever.'

The commander nodded, appreciating the sentiment. He swivelled in his chair, turning straight on.

'What did you Brits call those things again?' he asked

casually, but the years of supervising interrogations had given him an intuitive need to verify every fact. He had done two tours of Iraq himself and once been briefly seconded to the Regiment, as the British liked to refer to the SAS.

'The 110s?' Bates asked. 'Pinkies. Comes from the old desert rat days.'

The American smiled at the British penchant for eccentricity. 'Yeah, that's right. Pinkies,' he repeated. 'Anyway, we still got the VHF up and running, so you should be able to radio in if the first bit's too much.'

'Got it,' Bates said, nodding. 'I'll call this into Langley myself as soon as I get a signal. I'm guessing that'll be a few hours from now, or I can do it when I arrive in Cape Town.'

'Just call it in as soon as you can,' the commander replied. 'You know that technically no one moves without *their* say so. But I'll let you go as long as she's strapped down and sedated. You need me to send someone with you? Real fighter this one.'

'She's already out cold. Drugged her myself. And don't worry, your man's already given me the contact for the hospital. I'm all set.'

Taking a hooded, windproof jacket off one of the pegs by the door, Bates shoved his arms through the sleeves before pulling a handkerchief from his pocket. It was spotted, the ends tied into small knots. The American's smile returned at the thought of an Englishman actually carrying such an item of clothing, and he looked on as Bates secured it across his mouth like a highwayman to protect himself against the dust.

'Take it easy out there,' the commander called. Bates nodded as he grabbed a rucksack off the floor and stepped outside.

Sand hit the metal bodywork of the van in a constant, driving gale. With the windscreen wipers on full, Bates peered over the top of the steering wheel, trying to decipher the edge of the dirt road. Every so often, the right side of the car would dip down as they veered a little too close to the drainage chute, before he quickly corrected their course.

In the passenger seat beside him, Bear was slowly getting dressed. Only a mile out from the farm, Bates had stopped and undone the strapping on the stretcher, allowing her to climb through to the front. Now, she shuffled silently from side to side on her seat, pulling a pair of trousers on under the hospital gown, followed by a sand-coloured shirt that was a few sizes too large.

The whole process required effort, and Bear felt weaker than ever. Every few seconds she was forced to lean against the window for support while a sick line of perspiration welled out across her forehead. Then, just as she was pulling a grey hooded top over her head, the vehicle dipped down into a rut, causing a spike of pain to shoot up from her stomach. Bear groaned, reaching down to support her sides, before finally shutting her eyes and curling up in the seat.

'You OK?' Bates asked, but there was no response.

Reaching his hand into a rucksack that was sitting between them, he dug out a sandwich, followed by a can of Coke.

'I thought you might be hungry.'

Bear took the food without a word, slowly chewing on the thick wad of cheese and the dense bread, her dry throat bulging with the effort. She then drained almost the entire can of Coke, grateful for the sugar and caffeine as the treacly mixture went down.

'I got you some painkillers,' he added, folding his fingers into his trouser pocket and retrieving a plastic sleeve. 'They're strong, but they won't make you drowsy.'

There was silence as Bear stared at the proffered drugs.

'Go on, take them. It's OK.'

'It's not OK, you fucking piece of shit!' she snapped. It was the first time she had spoken in the entire journey and the sudden aggression took Bates by surprise. 'All you've done is set me up,' Bear continued. 'So what's next? You taking me over to the British now?'

He didn't respond but instead let his eyes settle back on the road. After a long pause, he nodded.

'You're right. I did set you up. And Luca too. But that's over now.'

At the mention of Luca's name, Bear turned towards Bates. Despite her utter hatred of this man, she was desperate for some news. 'Have you heard from him yet?'

'The last plane left Antarctica yesterday. Luca wasn't on it. When the main crew got back to Cape Town, they said that the British team hadn't come back in from the field.'

As he said the words, Bear slowly turned her head to gaze out of the window. She stared blankly at the sand whipping furiously across the glass, her face so close that she could feel the minute drafts of air against her cheek. Her jaw clenched as she tried to fight back the sweeping sense of grief that welled up within her. Could life really have turned so cruel as to take her lover from her, along with her unborn child?

'*Reviens, chéri. S'il te plaît, reviens,*' she muttered, her breath misting across the pane.

'He will make it back,' Bates replied as if the words were intended for him. 'If anyone's got a chance of surviving out there, it's Luca.'

This attempt to comfort her had the reverse effect. Bear's head snapped back and she glared at Bates.

'But now we'll have to wait ten months to find out!' she roared, spitting the words out. 'Ten months, before the winter ends. Just to find out if he froze to death or not!'

She raised her arm, but her abdomen immediately buckled in pain. Grabbing on to her side, her mouth hung open as she tried to steady herself. Bates watched, wincing with concern.

'Please,' he said, crinkling back the plastic cover of the painkillers. 'They'll help.'

He gently placed the packet between them. Grabbing hold of it, Bear pushed four pills from their protective sleeve and washed them down with the last of the Coke.

'Why are you helping me now?' she said. 'You fucked me over before, so what's changed?'

Bates' gaze switched back from the road and towards her dark brown eyes, wondering if she would believe the truth even if he told her. Something had snapped in him when the American had said she was dying. He had stayed awake the entire night, trying to decide what to do. As a murky dawn had broken over the Karoo Desert, he had been certain of only one thing – he couldn't just sit by and watch her rot in the American rendition programme. When the storm hit, he had seized his opportunity.

'You can either trust me or not,' he replied evenly. 'It doesn't matter.' He gestured towards the rucksack. 'You'll find eight thousand rand in the bag, plus a clean mobile phone. With your skill, I'd have thought that would be more than enough to give you a head start.'

Bear ignored the compliment and instead rummaged through the bag, pulling out the contents one by one. 'How do I know the phone's clean and that you're not tracking me again?'

'You don't. But it doesn't make sense for me to be busting you out of the farm like this if so. Don't kid yourself. The Americans would have got the information out of you eventually and found that flashcard.'

Bear looked across at him, a flash of genuine fear passing across her eyes. She had already reached rock bottom in that terrifying room and would have told that interrogator anything he wanted to hear, but then events had overtaken them and instead she had passed out. Now the mere mention of the farm made the muscles of her back go rigid. She knew that she would do anything to avoid being dragged back into that room. There was nothing but despair to be found there.

She continued rifling through the bag. There were some

more clothes, mostly man-sized T-shirts, a charger for the phone, and a small, razor-sharp knife in a leather pouch. She weighed up the contents and, despite Bates' assurances, wondered if this would be enough to get her beyond the reaches of the Americans. The storm would only last so long. Soon, as the satellite communications came back up again, they would know that she had escaped.

The painkillers were starting to take effect and Bear eased herself back in the seat. The release from continual pain allowed her to contemplate other things and she wondered where she could go. There was really only one place – the Congo. Although the Americans might anticipate she would return to her home country, the very lawlessness of the Congo meant she had a better chance of disappearing without trace there. It was the one place on earth where she might be able to tilt the playing field against them.

For the longest time, they continued travelling in silence. There was only the bouncing of the van as it rolled on and on along the dirt road. With each kilometre that passed the storm gradually abated until they reached the outer limits of the Karoo Desert and eventually turned on to a tarmac road. At the junction, Bates swung the vehicle round and parked at a desolate farm stall, manned by a charming Afrikaans couple in their late-seventies. They were horrified that anyone should be attempting to drive in such conditions and repeatedly pressed them to stay until the worst of the storm had passed. Both Bates and Bear smiled awkwardly before managing to excuse themselves and leave, this time armed with more provisions and diesel.

Six hours later they came down the winding turns of Sir Lowry's Pass and on to the N2 motorway heading past Somerset West. Ahead of them was Cape Town itself, with the wide expanse of Table Mountain spread across the horizon, for once free from its habitual cloud. As they kept to the speed limit along the last stretch, Bates turned in his seat.

'I'll take you into the bus terminal in the centre of town. After that you can connect to where you need to go. I'm afraid I couldn't get you a passport. Even with my connections, they'd piece it together too soon.'

Bear stared at him, still unsure whether or not to trust him. Could this be a trick, the whole escape part of an elaborate scheme to get her to lead them to the flashcard? But as she stared back at the man before her, she realised that Bates was risking everything to break her out of the farm. And if the Americans found out, they would hunt him down with equal zeal.

Ahead Bear could see the smoke trails of a heavy 747 jet coming in to land at Cape Town International. She watched as the plane's landing gear unfurled from its bulbous undercarriage and the pilots flared the nose before touching down. On the other side of the motorway, just past the offices of Interjet, she spotted the first line of ramshackle shacks.

There was Nyanga. She could feel her pulse begin to quicken.

'Pull up here,' she whispered. Bates looked confused before suddenly twisting round in his seat to look at her.

'What?' he asked incredulously. 'You're going back?'

'Slow the car,' Bear ordered, trying to keep her voice from wavering. 'Do it!'

He released his foot from the accelerator and as he drifted across the lanes, the car gradually slowed to a halt. Before the wheels had even stopped moving, he had turned fully to face her.

'This is madness!' he protested. 'You nearly died in there, for Christ's sake! You can't be thinking about going back in.'

Bear stared past him towards the sea of iron roofs. She tried to steady her breathing, but her heart was pounding in her chest.

'Bear,' Bates said. 'Listen to me. You're in no state to go in there and I can't come and rescue you again. If you walk out of this car, there's no going back.'

'I've got to get the flashcard. The only way this means anything is if that bastard Pearl goes down.'

'You go back in and they'll kill you. I can't protect you any more.'

'Then we've got nothing left to talk about,' she replied, grabbing hold of the rucksack he'd given her. Just as she clicked open the car door and the noise of the traffic suddenly filled the interior, Bates grabbed her arm. Bear went rigid at the contact.

'Take this,' he said, reaching under the seat and pulling out his Glock 9mm pistol. He handed it to her, followed by a spare magazine. Bear hesitated for a second before reaching forward and taking the weapon, the dulled black metal weighing heavily in her hands.

'Goodbye,' she said, the word flat with finality. Checking

back across the stream of traffic, she limped across the dead area on the opposite side of the motorway before slipping through the line of broken concrete pillars that marked the boundary of the township.

Bates watched her go, knowing that whatever happened from now on, he would never see Beatrice Makuru again.

Chapter 31

Luca stared through the opening in the hatch, eyes narrowed against the gloom. Somewhere below them, Vidar Stang was silently searching the base.

'Close it,' Dedov warned, his voice no more than a low hiss. Luca looked up briefly before wiping the sweat from his eyes. He inched the hatch down, but left it unlocked so that there was a thin crack through which he could make out a stretch of the corridor below.

His gaze switched between the three other men in the darkness. Next to Dedov was Katz and slightly set back from them both was Joel's wiry frame. Their faces dipped in and out of the shadows as a weak light filtered down from the glass porthole directly above. For want of any other hiding place, they had all clambered up into the attic space that Hiroko had inhabited and now lay on top of the piles of meticulously folded plastic bags, their limbs cramping in the confines of the narrow room.

Dedov had his hand firmly clamped across Joel's mouth.

The injured man was now conscious, but struggling to understand what was happening. The sudden move and hushed whispering had done little to relieve his sense of confusion and he stared from one person to the next, squinting without his glasses.

Beside him, Katz was seated with his arms folded across his chest. Despite having already been told about Stang and the generator house, he was still insistent that there was a better alternative to hiding.

'Look,' he whispered, 'there are four of us, right? So I say, we go down there and reason with him. It's not like before. We were sleeping then and he was able to sneak around.'

Dedov's gaze remained fixed on the hatch. 'The man down there is not here to reason or to talk. He is here to silence us.'

'But we could overpower him,' Katz persisted. 'I mean, it's four to one.'

'He is a monster of a man. And last time I saw him on barrier, he carried rifle over his shoulder. This is not a man who can easily be overpowered. He is a trained hunter.'

The news was greeted by silence, with Luca checking down through the crack in the hatch once more. When they had first climbed up into the attic, he had taken a light bulb off the wall and carefully cracked it under his boot. He had then spread the glass across the narrow corridor, hoping that if anyone tried to sneak up on them, they would hear him first.

'Is there anything we can use as a weapon in the base?' he asked.

Dedov shook his head. 'This is science station. We do not keep them.' His eyes widened then as a flash of inspiration came to him. 'But we have some flare cartridges in hangar unit. We use them for runway emergencies.'

Luca thought about how ineffectual a flare would be against a rifle in the hands of a trained killer. It was hardly a fair fight. But they were going to have to do something as there was only so long they could hide unnoticed. Stang knew that they were somewhere in the base. It was only a matter of time before he figured it out.

Picking up one of the hundreds of carefully folded plastic bags at his feet, Luca ripped it open and checked inside. Holding the contents up to the light, it took him several seconds to realise that it was a collection of jam-jar tops that had been wrapped in tissue paper as if part of a Christmas present. He let his hand drop to his lap, allowing the contents to scatter across his thighs. For all the hundreds of bags Hiroko had collected, he was sure not one of them would be of any use.

'We're just going to have to make a run for it,' he said eventually. 'Somehow create a diversion and get down to the garaging unit. Dedov didn't get through on the radio to the ship's captain yet, so unless we are standing at the barrier when the boat arrives, it'll leave without us.'

'And without the generators, we're fucked if we come back here,' Katz added.

Dedov ignored the comment, instead focusing on Luca. 'So what do you suggest?'

'I don't know yet, but there's nothing for us here at GARI.'

There was silence as they all tried to think of a way out. They would have to somehow get Stang off the base or, even better, try to trap him in one of the other modules. But that meant sneaking up on a man who moved as silently as a ghost and was armed with a rifle.

Joel signalled that he wanted to speak, gently pulling away Dedov's hand. He was still incredibly weak from having been unconscious for so long, his skin deathly pale. His eyes slowly sought Luca's.

'We need to get help,' he murmured. 'There must still be some sat phones in the radio room. They'll have batteries and we can call . . .'

'Call who?' Katz countered. 'The Ilyushin's gone! And the nearest overwintering base is the South Africans' at SANAE. That's a two-hour flight and we don't have any goddamn planes!'

Luca surged forward, grabbing Katz by the front of his jacket and dragging him close. 'Keep your fucking voice down,' he hissed.

Just as Joel was about to say something more, Luca heard the soft crunch of glass. He raised his hand, signalling for silence, and slowly crouched forward so that his nose was almost touching the hatch itself. He listened, straining to hear anything from the corridor below, but there was nothing. He was about to gesture to Joel to continue when he heard the faintest scrape of a boot nudging the glass carefully to one side, before pressing down its weight. Stang must be there, somewhere below them.

Then Luca saw him.

First, he saw Stang's brawny legs inching along the corridor, then the dull grey streak of the hunting rifle. Finally, he saw his face. Stang had his chin tilted upwards as he stared out along the corridor, searching for the slightest sign of life. He glided past, moving so steadily as to be almost unnoticeable. Luca had never seen anything like it. The control was like a snake poised to strike. In that one moment he knew that Dedov was right. There was no reasoning with such a man.

The others waited, heartbeats thudding in their chests. They watched as Luca bent his head to one side and lowered it even closer to the opening. Stang had dipped out of sight and was now moving through the anterooms along the corridor, searching every last nook and cranny.

The seconds dragged by interminably, with nothing to do but wait. They had to fight every impulse to flee, knowing that if they did throw back the hatch and make a run for it, Stang would simply pick them off one by one. Even if some of them did make it past him, they would probably end up getting lost somewhere outside in the dark and simply freeze to death.

Seconds became minutes, while all around them the darkness seemed to deepen.

Katz went to move but Luca's hand shot out, gripping him tight. Finally, there was the slightest squeak of metal as the door at the end of the corridor was opened and a soft wash of cold air ran through the base. Stang was on to the next module.

'He's gone,' Luca whispered, and everyone seemed to breathe for the first time in minutes.

'Dedov's right. I saw his rifle. This guy's only here for one reason.'

The Russian leant forward so that his broad face caught the light. 'There's nothing else for it. We're going to have to split up.'

The four men filed along the corridor, moving as silently as they could. The glass that Luca had sprinkled now came back to haunt them and each movement was dogged by a crunching sound that seemed to reverberate across the entire module, threatening to summon Stang. But the soundproofing of the heavy doors was enough to conceal their passing and, after taking the stairs, they eventually found themselves in front of the internal door to the garaging unit.

As they entered, they felt the cold of the bare concrete walls. There were no windows and inside it was pitch black with a pervading smell of old engine oil. They groped forward with hands outstretched until they heard Dedov murmur something unintelligible before heaving open one of the tractor doors. Suddenly, the entire garage was lit up with dazzling intensity as the tractor's halogen beams shone directly on to the metal runners of the roller door.

The garaging unit was huge, with three massive tractors parked side by side, as well as five Ski-Doos roped down by stretches of tarpaulin. In the far corner they could see the outline of the R-44 helicopter that Pearl had used. Dedov's men had returned it to the garage before heading up to the runway and now its Perspex windscreen and long tailfin looked pathetically brittle against the heavy machinery parked either side. It would have been the perfect means of escape to the nearest science base but none of them knew how to fly.

Dedov stood on the footplate of the tractor, arm raised like an orator.

'We drive one tractor out first,' he said. 'And bring it round towards the runway. There are some overwintering containers up there with radio equipment and a portable generator. Stang knows this and maybe thinks we try to reach them.'

His gaze turned towards Joel and Katz. 'Meanwhile, others take Ski-Doo and head in opposite direction towards ice barrier.'

'We drive the tractor?' asked Luca.

Dedov stared at him for a moment. 'I,' he countered.

Luca moved forward. 'But there's no way you are going to outrun Stang in that thing. If he made it over here from the lake, then he must have a Ski-Doo parked somewhere nearby.'

'I do not need to outrun him. I just need him to follow me.'

'But you know that if he catches up, you won't be safe inside the tractor.'

'Safe?' Dedov mocked. 'None of us are safe. But this way, there is a chance for you.'

Luca stared at him, trying to understand the Russian's motives. It seemed odd for him suddenly to suggest he go it alone. Was it really altruism or could he have some other reason for wanting to split up the group? Katz appeared alongside the tractor and, true to his nature, was obviously having the same doubts.

'So why head for the runway?' he asked, edging closer.

'There is a big ice disturbance on the far side. Is caused by the meltwater in summer and the tractor has big enough tracks to cross over. The Ski-Doo does not and he will get stuck.'

'That's *if* he follows you,' Katz pointed out.

'If! If! If!' Dedov repeated, slamming his fist into his palm with each word. 'We have no time for this. Now get me the flares!'

His gaze switched to the emergency kits stacked up against the nearside wall of the garage. 'I need two. The rest you take for yourself. Now go!'

For the moment Luca and Katz let the issue drop. They moved over to the shelving unit, slid one of the massive bags on to the floor and began spilling out its contents. There were survival rations, tents and sleeping bags, all designed to sustain a crew in case one of the DC-3 planes went down. After a moment more, Katz found the bundle of orange and yellow tubes.

'I don't like this,' he whispered, pressing the flares into Luca's hands. 'That Russian knows something. He's going to stab us in the back the moment those garage doors are opened.'

Luca hesitated, torn as to what to believe. He didn't understand Dedov's motivation, but by the same token, couldn't see how he would gain anything by splintering off and driving up to the runway alone. Stang would surely chase the tractor and, once past the runway, where was there to go?

Moving back to the tractor, Luca passed two of the flares through the window.

'We were straight with each other before,' he said, staring directly into the Russian's eyes. 'So tell me, why are you doing this? Why not make a run for it with all of us?'

Dedov gave a faint smile. 'Not this time, Snow Leopard. You must trust that I have my reasons. Just promise me you will tell my son about this. That I am not the one who launched the seed.'

Reaching into his pocket, he pulled out the old gas lighter that his own father had given him and slipped it into Luca's hand. The brass was smooth from age and still warm from Dedov's body heat.

'Give him that. And whatever you say, he will know that you are telling the truth.'

Luca stared at him, knowing in that one instance that Dedov's motives were pure. And, as he saw this gesture for what it was, Luca admired the man even more. There was no great speech or fanfare, just the quiet courage of someone prepared to go out into the dark alone.

'I will tell him,' Luca promised.

'Now, get ready,' Dedov ordered, jamming the key into the ignition.

Luca moved across to the nearby Ski-Doos. They were going to have to move fast if they were to have any real chance of escape. Stripping back the tarpaulin, he checked the fuel levels while, behind him, Katz and Joel did the same.

'Open it up,' Dedov called out, and Luca strode back towards the main garage door. Clicking down the manual override, he gripped the cold metal runners and was just about to heave them upwards when a sudden premonition hit him. He could picture Stang waiting beyond the metal door, his monstrous silhouette framed against the dark snow.

'Now!' Dedov shouted, turning the key and triggering the engine into life. The whole garage echoed to the roar of the engine and the grinding of cogs. He slammed the gear lever into first. It was too late for Luca to procrastinate any longer. As soon as he heaved the door up, Dedov sent the colossal machine charging out of the garage and into the snow.

The others stood motionless, watching the tractor lights quickly fade. Only the remnants of the diesel fumes hung in the freezing air.

The barrier was five hours away and Dedov would have bought them only so much time.

Chapter 32

The tractor powered on, sending vibrations rattling through the interior of the cabin. Up ahead, Dedov could see the dark landscape illuminated in the tunnel vision of the headlights. He peered out towards the horizon, searching for the next in a long line of wooden markers that ran from GARI all the way to the runway.

The noise of the tractor's engine was so loud that it took a while before he even realised he was being followed. Winding down the window, he felt the freezing air wash into the cabin and looked out. About fifty yards behind, he could see the single beam of a Ski-Doo travelling in his wake, light blurred from the haze of snow churning up from his rear tracks.

'Come on, you son of a whore!' Dedov shouted. He had his foot stamped down on the accelerator, red-lining the throttle, yet the speedometer only registered twenty-eight kilometres an hour. He gave a snort, the sound originating from somewhere deep within his throat, at the sheer insanity of it all. This must be the slowest vehicle chase in history.

Slamming his fist down on the steering wheel, Dedov urged the tractor on with a string of Russian expletives. Then, from over his shoulder, he saw the Ski-Doo venture closer. It sniped forward, easily accelerating past the lumbering tractor, until the two drivers were level. There was the unmistakable outline of Stang. His shoulders were hunched bearlike over the handlebars while his head was turned, staring directly at the Russian.

As their eyes met Dedov swung the steering wheel, sending the tractor careering to the left. The great machine bore down on the Ski-Doo but with a touch of the brakes Stang dipped back, disappearing somewhere behind the tractor's rear end. A second later he re-emerged, but this time with rifle raised.

There was a sharp crack, the noise of the rifle barely audible over the combined roar of the engines, before Stang reloaded and aimed again. He was no more than five feet away from the side of the tractor, drifting in so close that, through the fog of ground snow, the beams of their headlamps merged as one.

Just as Stang heaved the muzzle of his rifle up, Dedov sent the tractor pitching towards him once again, missing the front tracks of the Ski-Doo by only a few inches. He pulled back, craning his face against the side glass to peer down at his adversary, when the entire window exploded. The bullet smashed through to the interior of the cabin in a spray of splintered glass, sending fragments searing into the left side of Dedov's face. He cried out in pain as the tractor swerved wildly and ran off the ice road.

There was a violent dip, then the machine skidded across a patch of raw ice. Its massive tracks slipped, failing to gain any purchase, until the whole machine was nearly side on to the direction of travel. On it went across the icefield, before finally smashing into a snow bank on the opposite side. As it hit, the entire tractor listed over, nearly toppling completely and sending Dedov crashing across the inside of the cabin. His chest smashed into the dashboard opposite, driving the wind out of him.

By some freak of physics, the tractor managed to right itself and swung back towards the road. It ploughed on, riding directly over one of the road markers. There was a splintering of wood, before the remnants were summarily spat out by the rear axle.

Dedov fought to keep hold of the steering wheel, but with each new contact with the ground it spun violently in his hands. With his left eye closed by streaming blood, he squinted ahead through the windscreen, but all the while he could hear the whine of the Ski-Doo engine nearby. Stang was driving even closer now, so close as to be almost under the arches of the tractor itself.

Dedov swung his head round, trying to look out of the broken window with his one good eye. Suddenly, he saw Stang lunge upwards from the seat of his Ski-Doo and clamp his hand on to the tractor's wing mirror. Heaving with one arm, he dragged the rest of his body higher until he lay flat against the side door.

Dedov roared with anger, slamming his entire weight into the door and trying to shunt the Norwegian away. Stang's body was briefly pushed out with it, before he came crashing back in once again and this time managed to get his fist through the broken window and on to Dedov's throat. His fingers curled around the windpipe, biting deeper and deeper into the flesh, while the Russian frantically twisted in his grip.

Dedov felt his whole throat being crushed. His eyes bulged from the pressure. He reached up with both hands, trying to prise Stang's grip away, but the man was just too strong. Instead, Dedov flung his whole body forward, using his weight to finally break free and drag himself on to the far passenger seat. Across from him, the Norwegian reached further inside and, turning the key in the ignition, killed the engine.

The tractor slowed, grinding to a halt only a few hundred feet from the edge of the runway. There was silence.

Dedov stared across the cabin as Stang pulled back the door and craned his head inside. His grey eyes seemed to pass over the Russian, instead turning towards the rear seats of the cabin as he searched for the others. When he realised that none were to be found, his lips pulled upwards in a faint smile.

'The barrier?' he said, his tone flat and unhurried. Dedov stared at him, realising that despite everything he had done Stang was barely out of breath.

'They're gone, Stang. You won't catch them now.'

He nodded pensively, weighing up the information, before his forehead creased in confusion. 'Yet you went alone?'

Dedov glowered at him. Behind his back, his hands groped across the seat, searching for the flares he had taken from GARI. A second later, his fingers curled around the plastic cylinder and he snapped off the lid with his thumb.

'I was never going to leave this place anyway,' he replied, thrusting the end of the flare towards Stang's face. There was a split-second's delay in which Stang's hand instinctively shot out and locked on to Dedov's wrist, bending it sideways. The flare exploded in a flash of blinding light, missing the side of Stang's face by less than an inch. It ricocheted off the roof of the cabin before thudding into the upholstery of the seat behind and fizzing out a dense cloud of red smoke.

Soon, the entire cabin was engulfed in smoke. Dedov was the first to take advantage of the confusion and viciously kicked out towards the Norwegian. The heel of his boot connected with Stang's face, sending him sprawling back and out of the cabin. As Dedov turned towards the opposite door and frantically tried to open it, he heard Stang scream with rage. It was as if something had snapped inside the man and he burst back into the cabin, ripping and clawing at Dedov's legs like a wild animal. Dedov desperately felt along the door for the handle, but the smoke was too thick for him to see.

In a single movement, he felt his entire body being wrenched back across the cabin and flung out on to the snow. He wriggled back across the ground but Stang crashed down on top of him, his knees cracking several of the Russian's ribs on impact. The Norwegian then rained his colossal fists down on Dedov's face and neck in a blind fury, bludgeoning him with each mighty blow. On and on they went, one after the other, the sheer weight of his fists splintering bone and thudding down on to the flesh with sickening force. There was a muffled scream, but the next three blows fell directly on to Dedov's mouth, snapping his front teeth and ripping open the whole front section of his jaw.

Stang didn't stop, even when Dedov's legs had ceased to kick and his arms had gone limp on the cold snow. The only movement came from the next blow, which sent ripples the length of Dedov's inert body like the twitch from a long-exhausted muscle.

Behind the tractor the sun slowly re-emerged, sending the first rays of light cautiously across the landscape. It was one of the last few days of autumn and the grey snow was gradually brushed with a faint streak of orange, growing warmer with each minute that passed. Slowly, the sun was awakening the new day.

As the red smoke from the flare hung lazily in the sky, Stang finally stood up. With his chest heaving and his knuckles soaked in blood, he turned his gaze towards the distant sun and shut his eyes, letting the warmth touch his cheeks.

For the first time in weeks, he felt absolutely at peace.

Chapter 33

Bear stood in the sparsely furnished shop with her hood pulled low over her face. She had been staring out of the window for nearly an hour, watching the flow of traffic on Nyanga's main road. Every once in a while she would retreat back to the makeshift counter and buy one of the few chocolate bars on display. She did it to appease the old woman running the shop but, by and large, she seemed content to let her customer loiter inside. Only one other person had entered in all the time she had been waiting, and Bear suspected the old woman was glad of the company.

Outside the taxicabs went back and forth in their usual, chaotic way, with the drivers hanging their arms out of the window and beeping the horn at the slightest provocation. But for all the movement, the atmosphere on the streets seemed less charged than she remembered. The battle in Nyanga had come and gone, and despite the appalling violence it had somehow released the tension that had been mounting for weeks across the township. Undoubtedly the lull would only last so long, but for the moment a strange calm reigned on the streets.

Bear watched as the latest in a long line of taxicabs jerked to a halt, disgorging its passengers like cattle. Each vehicle was hand painted with its own unique design. Often the driver's football team colours were plastered across the bonnet or there was some cryptic affiliation to a local gang. Bear remembered that the words *Lonely Boy* had been stencilled in yellow across the front bumper of the vehicle she had been in. She had even managed to catch the first two digits of the number plate. But Lonely Boy was nowhere to be seen today and, after an hour of waiting, she wondered how she might track it down.

Turning back to the shop owner, she summoned up a smile.

'I'm looking for a taxi,' Bear said. The woman nodded encouragingly, suggesting she was in the right place given the goings on outside. 'This taxi has "Lonely Boy" written across the front. Do you know it?'

The old lady's face immediately darkened and she wagged her finger under Bear's nose.

'Bad men,' she whispered, lips curling down. 'Those men are bad! Never go to church. And a girl like you . . .' Her voice trailed off. She began adjusting the woollen hat perched on top of her head, as though the mere thought could unsettle it.

'I know,' Bear agreed, with absolute conviction. 'But I need to find them. Can you help?'

She pulled a hundred-rand note from her pocket and

slid it on to the counter. The woman bristled at the sight of it, before poking it back towards Bear with her stubby forefinger. 'They run the route from here to Wynberg,' she said. 'Everyone knows that.'

'How often do they do it?'

'Every few hours. But with that kind of money, you can take the bus.'

Bear nodded in thanks, instead buying another chocolate bar with the hundred-rand note. Going back to the window, she looked out once again, but this time her right hand curled around the weighty handle of the Glock 9mm that Bates had given her. She held it under her hooded top, the hard profile of the pistol pressing up against her sore stomach as she thought back to the taxicab and the brutality of her journey in it. As each detail flashed across her mind, her lips moved in quiet resolve – this time, things would be different.

Nearly forty minutes later, 'Lonely Boy' pulled up. It stopped like all the others, with the side door swinging open as the driver harangued his passengers to hurry up and get out. Grabbing her rucksack off the floor, Bear sprinted out of the shop and climbed on board, all the while keeping her gaze locked on the ground and her face concealed behind the hood of her jacket. As she settled into the first row of seats, she caught a glance between the driver and a young man seated beside him. Then, with only two other passengers on board, the door was abruptly slammed shut and the vehicle pulled out on to the main road.

Bear stared out of the window as the taxi lurched through

the flow of traffic, wiggling on to the bus lane of the motorway and accelerating hard along the N5 in the direction of Muizenberg beach. She heard brief mutterings, spoken in Xhosa, between the driver and his companion, with an occasional furtive glance in her direction. But with her gaze averted and her head held low, she doubted whether they recognised her.

As the taxicab took the off-ramp and started across an area of scrubland that eventually came out into the hub of Wynberg, Bear suddenly yanked the pistol from her pocket.

'Pull over,' she ordered, jamming the barrel into the back of the driver's neck. He swerved in surprise and a cry of alarm went up from the other passengers.

'Silence!' Bear roared, and immediately everyone fell quiet.

In the front seat, the driver soon regained his composure. He began acting entirely indifferent to the fact that he had a gun pressing into the base of his skull and made a show of lounging back in his seat. But every few seconds he would try to sneak a glance behind him and see what was happening.

The taxi ground to a halt.

'Everyone out,' Bear shouted, and without a word the side door was run back on its hinges. As a waft of fresh air drifted into the sweaty cabin, the other passengers and the driver's accomplice spilled out on to the road and began hurrying down a manmade slope towards a narrow stream. They jumped across the insipid brown water, dodging the plastic bags and occasional shopping trolley, as they tried to put as much distance as they could between themselves and the goings on in the taxicab.

The driver shifted in his seat, pulling his vest a little lower to give full prominence to the 28 tattoo running in heavy blue ink across his chest. The tattoo was usually enough to intimidate most people but he smiled for show, revealing two gold teeth at the side of his mouth.

'Haven't got much,' he said, pulling a small wad of notes out of his jeans. 'Two hundred, maybe three.'

He was stalling for time, having now recognised Bear's face. He had moved tens of girls in his taxicab and never once considered that any of them would come back for revenge. Most overdosed in the brothels or, if they did eventually make it out of the township, fled back to their villages in the countryside. No one ever came back.

'Take it,' he said, jiggling the money in his hand. With her spare arm, Bear sent the notes spinning into the opposite footwell and dug the barrel harder into his neck.

'I don't want your fucking money,' she hissed, causing the driver's tight smile to fade.

'It wasn't my idea,' he stammered. Now alone, his gangster demeanour evaporated and Bear could see sweat running down through his cropped hair. 'I just . . . get orders . . .' he managed, staring fixedly ahead.

'Shut up,' Bear snapped. Unclipping the knife that Bates had given her, she raised it in front of the driver's face. Gently tilting the blade from side to side, she let the razor-sharp metal glint in the light, watching as the driver's pupils widened with each turn. She held him like that for several seconds, moving her mouth a little closer to his ear despite the rank odour of his skin.

'Never pick up another girl again,' she whispered, 'or I will cut off the only thing that makes you a man.'

The driver nodded frantically as she whipped the knife back and jammed the blade into the underside of his seat. He squealed in fright, jolting upwards as he expected the knife to go straight through the padding and into his crotch. But the blade was only three inches long and instead Bear jerked it back, tearing at the lining. She felt underneath the seat, fingers splaying out across the padding as she tried to find the flashcard Lotta had given her.

When the gang had originally bundled her into the taxicab, she had been thrown under the first row of seats, while they kept her down with their boots. They had stamped on her face and dug their heels into her stomach, but she had managed to get the flashcard out of her bra and tuck it somewhere beneath the floating lining of the driver's seat.

As her fingers moved back and forth, the driver stayed stock-still, unable to understand what she was doing. Finally, her forefinger caught on a little piece of plastic that had jammed right up against the adjustment bar of the front seat. Bear had been lucky. Had the driver moved his seat back a single inch, he would have slid over the flimsy plastic and crushed it. Holding it up to the light, she checked that it was intact before returning it once more to her bra.

'Get out,' she said.

Without a second's hesitation, the driver groped for the door handle and fell out on to the road.

Bear climbed through into the driver's seat and sat down, trying to ignore the stench impregnated into the worn plastic cover. As she started the engine and rammed the gear lever into first, she looked across to the opposite side of the road. The driver was hunched over, staring at her in a mixture of fear and emasculated horror, his crotch dampened by a small circular mark from where he had wet himself.

She kept the pistol trained on him as she swung the vehicle round and headed back towards the centre of town.

Long Street was its usual bustle of tourists and half-price bars. The entire stretch had evolved to accommodate the endless migration of backpackers, with everything conveniently crammed into one place. From adverts for shark diving to happy hours that lasted well into the night, it was a magnet for transitory partygoers or the African traveller trying to see the sights on a shoestring.

Bear pulled off the main drag and turned left into one of the smaller side streets. Right at the end of Keerom Street, she parked in front of some heavy iron security gates and, leaving the keys in the ignition, walked back the hundred yards to the nearest in a long line of internet cafés. It was almost empty, with only a couple of teenagers busily tapping away in the far corner.

The manager was a skinny nineteen-year-old with tattoos covering both arms and a hat angled jauntily to one side. As Bear approached, he looked up and smiled. 'How can I help?'

'I've got some holiday snaps on here,' she said, raising the flashcard in her hand, 'but my camera's bust and I can't download them. You don't have one of those card reader things, do you?'

He smiled, giving her an 'I really shouldn't' look that he hoped would gain him a few points when Bear had finished whatever it was she needed to do. Rummaging behind the counter, he reappeared with the device in his hands.

Moving over to the far corner of the room, she plugged it in and watched as a single red dot flashed on the side of the card reader. After everything she had been through, she suddenly had a premonition that the flashcard would be empty or broken, but then a folder appeared on the screen in front of her. Clicking through, she started scanning the files, marvelling at how fastidious Lotta had been. Everything was there, from the initial research phase of the project, to several images of Pearl at the laboratory, congratulating the staff.

Quickly checking over her shoulder and seeing only the hopeful smile of the manager, Bear went online and opened the WikiLeaks website. The not-for-profit media organisation had blown almost every major story on the West's covert operations since its inception in 2007. They were also no friend to the USA. As news was breaking of the catastrophic situation in the South Ocean, Bear was sure that WikiLeaks would be able to get the story out to the world's press without being bought or silenced. The only way forward was to go public with the information, and fast.

Dragging the files into their electronic dropbox account, Bear watched as the upload icon spun round and round.

Minutes passed while she waited for the data to channel through the ether, expecting that at any moment the door of the internet café would suddenly swing back and the place would fill with shouting soldiers. But none came. There was only the sound of the café's background music and the occasional burst of laughter from the teenagers in the far corner of the room.

Thirty minutes later, Bear slid her chair back under the desk and, ignoring the attempt at conversation by the manager, walked out. She had one more visit to make.

Her son lived only six streets away. If she was going into hiding, he was coming with her.

Chapter 34

Luca stood on top of a single tabular iceberg staring out to sea. Amongst the miles and miles of flat sea ice, the iceberg stood like a fortress held captive by the last winter freeze. Its sides were sheer, with crumbling slabs of snow that threatened to splinter off at any moment, forcing him to circle it twice on the Ski-Doo to find a way up. Eventually he had seen a sloping ridge on the southern flank, built up from wind-hardened snow. After ten minutes of climbing, he had reached the top.

Forty feet below he could see Katz and Joel slumped across the saddle of their Ski-Doo with the black Pelican case of lake water jammed into the luggage tray behind. They were staring up at him, desperate to hear some good news after so much time spent driving in the continuous cold. The sun was now up, gradually pulling along the horizon in a low arc, but it did little to warm them. All it left was an orange glow filtering across the clouds, the rays so weak they barely had the strength to touch the ground.

'Can you see the boat?' Katz shouted, raising his hand to his mouth to funnel his voice.

Luca didn't respond. They saw him check his footing, then move over to the far side of the iceberg and out of sight.

'Jesus Christ,' Katz swore, slamming his fist down on the handlebars in front of him. His head turned back in the direction they had come, following the long trail of their Ski-Doos. They all knew that unless something miraculous had happened, Stang would be coming for them, and soon. In such a landscape, there was no way to hide their tracks and, with each passing minute, they expected to see his outline suddenly appear on the horizon.

'We're wasting too much time,' Katz growled. 'Too much time.'

'Give Luca a chance. He's doing all he can.'

Joel was seated beside him, still bundled up in the protective down jacket and pants they had taken from GARI. The thick padding engulfed his whole body, leaving only the narrow point of his nose visible, along with the shadowed outline of his eyes. He had said almost nothing on the entire drive out, as the scenery swept past in a continuous blur. Without his glasses, he could barely distinguish the outline of the massive icebergs, let alone help find the ship that was supposed to have docked somewhere nearby.

'We need to keep moving,' Katz continued, ignoring him. 'That bastard will be on our tracks before we know it.'

'And go where? This is the barrier. There's nowhere left to run.'

Katz's gaze snapped back to him, brimming with scorn.

'Just think of something! What the hell else have you got to do while I do all the driving?'

Joel bristled, but resisted the temptation to respond. All that would do was waste more time. Instead he remained silent, clamping his arms tight around his body for warmth. With a shake of his head, Katz went back to staring up the sheer-sided wall of the iceberg, willing Luca to reappear.

High above the two scientists, he had moved to the very northern edge of the iceberg and was staring out across the water. Open leads ran in between the snow-covered ice, snaking out in all directions like veins around a body. His gaze scanned the horizon, searching for the slightest trace of the ship, while his lips moved in silent prayer. There had been no radio contact with the crew and all Dedov had given him was the GPS coordinates of the ship's intended docking site. What if the captain had decided to unload somewhere else or had even arrived early and already turned for home?

As endless doubts passed across his mind, Luca suddenly spotted a dark smudge against the otherwise pristine sky. It was like a thumbprint blotched across his vision and he squinted, wondering what it could be. Then, he realised. It was the exhaust plume from the ship's engines. As he moved a little to one side he could see the tip of the vessel's prow nestled behind one of the icebergs, slowly bobbing up and down in the sea. The red paint of the hull was there, a streak of colour against the otherwise monochrome landscape.

'Yes!' Luca cried, throwing his hands into the air. For a fleeting moment he felt the same sense of release as he had done when climbing out of the old base. The end was so tantalisingly close. Here, right before them, was the way out.

'I see it!' he bellowed, despite guessing that the others wouldn't be able to hear him from such a distance. Turning back, he starting striding across the top of the iceberg, his gaze switching to the sweep of their Ski-Doo tracks in the distance.

He stopped. Something was moving towards them, but so tiny as to be nothing more than a dot on the landscape. The dot blurred, caught between the horizontal line of the ground and the grey sky above, and for a moment he lost sight of it altogether. He trained his eyes a little higher, unsure if it was just a figment of his imagination.

But then he saw it again. Stang was on their trail, and at that distance no more than an hour behind.

Running towards the far edge of the iceberg, Luca saw the others and skidded to a halt. For the briefest moment his mind refused to function, caught between joy at the ship's sighting and the certainty of Stang's pursuit.

'The boat!' he shouted, stabbing his hand towards a far iceberg.

There was a roar of excitement from Katz, and Joel jerked his head round in the massive hood of his down jacket. But before they could reply, Luca swung round and motioned towards their tracks. The meaning was only too clear – Stang was upon them. Without another word he disappeared from view, retracing his steps along the ridge and eventually reaching ground level.

By the time he arrived at the parked Ski-Doos, his cheeks

were flushed from running and his breath came out as great clouds in the freezing air. Katz started to say something but Luca brushed past him, immediately jumping on top of his Ski-Doo.

'Come on, move!' he shouted, slamming his thumb into the throttle. In a spray of snow from the rear tracks, he swung the machine round, powering across to the distant promise of the Russian ship that, against all odds, was right on schedule.

The *Akademia Federov* was a vessel of icebreaking class, constructed deep in the Soviet era when economic viability came a distant second to function. Its immense aft deck could fit two helicopters simultaneously, while its prow had a flattened, hammerhead design used to force the ship up on to the top of the ice floes and so break them under its weight. A collection of steel turrets and navigation equipment crowded the deck two-thirds of the way along the main hull, nestled directly below the piloting bridge.

Behind the panels of reinforced glass sat Nikolai Serov, the ship's captain for over eight years. He leant back in his usual chair with a cup of stale black coffee in his right hand, his hawk eyes following every inch of the unloading process that had been going on all morning.

His naturally weathered face had been locked in a continuous scowl for the last two days as their ship had passed along the coastline of Droning Maud Land and through a genocidal mass of dead fish and marine life. Nikolai was not a man to be shocked easily, but he was a man of the sea, and the sheer level of destruction had shaken him to his core. He had immediately phoned back reports to the main office in Saint Petersburg and even emailed some of the more ghastly images, but all that they had received in response was a note informing them that the Polar Academy was 'aware of the situation'.

Nicolai could barely believe that any of the bureaucrats back home were really aware of the cataclysmic scale of the destruction. It looked as if the whole ocean had been emptied of fish. Already the stench of the rotting carcasses was overpowering and, despite the recent spell of clement weather, all the crew had preferred to stay inside with the storm doors closed against it.

But Nicolai had been mesmerised by the carnage and unable to pull himself away. For hours he had leant over the bow rail, just watching the dead fish lap against the hull, unable to comprehend what might have triggered such a disaster. As they trawled along the edge of the world, surrounded by only ice and death, it felt as though some kind of biblical apocalypse were finally upon them.

He had stayed up most of last night, drinking viscous black coffee and staring out across the endless miles of broken pack ice. After much deliberation, he had decided to continue with their mission and reach the docking site. His reasoning was simple: what could be gained by turning back? The fish were already dead.

For the last three hours the main crane had been working ceaselessly, raising the containers off the deck before swinging them across to the land-fast ice of Antarctica on their port side. The ship was docked parallel to the cliff and although the sea was calm, it was a complicated procedure and the ship's pilot was constantly throttling backward or forward in an effort to keep them steady.

Worse still was the fact that only two days ago he had been forced to repair the crane's main hydraulic system and had personally rewired almost the entire system. Now a mess of black pipes lay exposed on the deck and Nicolai was convinced that it would only last so long. As if to aggravate matters, the new crane driver, Andrey, was swinging the containers around like a child with a toy.

Nicolai watched as a twenty-foot shipping container swung in front of him, ends pivoting so high as almost to twist the steel cables. Jumping up from his seat, he jammed his thumb down on the radio switch.

'Andrey!' he thundered. 'Take it easy on the unloading or you'll be repairing that winch by yourself.'

A voice crackled in response. '*Da*, Captain. But it's Muller's fault. There's too much tension on the line.'

Nikolai rolled his eyes at his men's petty squabbles. There was nothing else for it. He was going to have to transfer Andrey off crane duty, but right now he couldn't think of a single other task the lad could do adequately.

As his brow furrowed even further, he suddenly saw someone moving on the edge of the ice cliff. He peered closer, knowing full well that nobody should be out there at this time of year and wondering if one of his own crew had somehow made it across.

The ship rolled in the current, causing the figure to

disappear from view. Nicolai waited, half wondering if he might be seeing things. With all the goings on over the last few days, he barely trusted himself any longer. Then, as the boat righted itself, he caught sight of the figure once more, but this time it wasn't just one man. There were three of them.

Grabbing the radio, he raised the mic to his unshaven chin.

'Muller and Balakin, get on to the aft deck. There's someone on the barrier.'

There was a puzzled pause. 'But what are they doing there, Captain?'

Nikolai gritted his teeth. 'Just get down there, Muller! And I do mean *now*.'

A few minutes later, the three Russians were standing on the deck of the mighty vessel. They stood right up against the freezing metal rail, trying to listen over the gentle roll and splash of the ocean. They could hear the voices of the men on the barrier, but were just too far away to be able to understand what was being said.

'They're not Russian,' Balakin offered, wrinkling his nose against the smell of fish.

'German maybe,' Muller suggested, seemingly content to spend the next few minutes discussing the men's nationality despite the obvious urgency with which they seemed to be signalling.

'Wherever they're from,' Nicolai cut in, 'we can't just leave them on the ice. So we're going to have to figure out a way to bring them over.'

'It's too far for the gangplanks,' Balakin said. After a pause, Nicolai grunted in agreement.

There was only one way they were going to get them across and that was using the crane, but with Andrey's haphazard control it was a dangerous proposition. Already the captain was wondering how the hell he would write this up in the ship's log.

'Ditch the container already on the crane,' he ordered, 'and send over some cargo strapping. They're just going to have to tie themselves on.'

The two crew members nodded but both remained still, thinking ahead to the host of things that could go wrong.

'Go!' urged the captain, sending the men scurrying across the deck in search of the equipment.

With Andrey perched high in the open-sided cabin, the massive crane arm swung out across the water. Nearly a hundred feet below, the dark waves of the Southern Ocean rolled under the ship's hull before reflecting off the immovable ice of the barrier. It was a choppy mess of conflicting currents, interspersed with chunks of ice and the occasional dead fish. Without survival suits, the men on the opposite bank would only last a few minutes in the water. That was *if* they survived a fall in the first place.

Nicolai stared through a pair of binoculars he had retrieved from his cabin, watching as Andrey inched the crane hook down on to the other side. He saw one of the men tying in the other two, ratcheting the cargo belts tight around their thighs so that they were locked into a sitting position. Nicolai cursed his own men's stupidity again, realising that despite there being three men on the opposite bank, they had only sent across two straps. Now they were going to have to repeat the whole process.

He turned, about to reprimand Andrey, but then, as he looked up into the open cabin of the crane, he could see the concentration on the lad's face. His tongue was poking out of the corner of his mouth and his whole body was tilted forward, almost dangerously so. Nicolai shook his head, regretting having been so hard on him. He was obviously trying his best.

As the crane arm slowly swung back across the divide, the two newcomers became clearly visible. Both were gripping on to the metal hook above, while their heads were angled down towards the dark waters below. One of them was holding a black Pelican case in his left hand, which swayed with the natural roll of the ship.

With a whirr of the winch cables, they slowly descended towards the deck.

'Easy now,' Nicolai shouted. 'Easy.'

The two men landed in a crumpled heap and Balakin smiled at the incongruous tangle of legs and arms. As they tried to get up, the Pelican case slipped from the grasp of the larger man and spun a few feet across the deck.

'Welcome,' Nicolai said, his voice thick with a Russian accent. He grabbed the forearm of the tall, skinny man, easily hoisting him to his feet, while Balakin cranked the locking mechanism of the cargo strap, releasing them.

'Holy shit!' Joel stammered, eyes wide with manic energy.

Nicolai stared across at him, suddenly wondering if the

newcomer's fear resulted from something more than being craned across. Next to them, Katz clambered to his feet and immediately staggered towards the case. Snatching it up, he held it close to his chest.

'There's a lunatic after us,' Joel blurted out. 'Send back the crane for Luca. We could hear the sound of his Ski-Doo. He's got to be close by now . . .'

The Russian stared between them both, having only partially understood what was being said.

'Slowly, slowly,' he said, trying to reassure them. 'We collect other man. No problem.'

'Now!' Katz shouted, gesticulating wildly towards the cliff. 'Another man is after us. He has a rifle.' He then mimed firing a gun with his spare hand.

The Russian's eyes narrowed in confusion.

'OK, OK,' he said, more to try and placate them than with any real understanding. His eyes switched across to the ice cliff, searching for any sign of danger, but there were only the three containers they had already unloaded that morning, with the remaining Englishman standing nearby.

'We send crane now. Pick up other man,' Nicolai added, smiling good-naturedly. He then signalled up to Andrey once more and they all watched as the mighty crane arm swung back across the divide. Just as it was in position over the ice and Luca started moving towards it, there was the crack of gunfire. The noise echoed out across the open area, making everyone jump. Then Andrey's body came crashing down from the crane cabin, hitting the ship's deck face-first only a few feet away from them. The weight of the impact snapped his head back and he lay bunched unnaturally to one side. Beneath him, blood slowly fanned out in a semi-circle across the deck.

'*Mother of God,*' Nicolai breathed.

There was another shot and this time Joel spun round as the bullet passed through his left shoulder blade. His whole frame pivoted as though caught by some unseen wire and he collapsed on to the deck, screaming wildly.

'Run!' Katz shouted, sprinting full tilt across the deck with his back arched and the Pelican case swinging wildly in his grasp. A few seconds later he reached the first of the steel turrets lining the control bridge and dived for cover, bruising the entire left side of his body as he smashed on to the ground.

Out on the open deck, Nicolai finally jerked into action. Joel was crawling helplessly across the ground, his vision so blurred he couldn't tell which way to go. His right arm was raised, pressing down on the wound, while his mouth was wide in a constant scream. As Nicolai ran past, he grabbed hold of the wounded man and shunted him forward towards the shelter of the ship's bridge.

Nicolai ran with his head down, expecting the next bullet to strike at any moment. But the sea takes care of her own and, as if on cue, the ship slowly rolled in the opposite direction causing Stang's next bullet to miss by a few inches. They reached the cover of the steel doors just as the other member of the crew, Balakin, crashed down next to them.

'*What's happening, Captain?*' he cried out, stuttering from fear.

Nicolai looked across to the big man for an answer, but he was staring up at the cabin of the crane, grey sky now visible through its open side. After a moment, his gaze switched back towards the Russians.

'If we don't pull back the crane arm,' he said, 'Stang will be able to climb across and get on to the boat. You can't allow that to happen.'

Nicolai followed his gaze, his mind racing. He was an old navy man who many years ago had seen some action in the Baltic Sea. Now, he tried to steady his nerves and, instead of panic, do what was right for his crew and his ship. He had no idea who Stang was, but knew enough to fear the accuracy of his rifle. 'Nyet,' he said. 'Too dangerous to go back up to cabin and operate the crane arm. We drive boat away, retract crane later.'

Joel stared up at them both. He was still clutching his shoulder, desperately trying to stem the flow of blood trickling through his fingers.

'But Luca?' he pleaded. 'You can't just leave him.'

Katz's gaze settled on Joel for a moment, then he looked away.

'We can't help him now,' he said flatly. 'He's just going to have to take his chances.'

Chapter 35

Luca stared in horror as the deck of the *Akademia Federov* emptied under a hail of gunfire. He had been standing directly behind the row of containers when the first shot rang out. Stang was close; so close that Luca could even hear the sharp metallic click of the bolt-action rifle reloading with merciless repetition.

As it finally fell silent, Luca stared out towards the metal hook on the end of the crane. It swung idly in the breeze, no more than ten feet away. But as close as it was, he knew that if he broke cover and tried to reach it, Stang would simply gun him down.

He could only presume that Stang thought he was already on board the ship and had been winched across like the others. But that would only last so long. It was simply a matter of time before he rounded the side of the containers and discovered Luca cowering there.

Seconds passed. Sweat was running the length of Luca's spine. His mind raced as he tried to think of a way out of the situation, but there was nowhere left to go. He could hurl himself into the water to be picked up later by the others, but the drop looked absolutely terrifying. He doubted whether he would even survive it.

He turned his gaze up to the roof of the container, wondering if he could hide there instead. Tracing his fingers over the smooth side, he searched for a handhold but there was nothing to grip on to. The only way to get up there would be to leap for the edge and pull himself higher, but at such close range, Stang would be bound to hear.

So Luca waited. Second followed second, each filled with the gut-wrenching certainty that Stang would suddenly appear around the side of the container. Curling his hands into fists, Luca tried to steel himself for a fight, but already he knew it was pointless. Rifle or not, Stang was a giant of a man and Luca wouldn't stand a chance in a fistfight. The mere thought of it made his legs go weak and Luca just stood there, feeling physically sick with fear.

Turning his gaze out towards the ship, he willed someone to notice him. But the decks were deserted. There was only the broken form of the Russian who had fallen from the crane, his body haloed by a dark stain of blood.

Then Luca heard footsteps. There was a soft crunching of snow and he screwed his eyes shut, feeling terror rise within him. This was it. Another second and Stang would be on him. As he listened, he realised that the footsteps were heading away from him, not towards, and poking his head around the side of the container, he saw the

Norwegian shuffling back towards his Ski-Doo parked nearly a hundred metres away. He had his rifle slung across his back and his head bowed low. As Luca watched, he flipped open the saddle of the machine and began digging through the contents stored within. A few seconds later, Stang re-emerged with a rope, snapping the ends together as he tested its strength.

Luca stared at it, wondering if the rope was somehow meant for him. Did Stang now plan to garrotte him? Then he realised what it was for. The man needed it to secure himself as he climbed across the crane arm and on to the ship.

Ducking back behind the container, Luca stared across to the ship's empty deck. He *had* to get on board or risk being left behind. The generators at GARI were destroyed, meaning no heat, no water and no chance of surviving more than a few days.

The ship was his only way out.

Just as he tried to galvanise his legs into action, there was a deep roar from the engines. A dark plume of exhaust belched out and there was the sound of churning water. A second later, a great, foamy spray erupted beneath the hull as the propellers fought against the ship's mighty inertia to move her backwards.

Luca stared in disbelief. They were leaving without him! The fear of being abandoned finally triggered him into action and he pushed off against the container, sprinting headlong towards the hanging crane arm.

As soon as he broke cover, there was a yell of surprise.

Stang was still standing by the Ski-Doo, looping the rope over his hands as he considered the best way to attach himself. It took several seconds for him to shake himself free before dropping down on one knee and readying his rifle. In a single, finessed movement, he clicked off the safety and aimed.

But Luca was moving fast. With his arms pumping at his sides, he reached the metal hook of the crane in just a few strides. Flinging himself up, he grabbed on to the main cable and dragged his body on top of the crane arm. He began shuffling along, legs dangling to each side, while beneath him the ship started moving in earnest. The engines were on full reverse power, finally gaining momentum through the dark, frozen water.

There was the sound of the rifle once more, and Luca heard a low clang as a bullet smacked into the metal just ahead of him. However, there was only time for one shot. The speed at which the ship was retreating meant Stang didn't have time to reload. Instead, he gave chase, his mighty thighs powering through the deep snow.

Luca had managed to get nearly halfway along the crane arm when he suddenly heard another shot. He froze, with his upper body bent so low as to be touching the metal arm of the crane. Reaching behind him, he fumbled in his jacket pocket for a few seconds before grabbing hold of one of the emergency flares they had taken from GARI. He twisted round, searching for any sign of his adversary.

At first Stang was not visible. Then, as the ship rolled to one side, Luca suddenly saw him, dangling from the end of the crane winch. His military boots were clamped either side of the metal cable and he was staring fixedly ahead, right into Luca's eyes. It was the first time Luca had seen him in the full light of day and the sight of his blackened skin with red welts laced across his face was almost mesmeric. Luca stared back into Stang's pallid eyes and saw a look of absolute hatred. It was pathological, like a predator incensed by the lucky escape of its kill.

There was a sudden whoosh of light as the flare rocketed along the length of the crane. Luca stared after it through the clouds of red smoke, coughing violently as he tried to see whether it had struck its target. But a moment later he caught sight of Stang's outline. He was still there, gripping on to the end of the winch cable.

Turning back once more, Luca dragged his body hand over fist along the crane arm. A few feet further on he passed the threshold of the ship's rail below. Now, at least if he fell, he would land on deck instead of falling all the way to the water.

Behind him, Stang heaved his body up. He managed to get his barrel chest over the edge of the crane arm, then jerking his legs back and forth, wormed the rest of his body on top. Now astride the metal beam, he steadied his aim with the rifle. This time, he would not miss.

'Hold on!'

The shout came from somewhere directly beneath Luca and he saw a figure standing on the main deck. The captain was there, holding a fire axe above his head. In a single movement he severed one of the rubber pipes feeding into the crane's main controls. There was a loud hiss of escaping air as the hydraulic pressure suddenly drained from the system, sending a jolt through the entire crane and spoiling Stang's aim. Then the massive crane arm came pitching down, accelerating under its own weight. It smashed into the side of the ship, crumpling the side rail like a twig and sending a huge reverberation across the ship's metal hull.

Luca slipped, but managed to grab on to one of the running cables to break his fall. He tumbled down on the deck and lay in a heap until a second later he felt a pair of hands grab his shoulders as Nicolai wrenched him clear of the destruction.

On the opposite end of the crane, Stang was ripped from his perch and sent spinning off into the void. He fell nearly sixty feet down the side of the ship, with his body striking the surface of the water at an angle and immediately snapping his right knee joint. On he went, tunnelling deeper and deeper into the icy depths, as clouds of bubbles blinded him.

Finally resurfacing, Stang gasped for air. The force of the fall had winded him and he bobbed up and down in the swirling current, using his one good leg to try to keep afloat. All the while, he stared up at the towering expanse of the ship's hull just in front. The helmsman had killed the engines and now the ship lay stationary in the water only a few feet away. He wondered if he could climb on board somehow, but the hull's sheer sides looked utterly unassailable.

Swivelling round in the water, he stared across at the ice cliff directly behind, hoping it would offer a better chance of escape. But he couldn't see a single handhold in the glistening wall of ice, let alone a route up to the top. As he turned slowly in the current, he could feel water lap over his cheeks and mouth, while the cold seemed to wrap around his body, robbing him of every last ounce of his heat. Turning full circle once more, he frantically searched for some means of escape, but there was nowhere left to go.

Seawater washed over his head and Stang gulped as he sank beneath the surface. By the time he came up for air once again, he was shivering uncontrollably. His teeth were chattering and his back muscles were rigid from hypothermia. Already the cold was starting to confuse his mind, while the constant ebb and flow of the water was making him feel sick and disorientated.

Staring up towards the ship's rail, Stang suddenly spotted a figure gazing down at him. Its face was blurred by distance and he squinted harder, trying to make out the features. The figure on the boat moved a little to one side, causing him to cry out in recognition. He was convinced that the rough features of the Russian captain were, in fact, Richard Pearl's.

'Richard!' Stang cried, raising his hand. But there was no reply. The figure only stared down at him impassively. 'Please,' Stang begged, spluttering mouthfuls of icy water. 'Richard!'

He dipped below the surface and this time stayed under, sinking lower and lower into the depths. As his vision blurred, he held the image of Pearl in his mind, bewildered as to why he hadn't done anything to help, or even uttered a single word. Sinking further now, Stang could feel the weight of the water pressing on his skull. The pressure grew and grew, with each atmosphere building on top of the next, until finally he screamed. As his mouth opened in panic, the water rushed in, surging down his throat and filling his lungs, until at last everything went black.

Chapter 36

A week later, the helmsman of the *Akademia Federov* sighted land.

The four-thousand-kilometre journey from Antarctica to Cape Town had been a frustrating period of enforced in-activity. Luca had spent most evenings alone in his tiny cabin, just staring at the ceiling and thinking, while the soporific noise of the engines droned on and on. He knew he needed time to make sense of all that had happened. To make matters worse, he had broken three ribs falling from the ship's crane and, whenever he moved too quickly, a spike of pain shot through his abdomen. The constant discomfort put him in a foul mood, while the frustration of trying to track Bear down only made things worse.

During the day, he spent hours on the ship's satellite phone trying to garner the slightest information as to where she might be, but it seemed as though she had simply fallen off the planet. All he had managed to find out was that her last known location was in the Nyanga Township on the

Cape Flats. After that, she had simply disappeared. Luca's repeated calls to Kieran Bates at the British Foreign Office always ended with assurances from a secretary that his friend would get back to him, but nothing happened. As the silence continued, his frustration mounted. Soon, he was willing the days to pass, desperate to reach land and the chance to actually *do* something.

When not in his cabin or pressing the satellite phone to his ear, Luca found himself drinking coffee with Nicolai. The Russian captain was a quiet and steady companion, and helped to calm Luca's mercurial mood. Silence punctuated their conversations as they stared out at the uninterrupted view of the Southern Ocean and discussed all that had happened.

But this contemplative calm only lasted so long. Three days into the voyage, a flood of news bulletins appeared on the ship's computers as they came close enough to land for their internet systems to connect properly. Every few minutes, another bulletin would ping across the screen as the situation played out in the world's media. All eyes were on Antarctica and events there were unfolding fast.

Already the Russian Duma had insisted that a joint task force be used to clean up the disaster, and not just the American fleet as previously agreed. Although the full extent of the Americans' involvement had yet to be established, the Russians had tabled a motion that the Antarctic Treaty should be held in effect until such time as a full investigation was completed. It was passed the next day.

With the Treaty now back in force, the situation was fast

turning against the Americans. Newsfeed followed newsfeed, and with each one their position seemed to weaken further. Soon even the most patriotic US newspapers had conceded that 'an American citizen had been involved in the environmental disaster down south'.

Richard Pearl quickly came under the spotlight, with WikiLeaks churning out a plethora of information about how he researched and financed the production of the seed. Although none of this evidence directly linked Pearl to the US administration, it did lift the stain of suspicion from the Russians, who then acted quickly to regain the moral high ground. While they forced themselves centre-stage, the Americans, by contrast, were in full damage-control mode. Already, they were confining themselves to the occasional press conference where they emphatically denied any link to Pearl, despite his status as a US senator, and gave repeated calls for 'calm and the chance for a full and proper investigation'.

As Luca and Nicolai scanned each headline, the vilification of Richard Pearl became ever more complete. Someone in the American government was doing everything they could to serve him up on a plate and paint him as the Lee Harvey Oswald of his generation – the lone gunman responsible for the whole tragedy. Reports poured on to the news screens, documenting everything from Pearl's early childhood to discrepancies in the official report filed on the submarine incident all those years ago.

The reversal of Pearl's fortunes was extraordinary for both its speed and its scope. Arrest warrants were issued in the

US and almost every other signatory of the Antarctic Treaty followed suit. By virtue of the fact that so many countries were involved, Pearl was left with almost nowhere to run.

But for now he had disappeared. His Bombardier jet had altered course en route for America and that had been the last anyone had heard of him. While the news channels featured his image on a near-hourly basis, for now one of the world's greatest manhunts continued.

While all this unfolded via the ship's email, elsewhere on board Joel had been confined to bed. The ship's doctor had worked on his shoulder for much of the time they had been at sea and although the bullet from Stang's rifle had passed through relatively cleanly, splinters of collarbone still remained. They were beginning to become infected and so, like Luca, Joel was counting the days until they reached Cape Town and the chance for proper medical treatment. For now, his only release from the pain was an occasional shot of morphine, which blurred time and made him waft through the days in a detached haze.

Katz, meanwhile, skulked around the ship, avoiding contact with Luca at all costs. Shamed by his assertion that they should just leave him on the barrier, he only spoke to Joel and Nicolai occasionally, while the rest of his time was spent inside his cabin. He was filing a report that ran into hundreds of pages, detailing every facet of the expedition and allocating blame for each part of it.

Aside from the report, Katz's other main motivation for staying inside his cabin was the two remaining cylinders of lake water. They had survived intact inside the Pelican case and now he guarded them like a dragon might his treasure. He mumbled his plans for what he would do with them as if they were his alone and not the product of years of research by an international team. The closer they got to dry land, the more Katz withdrew into himself. The flash of humility that he had shown to Luca in the old Soviet base was long-since gone, replaced by his habitual sneer and brooding self-interest.

As the helmsman sighted Table Mountain and the boat drew ever closer to Africa's southernmost tip, Luca and Nicolai went out on deck. They stood side by side, letting the heat of Africa beat down upon their backs. There was silence for a moment, before Nicolai turned away from the view.

'The winter is finally over,' he said. 'We are free from the ice once more.'

Luca nodded. 'Thank you. For everything, I mean.'

As he spoke, his eyes drifted across to the heap of crane wreckage still littering the deck. The crew had lashed down the smaller parts, but the main arm of the crane lay buried in the side rail.

'We receive radio message that helicopter will be coming as soon as we are in range,' Nicolai said, ignoring his thanks. 'As soon as we pass out of international waters, I have to comply with their demand.' He shrugged. 'And I do not have enough fuel to take you anywhere else.'

'I guessed they would be coming,' Luca replied. Despite the lack of contact with Kieran Bates, he was sure the British Foreign Office would want to debrief them, but the idea of being cramped in a tiny room while some bureaucrat went through every detail of what had happened only filled him with dread. He didn't have time to waste. He needed to find Bear.

'After all that's happened,' Luca added, 'I'm not sure which country's worse.'

'*Individual* worse,' Nicolai corrected. 'Country is just country.'

Luca nodded again, now accustomed to the Russian's straight-talking philosophy and, as many times before in their conversations, a long spell of silence ensued.

It was some time later that they heard the first sounds of a helicopter coming in low across the water. As the aircraft slowed to a hover and then carefully touched down on the deck, a bulbous man dressed in a white shirt and flannel trousers stepped out. Keeping his back arched against the swirling rotors, he came close, revealing a bright streak of sunburn across his nose and a shirt stained at the armpits by sweat. As he stood in front of Nicolai, he raised a hand in greeting.

'The name's Jacobs,' he said, voice raised above the noise of the helicopter. 'My men radioed ahead.'

Nicolai nodded.

'I'm here to pick up Joel Cable-Forbes and Jonathan Katz,' Jacobs continued, with a lopsided smile on his face that suggested he might be dealing with a halfwit.

He motioned back to the helicopter and a side door was opened. Another two men clambered out. As Nicolai signalled to one of his crew to lead them to Joel's and Katz's quarters, Jacobs stayed on deck, eyes switching between Luca and the captain.

'So, where we headed?' Luca asked.

'Afraid you're being picked up later,' Jacobs replied. 'I have orders just to bring in the other two.'

'And where are they going?'

Jacobs' smile widened a fraction. 'Don't worry, they'll be well looked after.'

Luca knew there was little to be gained by pressing the point and the next couple of minutes passed in silence. Jacobs stood patiently, his gaze turned out towards the sea, until Katz appeared through one of the storm doors under the main bridge. He was clutching a thick file of A4 paper taken from the ship's printer and tied tightly with string, while in his other hand was the Pelican case.

Moving out on deck he kept his eyes down, still unable to meet Luca's gaze. He walked straight across to the helicopter and, without looking back, climbed on board.

Joel emerged a moment later, shuffling out into the bright sunshine. He looked pale and drawn, his gaze drifting unsteadily. The morphine made him barely aware of what was happening and for a moment, he paused halfway to the helicopter before spotting Luca standing to one side. Then a weak smile appeared on his face.

'I'll see you soon,' he said, reaching out his good arm to shake Luca's hand.

'Yeah, I'll be right behind you in the next chopper,' Luca lied. He knew it would only confuse Joel further to tell him they were being split up. 'Take care of yourself, Joel.'

His smile widened as he raised his wounded shoulder a fraction. 'That's easy. Just got to stay clear of psychotic Norwegians.'

As Jacobs gave a terse nod and shepherded him over to the helicopter, they heard the engine pitch rise and the rotors begin to quicken. Soon the downdraft washed across the deck, causing Luca and Nicolai to cover their eyes. No sooner had the aircraft gone than they saw another approaching, following the same trajectory but this time much faster. It landed on the deck with military precision and, glancing across, the pilot gestured for Luca to climb on board. 'I have no doubt that we will see each other again,' Nicolai shouted above the noise. 'Now go!'

Gingerly moving across the deck with his right hand clamped against his ribs, Luca climbed on board. He looked across at the pilot, but the man didn't return his gaze. As soon as the door was closed, he sent the machine pitching forward. Skimming the ship's rail, he headed straight towards the mountain and the distant silhouette of Cape Town.

Kieran Bates was waiting by the side of a warehouse in Cape Town's harbour. The giant building was flanked by a series of crane derricks that looked so old as to be long-since defunct, but still, they turned slowly, disgorging each ship's contents on to the quayside. There was a lazy, mid-afternoon feel to the whole dockyard. Most of the workers sat in the shade eating their lunch, while others dozed on the waiting pallets of freighted goods.

Bates stood by two parked Mercedes 4x4s, each containing

three men. They were a close-protection unit largely made up of former SAS soldiers that Bates had specifically requested for this meeting. As the helicopter landed and Luca slowly got out, the men exited the vehicles, looking alert and ready. Bates stepped forward, coming to a halt just a few paces from his old friend.

'Back on dry land,' he said.

'I see you brought a whole welcome committee,' Luca replied, with a shake of his head. 'So what happens now, Norm? You going to make me disappear too?'

'They're here because I know how dramatic you can be,' Bates countered. He paused and stared into Luca's eyes. He had been anticipating this encounter for days and, while he already knew that Luca would never forgive him for the deception, part of him wanted his old friend to understand the risks he had taken to get Bear out of Nyanga, and then, later, to break her out of the interrogation centre. Already the Americans were starting to pick holes in his official report. There was only so long that they would believe that Bear had 'overpowered him' on the drive back to Cape Town, given the condition she had been in and the supposed level of sedation. He knew he was going to have to work hard to stay a step ahead of the game.

'I know you think I set you up and that's all there is to it,' Bates continued, 'but when the dust settles, you're going to be thanking me.'

Luca gave a humourless smile. 'Thank you? You fucking lied to my face about Dedov and the smuggling. You used me to pin the whole thing on him and now the man is dead.

So what do I have to thank you for, Norm? You screwed us all over, pure and simple.'

'For Christ's sake, Luca. Don't be so naïve. Nothing is that simple. And it would have happened whether you did it or someone else. My way, you get paid nearly fifty grand.'

'You know I never gave a shit about the money!' Luca shouted. As his voice rose, his hand went to his painful ribs. 'You nearly had me killed out there!'

'I never meant for anyone to get hurt. I only knew some of the picture and had no idea how things would turn out. I thought you'd be sitting at the base just waiting out a storm for a few days.'

'How do I believe that? How do I believe anything you're saying to me?'

'Because I am here now,' Bates countered. Then his voice softened a little. 'I do care about what happens to you, Luca. Don't make that mistake.'

'Care?' he repeated incredulously. 'You don't give a shit about me. You just manipulate the situation to get things done. And you know what? I could almost forgive you for what you did to me, but then you went ahead and dragged Bear into all this.'

'I did everything I could do to *stop* her from getting involved,' Bates seethed. 'You have no idea what I have risked to keep her safe.'

'Then you shouldn't have fucking started this unless you knew how it would end,' Luca countered. In his anger, he stepped forward and there was a ripple across the security team as the closest two went for their sidearms. After a moment's hesitation Bates raised a hand, signalling them to stand down.

Luca didn't even flinch. It was as if he hadn't noticed the armed men standing only a few feet away.

'Just take it easy,' Bates said, raising his hands. 'Bear is OK. She was on her way north to the Congo but then I managed to get hold of her. She's holed up in a hotel right here in Cape Town. She's safe and she's with her son.'

Luca didn't respond, reluctant to take anything Bates was saying at face value.

'This is her number,' he offered, pulling out a piece of paper from his trouser pocket along with a cell phone. 'Take this and call her. Then you'll see I'm telling the truth.'

He signalled to one of the men, who handed him a small brown package. Bates stepped closer and offered it to Luca.

'Forty-eight grand – minimum payment for four weeks' work. That's what was agreed.'

Luca remained motionless, making no attempt to take the package.

'Don't be a fool,' Bates added, knowing full well that it was blood money. This wasn't about payment for the work done – the whole project had unravelled anyway. This was Bates' attempt to make amends and alleviate some of his own insufferable guilt.

'Think about it, Luca. Don't throw this away out of misplaced pride.'

Luca reached forward and, ignoring the packet, grabbed the phone and piece of paper. Bates nodded slowly.

'Same old Luca,' he said, backing off. He then crouched

down and left the package stuffed with notes at Luca's feet. Signalling to the security team to start their engines, the men quickly climbed inside the 4x4s with Bates being the last to do so.

'Take care of her,' he called across, but Luca didn't hear. He had already dialled the number and was waiting for a reply. As the two vehicles moved off, trailing the edge of the quayside, the line finally connected.

'Hello?' came Bear's voice. At the sound of it, Luca's eyes slowly closed with pure relief.

Chapter 37

Eleanor Page unbuttoned her suit jacket and leant back in her padded office chair. She had been working for just over two days straight and now even her immaculately styled hair and careful make-up were starting to take the strain. Flinging her tortoiseshell glasses on to the open file on her desk, she pressed her finger on the intercom switch and called for one of her assistants. It took several seconds before there was any kind of response, her team equally strung out by the sheer avalanche of work that had befallen their desks.

'Hold all calls for two hours,' Eleanor instructed, before letting her eyes drift closed. She knew that she was utterly drained and had been for some time. The side effect of the perpetual jolts of adrenalin was a deep and lasting exhaustion that seemed to permeate all the way down to her bones. For the first time in as long as she could remember, Eleanor felt every single year of her age.

Despite being long overdue, her sleep was fitful, while a

sharp, repetitive twitch played at one corner of her mouth. The unshakable calm that had served her so well in the past seemed to have evaporated. Now, even while she was sleeping, her heart beat rapidly in her chest.

In the wake of the Antarctic Treaty being reinstated, the Director General of the FBI had tasked her to find a viable plan B and, as far as Eleanor could tell, there simply wasn't one. She had gone back over all of the original research notes, trying to find a single line of enquiry that would be worth pursuing, but so far had nothing. The reality was that in eighteen months' time, the USA needed to have an alternative supply of oil or it would face heavy selling on the stock market and the wholesale collapse of its economy.

Without any prospect of a solution, Eleanor had instead turned her focus to another fundamental and done everything possible to distance the administration from Richard Pearl. But distance wasn't enough. They were going to have to ensure he remained silent – permanently. That was the single unanimous resolution of the meeting she had held that morning. Pearl was never to be allowed to stand trial and lay bare their secrets. But to be sure of that, they first needed to find him.

Just as her head tipped forward and she succumbed to the deepest of sleeps, her phone rang. The sudden noise made her head jerk upwards and her eyes peeled open with a look of weary disorientation. Wiping away the line of spittle that had escaped her mouth, Eleanor reached forward and pressed the receiver to her ear.

'I said . . .' she managed, but her assistant cut her off.

'I think it's the call.'

Eleanor's eyes widened. Shaking her head slightly, she tried to dispel the fog of tiredness.

'Put her through,' she ordered. The line connected, but it was distant. She could only just hear the sound of a woman's voice, but then she recognised the strong Italian accent of Helena Coroni, Pearl's personal helicopter pilot. Eleanor breathed a sigh of relief. While the rest of the world would still be looking for the man responsible for the plight of the Southern Ocean, she would soon have his exact whereabouts.

But the conversation didn't follow its usual form. Normally Coroni would be brief by necessity, but this time there was something more. She wasn't just being furtive. She was terrified.

'He's totally . . . lost control,' Coroni was saying, her voice muffled by the distance. 'It's a rage like nothing I have ever seen before . . .'

'Your location?' Eleanor pressed, ignoring the complaint. 'What's your location?'

'Wait!' Coroni snapped. 'I need you to promise you'll send help. He's finally asleep and I think I can make it to the helipad before he realises what's going on. But I only have enough fuel to make it to one of the other islands. I'm not going to be able to reach the mainland.'

Eleanor forced her voice to sound steady. 'We've got your back, I promise. Now, tell me your location.'

Coroni listed a succession of GPS coordinates, repeating

them twice. Relaying them into her computer, Eleanor soon discovered that Pearl was hiding out on one of the outlying islands to the north-west of Madagascar.

'Please, Eleanor, after all I have done for you. You owe me.'

'We owe you,' she repeated. 'Just stay calm. We're sending in a team right now, but if Pearl attempts to flee the island, I'm going to need you to call it in. So don't attempt to leave. Just stay where you are.'

There was a pause as Coroni weighed up the prospect. 'OK, I'll do it. But please, come quick. You don't know what he's like.'

'Hold tight,' Eleanor soothed, but already her finger had moved to the console on her desk as she opened a separate phone line. She heard herself say 'We're coming for you' as she cut the line to Coroni and transferred directly to operations. A kill team had been on standby for the last three days, just waiting for Pearl's location to become known.

When she connected through to the Ops Manager his tone was dry and perfunctory, concerned only with the details necessary for his logistics. They spoke for nearly five minutes and Eleanor was about to sign off when the germ of an idea suddenly filtered through from her subconscious. She paused, allowing herself the luxury of ten seconds' pure thought and ignoring the questioning voice on the other end of the line.

'Change of orders,' she said abruptly. 'I want Pearl taken alive.'

'But this has already been . . .' the Ops Manager objected, before she cut him off.

'You bring him back in one piece. Are we clear on that point?'

'We are clear,' the Ops Manager replied evenly. 'I'll update you in one hour once the team are en route.'

As the line went dead, Eleanor brushed a strand of silver hair back from her face and inhaled deeply. It felt as if she were breathing new air into her lungs for the first time in days.

She wasn't sure exactly why she had put a stay on Pearl's execution, but something deep inside her suggested that he would be more use to her alive than dead. Somewhere in that diseased but brilliant mind of his, she was sure there lay the answer to this mess they were in. To kill him too soon would only narrow their options.

After all, putting bad people to good use was a specialty of hers.

Chapter 38

Luca sat on a couch in a suite of the One & Only Hotel in Cape Town. His face was illuminated by the dull glow of a computer screen as he booked plane tickets. Behind him the first of the morning sun filtered over the towering edifice of Table Mountain and shone through a gap in the curtains. It reached all the way across the plush carpets to where a double bed had been positioned against the far wall. There, curled up together on one side, lay Bear with her son, Nathan.

They were both asleep, with Bear's arms looped around her son, hugging him tight into her chest. It left only the top of his curly brown head visible above the sheets, which rose and fell with his steady breathing. There was a low murmur and Luca looked up to see Bear move in her sleep, legs breaking free from the covers and spreading out across the empty bed behind her. For a moment he let his gaze trace the line of her hips and back, marvelling at how beautiful she looked, even now after all that had happened.

Easing himself off the couch, he was about to go into the

adjacent room for a shower when he heard her voice behind him.

'Still haven't slept?' she whispered.

'No, but I thought you were.'

'I was,' Bear sighed, before stretching and gently uncoupling herself from her son. Pulling a dressing gown over her shoulders, she followed Luca out of the room and closed the connecting door. She then perched on the edge of the writing desk as Luca peeled off his T-shirt and turned on the shower. Frown lines deepened across Bear's forehead as she took in the angry purple bruising that covered the entire left side of his abdomen. Luca seemed to have lost even more weight than she remembered. Now, his triangular frame was nothing but a knot of sinewy muscle.

Just as he stepped towards the shower, Bear took hold of his hand and pulled him close. She kissed him, keeping his body pressed against hers with her legs slowly curling around his waist. She had never intended it to be anything more than a kiss, but as their bodies stayed locked together their passion grew. Bear hesitated, knowing how painful it would be to make love after all that had happened at the farm, but by the same token, she felt a physical need for Luca right then.

Wriggling her shoulders, she let the dressing gown fall to her waist. Her head tilted to one side as Luca kissed along the line of her neck, with his right hand gently curling into her hair. They made love. It was slow and unhurried, filled with a sense of longing that was tinged with regret. By the time they had finished, Bear found herself clinging on to

Luca's shoulders. It was only when he pulled back from her that he realised she was crying.

The physical release had been like a catalyst. For so long, Bear had been forced to hold it all together and bury her feelings deep. Now that she was finally with Luca, it all came flooding out. Her emotions were raw and unchecked, filled with a sadness that seemed to tremble right through her, until all he could do was hold her tight.

As he embraced her, a memory began to resurface in Luca's mind. It was of his time at the old Soviet base in Antarctica.

'When we spoke on the satellite phone you said you had something to tell me, but you wanted to do it face to face.'

Bear gave a tight smile, then sniffed, wiping away the streaks of tears with the back of her hand. She had already decided that this was a pain she was not going to share with Luca. The miscarriage was something she had to deal with alone. Only once she had processed it herself could she contemplate sharing it with him. To tell him right now that their unborn child had been lost would only fill her with a sadness that she knew she couldn't contain. Maybe with time, she told herself. Maybe then she might tell him the truth.

'I was going to tell you that I wanted us to be together again,' she replied, voice steady once more. 'That I regretted us ever having broken up.'

Luca stared deep into her eyes, unsure if she was telling him the whole truth.

'That's all you wanted to say?'

Bear nodded. 'Isn't that enough?'

Luca remained still for a moment, looking at her, before a smile appeared on his lips. He knew not to push her for another answer right then.

'It is enough. And now we *are* together,' he said, before his eyes flickered towards the neighbouring room. 'All of us, I mean.'

Bear's smile widened, her nose wrinkling slightly as she followed the direction of Luca's gaze. The thought of them being together as a family was something that immediately helped dispel the darkness. It was the promise of a future that was positive and filled with potential.

'But how did you convince your ex-husband to let you have Nathan?' Luca asked.

'I went to see him and we ended up speaking for a long time.' Bear shook her head. 'Christ, those lawyers love to twist everything around and keep you fighting. Anyway, we both agreed on one thing, and that was we should do whatever was right for Nathan and that I still had a right to be in his life.' She paused, weighing up the conversation in its entirety. 'It's not like Jamie's giving me full custody or anything, but I think we can come to an agreement about visiting rights and start putting together some kind of structure.'

'Structure would be good. I could do with a bit of that myself after all that's happened.'

Bear nodded her agreement, then seemed to drift into silence.

'What is it?' Luca asked.

'Do you think the Americans will ever let us go?' she asked. 'I know what Bates said, but we can't keep running indefinitely. I just won't live like that.'

Luca sighed, the same concerns having plagued him for most of the night.

'The flashcard is in the open and all the information in the public domain. The bottom line is that we don't have anything the Americans want, so why would they still come after us? They're not about revenge. With them it's about what happens next. As far as I can see, we're old news.'

'So that's it?'

He shrugged. 'Who knows? Nothing's ever certain. But to my mind, it wouldn't make any sense for them to come after us.'

After a moment's deliberation, Bear nodded. Perhaps he was right. Besides, if she spent her entire life second-guessing the Americans, all she would do was plague herself with paranoia. Better to let them make the first move, if indeed there was one to be made.

Moving off the desk, Bear went to the wardrobe while behind her Luca finally stepped into the shower. For the longest time he let the water run over his back and shoulders, still revelling in life's small luxuries after the deprivations of Antarctica. He started scrubbing his whole body clean with such determination that it was as if he were trying to rid himself of all the memories from the last few weeks.

Walking back into the main room with a towel around his waist, Luca found Bear sitting by the desk and staring into a mirror while she tied back her hair. She was about to say something when she suddenly noticed a brass cigarette lighter lying to one side. It looked old and well thumbed, with the metal slightly warped from age.

'Whose is that?' she asked, picking it up and turning it over in her hand.

Luca came up behind her. 'I've got to give it to someone.'

'Someone?' Bear asked, wondering why he was being so cryptic.

Luca nodded. 'I owe him that at least,' he said, gently taking Dedov's lighter from her grasp. 'I'll tell you all about it on the way.'

Turning back from the mirror, he started getting dressed. Their flight to San Diego was due to leave in three hours' time.